# TOKYO REDUX

*Also by David Peace*

*NINETEEN SEVENTY-FOUR*
*NINETEEN SEVENTY-SEVEN*
*NINETEEN EIGHTY*
*NINETEEN EIGHTY-THREE*
*GB84*
*THE DAMNED UTD*
*TOKYO YEAR ZERO*
*OCCUPIED CITY*
*RED OR DEAD*
*PATIENT X*

# TOKYO REDUX

DAVID PEACE

ALFRED A. KNOPF NEW YORK 2021

THIS IS A BORZOI BOOK PUBLISHED BY ALFRED A. KNOPF



www.aaknopf.com

Knopf, Borzoi Books, and the colophon are registered trademarks of Penguin Random House LLC.

Library of Congress Cataloging-in-Publication Data
Names: Peace, David, author.
Title: Tokyo redux / David Peace.
Description: London : Faber & Faber, 2021. | Series: Tokyo trilogy ; 3 | Includes bibliographical references.
Identifiers: LCCN 2020004957 (print) | LCCN 2020004958 (ebook) | ISBN 9780307263766 (hardcover) | ISBN 9781101947784 (ebook)
Subjects: LCSH: Tokyo (Japan)—Fiction. | GSAFD: Mystery fiction.
Classification: LCC PR6066.E116 T65 2021 (print) | LCC PR6066.E116 (ebook) | DDC 823/.914—dc23
LC record available at https://lccn.loc.gov/2020004957
LC ebook record available at https://lccn.loc.gov/2020004958



Ambroise from Typofonderie, designed by Jean François Porchez.


Jacket photograph by Shiho Fukada
Jacket design by John Gall

Manufactured in Canada
First United States Edition

For William Miller,
always,
and with particular thanks
to Shunichirō Nagashima and Junzo Sawa.

Later, one summer night in 1949,
again the Buddha appeared to me,
in my cell, beside my pillow.
He told me:
The Shimoyama Case is a Murder Case.
It is the son of the Teigin Case,
it is the son of all cases.
Whoever solves the Shimoyama Case,
they will solve the Teigin Case;
they will solve all cases.

"Sadamichi Hirasawa," a poem,
from *Natsuame Monogatari*, by Kuroda Roman,
translated by Donald Reichenbach

## In the Gardens of the West

In the twilight, at the border, they ducked down under the door and stepped inside the garage. The body was lying on the cement floor under a bloodstained white sheet. They put on their gloves. They turned down the sheet to the waist. The head and hair were soaked in blood. There was a black hole in the left side of the chest. A pistol lay on the floor by the outstretched fingers of the right hand.

Did you know him personally, asked the detective from the City of Edinburg Police Department, Hidalgo Co., TX.

The left hand was resting on the left leg of the pants. They turned the hand over. They touched the marks on the wrist. They shook their heads.

Well, lucky you guys got here as fast as you did, said the detective. We can easy hit eighty degrees in March. Stink can be something else, I tell you.

They looked up from the body. They stared around the garage: pistols and rifles in cabinets and on the walls, boxes and boxes of ammunition on shelves and on the floor.

We don't ordinarily like to leave them *in situ* so long, said the detective. Not if we can help it.

They looked back down at the body. They turned the sheet back up over the face. They got to their feet and walked over to a long workbench against the length of one wall.

We left everything just the way we found it, said the detective. Just like your field office told us.

Hanging over the workbench was a photograph in a frame, a photograph of a Japanese mask: *The Mask of Evil*.

No note, said the detective. Just that postcard.

They looked down at the workbench. The top of the workbench was covered by a single sheet of old newspaper: page sixteen of the *New York Times* of Wednesday, July 6, 1949. There was a photograph of American troops parading down a wide Tokyo street for the Fourth of July. Below the photograph, the headline: TOKYO'S RAIL CHIEF FOUND BEHEADED. On top of the sheet of newspaper, a picture postcard was propped up against an alarm clock. They picked up the postcard, a postcard of the Sumida River in Tokyo.

Guess our friend Stetson had a real thing about Japan, right, said the detective. Beats me why, I swear.

They glanced back down at the alarm clock on the table. The hands of the clock had stopped at twelve twenty.

Forty years ago, we were fighting the hell out of them. Now they're the second goddamned largest economy in the world. Makes you wonder why we fucking bothered. They must be spinning, all them boys that died for nothing. Half the country driving about in Jap cars, watching Jap TVs. Makes no sense to me, I tell you. No goddamned sense at all.

They turned over the postcard. They read the three words scrawled on the back: *It's Closing Time.*

# I

# THE MOUNTAIN OF BONES

# 1

## The First Day

---

*July 5, 1949*

The Occupation had a hangover, but still the Occupation went to work: with gray stubble shadows and damp sweat stains, heels and soles up stairs and down corridors, toilets flushing and faucets running, doors opening and doors closing, cabinets and drawers, windows wide and fans turning, fountain pens scratching and typewriter keys banging, telephones ringing and a voice calling out, For you, Harry.

On the fourth floor of the NYK building, in the enormous office that was Room 432 of the Public Safety Division, Harry Sweeney turned back from the door, walked back to his desk, nodded thanks to Bill Betz, took the receiver from him, put it to his ear and said, Hello.

Police Investigator Sweeney?

Yes, speaking.

Too late, whispered the voice of a Japanese man, then the voice was gone, the line dead, the connection lost.

Harry Sweeney replaced the receiver in its cradle, picked up a pen from his desk, looked at his watch, then wrote down the time and date on a pad of yellow paper: 9.45 – 07/05. He picked up the telephone and spoke to the switchboard girl: I just lost a call. Can you get me the number?

Hold on a minute, please.

Thank you.

Hello. I have it for you now, sir. Would you like me to try it for you?

Please.

It's ringing for you now, sir.

Thank you, said Harry Sweeney, listening to the sound of a telephone bell, and then –

Coffee Shop Hong Kong, said the voice of a Japanese woman. Hello? Hello?

Harry Sweeney replaced the receiver again. He picked up the pen again. He wrote down the name of the coffee shop beneath the time and the date. Then he walked over to Betz's desk: Hey, Bill. That call just now? What did he say?

He just asked for you. Why?

By name?

Yeah, why?

Nothing. He hung up on me, that's all.

Maybe I spooked him? Sorry.

No. Thanks for answering it.

Did you get the number?

A coffee shop called Hong Kong. You know it?

No, but maybe Toda does. Ask him.

He's not here yet. Don't know where he is.

You're kidding, laughed Bill Betz. Don't tell me the little bastard's gone and got himself a hangover.

Harry Sweeney smiled: Like all good patriots. Doesn't matter, forget it. Be a crackpot. I got to go.

Lucky you. Where you going?

Meet the comrades off the Red Express. Colonel's orders. You want to tag along, listen to some Commie songs?

Think I'll just stay right here in the cool, laughed Betz. Leave the Reds to you, Harry. They're all yours.

Harry Sweeney ordered a car from the pool, had a cigarette and a glass of water, then picked up his jacket and hat and went down the stairs to the lobby. He bought a newspaper, turned the pages, and scanned the headlines: SCAP BRANDS COMMUNISM INTERNATIONAL OUTLAWRY: SEES JAPAN AS BULWARK / RED-LED RIOTERS STIR DISORDERS IN NORTH JAPAN / RED LABOR CHIEF HELD / NRWU GETS READY FOR COMING FIGHT AS JAPAN NATIONAL RAILWAYS START PERSONNEL SLASH / ACTS OF SABOTAGE CONTINUE / REPATRIATES DUE BACK IN TOKYO TODAY.

He glanced up and saw his car waiting on the curb outside. He folded up his paper and went out of the building into the heat and the light. He got into the back of the car, but didn't recognize the driver: Where's Ichirō today?

I don't know, sir. I'm new, sir.

What's your name, kid?

Shintarō, sir.

Okay, Shin, we're going to Ueno station.

Thank you, sir, said the driver. He took a pencil from behind his ear and wrote on the trip ticket.

And hey, Shin?

Yes, sir.

Wind down your windows and stick on the radio, will you? Let's have some music for the drive.

Yes, sir. Very good, sir.

Thanks, kid, said Harry Sweeney as he wound down his own window, took his handkerchief from his pocket, mopped his neck and face, then sat back and closed his eyes to the strains of a familiar symphony he just couldn't place.

Too late, barked Harry Sweeney, wide awake again, eyes open again, sitting up straight, heart pounding away, with drool on his chin and sweat down his chest. Jesus.

Excuse me, sir, said the driver. We're here.

Harry Sweeney wiped his mouth and chin, unstuck his shirt from his skin, and looked out of the windows of the car: the driver had pulled up under the railroad bridge between the market and the station, the car surrounded on all sides by people walking in all directions, the driver nervously glancing into the rear-view mirror, watching his passenger.

Harry Sweeney smiled, winked, then opened the door and got out of the car. He bent down to speak to the driver: Wait here, kid. No matter how long I'm gone.

Yes, sir.

Harry Sweeney wiped his face and neck again, put on his hat and found his cigarettes. He lit one for himself and passed two through the open window to the driver.

Thank you, sir. Thank you.

You're welcome, kid, said Harry Sweeney, then he set off through the crowds, into the station, the crowds parting when they saw who he was: a tall, white American –

*The Occupation.*

He marched through the cavernous hall of Ueno station, its crush of bodies and bags, its fog of heat and smoke, its stink of sweat and salt, marched straight up to the ticket gates. He waved his PSD badge to the ticket inspector and walked on through to the platforms. He saw the bright-red flags and hand-painted banners of the Japanese Communist Party and he knew which platform was his.

Harry Sweeney stood on the platform, in the shadows at the back, mopping his face and neck, fanning himself with his hat, smoking cigarettes and swatting mosquitoes, towering over the waiting crowd of Japanese women: the mothers and sisters, the wives and daughters. He watched as the long, black train pulled in. He felt the crowd first rise onto the tips of their toes, then surge toward the carriages of the train. He could see the faces of the men at the windows and doors of the carriages; the faces of men who had spent four years as Prisoners of War in Soviet Siberia; four years of confession and contrition; four years of re-education and indoctrination; four years of hard, brutal, pitiless labor. These were the fortunate ones, the lucky ones; the ones who had not been massacred in Manchuria in the August of 1945; the ones who had not been forced to fight and die for either of the Chinese sides; the ones who had not starved to death in the first postwar winter; the ones who had not died in the smallpox epidemic of April 1946, or of typhus in the May, or of cholera in the June; these were some of the 1.7 million fortunate ones who had fallen into the hands of the Soviet Union; a few of the one million very lucky ones the Soviets had now decided to release and have repatriated.

Harry Sweeney watched these lucky ones step off the long, black train and into the hands and tears of their mothers and sisters, their wives and daughters. He saw their own eyes were blank, embarrassed or looking back, searching for their fellow soldiers. He saw their eyes lose their families and find their comrades. He saw their mouths begin to move, begin to sing. He watched the mothers and sisters, the wives and daughters step back from their sons and brothers, their husbands and fathers, step back to stand in silence, their hands now at their sides, their tears still on their cheeks, as the song their men were singing got louder and louder.

Harry Sweeney knew this song, its words and its tune: the Internationale.

Where the fuck you been, Harry, the fuck you been doing all this time, whispered Bill Betz, the second Harry Sweeney came in through the door to Room 432, Betz taking his arm and leading him back out through the door, back down the corridor. Shimoyama's gone missing and all hell's broke loose.

Shimoyama? The railroad man?

Yeah, the railroad man, the goddamn President of the railroad, whispered Betz, stopping in front of the door to Room 402. The Chief's in there now with the Colonel. They've been asking for you. Been asking for an hour.

Betz knocked twice on the door to the Colonel's office. He heard a voice shout "Come," opened the door, and stepped inside ahead of Harry Sweeney.

Colonel Pullman was sat behind his desk facing Chief Evans and Lieutenant Colonel Batty. Toda was in there, too, standing behind Chief Evans, a bright-yellow pad of paper in his hand. He glanced round and nodded at Harry Sweeney.

I'm sorry I'm late, sir, said Harry Sweeney. I was up at Ueno station. The latest repatriates were arriving.

Well, you're here now, said the Colonel. One less missing man. Mister Betz told you what's happened?

Only that President Shimoyama is missing, sir.

We came straight here, sir, said Betz. The minute Mister Sweeney got back.

Well, isn't a whole lot else to tell, said the Colonel. Mister Toda, would you be so kind as to recap for the benefit of your fellow investigator what little we do know.

Yes, sir, said Toda, looking down to read from his pad of yellow paper: Just after thirteen hundred hours, I received a call from a reliable source at Metropolitan Police Board Headquarters that Sadanori Shimoyama, President of the Japanese National Railways, disappeared early this morning. I then confirmed that Mister Shimoyama left his home in Denen Chōfu around 0830 hours, en route to his office in Tokyo, but has not been accounted for since. He was in a 1941 Buick Sedan, License Number 41173. The car is owned by the National Railways and was being driven by Mister Shimoyama's regular driver. My source has since told me that the MPD were first informed of the disappearance at approximately thirteen hundred hours and that a police check showed no accident involving the vehicle in question has been reported. We were officially notified of the disappearance an hour ago, at 1330 hours, and were told that all Japanese police have been informed and are making every effort to locate President Shimoyama. As far as we are aware, no information has been given to the newspapers or radio stations, not as yet.

Thank you, Mister Toda, said the Colonel. Okay, gentlemen. Top down, we got a bad feeling about this. Yesterday, as you are all no doubt aware, Shimoyama personally authorized over thirty thousand dismissal notices to be sent out, another seventy-odd thousand scheduled to go out next week. This morning he doesn't show up for work. You take a walk down any street in this city, take a look at any lamp post or wall, and there you will see bills posted saying KILL SHIMOYAMA, is that not correct, Mister Toda?

Yes, sir. It is, sir. My source also told me that President Shimoyama has been repeatedly threatened by employees opposed to the mass dismissals and retrenchment program, sir, and that he has received numerous death threats.

Any arrests?

No, sir, not as far as I am aware, sir. It is my understanding that all threats were made anonymously.

Okay, said the Colonel. Chief Evans –

Chief Evans stood up, turned now to face Bill Betz, Susumu Toda and Harry Sweeney, careful not to be standing directly in front of Colonel Pullman: You are to drop all other cases or work with immediate effect. You are to focus only on this case until further notice. You are to assume that Shimoyama has been kidnapped by either railroad workers, trade unionists, Communists or a combination of the three, and that he is being held against his will in an unknown location, and you are to conduct your investigation accordingly until you receive orders to the contrary. Is that understood?

Yes, Chief, said Toda, Betz, and Harry Sweeney.

Toda, take your eyes and ears over to Metro HQ. I want to know what they know as soon as they know it, and what they're going to do before they do it. Understood?

Yes, sir. Yes, Chief.

Mister Betz, go over to Norton Hall and see what CIC have got on these death threats. Be the usual big fat nothing, I reckon, but least no one can say we didn't try.

Yes, Chief.

Sweeney, get yourself up to Civil Transport. Find out who we got there, find out what he knows.

Yes, Chief.

The Colonel, Lieutenant Batty, and myself will be in a meeting at the Dai-ichi with General Willoughby and others. But any information whatsoever you receive, pertaining to the whereabouts of Mister Shimoyama, then you call the Dai-ichi building immediately and you ask to be put through to speak to me as a matter of extreme urgency. Is that understood?

Yes, Chief, said Toda, Betz, and Harry Sweeney.

Thank you, Chief Evans, said the Colonel, coming round from behind his desk to stand beside the Chief, standing in front of William Betz, Susumu Toda, and Harry Sweeney, to look from one man to the other, to stare each man in the eye: General Willoughby wants this man found. We all want this man found. And we want him found today and found alive.

Yes, sir, barked Toda, Betz, and Harry Sweeney.

Very good then, said the Colonel. Dismissed.

Harry Sweeney pushed his way through a crowd of people up to the third floor of the Bank of Chōsen building. The corridor was full of Japanese staff, running this way and that, in and out this door and that, answering telephones and clutching papers. He weaved his way toward Room 308. He showed his PSD wallet to the secretary outside the room and said, Sweeney, Public Safety Division. Colonel Channon is expecting me.

The man nodded: Go right in, sir.

Harry Sweeney knocked twice on the door, opened it, stepped into the room, looked at the flabby man sat behind a spartan desk, and said, Police Investigator Sweeney, sir.

Lieutenant Colonel Donald E. Channon smiled. He nodded. He got up from behind his desk. He pointed to a chair in front of the desk. He smiled again and said, Take a load off, Mister Sweeney, and sit yourself down.

Thank you, sir.

Colonel Channon sat back down behind his desk, smiled again, and said, I know you, Mister Sweeney. You're famous, you were in the papers: "the Eliot Ness of Japan," that's what they called you. That was you, right?

That was me, sir, yes, sir. Before.

Used to see you around town, too. Always some able Grable on your arm. Can't say I've seen you recently, though.

I've been away, sir.

Well, we sure picked a fine day to finally hook up. Goddamn Bedlam out there. Like Grand Central Station.

I saw that, sir.

Been like this since old Shimoyama decided not to show up for work this morning.

Why I'm here, sir.

He sure picked his day, too. Goddamn morning after the Fourth of July. I don't know about you, Mister Sweeney, but I was hoping for a quiet day. A very quiet day.

I think we all were, sir.

Colonel Channon laughed. He massaged his temples and said, Jeez, do I wish I'd taken it easy last night. Lucky I ain't got the old katzenjammers.

You and me both, sir.

Colonel Channon laughed again: You look like you seen better mornings. Where you from, Mister Sweeney?

Montana, sir.

Hell, this must be a change of pace.

It keeps me busy, sir.

You bet it does. I'm from Illinois, Mister Sweeney. Used to work for Illinois Central Railroad. Now I got the whole of Japan. Been here since August '45. My first office was a carriage on a cargo train. I've seen the whole country, Mister Sweeney. Top to tail. Every goddamn station, I reckon.

Some job, sir.

Colonel Channon stared across his desk at Harry Sweeney. He nodded: You bet it is. But you didn't come here for a history lesson, did you, Mister Sweeney?

No, sir. Not today, sir.

Colonel Channon had stopped smiling, stopped nodding. He was still staring at Harry Sweeney: Colonel Pullman send you over, did he?

Chief Evans, sir.

Same game, different name. You all answer to General Willoughby anyways. But they must be spooked if they've sent you over, Mister Sweeney. They're worried, yeah?

They're concerned, sir.

Well, swell as it is to finally meet you, Mister Sweeney, you could have saved yourself the trip here.

Harry Sweeney reached inside his jacket. He took out a notebook and a pencil. How's that, sir?

Colonel Channon glanced at the notebook and the pencil, then looked up at Harry Sweeney: You a gambling man, Mister Sweeney? You ever like to take a bet?

No, sir. Not if I can help it, sir.

Well, that's a shame, a real damn shame. Because I'd bet you a hundred bucks, a hundred of my US dollars, Mister Sweeney, that good old Shimoyama will make like Cinderella and be back home sweet home before midnight tonight.

You sound very certain, sir?

You bet I am, Mister Sweeney. I know the man. I work with him every day. Every goddamn day.

He often go AWOL, does he?

Listen, here's the thing: last night my secretary comes in, he tells me he's heard from someone in their head office that Shimoyama is going to jump. No surprise to me, Mister Sweeney. No surprise to you either, I'm guessing. You read the papers. The man is under pressure. He's the President of the Japanese National Railroads for Chrissake. He's firing over one hundred thousand of his own goddamn men. Shimoyama didn't even want the job. Straight up, I didn't want him either. Anyway, I get a jeep, go out to his place. Talk him back down.

That would be his house in Denen Chōfu, sir?

Somewhere out that way, yeah.

And what time was this, sir?

Sometime after midnight, I guess.

And you saw him?

You bet I did. His wife and his son were still up, so we went into this little old reception room they have. It's a big house, you know. Nice place. So anyway, me and him, we go in there, just me and him, and we talk.

He speaks English?

Better than you and me, Mister Sweeney. But he was exhausted. The man was shattered. The pressure he's under. But you see, this pressure is not from the union, not from the workers. There is that, but he can handle that. What he can't handle is all the goddamn internal bullshit.

Internal?

Inside the Railroad. That place is a goddamn nest of vipers, I'm telling you. They could do with someone like you in there,

Mister Sweeney. Clean the place up. Now old Shimoyama, he's Mister Clean. But he's not like you, he's not like me, he's no tough guy. See, this is why he didn't want to be president. Why no one wanted him. Too goddamn clean.

Someone must have wanted him?

Yeah, right. But see, the feller who's his deputy, Katayama, he's the one they all wanted. But his wife's father, he's caught up in some bullshit scandal. Goddamn press would never have bought it. So they picked on good old Shimoyama. Thought he was easy, thought he was soft. They know they're going to have to cut all these men. They figure old Shimoyama does the dirty work for them, then they'll cut him, too.

He took the job knowing all this?

Yes and no, Mister Sweeney. Yes and no. See, cutting the work force is only one part of the goddamn mess. They're losing money hand over fist. For my sins, I got to get them back on track. That's me, Mister Sweeney: Colonel Back-on-Track. Then keep them on the goddamn rails. That means restructuring, massive restructuring. All the kickbacks, the handouts, the extra pay days and usual graft: all that's got to go, got to stop.

And they don't like it?

You bet they don't, Mister Sweeney. They don't like it one bit. So they're freezing the guy out, giving him the shoulder, leaving him swinging. Him taking all the heat from the unions, him getting all the hate mail. All that crap on him.

So you're aware of all the threats that have been made against him then, sir?

You seen the posters all over town?

Yes, sir.

So you know, I know, the whole goddamn country knows. But like I say, that's not why he wanted to quit, why he wanted to walk. Old Shimoyama's tougher than he looks.

You said he was no tough guy, sir?

I mean not like you, not like me. You saw combat, yeah? Well, that was my second war, Mister Sweeney. Old Shimoyama, he sat the whole thing out behind his desk.

But he's tougher than he looks?

Look, he can handle all the threats. No problem. It's all this internal bullshit he can't take. They all nod along, all agree with his plans. But then they just sit on their hands and scheme against him. Den of goddamn thieves, I'm telling you.

But you went out to see him last night, sir?

Yeah, like I say. I go out there. We talk. He tells me the burden's too heavy. Apologizing away, but telling me he's had a bellyful. So I give him the spiel, you know, how what he's doing is so important for Japan, rebuilding his country. How if he resigned, it would screw the whole thing up.

And he bought it?

You bet he did, Mister Sweeney. I could sell a Bible to the Pope. We were laughing and joking when I left.

And what time was that, sir?

About two, I reckon. See, I'm guessing he didn't sleep too good, so he's just off resting someplace, waiting for all the heat to blow over. He'll turn up, Mister Sweeney.

You seem very certain, Colonel.

You bet I am. A hundred bucks says I am, if you still want it? I know the man, Mister Sweeney. Work with him every day. See him every day. Every goddamn day of the week.

Except today, sir.

Colonel Donald E. Channon stared across his desk at Harry Sweeney. Then he glanced at his watch, stood up and said, I need the can, Mister Sweeney. Then I need to get back to running my railroad.

Harry Sweeney put his pencil inside his notebook. He closed the notebook: May I use your telephone, sir?

Knock yourself out.

Thank you, sir.

Colonel Channon stopped beside Harry Sweeney's chair. He put a fat, wet hand on Harry Sweeney's shoulder: Believe me, Mister Sweeney. He'll turn up.

I believe you, sir.

Harry Sweeney could see Toda up ahead, standing outside Metropolitan Police HQ, smoking a cigarette next to a car. Harry Sweeney wiped his face and neck again, then lit a cigarette of his own as he came up to Toda: You got anything?

Nothing new, said Toda. Both Rooms One and Two are on it, acting like it's the biggest thing since Teigin. They're putting it out on the radio at five. It'll make the evening papers. So they're just sitting around, waiting by the telephones.

Harry Sweeney dropped his cigarette on the ground, stood on it, then pointed at the car: This for us?

Yes, said Toda. You got something?

Maybe. Maybe not. I don't know.

Does the Chief know?

He's in a meeting.

You should call him, Harry, tell him.

Harry Sweeney opened the back door: Tell him what?

Tell him where we're going.

Harry Sweeney got into the back of the car. He slid across the seat. He wound down the window. He leaned forward. He recognized the driver: Hey, Ichirō.

Hello, sir.

Harry Sweeney took out his notebook. He opened it, turned the pages, then said, 1081 Kami-ikegami, Ōta Ward.

Yes, sir, said Ichirō.

I don't think that's a good idea, said Toda, getting in beside Harry Sweeney, closing the door.

Harry Sweeney smiled: You got a better one?

*

It took thirty minutes to drive out along Avenue B to Senzoku Pond, then a couple more minutes to find the Shimoyama residence, down the hill from the pond, in a quiet, shaded street, one uniformed officer standing in front of the gate to the house. No crowds, no cars, no press, not yet.

Nice neighborhood, said Toda. Must cost a fortune to live round here. A fortune, Harry.

Harry Sweeney got out of the car. He wiped his face and neck. He looked up at a large British-style house, shielded by high hedges and tall trees.

Harry Sweeney and Susumu Toda showed their PSD badges to the uniformed officer at the gate. They walked up the short drive, showed their badges to the officer at the door, then stepped inside the house, their hats in their hands.

A maid showed Harry Sweeney and Susumu Toda into a Japanese-style reception room. Detective Hattori from the MPD was there. He introduced them to another detective, one from the Higashi-Chōfu station, and then to Ōtsuka, the secretary to President Shimoyama. Ōtsuka bowed, thanked them for coming, then asked, Is there any news?

No, said Harry Sweeney. I'm sorry.

Ōtsuka sighed, Ōtsuka shrank. He was a young man, in his twenties, but aging fast.

Harry Sweeney asked them all to sit back down, their knees at the low table. The maid brought in tea, the maid served the tea. Harry Sweeney asked, Where are the family?

Upstairs, said Detective Hattori.

Harry Sweeney looked across the low table at the young secretary. This anxious man, this nervous man. Harry Sweeney took out his notebook and pencil: Tell me about this morning, please. Mister Shimoyama's schedule.

Well, we were expecting the President at Headquarters as usual. The President usually arrives sometime between eight forty-five and nine o'clock. I was waiting for the President at the back entrance, as I always do. I waited there until about nine fifteen. Then I went back to my office and called Missus Shimoyama. She told me the President had left home as usual, at around eight twenty. Occasionally, the President does go somewhere before arriving at the office. So I thought maybe the President had gone to CTS, to the Bank of Chōsen building. But when I called there, they said the President was not there, and he'd not been there. So then for about the next hour or so, I was just calling any place I could think the President might have gone. I must have disturbed Missus Shimoyama three or four more times, to check if she'd heard from the President. Because by this time, we were worried, very worried. Then I met with Vice President Katayama and with two of the other directors. The Director of Security spoke with Lieutenant Colonel Channon, and I believe Vice President Katayama then visited GHQ. We also called the Metropolitan Police Headquarters, of course. And then, about three o'clock, I came out here to visit Missus Shimoyama and to meet these officers.

Harry Sweeney stopped writing. He looked up from his notebook: But what appointments did Mister Shimoyama have scheduled for this morning?

Well, apart from our morning meeting, the regular one we have every day, the President had an appointment at GHQ with Mister Hepler, the Chief of the Labor Division.

What time was that scheduled?

Eleven o'clock.

At GHQ?

Yes.

Has Mister Shimoyama ever failed to keep any appointments before?

This young man, this anxious, nervous man, shifted on his knees, looked down at his hands, and said, Not usually, no.

But sometimes, yes?

Ōtsuka looked up from his hands, Ōtsuka looked across the table at Harry Sweeney: The President has a very difficult job. His work is very demanding, his work is extremely tiring. For these past few weeks, the President has been working without rest. These past few weeks, there have been occasions when the President has had to suddenly adjust his schedule at short notice. The President has often been summoned to the CTS, or to GHQ, and at very short notice. It is a very difficult time for us all, and for the President more than anybody. We are having to dismiss over one hundred thousand members of our staff. Over one hundred thousand men. The President carries this weight personally, feels this responsibility, this burden. Every day. It's a very difficult time for him.

Harry Sweeney nodded: We are aware of how difficult the present situation is for Mister Shimoyama. That is why we are here. Thank you for answering my questions.

Harry Sweeney turned to Detective Hattori and said, I'd like to speak with Missus Shimoyama.

Detective Hattori led Harry Sweeney and Susumu Toda out of the room, up the stairs to another, larger Japanese room. There was a wooden desk, there was a large wardrobe. An elderly woman, two teenage boys, and a middle-aged woman in a somber kimono were sitting in the room. Detective Hattori introduced Harry Sweeney and Susumu Toda. He asked the elderly woman and the two boys to come downstairs to wait with him. The boys looked to their mother, the mother smiled at her boys. The boys followed their grandmother and Detective Hattori out of the room. Harry Sweeney and Susumu Toda knelt down at another low table. Harry Sweeney said, Excuse us for disturbing you in this way, Missus Shimoyama.

Missus Shimoyama shook her head: You are very welcome, Mister Sweeney. But do you have any news for me?

I'm sorry. Not yet.

So my husband is not at GHQ?

Not as far as we are aware.

I thought he must be. Recently, there have been a number of occasions when he has been summoned there. Suddenly. I thought maybe . . .

Can you think of anyplace else he might be?

No, but I am sure he must be just sleeping, just resting somewhere. So I am sorry for all the trouble he is causing. He took some sleeping pills last night, but I don't think they worked. So he must have needed a rest, a nap somewhere.

Yes, said Harry Sweeney. I heard he was very late to bed. I heard Colonel Channon visited you.

Missus Shimoyama shook her head: Not last night, no.

Are you certain, ma'am?

It was the night before.

Are you sure it was not last night?

It was the night before last. I'm certain, Mister Sweeney.

But your husband did not sleep well last night?

No, he did not sleep well, Mister Sweeney. Recently, he has been working so hard, and it's affected his sleeping.

I'm sure, said Harry Sweeney. But this morning, how did your husband seem this morning, ma'am?

Missus Shimoyama smiled: He was tired, I know. But he got up at seven o'clock, as he always does. I heard him speaking quite cheerfully with our second son, Shunji, while he was shaving in the bathroom. Then he came down to the dining room and he ate breakfast as usual.

And did you speak with your husband, ma'am?

Of course. Our eldest son is studying law at Nagoya University. But he's coming home this evening. My husband was very much looking forward to seeing him. It's been a long time since we last saw our son. A long time since my husband saw him. We were talking about his visit. About tonight.

I see, said Harry Sweeney. And so you're expecting your husband home for dinner this evening then, ma'am?

Missus Shimoyama nodded: Yes. But we are never quite sure when my husband can return home these days . . .

Down the stairs a telephone rang briefly –

Missus Shimoyama turned to look at the door: I am just sorry for all the trouble. I just wonder what is going on. He should have arrived at his office. He should have been there by nine thirty. Surely no one could have abducted him, not in broad daylight. I can't believe they would try . . .

Up the stairs feet were coming quickly –

Not from his car. In broad daylight . . .

Susumu Toda got up from the table and stepped out of the room, Missus Shimoyama watching him go, Missus Shimoyama staring at the doorway, Missus Shimoyama wringing her hands, Missus Shimoyama getting to her feet now –

What is it? What is it? Please . . .

Harry Sweeney on his feet too, his hands out toward Missus Shimoyama, asking Missus Shimoyama to sit back down. To wait, to please just wait –

Viscount Takagi disappeared, she was saying. He disappeared, too. And then they found him, found him dead in the mountains. I hope . . .

Susumu Toda stepped back into the room. He looked at them both, he said to them both, They've found the driver.

The hell you playing at, Sweeney? You should've left Toda where he was, where I sent him, where I told him to stay.

I'm sorry, Chief. But he's back there now.

Too goddamn late, sighed Chief Evans.

He called in, Chief. I've got it all here.

You better hope you have. Go on.

Harry Sweeney looked down at the yellow pad of paper in his hand and began to read: They've got the driver at Metro HQ and they're still questioning him. But so far the shorthand from Toda is the driver picks up Shimoyama as usual at eight twenty. But instead of going straight to the office, to Railroad HQ by Tokyo station, Shimoyama tells him to head to the Mitsukoshi department store in Nihonbashi. They park up there, wait for the store to open at nine thirty, then Shimoyama goes inside. He told the chauffeur to wait. Said he'd be back in five minutes. Driver hasn't seen him since.

And what time was that?

Nine thirty, Chief.

So what the hell's the driver been doing?

Says he was just sitting there, waiting in the car outside the store. He switches on the radio at five o'clock, hears the news his boss is missing, then runs straight inside the store to telephone head office.

He's just sitting in that goddamn car for over seven hours, doesn't think to get out and look for his fucking boss or to pick up a telephone and find out what the hell is going on? That's his goddamn story, is it? Jesus Christ.

He was told to wait, so he waited.

For over seven hours?

That's what he's saying, Chief. So far.

What do we know about him?

Name is Ōnishi. Forty-eight years old. Twenty years' service with the railroad. Clean as can be. Not even a parking ticket. Doesn't drink, doesn't gamble. No hint of any left-wing sympathies or associates. Loyal, trusted. That's why he's the chauffeur for the President. But they're still questioning him, and Toda will call the minute there's anything more.

Chief Evans rubbed his eyes, squeezed the bridge of his nose, then looked back up at Harry Sweeney: What do you think, Harry? What's your gut telling you?

Don't know. I spoke with Colonel Channon at CTS. He says Shimoyama wants to resign. Lot of internal railroad politics going on. That's on top of the rest of it. And I spoke with his wife. The man's not been sleeping, been taking pills. The pills aren't working. She's just praying he's off someplace resting, that he'll be back for his dinner.

The Chief sighed again: You reckon he's just gone and wandered off reservation then?

Maybe. Hopefully.

You don't sound so convinced, Harry?

Just not so sure he'll wander back, Chief.

Well, we need him back, Harry. And back now.

Hot and humid still, it was getting dark now, the city closing down, the city going home. Ichirō drove Toda and Harry Sweeney along Avenue A, then up Avenue W, under the railroad tracks, through the crossroads at Gofukubashi and on past the Yashima Hotel, turning left by the Shirokiya department store, then over the river at Nihonbashi, before turning left again, up one side street, then right and right again, down another side street, until Toda said, This is the place.

In the shadows of the Mitsukoshi department store, alongside the doors to its south entrance, Ichirō parked up.

In this narrow side street, the car facing the main street, from the back seat Harry Sweeney stared past Ichirō, out through the windshield, down through the shadows, up toward the lights on the main street: traffic heading home, people going home; men heading home, returning to their homes.

Hell of a tour to get here, said Toda.

Harry Sweeney turned to his left and looked out at the doors to the store, glass and gold, dark and closed. The doors closed, the store closed. Everything closed, everything dark. He nodded, then said, Tell me again.

Okay, so according to Ōnishi, said Toda, taking out his notebook, opening up his notebook, Shimoyama wanted to do some shopping, said something like it was okay for him to arrive at the office by ten. So first he tells Ōnishi to drive to Shirokiya; when they get there, the store's not open. So Shimoyama tells him to drive here. Ōnishi says Mitsukoshi won't be open either. This is all before nine o'clock. So Ōnishi starts to head back toward railroad HQ, but Shimoyama tells him to go to Kanda station. They pull up there, but Shimoyama stays in the car. Ōnishi asks if he's going to get out; Shimoyama says no. So Ōnishi starts back to HQ again. But when they're crossing Gofukubashi, Shimoyama tells him to go to the Chiyoda Bank. They park in front, Shimoyama gets out. He goes into the bank; he's inside for about twenty minutes. He comes back out. It's now about nine twenty-five. Shimoyama says something like now is the best time to go. Ōnishi assumes he means back here, back to Mitsukoshi. When they get here, when they park up here, Shimoyama just stays put again, says the store isn't open yet. Ōnishi can see there are already customers inside and tells Shimoyama the store's open. Shimoyama gets out. He tells Ōnishi to wait. He says he needs to buy a present, a wedding present, but he'll be back in five minutes. Then Shimoyama walks off, in through those doors.

Harry Sweeney stared out at those dark doors, those closed doors. Everything closed now, everything dark now.

They've sent in Hattori with a whole squad to search the building, said Toda. Top to bottom, every floor, every room, the restrooms and the roof. Not a trace of the man. But they've kept all the staff back. They're still in there, as far as I know, still questioning them. Someone must have seen something. The man can't have just vanished into thin air.

Harry Sweeney nodded again. He opened the door of the car: You go back to the office, wait there. I'll call you.

But what if he turns up? Where will you be?

Then you won't need me, said Harry Sweeney. He got out of the car and closed the door. He stood on the side street and stared up at the Mitsukoshi department store –

The seven stories, the tower on the roof. The darkening sky above, the lengthening shadows below.

Harry Sweeney turned and walked away from the car, the car heading off toward the main street and the bright lights. He walked down the side street, down the side of the store, toward the end of the building, deeper into its shadows. He turned to his right and walked down another side road, along the back of the building, the length of the store, past the loading bays, the platforms, and the shutters. Everything closed, everything dark. He turned right again at the end of the building and walked down another side road, down the north side of the building, the north side of the store, past the windows and past the doors. Everything closed, everything dark. He walked through the shadows, back toward the lights, the bright lights of the main street. He reached the corner of the building, the junction with the main street. He turned right onto the main street and walked along the front of the store, past the dark windows to the front doors, the main entrance with its bronze statues of two lions, poised there, sitting there, guarding the store, on their marble plinths with their mouths open, their eyes open, watching the street, the passing traffic, the passing people, the traffic heading home, the people going home.

Under the lights of the street, at the entrance to the store, Harry Sweeney reached out to touch the two front paws of each bronze lion. He rubbed each paw and he said a prayer, then he heard a rumbling underground, felt a trembling in the ground. He turned away from the lions, turned away from his prayers, and he walked toward the entrance to the subway.

Harry Sweeney went down the steep stone stairs to the subway below, under the ground, along a corridor. There were marble columns and a tiled floor, the basement of the store to his left, other shops to his right. Everything closed, everything dark. The corridor led to the subway, a passage to Mitsukoshimae station. He could see the station up ahead, down the corridor. He walked along the corridor toward the station, past the basement windows of the Mitsukoshi department store, to the basement doors of the store; the doors from the department store to the subway station, from the station to the store: an entrance and an exit. He walked toward the ticket gate to the subway and was about to show his PSD badge, was about to go through the gate, when he saw some more shops in the gray shadows down the corridor, beyond the station and the store. He saw a hair salon, he saw a tea shop, and he saw a coffee shop: COFFEE SHOP HONG KONG.

Harry Sweeney turned away from the ticket gate, walked down the corridor, beyond the station and the store, to the coffee shop in the gray shadows. He stood before its dark window and its closed door. He knocked on the door and waited. Everything closed, everything dark. He knocked again and tried the door. No light went on, no answer came –

*Too late, whispered the voice of a Japanese man, then the voice was gone, the line dead, the connection lost.*

Harry Sweeney heard a rumbling underground again, felt a trembling in the ground again. He turned away from the door, turned away from his petitions, and walked back toward the ticket gate. He showed his pass, went through the gate and down the steps, onto the platform. The trains for Asakusa to his left, the trains for Shibuya to his right. East or west, north or south, under the ground, under the city, people going home, men heading home, returning to their homes.

But not tonight, not here: the platform was deserted, and Harry Sweeney was alone, waiting for a train, looking into the mouth of the tunnel, staring into the darkness, watching for the light, waiting for the light. A solitary Japanese came slowly and unsteadily down the stairs onto the platform. He was short but stocky, in a pale summer suit darkened by grime and stains, sweat and drink. He walked up close to Harry Sweeney, foisting his face up to his face, smelling as bad as he looked, as drunk as he sounded: America! America! Hey you, America!

Harry Sweeney took a step back, but the Japanese took a step forward: You hairy coward! You think you won the war, but we Japanese are not so easily defeated!

He stood there, glaring up through his spectacles at Harry Sweeney, and repeated the same sentence, but more slowly and much louder. Then he made a sudden lunge and gripped Harry Sweeney in both arms, maneuvering to throw Harry Sweeney onto the live electric line. He was too weak and too drunk, but Harry Sweeney was locked in his embrace.

Another man, also drunk, now joined the party: I Korean, America's friend, he shouted, and pulled the Japanese off Harry Sweeney as a blast of wind came rushing out of the tunnel and along the platform, picking up scraps of paper and ends of cigarettes, making small tornadoes of trash around their feet. Harry Sweeney gripped his hat, held it tight as the train pulled into the station, the screams of its wheels and brakes piercing his ears. At that moment, the Japanese made another sudden, wild rush, but the young Korean knocked him out with one punch. Go, said the Korean. Just go.

Harry Sweeney got onto the train. The doors closed and the train began to move. He looked back at the platform: the young Korean standing over the still-prone Japanese, going through the man's pockets, and then they were gone. Harry Sweeney turned back to the brightly lit carriage of half-empty seats. He sat down and took off his hat. He took out his handkerchief and wiped his face and then his neck. He put away his handkerchief and then his hat back on. He looked up and down the carriage, then across the aisle, at the passengers. A man here, a man there, in jackets, in ties, sleeping or reading, a book or a paper. Back pages and front pages, in their hands or at their feet: one left on the floor of the carriage, a single sheet of newspaper, an extra *Mainichi*. Harry Sweeney leaned forward, reached down to the floor, picked up the sheet, and read the headline: PRESIDENT SHIMOYAMA MISSING; *On The Way To JNR Headquarters From His Home; Police still investigating as of 5pm.*

Harry Sweeney looked back up at the passengers, the men here and there, in their jackets and their ties, reading or sleeping, sleeping or not. Men after their work, men going back home. Maybe, maybe not. Harry Sweeney folded up the paper and put it in his pocket. The train stopped in Kanda. Harry Sweeney took off his hat again. He reached back into his pocket and took out his handkerchief again. He wiped his face and then his neck again. The train stopped in Ueno. Harry Sweeney put away his handkerchief and put on his hat again. He stood up and walked through the carriages toward the front of the train, to the end of the line. The train terminated in Asakusa and the doors opened. Harry Sweeney stepped onto the platform. He walked up the steps to the ticket gate, showed his pass, and went on through the gate. There was another basement entrance to another department store: the Matsuya department store closed, the Matsuya department store dark. Harry Sweeney walked up the steps to the Tōbu line station, but he did not take the second staircase up to the platforms. Harry Sweeney turned left, out of the station, onto the street, and stopped. His back to the station, his back to the store, the Kamiya Bar to his right, the Sumida River to his left, the shops already shut, the stalls now packing up, he watched the people walking past, the people going home. Harry Sweeney watched them pass, he watched them go. Into the night and into the shadows. Men disappearing, men vanishing.

Harry Sweeney turned and started to walk away from the station, away from the store, across Avenue R, toward the river, the Sumida River. He walked into the park, through the park, the Sumida Park. He came to the river, the banks of the river. He stood on the bank and he stared at the river. The current still, the water black. There was no breeze, there was no air. Only the stench of sewage, the stink of shit. People's shit, men's shit. The stench always here, the stink still here. Harry Sweeney took out his pack of cigarettes and lit one. By the river, on her bank. The streets behind him, the station behind him. All the streets and all the stations. He stared down the river, into the darkness, where its mouth would be, where the sea would be; across the ocean, there was home. A dog barked and wheels screamed, somewhere in the night, somewhere behind him. A yellow train was pulling out of the station, the yellow train crossing an iron bridge. The bridge across the river, a bridge to the other side. Going east, going north. Out of the city, away from the city. Men disappearing, men vanishing. In the city, from the city. On its streets, in its stations. Their names and their lives. Disappearing, vanishing. Starting afresh, starting again. A new name, a new life. A different name, a different life. Never going home, never coming back. The train disappearing, the train vanishing.

Harry Sweeney looked away from the bridge, stared back down at the river, the Sumida River. So still and so black, so soft and so warm. Inviting and welcoming, tempting, so tempting. No more names and no more lives. Memories or visions, insects or specters. So tempting, very tempting. An end to it all, an end to it all. The pattern of the crime precedes the crime. The end of his cigarette burning his fingers, blistering their skin. Harry Sweeney threw the butt of his cigarette into the river. This dirty river, this stinking river. People's shit, men's shit. He turned away from the river, walked away from the river, the Sumida River. Back to the station, back down the steps. Away from the river, the Sumida River, and away from temptation, away from temptation. The pattern and the crime. Disappearing, vanishing. Into the night, into the shadows. Under the city, under the ground.

*

Back again, laughed Akira Senju, the man who would not die, the man who really ruled this city, its Secret Emperor. In plain sight, in his Shimbashi Palace, at the heart of his thriving empire, at the top of his shiny new building, in his luxurious modern office, at his antique rosewood desk, in his expensive tailored suit, with his fat foreign cigar, he reached into a drawer, took out a piece of paper, and handed it across the desk to Harry Sweeney: That should keep you occupied, Harry-san.

Harry Sweeney glanced down at the piece of paper, its list of names: Formosan names, Korean names. Harry Sweeney folded the paper in half, put it in his jacket pocket, and started to get to his feet, to turn to the door, the exit.

Not staying for a drink tonight, Harry, said Akira Senju. Of course not, excuse me, you're a busy man, I know. I was actually surprised you called, surprised you came. I thought you'd have had your hands full, trying to find your missing president. Very careless that, I must say, Harry. Losing a president. All over the radio, all over the papers. Looks very bad, very careless. Makes people nervous, makes people worried. Our imperial masters, our foreign saviors, and you go and lose your president, your own little lapdog, your little puppet. I mean, if you can't protect the President of the National Railroads, if he can be abducted in broad daylight, then who can you protect, Harry? And if you can't find him, can't save him, then who can you save?

Harry Sweeney turned back from the door. He said, You're so certain he's been abducted, are you?

What else could have happened, Harry? You fire a man, you expect a reaction. You fire thirty thousand men, you expect thirty thousand reactions, no? Extreme reactions, violent reactions. I mean, a man doesn't simply disappear, simply vanish. Well, some men, yeah. But not presidents. Presidents, well, they tend to . . . Well, they tend to get assassinated, Harry.

Harry Sweeney smiled: We'll see.

We will, Harry, we will. I'm just surprised you're not out there now. Cracking union skulls, breaking red bones. That's what I'd be doing. Cracking skulls and breaking bones. Turning this city upside down, burning it down, if I had to. If that's what I had to do, if that's what it took to get my man back. That's what I'd be doing, Harry.

Harry Sweeney smiled again: Well, I'm not you.

Really, laughed Akira Senju. Well, you keep telling yourself whatever you need to tell yourself, Harry. I know how it is, I understand. But remember: you ever need a list of Communists, of Reds, of skulls to crack, of bones to break, then you know where to find me, Harry. You know where I am. And I am here to help. So you be sure to tell the General, General Willoughby, I'm your man, Harry-san. I'm your man.

Fuck, cursed Harry Sweeney in a telephone booth in the lobby of the Dai-ichi Hotel. He replaced the receiver and stepped out of the booth. He walked across the lobby and handed his hat to the checkroom girl. The Japanese girl gave him a ticket and bowed. Harry Sweeney smiled, thanked her, then turned and walked down the stairs into the cellar bar. Low lights and loud voices. Foreign voices, American voices. Americans playing poker in one corner, Americans playing ping-pong in another, Americans singing "Roll Me Over in the Clover," Americans clapping and Americans laughing; Americans drinking, Americans drunk. Harry Sweeney took a stool at the bar and nodded to the Japanese barman. In his white shirt and black bow tie, the barman came over: What'll it be, Harry?

The usual please, Joe, said Harry Sweeney.

Joe the barman put a glass down on the counter in front of Harry Sweeney. He picked up a bottle of Johnnie Walker. He filled the glass: You still never say when, Harry?

That's me, Joe. No ice, no soda, no when.

Joe the barman filled the glass to the brim. He put the bottle down. He said, She's been and gone, Harry.

Harry Sweeney nodded. He reached out toward the glass. He gripped it in his fingers. He leaned forward, bowed over the drink. He smiled and nodded again.

Joe the barman shook his head: And you won't find her in there, Harry. You know that.

No harm in just looking, is there, Joe?

Joe shook his head again.

A young woman in a red dress walked down the length of the bar. She had large eyes, a large nose, and she was smoking a cigarette, holding a glass. She put the glass on the counter next to Harry Sweeney, put her hand on the stool next to Harry Sweeney, and said, You expecting company?

I try to avoid expectations, said Harry Sweeney.

But you don't mind some?

Mind some what?

Some company?

Depends on the company.

The woman sat down on the stool, turned and held out her hand toward Harry Sweeney. She had a wide mouth and full lips. She smiled and said, Gloria Wilson.

Harry Sweeney.

I know, said Gloria Wilson. We're neighbors.

You don't say.

I do say, laughed Gloria Wilson. You're on the fourth floor, I'm on the third. At the NYK building.

Well, fancy that.

Not really, said Gloria Wilson. It's such a small world, don't you think, Mister Sweeney? This world. And it's all Sir Charles's world. We're all his children. You, me, and everyone here. We're all his children, Mister Sweeney.

You should be careful, Miss Wilson. Walls have ears. The General might not like it if he heard you talking that way. He might take offense.

I'm sure he would, Mister Sweeney. But he wouldn't like the color of my dress either, would he? He'd be offended by that. He's so easily offended. Poor man.

Harry Sweeney nodded at Joe the barman: Give the lady another of whatever she's drinking, please, Joe.

I hope you're not implying I'm some kind of lush, Mister Sweeney, said Gloria Wilson. Because I'm not.

Harry Sweeney shook his head: Not at all, Miss Wilson. It's just called being friendly where I come from.

And where's that, Mister Sweeney?

Montana.

Billings? Missoula? Helena?

Nope.

Great Falls? Butte?

No.

Well, that's me stumped, Mister Sweeney. You win.

Not really, said Harry Sweeney. Anaconda.

It must be very beautiful. The Big Sky.

You've never been to Montana.

No, but I'd like to go.

What makes you say that?

Oh, no reason, sighed Gloria Wilson. No reason except it isn't Muncie, Indiana, I guess.

Muncie, Indiana's that bad?

Yes, laughed Gloria Wilson. That bad.

So how long you been free of Muncie, Indiana?

Probably too long now.

Too long? So you want to go home?

No, Mister Sweeney, said Gloria Wilson. I do not want to go home. I sometimes dream I'm back home, back in Muncie. But then, when I wake up, when I open my eyes and I look around my room, I'm so very glad I'm not back home in Muncie. I'm so very relieved I'm still here, here in Tokyo.

In the Kingdom of Sir Charles?

Well now, we can't have everything now, can we, Mister Sweeney? That just wouldn't be fair.

But you feel guilty you don't want to go home.

Yes, I do, Mister Sweeney, I do! I feel so very guilty.

Harry Sweeney slowly raised his glass, careful not to spill the whisky: Nice to meet you, Miss Wilson.

Gloria Wilson raised her glass, gently touched it against the glass in Harry Sweeney's hand, smiled, and said, Nice to meet you, too, Mister Sweeney.

And here's to not being in Anaconda or Muncie, said Harry Sweeney, gently touching glasses again, then carefully putting his own back down on the counter.

You bet! But you're not drinking your drink?

I just watch these days.

You see much happen, laughed Gloria Wilson.

More than you'd think.

But you don't mind if I drink mine?

I'd be heartbroken if you didn't, Miss Wilson.

Then I surely shall, said Gloria Wilson. She took a sip from her glass, and then another: If only to keep your heart from breaking, Mister Sweeney.

You're very kind, Miss Wilson. Thank you.

I'm not really, said Gloria Wilson. But thank you for saying so. And please, call me Gloria, Mister Sweeney.

Then call me Harry, if you don't mind.

I don't mind at all, Harry. You're famous.

For what, Miss Wilson? Sorry, I mean Gloria.

Now you're being a tease, Harry Sweeney. You know full well for what. You were in the papers. You're the man who's busting all their gangs. Everyone knows that.

You really shouldn't believe everything you read, said Harry Sweeney. But what about you? What do you do, Gloria? Down on the third floor?

Well, nothing so exciting or glamorous as you, Harry, laughed Gloria Wilson. I'm just Miss Plain Jane the librarian. In the Historical Branch. That's dull little me.

I very much doubt that, said Harry Sweeney. You sure don't dress like any librarian I ever saw. Not in Montana.

Gloria Wilson laughed: And not in Muncie, Indiana, either. Then she nodded at the poker game over in the corner: But we're having an historical night on the town.

Harry Sweeney glanced at the corner, at the faces round the table. Three Americans, one Japanese. No one clapping, no one laughing. Not joining in the songs, just playing their cards. Harry Sweeney smiled: Looks like a swell old party.

You're kidding me? Worse than the library. But my friends Don and Mary, they said they'd swing by. They're a blast, you'd like them . . .

Harry Sweeney smiled again. Harry Sweeney looked at his watch. Then Harry Sweeney nodded to Joe the barman again as he stood up: Freshen up the lady's glass for her, will you, Joe, and stick it on my tab, please.

Don't tell me you're leaving, said Gloria Wilson.

Harry Sweeney bowed: Back to work for me, I'm afraid. But it's been real nice to meet you, Gloria.

Just my luck, laughed Gloria Wilson. I finally run into someone in this town who'll still buy a drink for a round-eyes and make nice, and you're a workaholic. But thank *you*, Harry Sweeney. Thank you. It's been a pleasure . . .

Harry Sweeney smiled: See you around, Gloria.

You bet you will. I'll come find you . . .

You're welcome to try, laughed Harry Sweeney, then he walked away from the woman, the bar, and the drink, and up the stairs. He handed his ticket to the checkroom girl. The girl gave him his hat with a smile and a bow. Harry Sweeney smiled back and thanked her. He walked across the lobby, out through the doors, and straight into a couple: a Japanese woman in a kimono and an American man in uniform –

Well, hell, the odds of that, laughed Lieutenant Colonel Donald E. Channon. We don't meet for four years, then twice in the same goddamn day. You find my president for me, did you yet, Mister Sweeney?

Your president, sir?

My railroad, my goddamn president.

Not last I heard, sir, no.

Colonel Channon put a hand in his pocket, took out a wad of notes, and waved them about in front of Harry Sweeney: A hundred goddamn dollars, Sweeney.

Donny, please, said the Japanese woman at his side. Come on, Donny. Let's just go home, please, Donny . . .

Jesus Christ, spat Colonel Channon, pushing the woman away, staggering on the step, scattering the notes, swinging at the woman, and shouting, What did I tell you about speaking when I'm speaking! And calling me . . .

Harry Sweeney took the Colonel's arm, pulling him away from the woman: It's late, sir. I think –

Don't you goddamn tell me what you think, Sweeney. I know you, Sweeney, you're no saint. Just a pack of lies, a goddamn pack of lies. That's you, Sweeney, same as all the goddamn rest of them. I don't give a crap what you think, what any of you fucking think. I love this woman! Goddamn fucking love her, Sweeney. You hear me? You all fucking hear me! And I love her goddamn fucking country, too! So screw you, Sweeney. Screw you and goodnight.

Harry Sweeney put the key in the lock of the door to his room in the Yaesu Hotel. He turned the key, he opened the door. He shut the door behind him, he locked the door behind him. He stood in the center of the room and he looked around the room. In the light from the street, in the light from the night. The screwed-up envelope, the torn-up letter. The open Bible, the fallen crucifix. The upturned suitcase, the empty wardrobe. The pile of damp clothes, the bundle of soiled sheets. The bare mattress, the empty bed. He heard the rain on the window, he heard the rain in the night. He walked over to the washstand. He looked down into the basin. He saw the shards of broken glass. He looked back up into the mirror, he stared at the face in the mirror. He stared at its jaw, its cheek, its eyes, its nose, and its mouth. He reached up to touch the face in the mirror, to trace the outline of its jaw, its cheek, its eyes, its nose, and its mouth. He ran his fingers up and down the edge of the mirror. He gripped the edges of the mirror. He prized the mirror off the wall. He crouched down. He placed the face of the mirror against the wall beneath the window. He started to stand back up. He saw spots of blood on the carpet. He took off his jacket. He threw it onto the mattress. He unbuttoned the cuffs of his shirt. He rolled up the cuffs of his shirt. He saw the spots of blood on the bandages on his wrists. He undid the buttons of his shirt. He took off his shirt. He tossed it onto the mattress. He took off his watch. He dropped it on the floor. He unhooked the safety pin that secured the bandage on his left wrist. He put the pin between the faucets of the washbasin. He unwound the bandage on his left wrist. He threw the length of bandage on top of his shirt on the mattress. He unhooked the safety pin that secured the bandage on his right wrist. He put it next to the other safety pin between the faucets. He unwound the bandage from his right wrist. He tossed this length of bandage onto the other bandage on top of his shirt. He picked up the trash can. He carried it over to the basin. He picked out the pieces of broken glass. He put them in the trash. He turned on the faucets. He waited for the water to come. To drown out the rain on the window, to silence the rain in the night. He put the stopper in the basin, he filled the basin. He turned off the faucets. The sound of the rain on the window again, the noise of the rain in the night again. He put his hands and his wrists into the basin and the water. He soaked his hands and his wrists in the water in the basin. He watched the water wash away the blood. He felt the water cleanse his wounds. He nudged out the stopper. He watched the water drain from the basin, from around his wrists, from between his fingers. He lifted his hands from the basin. He picked up a towel from the floor. He dried his hands and his wrists on the towel. He folded the towel. He hung the towel on the rail beside the basin. He walked back into the center of the room. In the light from the street, in the light from the night. He held out his hands, he turned over his palms. He looked down at the clean, dry scars on his wrists. He stared at them for a long time. Then he knelt down in the center of the room. By the screwed-up envelope, before the torn-up letter. The scraps of paper, the scraps of phrases. Betrayal. Deceit. Judas. Lust. Marriage. Sanctity. My religion. You traitor. Will never give up. Give you a divorce. I know what you are like, I know who you are. But I forgive you, Harry. The children forgive you, Harry. Come home, Harry. Please just come home. Harry Sweeney brought his palms together. Harry Sweeney raised his hands toward his face. He bowed his head. He closed his eyes. In the middle of the American Century, in the middle of the American night. Bowed in his room, his hotel room. The rain on the window, the rain in the night. On his knees, his stained knees. Falling down, pouring down. Harry Sweeney heard the telephones ringing. The voices raised, the orders barked. The boots down the stairs, the boots in the street. Car doors opening, car doors closing. Engines across the city, brakes four stories below. Boots up the stairs, boots down the corridor. The knuckles on the door, the words through the wood: Are you there, Harry? Are you in there?

Harry Sweeney opened his eyes. He got to his feet and he steadied himself. He walked to the bed. He picked up his shirt, he put on his shirt. He stared across the room at the door. Then he walked to the door and he put his hand on the key. He breathed in, he breathed out. He turned the key, he opened the door, and said, What you want, Susumu?

Toda standing in the corridor, Toda soaked from head to toe: They've found him, Harry.

Thank Christ.

He's dead.

# 2

## The Next Day

---

*July 6, 1949*

They drove as fast as they could through the night and the rain: Harry Sweeney in the back beside Bill Betz, Toda up front with Ichirō at the wheel, north through Ueno and up Avenue Q, then east at Minowa and across the river, the Sumida River.

Harry Sweeney looked at his watch again, its face cracked and hands stopped: What time is it now?

Just gone four, said Toda.

Harry Sweeney turned back to the side window, to the night and the rain, the city and its streets, deserted and silent, buildings ebbing as fields emerged, heading north again now, to the edge of the city, as fast as they could.

It's here, said Toda, as Ichirō pulled in and parked up behind Ayase station. There were cars on either side of them, standing black and empty under buckets of water.

Fuck, said Betz. Look at the rain.

Toda, Betz, and Harry Sweeney got out of their car into the night and the rain, the end of the night and the sheets of rain. Jesus wept, said Betz. And not an umbrella between us.

They turned up the collars of their jackets, they pulled down the brims of their hats, and again Betz said, Fuck.

That way, said Toda, pointing west.

How far that way, said Betz.

I don't know, said Toda.

We'll find out soon enough, said Harry Sweeney. Come on. We're wasting time.

They walked away from the station. Beside the tracks, following the tracks. They crossed a footbridge over a narrow river. Beside the tracks, following the tracks. The tall, dark walls of Kosuge Prison rising up to their left, the wide, dark void of open fields gaping to their right. Beside the tracks, following the tracks. In the hard rain, amid the heavy sheets. They were drenched in their clothes, they were soaked to their skins. Into their blood, into their bones. The rain falling, the rain wounding. Betz said, How much goddamn further?

There, said Toda. That must be the place.

They saw lanterns up ahead, they saw men up ahead. Before a bridge, below an embankment. In their oilskins and in their raincoats. In their rubber boots, up and down the tracks, in their rubber boots, back and forth across the tracks. In the sheets of rain, by the light of their lanterns. They were picking up pieces of clothing, they were throwing down pieces of flesh. Up and down, back and forth, this way and that, all over the place, clothing and flesh, strewn about and ripped apart –

Jesus, said Betz. Will you look at that –

A severed arm between the outbound tracks.

Jesus, said Betz again. Poor bastard.

In the night and in the rain, Harry Sweeney said nothing. Harry Sweeney stood there, wishing the night would end and the rain would stop, staring up and down the tracks, trying to see as much as he could see, desperate to remember as much as he could remember. In the night and in the rain, Harry Sweeney took out his notebook and his pencil, and in the night and in the rain, Harry Sweeney began walking along the tracks, pacing out the distances, sketching the scene and jotting down details: the tracks passed under a bridge carrying another railroad; three yards from the bridge, there was a large amount of oil on the sleepers and the ballast; six and a half yards from the bridge, a right ankle in a torn sock lay on the ballast; twelve yards from the bridge, between the tracks, was the garter of a sock; approximately fourteen yards from the bridge, in the grass beside the outbound track, was a crushed right shoe; eighteen and a half yards from the bridge, the left shoe lay between the outbound tracks; twenty-six yards from the bridge, between the outbound tracks, Toda identified a strip of material as being a *fundoshi*, or loincloth, traditional Japanese underwear; thirty yards from the bridge was a white shirt, its back torn; forty-seven yards from the bridge, the left ankle again still in its sock lay on the ballast between the tracks; fifty yards from the bridge, between the tracks, was the jacket of a suit, its back torn in a way similar to the tear in the white shirt; fifty-nine yards from the bridge, on the ballast between the outbound and inbound tracks, was the face of a man, severed from the top of the head down to the chin, one eye still attached, staring up, up into the night and the rain –

Fuck, said Betz.

Toda nodded: Things a train does to a man.

Harry Sweeney said nothing, still walking, still writing: there was brain matter, too, beside the face; intestines scattered between the tracks for the next ten yards or so; seventy-five yards from the bridge, the right arm and part of the shoulder lay on the ballast between the outbound tracks; finally, ninety yards from the bridge, on the ballast between the outbound tracks, there was the torso, stripped and twisted, its back and its knees both contorted against the ballast, almost severed at the waist, the flesh open and the bones crushed –

Fuck, said Betz again. What a way to go. Jesus.

Harry Sweeney said nothing, watching a faint light now spreading from the east, watching it pick out the white pieces of wet skin and the gray chunks of damp flesh all scattered and strewn back down the tracks. In the grayer light and in the quieter rain, Harry Sweeney turned away from the skin and from the flesh, from the tracks and from the ballast. More men arriving, some men leaving, coming and going, up and down, back and forth, across the tracks and over the scene. He watched the Metropolitan Police investigators now taking charge of the scene, the public prosecutors and medical examiners now arriving, and asked Toda to find out their names and ranks, their positions and functions, what they had heard and what they had seen. And then Harry Sweeney stood in the dawn and in the drizzle, soaked through to his own skin and bone, and he looked to the east, and then turned to the south, to the west, and to the north, looking at a crossing and the station up the line, a building and the prison beside the tracks, the bridge and the embankment down the line, and the fields, the low, flat fields which stretched to the north, Harry Sweeney looking and turning, again and again, turning and looking at this silent, empty, and godforsaken landscape of a death –

What are you thinking, Harry, asked Betz.

Why here, Bill? Why here?

They were walking back down the tracks, back toward Ayase station, back toward the car, Toda reading from his notes, telling them what he'd learned at the scene, saying, I'll spare you the names for now, but the driver of the last freight train from Ueno to Matsudo stopped at Ayase station to report that he thought he'd glimpsed some scarlet objects scattered across the tracks where they run parallel to the prison. Apparently, the place is known as Demon's Crossing or Cursed Crossing –

You don't fucking say, laughed Betz.

Yeah, said Toda. It's notorious for accidents and suicides, so the locals keep away. Especially when it rains. That's when the ghosts of the wronged gather by the bridge or the crossing. They reckon you can hear them all weeping.

When was the last one, asked Harry Sweeney.

The last what?

Suicide.

They didn't say, and I didn't ask. Sorry, Harry.

We can find out. Go on.

So the driver stops at Ayase to say he thinks he's seen a "tuna," that's their slang for a corpse on the line. This is at approximately half past midnight. So the assistant stationmaster sends the ticket inspector and another member of staff down the line to the Cursed Crossing to investigate. They only had a hand lantern between them but they could see a body on the tracks, so they go straight to the police box by the prison to telephone the assistant stationmaster and report what they've seen. The assistant stationmaster then forwards the report up the chain of command to the chief of the maintenance team for the Kita-Senju area. I need to confirm this, but I think they were at Gotanno, on the Tōbu line, that's the next station on the line which runs over that bridge. Anyway, the chief and one of his men set off down the Tōbu line, eventually coming down the embankment beside the bridge, arriving at the scene at half past one. It's already raining by then, but they find the badly mutilated, partially severed body of a well-built man. They search through what they describe as the shredded, oil-stained clothing strewn about the scene, looking for a means of identification, and find name cards and travel passes in the name of Sadanori Shimoyama, President of the National Railroads. They immediately head for the nearest police box – which is Gotanno Minami-machi – and report what they've found to an officer named Nakayama. It's now two fifteen. Nakayama immediately notifies the Nishi-Arai police station and then heads to the scene himself, which is where I found him; Nakayama's the officer I spoke to who told me all this. When he got there – which was about two forty, he reckons –

there were some other men there, men from Ayase station and the maintenance division. The stationmaster also arrived while Nakayama was there, and they all began to search for other means of identification. Found a wristwatch by the torso, a gold tooth, too. At some point, the stationmaster turned over the torso, found a wallet in one of the pockets of the pants. The rain was really coming down by now, but Nakayama said the ballast beneath the torso was dry when they turned it over.

They had reached their car. Ichirō sat waiting at the wheel; four or five more cars parked up, all empty.

I don't know about you two, said Betz, but I want a hot bath and breakfast, and then my bed. Be lucky if we aren't off sick for a week, way that fucking rain came down.

Harry Sweeney looked at the empty cars, looked at the station building, and said, You wait in the car, Bill. I'll be back as quick as I can, okay? You come with me, Susumu.

Better be quick, Harry, I swear. I'm shivering.

Be as quick as we can, said Harry Sweeney again, lighting a cigarette, walking off toward the station buildings, asking Toda, These cars? They belong to the Railroad, yeah?

Toda glanced back and nodded: Yeah. Most of them.

Harry Sweeney smiled: Let's save some legwork –

Inside the stationmaster's office at Ayase station, three men from the Head Office of the National Railways were gathered around a small *hibachi*. Pale and wet, silent and mourning, they were drying their suits, drying their skins. Harry Sweeney took out his PSD badge and said, I believe one of you gentlemen identified President Shimoyama?

Yes, said one of the men. I did.

And your name is . . . ?

Masao Orii.

Harry Sweeney said, Mister Orii, I want you to tell me exactly how you came to be here. Tell me who called you and when. And then everything you saw when you arrived here, and all that has happened since then. Everything, please.

Well, began Mister Orii, I received a phone call at the President's house at three –

I am sorry to interrupt you, Mister Orii. I should have been more specific. I want you to go back through the whole day for me, tell me everything you can.

Well then, began Mister Orii again, I first heard the President was missing at around eleven o'clock this morning. Sorry, yesterday morning. Mister Aihara called me to say that the President had not yet shown up for work, for the daily morning meeting. But to be honest, at the time I did not pay particular attention to what he was saying, or take it very seriously. I thought it was ridiculous and forgot about it.

And why was that, Mister Orii?

Well, because I was so busy. It is my responsibility to arrange the extra trains for the repatriates who have been returning. There has been a lot of trouble, a lot of confusion at various stations. At Shinagawa, Tokyo, and Ueno. And I had men from the Ministry of Transport calling me, the police, and so on. Many people to deal with, a lot of calls, a lot of visitors. But around one o'clock, Mister Ōtsuka, the personal secretary to the President, he called me. He said that the President had still not shown up and could I think of anyone or anywhere the President might visit. I just told him what he had already heard from everyone else, what he already knew. But that was when I began to be worried, began to think something might have really happened to President Shimoyama.

Like what, Mister Orii?

Like he might have been kidnapped or something.

By whom?

Well, by people opposed to the cuts, the dismissals. I know there have been a lot of threats. Letters and calls. And then there are the posters.

Any specific individual or group?

No, no names. Nothing like that. I wasn't thinking like that; I was just thinking, I hope nothing like that has happened to the President.

So after this call at one, then what did you do?

I had to stay in the office. As I say, I still had to deal with all the matters to do with the repatriates and their trains. And so I couldn't leave. But I was worried, and I was also aware that there had been an announcement on the radio, and the newspapers had printed extra editions.

So what time did you leave the office, Mister Orii?

It was after midnight. I couldn't tell you exactly when, I'm sorry. But after midnight, when things had calmed down. I went to the President's house in Kami-ikegami. It was about one when I arrived. There were about twelve cars parked outside the house. All from the newspapers. I went into the house. The reporters were inside the house, in the drawing room. About fifteen or sixteen of them. I went upstairs, into the living room. Missus Shimoyama and all four of their sons were there, and the President's younger brother. They were just sitting there, very worried, in silence. After a few minutes, Missus Shimoyama said she would like the reporters downstairs to leave. She said they had been there such a long time, and she had not even offered them any tea or anything. And she was sorry. So I went back downstairs and told them to leave. I said if we had any information, we would let them know. They all left, and I went back upstairs. Everyone was just waiting. No one talking, no one speaking. Just waiting. Then about ten past three, the telephone beside me rang. It was the Railroad Telephone. Our special phone. I picked it up immediately. It was Mister Okuda. He said a body had been found on the Jōban line, on the railroad tracks between Kita-Senju and Ayase stations, along with the President's pass . . .

In the warm and damp, close and suffocating air of the stationmaster's office, Masao Orii stopped speaking, rubbing his eyes and his face, struggling –

Did you inform the family, asked Harry Sweeney.

Masao Orii shook his head: I couldn't, no. I didn't want to believe it could be true, that it could be the President. I just said something like I needed to return to Headquarters, asked Mister Ōtsuka to step outside. I told him what I'd just heard, asked him not to say anything but just to wait with Missus Shimoyama and the children. But he wanted to come, too, and so we had no choice but to speak with the President's brother. We told him what had been found, but that nothing could be confirmed until we went to the scene ourselves. He agreed nothing should be said to Missus Shimoyama, not at that stage, and then myself, Mister Ōtsuka, and Mister Doi left.

And you drove here directly?

Yes, said Mister Orii. Well, one of our chauffeurs, Mister Sahota, he drove us.

What time did you get here?

Just after four, said Mister Orii. Soon as we got here, we were taken to the scene. We were shown the President's passes, his watch, his wallet. And then we were shown his body. What's left of it. And I confirmed it was the President.

In the close and suffocating air of the stationmaster's office, Harry Sweeney asked, And you are certain?

Yes.

Have the family been informed?

Yes, said Mister Orii again. Myself and Mister Doi came back here to call Headquarters and then the President's brother. Mister Ōtsuka is still at the scene, with the body.

May I ask what you think?

What I think?

You went to the scene, you identified the body, said Harry Sweeney. And you knew the man, you knew the President. I'd like to know what you think happened here.

Masao Orii looked up at Harry Sweeney and shook his head: I don't know what happened here. But I wish it hadn't happened. A good man, a devoted husband and father, is dead. I know that. And I know this changes everything.

They drove back through the morning, through its gray light and heavy air. Back across the river, back into the city. Bill Betz asleep in the back, Harry Sweeney staring out of the side window. The city drenched and dark, its buildings damp and dripping, Avenue Q turning to Ginza Street again, Ginza Street taking them past the Mitsukoshi department store again.

Harry Sweeney looked at his watch again, its face still cracked and hands still stopped. He took out his notebook, he turned its pages. He stopped turning the pages, he started reading his notes. Then he leaned forward to the front and said, Stop at the Chiyoda Bank, please.

Harry, pleaded Toda. The Chief's waiting . . .

It'll take five minutes, said Harry Sweeney. We're almost there, right, Ichirō?

Ichirō nodded and turned onto Avenue Y. They passed under some tracks and came to the corner with 4th Street. Ichirō pulled up and parked outside the Chiyoda Bank.

Harry Sweeney did not wake Bill Betz. He got out of the car with Susumu Toda. They closed the car doors quietly and walked into the bank. The bank just opening, their day just beginning. Harry Sweeney and Susumu Toda showed their PSD badges to a member of staff. Harry Sweeney and Susumu Toda asked to see the manager. The member of staff took them to see the manager. She spoke to his secretary, she knocked on his door. She introduced them to the manager –

The manager was already getting up from behind his desk, the manager already looking concerned, nervously asking, What is it I can do for you, gentlemen?

We're here about President Shimoyama of the National Railroads, sir, said Harry Sweeney.

The manager looked at Harry Sweeney, his clothes stained with rain, his shoes covered with mud, and the manager said, I heard on the radio that his body was found on the Jōban line?

Unfortunately, that is true, said Harry Sweeney. We understand from his driver that President Shimoyama called here yesterday morning. Is this information correct, sir?

The manager nodded: Yes. After the announcement on the news yesterday, the announcement that President Shimoyama was missing, Mister Kashiwa, who is in charge of our safety-deposit section, came to see me. He told me that the President had stopped by yesterday, just after we had opened.

And so yesterday morning, did Mister Kashiwa deal with the President personally?

The manager nodded again: I believe so, yes.

Is Mister Kashiwa at work today?

Yes, he is.

Please can you take us to him then, sir, said Harry Sweeney. Thank you.

Of course, said the manager. And he led them out of his office, and he took them down a corridor. He opened a door, he showed them in. Another man already getting up from behind his desk, another man already looking concerned, the manager telling him, Mister Kashiwa, these gentlemen are from GHQ, investigators from the Public Safety Division. These gentlemen are here about President Shimoyama. These gentlemen wish to speak with you about the President.

Is it true the President is dead, asked Mister Kashiwa. I heard it on the radio. They found his body on the Jōban line.

Unfortunately, it's true, said Harry Sweeney again. We are trying to account for the President's movements yesterday. We understand that he visited your bank early in the morning and that you dealt with him personally?

Yes, said Mister Kashiwa.

Did you notify the Metropolitan Police?

Er, no, said Mister Kashiwa, looking at the manager, his superior. After I heard that the President was missing, I spoke with the manager. I told him that President Shimoyama had visited the branch yesterday morning, and we discussed what we should do –

Yes, interrupted the manager. That's correct. We discussed what to do, yes.

And so what did you do, asked Harry Sweeney.

Well, er, stammered the manager. We decided we should inform the Railroad Headquarters. So I telephoned them and I told them that President Shimoyama had visited our branch that morning. Just after we had opened.

And with whom did you speak?

The President's secretary, I believe.

And what did he say?

He thanked me and said he would notify the police.

Harry Sweeney nodded: I see. And so did the police contact you? Did they visit you?

The Japanese police, asked the manager. No. Not yet. But I presumed that's why you are here. Because we called.

Harry Sweeney nodded again. He turned to Mister Kashiwa again. He asked, What time exactly did President Shimoyama visit here yesterday?

Er, about five or ten past nine, I think. Yes.

And what was the reason for his visit?

The President asked for the key to his safety-deposit box. I gave him his key. He went down to the basement, to the safety-deposit boxes. And then he returned the key and left.

And what time was that?

Mister Kashiwa walked over to a cabinet. He opened a drawer. He took out a file. He looked down at the file and said, Nine twenty-five. We keep a record, a log.

So President Shimoyama was in the basement for approximately fifteen to twenty minutes then, asked Harry Sweeney. With his safety-deposit box?

Yes, sir, said Mister Kashiwa.

Was any member of your staff present?

No, sir.

Any other customers there at that time?

No, sir. Only one person can go down at a time.

So he was alone in the basement?

Yes, sir.

And that's the policy of the bank?

Yes, said both Mister Kashiwa and the manager.

Harry Sweeney nodded, then asked, And so how long has President Shimoyama had a safety-deposit box with you?

Actually, not very long, said Mister Kashiwa, looking down at the file in his hands again. Yes. He's only had it since the first of June this year. So just over a month.

And how often did he visit here?

Quite frequently, said Mister Kashiwa. At least once a week. According to this record, President Shimoyama was here the day before yesterday, for example.

At what time was that?

Er, two forty on the afternoon of the fourth.

And the last visit before then?

The thirtieth of last month.

Thank you, said Harry Sweeney. Now we're going to need to see the safety-deposit box. The contents of the box.

Mister Kashiwa looked at the manager, the manager looking at Mister Kashiwa, Mister Kashiwa saying, But . . .

We cannot open the box without the permission of the safety-deposit-box holder, said the manager. Or we would need the authorization of a family member . . .

President Shimoyama is dead, said Harry Sweeney. GHQ are investigating the circumstances of his death. That's all the authorization we or you need.

Both men nodded. Their faces drained, their faces pale, the manager whispering, I'm sorry. Of course, right away.

Harry Sweeney and Susumu Toda followed the manager and Mister Kashiwa out of the office. Down the corridor, down the stairs. To the basement, to the room. This narrow room of boxes, these high walls of boxes, each box numbered, each box locked. Where Mister Kashiwa turned one key, where Mister Kashiwa removed one box: box number 1261. Then Mister Kashiwa carried box 1261 to the private tables at the end of the room, placed box 1261 down upon one of the tables, put another key in the lock of box 1261, and then Mister Kashiwa stepped away from box 1261.

Harry Sweeney and Susumu Toda stood before the box, the key hanging, waiting in its lock. Harry Sweeney glanced at Susumu Toda, Susumu Toda staring down at the lid. Harry Sweeney turned the key in the lock, then Harry Sweeney lifted the lid of the box. He reached into box 1261 and took out a narrow package wrapped in newspaper. He unfolded the newspaper. Three bundles of one-hundred-yen notes lay on top of the paper in his hand. He counted out the notes. There were thirty one-hundred-yen notes. He placed the newspaper and the notes on the table beside the box. He reached into box 1261 again. He took out some share certificates. He placed them on the table beside the box. He reached into box 1261 again. He took out the registration for a house. He checked the address. The registration was for the family house in Ōta Ward. He placed it on the table beside the box. He reached into box 1261 again. He took out five one-dollar notes. He placed them on the table beside the box. He reached into box 1261 again. He took out a rolled-up scroll. He untied and unrolled the scroll. It was a woodblock print of a man and a woman engaged in a sexual act. He rolled and tied up the scroll again. He placed it on the table beside the box. He stared down at the box on the table. Box 1261 empty now. Harry Sweeney turned to Susumu Toda, Susumu Toda writing in his notebook. He asked, Are we done?

Yes, said Toda. I got everything, Harry.

Harry Sweeney turned back to the table. He picked up the scroll and put it back in the box. He picked up the dollar bills and put them back in the box. He picked up the registration for the house and put it back in the box. He picked up the share certificates and put them back in the box. He picked up the newspaper and the bundles of one-hundred-yen notes. He checked the date on the newspaper: June 1, 1949. He folded the newspaper around the money and put it back in the box. He closed the lid of the box, he turned the key in the lock. He stepped away from the box, he stepped back from the table –

Thank you for your cooperation, gentlemen, said Harry Sweeney, turning to the manager and Mister Kashiwa. Now the Metropolitan Police will also ask to see the contents of this box. But please ensure a member of the Shimoyama family is present when you open the box for the police. And please do not mention our visit to either the family or the police.

Mother of God, Harry, sighed Chief Evans. This is fucked up.

Yes, Chief, said Harry Sweeney. Very.

Chief Evans rubbed his eyes, squeezed the bridge of his nose, shook his head again, then sighed again and said, So go on then, what you got, Harry?

Harry Sweeney opened his notebook and read: Shortly after oh one hundred hours, the mangled and partially dismembered body of Sadanori Shimoyama was discovered near a railway bridge on the Jōban line, close to Ayase station, north of Ueno. Employees of the National Railroad identified the body at about oh three hundred hours by means of a railway pass, a name card, and other papers on the body. The identification was confirmed by senior staff from Railroad Headquarters at approximately oh four hundred hours. The family were informed soon afterwards. Preliminary investigations indicate that the body of Shimoyama had been run over by a train, though whether that was the cause of death has yet to be determined. The body has been moved to Tokyo University for autopsy.

When can we expect the results?

Harry Sweeney closed his notebook, shrugged, and said, Sometime this afternoon, Chief. Hopefully.

Chief Evans rubbed his eyes again, squeezed the bridge of his nose again, and said, So what do you think, Harry?

Harry Sweeney shrugged again: I don't know, Chief.

Oh, come on, Harry, said Chief Evans, banging down his hand on the top of the desk. Come on, you went out there, you saw the scene, you saw the body. Tell me what you think for Chrissake, man. What the fuck you think happened?

Harry Sweeney shook his head: Chief, sir, with all due respect, you never saw a more fucked-up or compromised crime scene. You got a real toad-strangler of a storm flooding the place, then a hundred goddamn pairs of boots tramping back and forth. Bits and pieces of the man up and down the track, his face hanging off. An arm here, a foot there. Clothes being picked up, moved here, moved there. None of it left *in situ*. Basic fucking procedures ignored. Last person to arrive at the scene is the goddamn medical examiner . . .

But you were there, Harry.

Yes, I was there.

So come on, what do you think? Was the man dead or alive when that train hit him?

Harry Sweeney shook his head again, shrugged again, and said again, I just don't know, Chief. But if it's not a suicide, then it's been made to look like one. And if it was staged, they've made a pretty good job of it.

Jesus, said Chief Evans, getting up from behind his desk, walking over to the window. He looked up at the gray sky over the city and sighed, It's a goddamn fuck-up, either way.

Harry Sweeney nodded: Yes, sir. Very much so, sir.

You see the papers this morning, Harry?

No, sir. Not yet.

Well, some six hundred union men occupied a railroad office in Fukushima. Dragged the officials out. Took two hundred police to sort it out. Same story in Toyama, Osaka, and Shikoku. Reports of some of these damn returnees joining them, all singing the Red Flag. So you can imagine what General Willoughby is going to say about all this.

Yes, sir.

What a fuck-up, said Chief Evans again, turning back from the window, walking back over to his desk. He sat back down, looked across his desk, and said, The General's called a meeting for this evening at GHQ. Colonel Pullman will be there, I'll be there, and I want you there with me, Harry. The General's office, seven o'clock sharp. I want you to bring all we have.

So you want me to stay on this, Chief?

You're even asking me?

I'm sorry, sir.

This is all there is now, Harry. Turns out the man jumped in front of that damn train, then we're done. You can go back to chasing gangsters. But if Shimoyama was murdered, and we'd all better hope he was, then this is all there is.

I understand, sir.

I damn well hope you do, Harry. Because I want your full attention on this. I want every single goddamn scrap of information you can get. I don't want to be walking into that meeting tonight with only bullshit excuses and a file full of nothing. We better fucking have something, yeah?

Yes, sir. I understand, Chief.

Then get to work . . .

*

Back in Room 432, back at his desk, Harry Sweeney went back to work. He had Susumu Toda on the telephone to Metropolitan HQ begging for scraps, anything at all. He had his own notebook open, turning the pages, back and forth, typing up bits, typing up pieces, just bits and pieces, all of it scraps, scraps of nothing, nothing at all, glancing at the telephone, waiting for it to ring, to ring with some news, with a break, with anything at all –

Listening to heels and soles up stairs and down corridors, toilets flushing and faucets running, doors opening and doors closing, cabinets and drawers, windows wide and fans turning, fountain pens scratching and typewriter keys banging, glancing at the telephone, waiting for it to ring –

Fuck this, said Harry Sweeney, putting on his jacket, picking up his hat. Susumu, you got anything?

Nothing, Harry. Body's up at Tōdai, but the autopsy won't start till this afternoon. They got every man they have either at Mitsukoshi or Ayase, canvassing.

Okay then, said Harry Sweeney. Get a car and bring the papers, too. No sense us just staying around here, waiting to play goddamn catch-up. Come on, let's go –

They drove away from the NYK building. They drove down Avenue B. No Bill Betz and no Ichirō. The new kid Shin at the wheel, Susumu Toda in the back with Harry Sweeney. The two side windows in the front of the car were open, blowing warm, damp air through the car, Harry Sweeney staring out at the road, the cars and the trucks, the motorcycles and the bicycles, the buildings passing by, the buildings passing away, the telegraph poles, the telegraph wires, a tree here and a tree there, the people coming, the people going, in browns and grays, in greens and yellows, Harry Sweeney listening to Susumu Toda translate the news, in black and white –

Early editions of all the papers still have Shimoyama missing, leading with what Ōnishi the driver said and statements from Railroad HQ and his wife. Nothing we don't already know, though the *Yomiuri* has the driver saying they were not tailed and that Shimoyama left his briefcase and lunchbox in the car. The *Asahi* and *Mainichi* both have extras out already, both carrying the news of the body being found, some details of the crime scene – the location, the identification, pretty graphic descriptions of the body – the *Asahi* even claiming "it was said" there's a bullet hole in the corpse.

Yeah, asked Harry Sweeney. Said by whom?

Doesn't say, said Susumu Toda.

You got the *Stars and Stripes* there?

Wasn't in yet, not when we left.

Excuse me, sir, said the driver. We're here, but . . .

Shit, said Susumu Toda. Look, Harry –

The quiet, shaded street was no longer quiet, the street lined with cars, filled with people. Cars parked two abreast, cars blocking the road, people pushing to get a better view, people straining to see over the walls. Through the hedges, through the branches. Journalists and cameramen, neighbors and spectators. Uniformed officers pushing the crowds away, struggling to keep the crowds at bay –

Park down the hill, said Susumu Toda, Shin the driver nodding, going down the hill, all the way down the hill, to pull up and then park. Harry Sweeney and Susumu Toda got out of the car. They took out their handkerchiefs, they wiped their necks. They put away their handkerchiefs, they put on their hats. And then they walked back up the hill, all the way back up the hill, to the house of grief, this house of mourning, its hedges dark, its trees bowed. They pushed their way through the crowds, they struggled to get to the stone gate. They showed their PSD badges to the uniformed officers, the uniformed officers ushering them through the stone gate, Harry Sweeney and Susumu Toda walking through the stone gates, going up the short drive. Hats off their heads, hats in their hands, approaching the door, the door to grief –

Two late-middle-aged Japanese men were leaving the house, the two men walking toward Harry Sweeney and Susumu Toda. One man tall and thin, one man short and fat. Both men in black, both men in mourning. They stared at Harry Sweeney and Susumu Toda but did not speak to Harry Sweeney or Susumu Toda. Just staring, walking past. Harry Sweeney turned to watch them go, the tall man turning to look back. Back at Harry Sweeney, staring at Harry Sweeney. Harry Sweeney turned to the officer on the door to the house. The house of grief, this house of mourning. His hat in one hand, his badge in the other, Harry Sweeney asked, Who were those two men?

The officer sucked in air through his teeth, shook his head, and said, I'm sorry, sir. I don't know.

You need to know, officer. From now on, you record the names of any visitor to this house. Understood?

Yes, sir. I understand, sir.

Harry Sweeney nodded, then Harry Sweeney and Susumu Toda stepped into the house. The house of grief, this house of mourning. The air heavy, the air thin. People in the hallway, people on the stairs. In every doorway, in every room. In black, in mourning. They turned to look at Harry Sweeney and Susumu Toda, they turned to stare at Harry Sweeney and Susumu Toda. Eyes filled with tears, eyes filled with accusations. That blame all Americans, that blame their Occupation. Susumu Toda was shaking his head, Susumu Toda whispering, Why the fuck are we here, Harry?

To pay our respects, said Harry Sweeney. And to look and to listen. So look and listen, Susumu. Look and listen.

Thank you for coming, said a man coming down the stairs. I am Tsuneo, the younger brother of Sadanori.

Harry Sweeney and Susumu Toda both bowed. They both expressed their condolences, they both apologized for the intrusion, and then Harry Sweeney said, May we speak with you for a moment in private, sir?

Yes, of course, said Tsuneo Shimoyama. He gestured to one of the rooms off the hall, and Harry Sweeney and Susumu Toda followed Tsuneo Shimoyama into the room. The four sons of Sadanori Shimoyama were sitting alone in this room. Their heads bowed in silence, their hands in their laps. Tsuneo Shimoyama asked the boys to step outside. They nodded, they stood up, and they left as Tsuneo Shimoyama asked Harry Sweeney and Susumu Toda to sit down, asked them if they would like any tea. They declined the tea, and then Harry Sweeney said, We are very sorry to intrude at this difficult time, but we do need to ask you some questions, sir.

Of course, said Tsuneo Shimoyama. I understand.

Thank you for understanding, said Harry Sweeney. We'll try to be as quick as we can. But could you tell us when you were first aware that your brother was missing, sir?

From the radio, on the news. The five o'clock news. I came here immediately, directly. I arrived about half an hour later. In fact, I was told I had just missed you, Mister Sweeney. And I've been here ever since.

How often did you see your brother, sir?

I saw him regularly, almost every week. Depending on his work and mine, of course. But I saw him often, yes.

And so when did you last see him?

About a week ago.

And how was he? How did he seem?

Tsuneo Shimoyama turned his head slightly to his right. He sighed, then said, Well, he was under a lot of stress. I knew that. We all did. Everybody did. But my brother always made a great effort to be cheerful. A tremendous effort, Mister Sweeney. But I knew he wasn't sleeping very well, that he also had an upset stomach. But then he often did at this time of year. But still he was always so cheerful. He always was.

Aside from the stress of his position, were there any other worries, financial or personal, that your brother had?

No, Mister Sweeney. Not that I'm aware of, no.

And you think you would have been aware if he'd had any other worries? You were close, right?

Yes, said Tsuneo Shimoyama. We were very close, and so, no, I don't believe he had any other concerns, any other worries. Just his work, particularly the dismissals.

I'm sorry to be blunt, sir, said Harry Sweeney, but did you ever hear your brother talk of suicide?

No. Never.

So just so we are very clear, you do not believe your brother would have killed himself, sir?

No, said Tsuneo Shimoyama again. But I know it is what people are thinking, what people are saying. But no, my brother would never take his own life. Furthermore, his wife and sons have said he was in particularly good spirits yesterday morning before he left here. My brother was looking forward to the visit of his eldest son, Sadahiko. He was returning from Nagoya last night. If my brother had had any intention of committing suicide, it would surely have been after seeing his eldest son, would it not?

Harry Sweeney nodded. Yes. I guess so.

It would have been natural, too, to have arranged his affairs so they were all in order, to spare his wife and sons and our family such work. But he had not even straightened his desk upstairs before he left the house. So despite what people are thinking, what people are saying, I am absolutely certain my brother did not kill himself, Mister Sweeney.

Thank you, said Harry Sweeney. I appreciate you being so forthright, so adamant, sir. That's a great help to us.

Tsuneo Shimoyama sighed. He shook his head, then said, Well, I'm sorry, Mister Sweeney. Maybe I am being too forthright, too adamant. But we are all so shocked. Utterly shocked. And for people to suggest my brother . . .

I know. I am sorry we have to ask –

No, no, Mister Sweeney. Not you, not the police. You are only doing your job. I know that, we know that. But we've had people, my brother's so-called friends even, calling on us, suggesting we should say that my brother had taken his own life. Even urging us to release a statement to that effect.

Really? Who? When?

Only a moment ago. Two gentlemen called, wishing to pay their respects, but then suggested we should write a suicide note and have it printed in the newspapers.

Saying what?

That my brother had not wanted to fire ninety-five thousand employees. That he would apologize with his death for the benefit of everybody concerned. For the good of Japan.

Who were these two men, sir?

A Mister Maki and a Mister Hashimoto. Mister Maki is a member of the Upper House, and Mister Hashimoto is a former director of the railroads. Mister Hashimoto is retired now, but my brother even lodged with him and his wife when they both worked in Hokkaido. I cannot believe they would even suggest such a thing. It's unbearable. Unbearable.

Why did they say that, sir? What were their reasons?

Tsuneo Shimoyama sighed again, then said, If we printed such a notice in the newspapers, and with a photograph of the note, then the union and the employees would all feel sorry, and then all the disputes with the Corporation would be settled. And then Japan and the world would remember my brother as a martyr and a great man. Or so they said.

And what did you say, sir?

I didn't say anything. I just kept picturing my brother's face, and his wife and his sons. I could not speak.

Well, thank you for speaking with us, sir, said Harry Sweeney. I'm afraid, though, I need to impose upon you further, to ask if we may speak briefly with Missus Shimoyama now.

We spoke with her yesterday, and we would like to express our condolences, if we may, sir.

Of course, said Tsuneo Shimoyama, getting to his feet. She is upstairs. I will show you up, Mister Sweeney.

Harry Sweeney and Susumu Toda followed Tsuneo Shimoyama out of the room, back into the crowded hallway. Through the tears and through the accusations. Up the stairs and into the room. The same room as yesterday afternoon: the same wooden desk, the same large wardrobe. Now devoid of hope, without a prayer, now soaked with grief, drenched in mourning. In her somber kimono, with her pale face, a framed portrait of her late husband on the low table before her, Missus Shimoyama looked up at Harry Sweeney, stared up at Harry Sweeney. But her eyes did not accuse, her eyes only pleading –

That this was not happening, no . . .

That none of this was true.

But Harry Sweeney and Susumu Toda knelt down at the low table, and Harry Sweeney and Susumu Toda bowed before the low table, before Missus Shimoyama, before the portrait of her husband, the portrait between them –

Please excuse us for disturbing you, ma'am, said Harry Sweeney. And forgive us for intruding at such a time, but please accept our sincerest condolences at this time, ma'am.

Thank you, said Missus Shimoyama, turning away from Harry Sweeney and Susumu Toda, looking down at the portrait of her husband on the table. Her fingers on the frame, her fingers to the glass, she said, she whispered, You know, when I heard that the car had been found at Mitsukoshi, but that my husband was still missing, when you were here, when you were leaving, I knew then he was dead. I knew then. In my heart.

Harry Sweeney nodded, silent, waiting –

I know my husband sometimes stops off at the bank on his way to the office. I know he sometimes goes shopping at Mitsukoshi. But I knew he would not have gone shopping yesterday morning. Not yesterday morning, not without saying. He would never just go without saying, and not when he was so busy. He was so extremely busy, Mister Sweeney.

I know, said Harry Sweeney.

So I knew, you see? I knew something was wrong. The car at the store, my husband not there. When you were here, when you were leaving, I already knew, I just knew. But then there was that call, that telephone call. And so then there was hope, I had hope again.

Harry Sweeney leaned forward at the low table. Before the portrait, the portrait between them. And Harry Sweeney asked, What call was that, ma'am?

You don't know? They didn't tell you?

No, ma'am. I'm afraid they didn't.

Someone telephoned here yesterday evening. They said they had heard the news about my husband on the radio, but he'd dropped into their place and he was fine, and so there was no need to be worried about him. No need for us to worry.

What time was this, ma'am?

I'm not sure exactly. I did not take the call myself. It was Missus Nakajima, our maid. She lives with us. She took the call downstairs. But it was just after nine o'clock, I believe.

Did the caller identify himself? Give a name, ma'am?

He did, yes. He said his name was Arima.

Do you know anyone called Arima, ma'am?

Not personally, no. But some time later, after the call, I did remember that my husband had once mentioned a Mister Arima. I can't remember in what context, but I'm certain he did. And there's one other thing, Mister Sweeney . . .

Yes, ma'am. Go on . . .

Well, yesterday morning, about ten o'clock, I took a call myself from someone who said his name was either Arima or Onodera. In fact, I'm certain he used both names.

And what did he say?

He asked me if my husband had left for work as usual.

And you say this was about ten o'clock, ma'am?

I think so, yes. But there were so many calls yesterday, yesterday morning, Mister Sweeney. All asking the same question: Had my husband left for work as usual? Calls from his office, calls from different colleagues. They kept calling . . .

Did this man say anything else, ma'am?

No, he just asked if my husband had left for work as usual. That was all. So I said yes, my husband had left by car for his office, at twenty past eight as usual. But then I asked the man's name as I did not catch it when I first answered the telephone. But I think the name he had said was Arima. And then when I asked him again, I am sure he said Onodera.

Did you recognize his voice, ma'am?

No, Mister Sweeney. I did not.

And later, when this second call came in the evening, did your maid recognize the caller's voice?

No, said Missus Shimoyama. But you see, for a moment then, after that call, I did believe my husband might be coming home again. I started to hope again. That's the worst of it.

I'm sorry, ma'am. So very sorry.

I'm just sorry they didn't tell you, Mister Sweeney.

So am I, ma'am, said Harry Sweeney. So am I.

Tsuneo Shimoyama coughed. Tsuneo Shimoyama said, After that telephone call, the one in the evening, my brother's secretary and I did search the desk and drawers, looking for any name card or address for either an Arima or an Onodera, but we were unable to find anything.

Harry Sweeney nodded. Harry Sweeney looked down at the table. At the portrait on the table, at the face of Sadanori Shimoyama. The thin smile, the raised eyebrows. The plaintive eyes and the round glasses. Harry Sweeney looked up again.

Harry Sweeney asked Missus Shimoyama, Did your husband always wear his glasses, ma'am?

Always, nodded Missus Shimoyama. He couldn't see without them. Couldn't see anything at all.

Thank you, ma'am, said Harry Sweeney, starting to get to his feet, saying again, Thank you, ma'am. We've taken up too much of your time already. We will leave you now.

Missus Shimoyama looked up from the portrait on the table, from the face of her husband. And Missus Shimoyama asked, Mister Sweeney, when will I be able to see my husband? When will they let him come home?

I'm sorry, said Harry Sweeney. I don't know. Not precisely. But as soon as they've completed certain formalities, I am sure they will then return him to you, ma'am.

Thank you, whispered Missus Shimoyama, turning back to the portrait on the table, staring down at the face of her husband. Her fingers on the frame, her fingers on the glass. Her eyes searching, still pleading, still hoping –

That this was not happening . . .

That none of this was true.

Harry Sweeney and Susumu Toda followed Tsuneo Shimoyama out of the room. Back down the stairs, back through the people. Still filling the rooms, still filling the hallway. Their eyes still filled with tears, their eyes still filled with accusations. Blaming all Americans, blaming their Occupation.

In the *genkan*, by the door, Harry Sweeney and Susumu Toda bowed to Tsuneo Shimoyama, Harry Sweeney and Susumu Toda thanked Tsuneo Shimoyama. Then they turned away, then they walked away. From the house of grief, from that house of mourning. Back down the drive, back through the gates. Through the journalists and cameramen, through the neighbors and spectators. Back down the hill, back to their car. And beside their car, standing in the road, Harry Sweeney took off his hat, Harry Sweeney took out his handkerchief.

He wiped his face, he wiped his neck. He put away his handkerchief, he took out his cigarettes. He lit a cigarette, he took a pull. And beside their car, standing in the road, Harry Sweeney looked back up the hill, looked back at the house. The house of grief, that house of mourning, the smoke in his eyes, the sting in his eyes. He blinked, turned, dropped and crushed his cigarette. He took out his notebook and pencil. He opened his notebook and wrote down three names and two times. Then he put away his notebook and pencil, and opened the passenger door.

What do you think, Harry, asked Toda.

I think you should go up to Tokyo University. Find out what's happening with the autopsy. Drop me off on the way.

Drop you off where, Harry?

Lieutenant Colonel Donald E. Channon looked up from his desk. His uniform stained, his face unshaven. His eyes red and ringed in black. He closed the file on his desk. He gestured at the empty chair before his desk: Sit down, Mister Sweeney.

Thank you, sir, said Harry Sweeney.

Colonel Channon put his hands to his face. He rubbed his eyes, shook his head, then said, I still can't believe it, Mister Sweeney. Jesus Christ. I can't believe it.

Harry Sweeney nodded.

You been out there, Mister Sweeney? To the place?

Yes, sir. I was there first thing. Have you, sir?

Colonel Channon rubbed his eyes again, shook his head again, and said, No. Not yet. Not sure I will now. No point, not now. So you saw the body, yeah?

Yes, sir. I did.

As bad as they say it was? In the papers?

Yes, sir. It was.

Jesus Christ, Sweeney. The poor man.

Yes, sir.

Where is he now?

The body's been taken to Tokyo University, sir. For the autopsy. Should be getting the results very soon now, sir.

Well, he didn't kill himself, Mister Sweeney. I can tell you that. I don't need to wait for no goddamn autopsy.

You sound very certain, sir?

You bet I am. Like I told you yesterday, Sweeney, I knew the man. I worked with him every goddamn day. The last time I saw him, the night I went to his house, that night I told you about, when I left him, he was in good spirits. But he knew the risks, of course he did. He even said, just as I was leaving, said he would carry out the readjustments at the risk of his own life. That was his exact phrase, Mister Sweeney: even at the risk of his own life. That was the kind of man he was. So he didn't commit suicide. No goddamn way did he kill himself.

So you believe he was murdered, sir?

You bet I do. Obviously.

Then by whom?

Colonel Channon leaned forward. His elbows on his desk, his fingers locked together. He sighed. He closed his eyes. He swallowed. He opened his eyes again. He stared across his desk at Harry Sweeney. He sighed again, shook his head, then he said, Look, he'd received threats to his life. Not only him, we all have. Katayama. Me, too. Why do you think I wear this goddamn pistol, why you think I only travel in an MP jeep?

So who are these threats coming from, sir?

Who the hell you think they're coming from, Sweeney? From inside their own damn union, from the goddamn Reds.

You have some specific information, sir? Names? Organizations? Anything? Anything at all?

Course not. They're always anonymous. But for Chrissake, Sweeney, who else, where else would they be coming from. Jesus Christ. That's your fucking job!

Actually, sir, with all due respect, it was not my job. But it is now, and any help you can –

Yeah, right, laughed Colonel Channon. I forgot: you were too busy busting gangs, getting your face in the papers. Meanwhile, schmucks like old Shimoyama, schmucks like me, we're getting death threats, just for doing our goddamn jobs!

I'm sorry about that, sir. But the Japanese police, they knew about these threats, yeah? They know, right?

Sure they do, Sweeney. They stuck a plainclothes guy outside Shimoyama's house, another in his office, one in his car. Fat fucking lot of good it did the poor bastard.

I don't believe they did, sir.

Bullshit, they didn't.

Sir, as far as I'm aware, with all due respect, there was no plainclothes detail assigned to President Shimoyama. Least not yesterday morning, not when he left his house.

Well, you'll have to go ask them about that, Sweeney. All I know is there was supposed to be. That's what I was told. There should have been someone.

Yes, sir. I agree. There should have been someone.

Colonel Channon shook his head again. He put his hands out, his palms up. He looked down at the papers on his desk. He sighed again. He stood up. And he said, Jesus Christ. This goddamn country, Sweeney, I tell you. The fuck am I doing here? The fuck any of us are doing here?

Harry Sweeney nodded. He put his pencil back inside his notebook. He stood up and he asked, Just one other thing, sir. You're certain it was Monday night you went out to the Shimoyama house? You're sure?

You bet I am, yeah. The Fourth of July. Why?

Just double-checking, sir. I'm sorry.

Well, if you're all done double-checking, Mister Sweeney, I've still got a railroad to run and now a new president to appoint. And you've a goddamn murderer to catch.

*

Again in the shadow of Tokyo station, again in the echoes of the train tracks. In another building, in another office. The headquarters of the National Railways Corporation, the office of Sadanori Shimoyama. The office he shared with his deputy. Before his deputy, before his desk, Harry Sweeney sat down, Harry Sweeney took out his notebook, and Harry Sweeney said, Thank you for seeing me at this time, Mister Katayama.

Yukio Katayama glanced past Harry Sweeney. Over his shoulder, across the room. At the other desk, at the empty chair. Yukio Katayama looked down at his own desk, his hands together on his desk, and nodded. Then he looked back up at Harry Sweeney and asked, You've just come from the Chōsen building, from the CTS, Mister Sweeney? So you've spoken with Lieutenant Colonel Channon then?

I have, sir. Yes, said Harry Sweeney.

Have you heard anything from the university yet, asked Yukio Katayama. Heard the results of the autopsy yet?

Not yet, sir. No.

I see, said Yukio Katayama. Again he glanced over the shoulder of Harry Sweeney, again he looked at the other desk, at the empty chair. And then he said, slowly said, It's all my fault, Mister Sweeney. All my responsibility.

Why do you say that, sir?

Because I recommended Shimoyama-kun for the position of Vice Minister for Transport, Mister Sweeney. This was when Shimoyama-kun was the Director of the Tokyo Railways Bureau. And because he accepted the position as Vice Minister, Shimoyama-kun then became the President when we were reorganized as a public corporation, when everybody else withdrew. Today I cannot help but feel that was the first step on the journey to his death. If I had not suggested his name to the

Minister for Transport, then none of this would have happened, Mister Sweeney. Shimoyama-kun would still be here.

And what do you think happened, sir?

Yukio Katayama staring at the empty chair again, Yukio Katayama talking to the empty chair now, Yukio Katayama said, slowly said, Ever since you were a child, you loved the railways. You were obsessed by the railways. You were mad about all machines, but you loved locomotives. You adored locomotives more than anything else. You had traveled the world, traveled on all the trains of the world. You had studied them all, and you loved them all . . .

Yukio Katayama looked away from the empty chair, Yukio Katayama turned back to Harry Sweeney, and Yukio Katayama said, quicker now he said, No matter how much pressure he was under, no matter how fraught his nerves might have been, there is no way a man who loved trains, a man who worked for the railways, no way he would ever use a train as the tool with which to end his life. Never, Mister Sweeney. Never.

So you believe the President was murdered, sir?

Yes, said Yukio Katayama. As soon as I heard Shimoyama-shi's body had been found, where and how it had been found, I knew he had been murdered. I knew.

Harry Sweeney nodded, then said, Both you and the President had received death threats?

Yes, said Yukio Katayama again. But not only the President and myself; many of our senior directors have. The Colonel too, I believe, Lieutenant Colonel Channon.

And these death threats, they came in the form of letters? Is that correct, sir?

Letters, yes. But also telephone calls. And then, of course, there are the posters that have been put up across the city. I'm sure you've seen them, Mister Sweeney?

Harry Sweeney nodded again: I have, sir, yes. Do you have any of these letters to hand, sir?

No, said Yukio Katayama. Not now, not here. We always hand such letters to our own security staff. They then forward them to the police.

Is it correct, sir, that the Metropolitan Police have provided you with extra security? Both here and at your home, and also in your car?

Again Yukio Katayama looked over the shoulder of Harry Sweeney, again he was staring at the empty chair as he said, Well, it was suggested and then discussed, yes. However, I don't believe Shimoyama-kun accepted the offer.

Did you accept the offer, sir?

Yes, Mister Sweeney. I did accept, yes.

And so why did President Shimoyama decline?

I am not sure.

You didn't discuss it with him then, at the time?

No, Mister Sweeney. But I believe he did discuss the matter personally with Chief Kita of the Metropolitan Police.

But there were many of these threats, sir?

Yes, Mister Sweeney. Many.

I am sorry, sir, but I have yet to see any of these letters, these threats. So could you give me an example of what kind of things they said, please?

Yukio Katayama nodded, sighed, and then said, That we would be assassinated, that we would meet Heaven's Justice. If we carried out the proposal to cut personnel numbers.

And these were all anonymous?

Usually anonymous or signed with names such as the Repatriates' League of Blood. Or something similar.

I see, said Harry Sweeney. Thank you. And in each case, you said you first handed them over to your own security staff. So were your own security staff able to find out anything at all about who might have been sending them?

Yukio Katayama smiled. Yukio Katayama shook his head. And then Yukio Katayama said, Not any names or addresses, no. But I think it's quite obvious where they were coming from, don't you, Mister Sweeney?

You mean from within the Railroad Union?

Yes, Mister Sweeney. From within the Railroad Union. Our own union, the union we helped set up and fund, yes.

And so then you believe President Shimoyama was abducted and murdered by members of the National Railroad Workers' Union, sir? Is that what you're saying, sir?

Yukio Katayama stared at the empty chair at the other desk, then he looked down at his hands, his hands together on his own desk. He shook his head, then looked back up. He stared at Harry Sweeney, stared at Harry Sweeney for a long time, before he said, Who else could it have been, Mister Sweeney? You have any other suspects, any other ideas?

Under the tracks, among the stalls. Under a canopy, on a bench. No more rooms, no more walls. Interviews or voices. Pushing him, pulling him. This way and that way. Just a bottle, just a glass. In the damp, in the heat. Everything stuck, everything wet. Clinging to him, clawing at him. Harry Sweeney picked up the bottle of beer. Harry Sweeney held the bottle in his hand. The bottle damp, the bottle wet. Clinging, clawing. The noise of the trains, the sound of their wheels. The stall shaking, the bench trembling. Harry Sweeney shaking, Harry Sweeney trembling. He gripped the bottle, he steadied his hand. He held it against his head, he pressed it into his skin. Damp and wet, damp and wet. The bottle and his head, his skin and his eyes. Damp and wet, damp and wet. He closed his eyes, he opened his eyes. Holding the bottle against his head, pressing the bottle into his skin. The noise of the trains, the sound of their wheels. Harry Sweeney shaking, Harry Sweeney trembling. He put down the bottle, the bottle still full. He pushed away the glass, the glass still empty. He looked down at his watch, the face still cracked and the hands still stopped. The noise of the trains, the sound of their wheels. Shaking and trembling, shaking and trembling. Harry Sweeney stood back up. He wiped his face, he wiped his neck. He picked up his hat, he picked up his jacket. He reached into his pocket, he paid the man in cents. The man smiled, the man bowed. Harry Sweeney smiled, Harry Sweeney bowed. Damp and wet, shaking and trembling. Harry Sweeney took out his cigarettes and Harry Sweeney lit a cigarette. He went back down the alley, he turned back round the corner. He turned left, onto Avenue Z. Under the heavy skies, in the gray light. Harry Sweeney walked down the avenue, Harry Sweeney passed the telegraph poles. The posters still on the poles, the words still on the posters. In Japanese, in English: KILL SHIMOYAMA. KILL SHIMOYAMA. KILL. KILL. KILL SHIMOYAMA. On every pole, on every poster. The words, the threats –

KILL, KILL, KILL SHIMOYAMA –

Words and threats, now made good.

Harry Sweeney sweating, Harry Sweeney shivering. In the damp, in the heat. He came to the Hibiya Crossing, he waited at the Hibiya Crossing. In the damp, in the heat. His eyes closing, his eyes opening. The black park and its trees, its shadows and insects. The still moat and its stench, its reflections and specters. The cars braking, the streetcars stopping. Shrill whistles and white gloves. Boots marching, feet moving. Harry Sweeney crossed over Avenue A, Harry Sweeney walked up 1st Street. In the damp, in the heat. His eyes closing, his eyes opening. The palace to his right, the park to his left. Still sweating, still shivering. In the damp, in the heat. Shaking and trembling, shaking and trembling. In the damp and in the heat. Harry Sweeney reached Sakuradamon, Harry Sweeney crossed 1st Street. Closing his eyes, opening his eyes. He walked up toward the Metropolitan Police Department HQ, could see Susumu

Toda waiting by the car. Susumu Toda stubbing out a cigarette, Susumu Toda walking toward him: You get my message, Harry? Heard what they're saying?

Still sweating, still shivering, but not shaking and not trembling, Harry Sweeney lit another cigarette, Harry Sweeney looked at Toda, and Harry Sweeney said, I've heard a lot of things today, Susumu. Let's go . . .

In the Dai-ichi building, on the fifth floor, half walking, half running, Harry Sweeney and Susumu Toda saw Chief Evans up the corridor, heard his voice down the corridor –

You're goddamn late again!

I'm sorry, sir, said Harry Sweeney, struggling to breathe, to catch his breath. The MPD briefing just finished.

Well, I hope for your sake it was worth it, said Chief Evans. They've been in there a goddamn half-hour already. General Willoughby does not like to be kept waiting.

I know, sir. I'm sorry, Chief.

Save it for the General, said Chief Evans. Just pull yourself together and let's go –

I'm ready, sir.

Okay then, let's go, said the Chief, knocking on the door to Room 525, the door to the office of the Assistant Chief of Staff, G-2, FEC & SCAP. Not you, Toda. You wait here.

Yes, sir, said Susumu Toda. Very good, sir.

If we need you, I'll call you, said Chief Evans, opening the door to Room 525, leading Harry Sweeney inside the office of the Assistant Chief of Staff, announcing to the room, Police Investigator Sweeney, sir. He's come here directly from the briefing at Metropolitan Police HQ, sir.

One of our very best men, General, said Colonel Pullman, smiling at Harry Sweeney –

Harry Sweeney glancing around the room, trying to take in the room, the men and their faces, the uniforms and their medals, looking now at the man at the head of the table: Major General Charles A. Willoughby, "Sir Charles" himself – born Adolf Karl von Tscheppe und Weidenbach, thus also known as "Baron von Willoughby" – much mocked but never to his face. Mac's right-hand man, his "loveable fascist," the Chief of Intelligence had the complete confidence and trust of the Supreme Commander, and thus "carte blanche" to do whatever he wanted, to whomever he chose –

The General looked Harry Sweeney up and down, smiled, and then, his German accent heavy and pronounced despite forty years in the United States Army, he said, I have heard good things about you, Sweeney. Very good things.

Thank you, sir.

But I did not imagine you would look like this, not from the things I had heard. You look like you have been sleeping in the ditch, Sweeney, like you have been digging in the dirt.

Yes, sir. I'm sorry, sir. It's been a long –

Spare us your excuses, Sweeney. Just tell us what you have found. In your ditch, in your dirt.

Yes, sir. The preliminary autopsy ended at seventeen hundred hours, sir, and the initial conclusion is that Sadanori Shimoyama was murdered, sir.

Well, that is good news, said the General. Very good news. Excellent, in fact.

Sir –

The General raised a hand, a finger, stared at Sweeney and then around the table: The murder of this man is a tragedy, of course. But it is an outrage, and we must turn this outrage into an opportunity. Only two days ago, in his speech on the Fourth of July, did not our Supreme Commander warn that Communism was a movement of national and international outlawry? Did he not warn that the Communist will always use assassination and violence to create chaos and unrest? And the very next day is he not proved correct yet again? The brutal assassination of this innocent man demonstrates to the whole of Japan and to the watching world that the nihilism and terrorism of the Communist knows no mercy, that he will stop at nothing in order to bring about his violent revolution! So we must show him no mercy, we must stop at nothing to crush him! We must meet force with force; we must outlaw their party, close down their newspaper, arrest their leaders, and bring the murderers of this poor man to justice, swift, merciless justice! Sweeney –

Yes, sir!

Tell us what steps are being taken, what progress is being made to hunt down the Communist assassins.

Sir, the preliminary autopsy results indicate that Shimoyama had been dead for some time before his body was run over by the train. However, the autopsy will resume tomorrow, when it is hoped that the precise cause of death can then be determined. In the meantime, the police consider this the most important case in recent years and are working all out to solve it. Because they believe that a number of people must have been involved in the murder, both the First and Second Investigative Divisions have been assigned to the case. They are presently canvassing both the areas around the Mitsukoshi department store, where Shimoyama was last seen, and around the crime scene itself. Important clues are expected shortly, sir.

Shortly, said the General. What is shortly, Sweeney? What about now? What about suspects? Arrests?

Sir, according to PSD sources within the MPD, the police are investigating a number of threatening letters which were sent to Shimoyama and also to Premier Yoshida and his cabinet, and to Police Chief Kita and Mister Katayama, the Vice President of the National Railways. The letters were all received on the

Fourth of July and were all signed "Repatriates' Blood League" or "League of Blood."

Colonel Batty, Colonel Duffy, said the General, turning to look down the table. Have you heard of this, er, Repatriates' League of Blood?

Colonel Batty shook his head, but Colonel Duffy nodded and said, General, sir, CIC are aware of these letters, and others of a similar nature, but, as yet, have no information about this particular group. According to our own intelligence, they would seem to have had no history prior to the sending of the letters in question. But we are continuing to investigate, sir.

General, sir, said a tall, thin man dressed in a dark, well-cut civilian suit, seated close to the top of the table, close to the General. If I may interject here . . .

Please, said the General, turning to smile at the man, to smile and say, by all means, Richard, please do.

Hongō are in possession of some information which might be of relevance here, sir.

Very good, said the General. Please, go on . . .

Well, sir, said the man, glancing down the table at Harry Sweeney, Harry Sweeney standing at the foot of the table. It's information of a somewhat confidential nature, sir.

The General nodded, looked down the table at Harry Sweeney, stared at Harry Sweeney at the foot of the table, nodded again, then said, You got anything else, Sweeney?

No, sir. Not at this stage, no, sir.

Then you are dismissed, Sweeney.

Yes, sir. Thank you, sir, said Harry Sweeney, turning toward the door, walking toward the exit –

One last thing, Sweeney, said General Willoughby.

Harry Sweeney turned back from the door: Yes, sir?

The next time you come before me, you make sure you are washed and shaved, your clothes are fresh and pressed, and your shoes polished and shined. You may think you are a civilian, Sweeney, but you work for SCAP and you represent the United States of America. Is that understood, Sweeney?

Yes, sir. I am very sorry, sir.

Oh, and Sweeney?

Yes, sir?

That next time, when you are standing before me, all washed and shaved, fresh and pressed, polished and shined, you better be bringing me the names of the assassins of Sadanori Shimoyama. Is that also understood, Sweeney?

Yes, sir. It is, sir.

Then go on, Sweeney. Go fetch!

He did not stop to speak to Susumu Toda, he did not wait outside for Chief Evans. He walked away from Room 525, he walked down the corridor. He did not wait for the elevator, he took the stairs, the ten flights of stairs, down and out of the Dai-ichi building. Down and out, he walked past the Imperial Hotel, then along the tracks, he walked past the Dai-ichi Hotel and on past the station, Shimbashi station. He walked past the shops and through the market, he walked past the restaurants and through the stalls. He walked and he walked, through a set of double doors and up another flight of stairs, walking and walking, until he was standing before a desk, until he heard Akira Senju say, Look at the state of you, Harry. You look like you've been hit by a train – Sorry! How very tactless of me. I'm sorry, Harry. Forgive me, please. Sit down, sit down . . .

Harry Sweeney sat down, slumped in the chair before that antique rosewood desk in this luxurious modern office at the top of that shiny new building, this Shimbashi Palace.

Twice in twenty-four hours, smiled Akira Senju. This is just like old times, is it not, Harry? Those good old times. So I hope you are bringing me good news, Harry. Just like you used to do, back in the old times, those good old times.

Harry Sweeney said, Good news?

About that little list of names?

Harry Sweeney reached inside his jacket, felt the folded piece of paper, that folded list of names, Formosan names, Korean names, and Harry Sweeney shook his head, shook his head and said, I'm sorry.

You've not had the time, said Akira Senju. Of course not, I know. I understand, Harry. No need for apologies, not between friends. Old friends like us, Harry. You take your time, take as long as you need, Harry. But then to what do I owe the pleasure of another visit, Harry? A little drink, perhaps?

Harry Sweeney shook his head again, Harry Sweeney sat forward in his chair and said, Shimoyama . . .

Of course, of course, said Akira Senju, nodding and smiling at Harry Sweeney. I heard the news. Terrible, terrible business. And I don't like to say I told you so, Harry, but I told you so; presidents, they do tend to get assassinated.

Harry Sweeney nodded: Yes, so you said. You were quite certain last night. Very certain, in fact.

Well, laughed Akira Senju, I'm no Nostradamus, no Sherlock Holmes. It was inevitable, it was obvious. You only have to walk down any street in the city, read the posters on the walls, on the poles. It's there in black and white, red and white, in Japanese and English: *Kill Shimoyama!*

He could have killed himself.

He could have, yes, said Akira Senju, nodding, then smiling and saying, But he didn't, did he, Harry.

You've already heard then?

I have my sources, Harry. You know that.

Harry Sweeney looked across the antique rosewood desk, Harry Sweeney stared at Akira Senju behind the desk, on his throne, in his palace at the top of his empire, and Harry Sweeney said, What else have you heard?

Ah, I see, said Akira Senju, nodding and smiling again at Harry Sweeney. You're still on the case then?

Yes. Unfortunately.

Unfortunately, indeed, said Akira Senju. This might prove rather distracting for you, Harry. Keep you from doing what it is you do best. From that little list, for example.

Harry Sweeney nodded, Harry Sweeney smiled and said, Exactly. So anything you have heard, any help you can give me in order to bring this matter to an end –

Would be to our mutual benefit, nodded Akira Senju.

Harry Sweeney nodded again, Harry Sweeney said again, Exactly. Last night you mentioned a list of Communists, of Reds? General Willoughby would be very grateful.

You've spoken with the General, Harry?

I was just there, in his office.

Akira Senju sat forward in his chair, stared across his antique rosewood desk at Harry Sweeney, and asked, Did you mention my name, Harry? My offer of help?

Not yet, said Harry Sweeney. But I can, I will.

Akira Senju got up from his desk. He walked over to one of the large windows in his luxurious, modern office. He stared out of the window, stared out across his empire, across the city and the night, then still staring out of the window, out across his empire, he nodded and said, Well, well. This could prove to be a most convenient death, could it not, Harry?

Harry Sweeney looked down at his hands, looked down at his wrists, the ends of two clean, dry scars visible beneath the cuffs of his shirt, beneath the straps of his watch, the face of the watch cracked, the hands of the watch stopped.

Akira Senju turned away from the window. He walked across the thick carpet of his luxurious, modern office toward the drinks cabinet. He opened the cabinet. He picked up a bottle of Johnnie Walker Reserve. He poured two large measures into two crystal glasses. He put down the bottle and picked up the glasses. He carried the glasses over to Harry Sweeney, saying, Convenient and fortuitous – that is the word, is it not, Harry?

Harry Sweeney turned to look up at Akira Senju, Akira Senju standing over him, holding out the glass to him –

Fortuitous, said Akira Senju again, smiling now, saying now, So let us drink to convenience and to fortuity, Harry. Just like old times, the good old times, Harry.

In the park, in the dark, among the insects, among the shadows, leaning against a tree, sliding down its bark, falling to the ground, lying in the dirt, Harry Sweeney made a pistol of his hand, Harry Sweeney held the pistol to his head, pulled the trigger but was not dead, he was not dead. In the park and in the dark, among the insects and the shadows, on the ground and in the dirt, Harry Sweeney took the barrel of his pistol, the two fingers of his hand, and Harry Sweeney put them in his mouth, forced them down his throat, down and back into his throat until he retched and he retched, retched and heaved, heaved and vomited, into the dirt and across the ground, among the insects and the shadows, the dark and the park, vomiting and vomiting, whisky and bile, over his fingers and over his hands, down his wrists and over his scars. And when there was no more whisky and no more bile, when he could vomit and heave no more, Harry Sweeney turned onto his side, then onto his back, and Harry Sweeney looked up at the branches, looked up at their leaves, stared up at the sky, stared up at its stars, and Harry Sweeney sobbed and Harry Sweeney screamed –

I'm sorry, I'm sorry, I'm sorry.

## 3

## And Then the Next Days

---

*July 7–July 10, 1949*

Night turned to day, cloudy and gray. Harry Sweeney had a hangover, but still Harry Sweeney went to work, with a clean shave and a fresh shirt, pressed pants and polished shoes, up the stairs and down the corridor, flushing the toilet and running the faucets, washing his hands and face again, drying his face and hands again, opening the door, then closing the door, walking across Room 432 of the Public Safety Division, the windows wide and the fans turning, taking his seat at his desk, listening to all the fountain pens scratching, all the typewriter keys banging, the telephones ringing, and a voice saying –

The hell got into you last night, Harry?

Harry Sweeney looked up from his desk, Harry Sweeney smiled at Susumu Toda, and said, Good morning to you, too, Susumu. How you doing this fine new day?

Me? I'm fine, but I was worried about you. The Chief was, too. Going off like that, without a word, disappearing.

I didn't disappear. I'm right here, aren't I?

You know what I mean, Harry. I went by the Yaesu Hotel, looking for you. Waited half the night.

You like worrying, you should have been my mother. I just needed some air, clear my head. That's all.

All night?

Hey, come on! What's with you?

I just thought maybe . . .

Maybe what?

Nothing. It doesn't matter.

Doesn't matter's right.

Whatever you say, Harry, said Toda. But the Chief was worried, too, said Willoughby gave you a hard time.

Harry Sweeney smiled, Harry Sweeney laughed: Turns out all we heard about Sir Charles is true. But I've had worse, Susumu, believe me. It was nothing I didn't expect.

You looked pretty cheesed off when you came out of the room. I mean, taking off like that . . .

It wasn't Sir Charles. I told you, just needed to clear my head. It'd been a long day. Up at Ayase, then the family. A very long day. Let's hope today's a better day, yeah?

What you want to do, Harry?

Where's Bill? Don't tell me he's off again?

No, said Susumu Toda. He's been in and gone out again. Chief sent him back to Norton Hall, to see what they've turned up on these Repatriates' Blood League letters.

Nodding to himself, taking out his cigarettes, Harry Sweeney said, That reminds me. You know anything about or anyone at Hongō House? They're CIC, too, right?

You're kidding, right, said Susumu Toda. Not those guys, no thank you. They're a law unto themselves. Why?

Harry Sweeney lit his cigarette, inhaled, then exhaled, shook his head, and said, Just something Willoughby said.

Yeah, asked Susumu Toda. Like what?

Harry Sweeney stood up, picked up his hat, and said, Nothing. Forget it. Who you been talking to at MPD HQ?

Hattori, all the good it does me.

Harry Sweeney laughed again: Beggars can't be choosers, Susumu. You know where he is this fine morning?

No, said Susumu Toda. But I can find out.

*

They drove north through Ueno and up Avenue Q again, then east at Minowa and across the river, the Sumida River again. The young guy Shin at the wheel this time, Harry Sweeney sat in the back with Susumu Toda, Toda going through the newspapers again: Well, they've all gone to town on it, as you'd expect. Only *Akahata* saying people shouldn't jump to conclusions, that suicide can't be ruled out . . .

They might want to think about changing that line, said Harry Sweeney, looking out of the window, watching factories turn to fields again, getting closer, nearer again. Willoughby's already talking about shutting them down.

Susumu Toda shrugged, smiled, and said, Be one less paper for me to translate, I guess.

Lucky you, said Harry Sweeney. Go on . . .

Well, the rest of them have a lot of pages, lot of columns, lot of what we already know: details of the crime scene, bits about the autopsy, the trains, etcetera. But a couple of them report witnesses hearing a "mysterious car" in the vicinity, around that Cursed Crossing, around midnight –

Yeah? That wasn't in the briefing, was it?

Susumu Toda shook his head: No.

Go on, read it to me then, said Harry Sweeney, turning from the window, turning to Susumu Toda and his papers.

So the *Asahi*, *Mainichi* and *Yomiuri*, they've all got interviews with a local fishmonger, a Mister Sakata, who lives in Gotanno Minami-machi, about two hundred yards from where the body was found. He says different things to different papers, but he seems to have heard a car pull up outside his house between midnight and one a.m., or it was turning round, then coming back past his house. According to the *Mainichi*, the tire marks from a U-turn are still visible outside the man's house. Despite the rain.

Well, that'll give us something to chew over with Hattori, said Harry Sweeney. Anything else?

Susumu Toda sighed, nodded, and said, Yeah. There's a few "I saw him" accounts, too. Both from the department store and in the vicinity of the scene –

At the crime scene? Alive, said Harry Sweeney, staring down at the papers in Toda's lap. You're kidding me?

Susumu Toda shook his head: No, Harry.

Jesus Christ, said Harry Sweeney. The fuck are the police doing? They got goddamn journalists doing their fucking jobs. Interviewing witnesses, printing what they say.

Susumu Toda smiled: Well, the *Asahi* has even got Kuroda Roman, Roman Kuroda on the case.

Who the hell is Roman Kuroda?

Susumu Toda laughed: The mystery writer.

It's not goddamn funny, Susumu, said Harry Sweeney. Next time, you go fucking explain this bullshit to Willoughby. Explain why journalists and writers are investigating the case while the Japanese police are sat on their asses, telling us goddamn nothing. Why we're the last to know –

Sir, said Shin. Excuse me, sir . . .

What is it, said Harry Sweeney. Why we stopped?

Sir, said Shin, gesturing with both hands toward the windshield, toward a line of backed-up cars up ahead –

Mother of God, said Harry Sweeney, staring over the front seat, shaking his head. Pull in and wait here. We'll get out and walk. Come on, Susumu . . .

And Harry Sweeney and Susumu Toda got out of the back of their car, putting on their hats and taking out their cigarettes, Harry Sweeney shaking his head, cursing out loud as he surveyed the scene: forty, fifty cars, all backed up, double parked, blocking the road to Ayase station, crowds of people walking back and forward between the cars, back and forward between the station and the so-called Cursed Crossing, some of the people in their Sunday best, with their parasols and umbrellas up, some of them chewing on sticks of grilled chicken, their kids carrying candyfloss, shouting and laughing, running here and there, from food stall to food stall, the hawkers and vendors calling out with their promises of tasty this and tasty that, get your Shimoyama candyfloss here –

You fucking believe this, said Harry Sweeney, pushing between the cars, pushing people out of his way, making his way through the crowds, fighting his way through the throng, knocking a man off a bicycle, a kid against a car, cursing and cursing, over and over, Get the fuck out my way! Move!

Susumu Toda following in his wake, Susumu Toda pleading, Harry, Harry, come on, don't . . .

But Harry Sweeney kept on pushing his way, kept on fighting his way until he came to Ayase station, until he saw a uniformed officer, until he took out his PSD badge, until he shoved it in the man's face and said, The fuck are you doing? I want to see the officer in charge and I want to see him now! And then get these fucking people out of here. This is a goddamn crime scene for Chrissake! Susumu, tell –

Yes, Harry, I'm telling him, I'm telling him, said Susumu Toda, Susumu Toda translating, speaking with the uniformed officer, listening to the uniformed officer, the uniformed officer apologizing and bowing, gesticulating and pointing this way then that way –

What is it? What's he saying, Susumu?

Susumu Toda nodded to the officer, thanked the officer, then took Harry Sweeney to one side and whispered, Seems there's been a breakthrough, Harry.

To avoid the crowds, to avoid the throngs, they crossed the tracks at Ayase station, the trains running again, up and down the tracks, back and forth over the scene. Then they crossed the Ayase River by the water gate on the other side of the tracks, heading west through a patchwork of fields, damp and empty, under a curtain of sky, gray and heavy, until they came to the Gotanno Minami-machi police box. There were cars here, were crowds here, but not as many, not so many. They showed their badges and got directions, then they walked beside the embankment of the Tōbu line, turned left, and passed under the metal bridge of the Tōbu line, following the road west until they saw more cars parked up ahead, saw more people standing up ahead, and saw Detective Hattori standing there, too, outside the Suehiro Ryokan, a traditional Japanese inn –

The property was surrounded by a narrow drainage ditch, shielded by a tall wooden fence, the tops of a few trees visible above the fence and the gate, further hiding the shabby, gloomy, two-storied wooden inn within, obscuring this place of shabby, gloomy trysts and assignations –

You got my message then, said Detective Hattori, walking toward Harry Sweeney and Susumu Toda.

No, said Toda. What message?

Really, said Hattori with a shrug and a nod. Soon as I heard, first thing I did was call your office. Like I said I would. Left a message that I'd be here –

Soon as you heard what, asked Harry Sweeney.

Well, it's a bit embarrassing to say, said Detective Hattori, taking off his hat and scratching his head. But these reporters, they've been canvassing the area, interviewing witnesses faster than we can. So this one reporter, from the *Mainichi*, I think it was, he shows a photograph of President Shimoyama to the wife of the owner, and she's like: Yeah, the man was here, afternoon of the fifth. Arrived about half one, stopped for about four hours. Makes sense, you know. We got umpteen witnesses now saying they saw President Shimoyama around here that night.

Yeah, said Harry Sweeney. We've been reading all about these witnesses. Not in your reports, not in your briefings, in the goddamn newspapers, detective.

I know, I know, said Detective Hattori, nodding his head, scratching his head. What can I say? It's embarrassing.

It's not embarrassing, said Harry Sweeney. It's fucking disgraceful, shameful. A stain on the Japanese police –

Hey, hey, said Detective Hattori, stepping toward Harry Sweeney, staring up at Harry Sweeney. With respect, you give us a free press, this is what you get.

Harry Sweeney stepped toward Detective Hattori, looked down at Detective Hattori: Bullshit. It's got nothing to do with a free press, and you know it. Basic, elementary police work. That's what this is about. The preservation and integrity of the crime scene. The allocation of manpower and resources. That's what I'm talking about.

Yeah, said Detective Hattori, taking a step back, pointing down at his feet. Well, you see these shoes? These were brand new. I ordered them specially, only picked them up the day before this thing broke. Cost me half my salary, they did. Be chump change, peanuts to you, no doubt. But look at them now, they're ruined. Ruined because they've been out to the Shimoyama house, down to the house of Vice President Katayama, then, ever since the body was found, they've been here, in the pissing rain, under the beating sun, walking this scene, working this case, until there's nothing left of them. So with respect, don't tell me I ain't been doing my job.

Harry Sweeney shook his head, smiled at Detective Hattori, and said, Well then, you've wasted a new pair of shoes, detective, because you doing your job like you say you been doing, that still don't explain why every goddamn newspaper in Japan has been doing a better job than you.

Look, said Detective Hattori, turning to Susumu Toda. You know me, Toda, I've just been doing what I've been told to do, going where I've been told to go. I don't decide nothing, I just do what I'm told. He wants to pick a fight, be my guest. But tell him to go pick it with my boss –

I will, said Harry Sweeney. Where is he?

In there, said Detective Hattori, nodding toward the Suehiro Ryokan. Doing his job.

Is that right, said Harry Sweeney. Come on then, lead on. Let's go see the great Japanese police force at work.

Detective Hattori said nothing, just nodded, then turned and led Harry Sweeney and Susumu Toda over the narrow ditch, under the wooden gate, through the tiny garden and into the *genkan* of the Suehiro Ryokan, shabby and gloomy. The three men took off their shoes, then stepped up into a dark, narrow hallway and walked down the corridor to a dim, humid room at the back of the inn where Chief Inspector Kanehara, the head of the First Investigative Division, and two other senior officers were sat sipping tea with a stick-thin, middle-aged woman in a somber kimono –

Excuse me, Chief, said Detective Hattori, bowing from his waist, gesturing toward Harry Sweeney and Susumu Toda. But Public Safety Division are here, sir.

In the dim, humid room, Chief Inspector Kanehara turned in his seat, looking toward the entrance, squinting in the weak light, then nodded, smiled, stood up, and said, Of course, of course, I know Police Investigator Sweeney. How are you, Harry? How you doing? It's been a long time, no?

Yes, sir, said Harry Sweeney. It's been a while.

Too long, said Chief Inspector Kanehara, then he turned to the stick-thin, middle-aged woman in the somber kimono and said, Would you excuse us, please?

The woman gave a brief nod, got to her feet, then shuffled out of the room, her eyes to the floor as she passed Harry Sweeney and Susumu Toda.

Gentlemen, please, said Chief Inspector Kanehara, sitting back down. Have a seat.

Harry Sweeney and Susumu Toda both thanked Chief Inspector Kanehara and sat down at the chipped, stained table in the center of this dim and humid room.

Well, I trust Detective Hattori has given you a full briefing on recent developments, Harry, said Chief Inspector Kanehara, glancing up at Hattori.

Broad strokes, Chief, said Hattori, nodding in the doorway. They were keen to speak with you, Chief.

Yes, sir, said Harry Sweeney. We – that is, Public Safety – would be very grateful for the latest information, sir.

Of course, Harry, of course, said Chief Inspector Kanehara. I imagine General Willoughby, even the Supreme Commander himself, is taking an interest in this case?

Yes, sir, said Harry Sweeney, nodding. General Willoughby is particularly interested, sir, yes.

Chief Inspector Kanehara nodded, then sighed and said, Well, Harry, things have been moving rapidly, very rapidly indeed. The lady you just saw, her name is Nagashima, she's the proprietress of this inn. Late yesterday, she came forward to say that she believes President Shimoyama visited here on the afternoon of the fifth. He appeared very tired and was asking for a room in which to sleep for a short time. Initially, she was reluctant, and so she checked with her husband. But because the man we now believe to have been President Shimoyama had the appearance "of being a gentleman," in her words, she agreed. She then showed the man up to one of the second-floor rooms, where a maid laid out the bedding and served him tea. The man – the man we now have reason to believe was President Shimoyama – stayed until approximately half past five, when he left, paying two hundred yen for the room, with a hundred-yen tip. Naturally, we have questioned Missus Nagashima, the maid, and also the son of Missus Nagashima – it was her son who initially answered the door. All three have accurately described President Shimoyama and the clothing he was wearing on the afternoon of the fifth, even down to the color of his socks. All three have also correctly identified the President from photographs. Of course, as soon as you and I have finished speaking, Harry, we will be taking all three witnesses back to HQ, where we'll take formal statements.

But your instinct is that she is telling the truth, sir, asked Harry Sweeney. You believe her, sir?

Chief Inspector Kanehara shrugged, smiled, and said, Put it this way, Harry: at this stage I have no reason to doubt her, can see no reason why she would make such a thing up. Furthermore, she is the wife of a former police officer.

I see, said Harry Sweeney, nodding; nodding, then saying, But – and forgive me if I'm mistaken here, sir – but she first spoke with a reporter, before she contacted the police?

No, you're not mistaken, Harry. That's true. You see, ever since the body of the President was found at Ayase, a number of journalists have been staying here. As you can imagine, the inn has been rushed off its feet. So last night, while helping the maids to serve dinner, Missus Nagashima happened to see a photograph of President Shimoyama on the front page of a newspaper one of the journalists was reading. Only then did she realize it was the face of the same man who had stayed here on the afternoon of the fifth.

I see, said Harry Sweeney again, nodding again; nodding again, then saying, And I believe a number of other witnesses have come forward, sir, also claiming to have seen President Shimoyama in the area that evening?

In the dim, humid room, at the chipped, stained table, Chief Inspector Kanehara nodded, smiled again, and asked, So you've read the witnesses' statements then, Harry?

Only in the newspapers, I'm afraid, sir, said Harry Sweeney. Unfortunately.

Chief Inspector Kanehara sighed, shook his head, and said, That is most unfortunate, Harry, yes. And I'm sorry. Very sorry indeed, Harry. But may we speak frankly, Harry?

Of course, sir, said Harry Sweeney. Please –

Chief Inspector Kanehara looked across the chipped, stained table at Harry Sweeney, stared through the dim, humid light at Harry Sweeney, and nodded, sucking in the air through his teeth before saying, This need go no further, Harry, should stay within these walls, between us, Harry, but, er – how can I put this? – the initial stages of this investigation, they have not been handled as well as they might have been.

I would agree, sir.

Chief Inspector Kanehara, still looking at Harry Sweeney, still staring at Harry Sweeney, nodded again and said, Of course, I know you know this, Harry. Being a policeman, a detective yourself. That is why I'm speaking frankly with you now, Harry, even though as a ranking officer in the Japanese police force it is an embarrassing, shameful thing to have to admit. Especially, if I may say, and with respect, to an American detective. But you see, Harry, and not to make excuses, nor to pass the buck, but the management of this investigation has not been in my hands, Harry.

I see, sir, said Harry Sweeney.

Yes, Harry, you see because there are three separate crime scenes to cover – the Shimoyama house, the Mitsukoshi department store, and then the tracks at Ayase – I was forced to divide my division, the First Investigation Division, even using both Rooms One and Two, you understand, Harry, between these three separate scenes. That meant Chief Kita had no choice but to enlist the help of the Second Investigative Division, in order to assist in the canvassing of the area around here, specifically around Ayase and Gotanno.

I see, said Harry Sweeney again.

Now I'm sure our colleagues in the Second Investigative Division have many qualities, but the specific nature of the fieldwork required here – canvassing neighbors and locals, taking down witness statements, and so forth – well, to be candid, Harry, it's not one of their strengths and has proved to be beyond either their capacity or capability.

So just to be clear, sir, said Harry Sweeney, the Second Investigative Division are responsible for interviewing witnesses then, not your division, sir?

They *were*, Harry, they *were*. But given their manifest inability to do what was being asked of them, either accurately or efficiently, I asked for them to be withdrawn, and Chief Kita agreed. Therefore, the First Investigative Division are now in complete control of this case. And so rest assured, Harry, we have immediately begun to right some of the initial wrongs created by the Second Investigative Division. Of course, this entails re-canvassing the entire vicinity, re-interviewing all the locals, but this time accurately documenting, then collating all witness statements and so forth.

That's very welcome news, sir, said Harry Sweeney. But not to jump the gun here, sir, but may I ask what your initial instincts are, sir? About these witnesses, their statements?

Chief Inspector Kanehara sucked in the air through his teeth again, glanced at the other two senior officers, then leaned forward in his seat and said, As I say, we need to re-interview the witnesses in question, but – between you and me, Harry, detective to detective – they seem pretty solid. Two in particular, both local – a Mister Narushima and a Missus Yamazaki, I think – they both saw a man fitting the description of President Shimoyama in the vicinity of the railroad tracks, both saw him between six and seven on the evening of the fifth, which would seem to fit with what Missus Nagashima says, about the man checking out of here around half past five. I mean, you have to remember, Harry, they're not used to seeing strangers round here, certainly not dressed the way President Shimoyama was. But we'll make sure you have copies of all the witness statements, Harry, then you can decide for yourself.

That would be very much appreciated, sir, said Harry Sweeney. Thank you, sir.

Chief Inspector Kanehara nodded, smiled, and said, Thank *you*, Harry, we appreciate *your* support. Furthermore, we'll also endeavor to keep you – and I mean you personally, Harry – up to date with all pertinent information, as and when we receive and process it. This should mean neither you nor I will be getting our news from the papers, Harry.

That would be very much appreciated, sir, said Harry Sweeney again, placing one hand on the top of each thigh, then leaning forward in a short bow. Thank you, sir.

Chief Inspector Kanehara shook his head, waving his right hand back and forward across his face: Please, Harry, really; you should not be thanking me. It should have been this way from the beginning. But I'll personally ensure you have copies of all the statements by the end of today.

We look forward to them, sir, said Harry Sweeney.

Chief Inspector Kanehara leaned forward in his seat again, bowed briefly, then said, But now, if you'll excuse us, Harry, we need to get Missus Nagashima, her son, and the maid down to Headquarters, to get their statements down.

Of course, sir. Thank you for your time, sir, said Harry Sweeney, standing up at the same time as Chief Inspector Kanehara, the two other men, and Susumu Toda.

I'll see you again soon, I hope, Harry, said Chief Inspector Kanehara, showing Harry Sweeney and Susumu Toda out into the dark, narrow hallway, then gesturing toward Detective Hattori: And, of course, remember Detective Hattori here; he's always available if I'm not, Harry.

Day or night, said Detective Hattori, nodding at Harry Sweeney, smiling at Harry Sweeney. Be my guest.

Harry Sweeney stopped, turned in the dark, narrow corridor to look at Detective Hattori, to smile at Detective Hattori and say, That's very professional of you, detective.

Just doing my job, sir, said Detective Hattori.

Aren't we all, detective, said Harry Sweeney, then he turned back toward the *genkan*, stepped into his shoes, and followed Susumu Toda through the tiny garden, under the wooden gate, across the narrow ditch, and out into the street.

What do you think, Harry, asked Susumu Toda, taking out his cigarettes, holding out the pack to Harry Sweeney.

Harry Sweeney shook his head, turning in the street to watch two men getting out of yet another car, the two men taking two suitcases out of the trunk of the car, carrying their suitcases across the narrow ditch, under the wooden gate, disappearing into the shabby, gloomy two-storied inn, that place of shabby, gloomy trysts and assignations –

Harry, asked Susumu Toda again.

Harry Sweeney shook his head again, took out his own cigarettes, and said, I think things just got a whole lot easier for us, Susumu. Or a lot more complicated.

Yeah, but which is it, Harry?

Harry Sweeney lit a cigarette, inhaled, exhaled, then shook his head again, smiled, and said, Dunno, Susumu, dunno. All I do know is we got a long walk back to the car, then a long day ahead of us. Another very long fucking day.

Long day turned to long night, caffeine-stretched under office light. Harry Sweeney requested and got extra bodies from Chief Evans: George, Dan, and Sonoko – two Nisei translators and a local-hire girl who could speak and type English; then Harry Sweeney waited for Bill Betz to come back from Norton Hall, with nothing but promises that intelligence would be shared; waited until Susumu Toda returned from the late-afternoon briefing at MPD HQ, bringing with him copies of all the witness statements to date; waited until the evening editions of the newspapers were in; waited until the rest of Room 432 had left, until the office was empty, until the office was theirs; then Harry Sweeney, Bill Betz,

Susumu Toda, and one of the Nisei translators pushed back the desks and the chairs in Room 432 to clear a space; then Harry Sweeney, Bill Betz, Susumu Toda, and one of the Nisei translators went down the corridors of the fourth floor, from room to room, until they had found and brought back three blackboards and a box of chalk to Room 432; then Harry Sweeney, Bill Betz, Susumu Toda, and one of the Nisei translators placed the three blackboards side by side in Room 432; then Harry Sweeney took a piece of chalk from the box and wrote a title in block capitals at the top of each board – THE SHIMOYAMA HOUSE, THE MITSUKOSHI STORE, THE CRIME SCENE; then he drew three vertical lines down the length of each board and one horizontal line across the top of the three vertical lines, creating four columns on each of the boards; then at the top of each column he wrote Date, Time, Name, Location; then Harry Sweeney distributed copies of all the witness statements and newspaper reports to date; he told Susumu Toda to focus on the Shimoyama house and the route to the Mitsukoshi department store; he told Bill Betz and one of the Nisei translators to focus on the Mitsukoshi department store; he and the other Nisei translator would take the lion's share and focus on the crime scene; he told them to read all of the witness statements and all of the newspaper reports, told them to make lists of dates and times, names, and locations, to list all possible sightings of Sadanori Shimoyama, then to write them in chalk in the columns on the appropriate board; then Harry Sweeney said, Okay. Let's get to work . . .

And then they went to work; they worked and they worked, through the evening into the night, reading and translating the statements and the reports, through the night toward the dawn, noting down dates and times, names and locations, listing all possible sightings of Sadanori Shimoyama in chalk in columns on the appropriate board, until the dawn had come and the work was done, in numbers and letters across three boards, white on black, before their eyes –

Red raw and smarting, exhausted, shattered, and dead on their feet, Harry Sweeney, Bill Betz, and Susumu Toda stood before the three boards, the twelve columns, their heads moving back and forth from board to board, their eyes going from left to right, column to column, up and down, then back and forth, over and over, each board, each column –

Maybe it's because I'm beat, said Bill Betz. But this makes no goddamn sense to me. I mean, we got this guy Ōtsu – he's the secretary to Eisaku Satō, a member of the Diet, ex-Minister of Transport, friend of Shimoyama; what you'd call a reliable witness – he's claiming he saw Shimoyama wedged between two men in the back of a car going past the Diet building, heading at speed toward Hirakawa-chō at about eleven o'clock that morning. Meanwhile, around the same time, over at Mitsukoshi, we got shop staff, housewives, and maids all claiming they saw Shimoyama walking round the store, or in the basement, by the entrance, or near the subway, either on his own or talking with three other men. But then, just two hours later, he's getting off a train at Gotanno, checking into this Suehiro inn and having a nap.

Harry Sweeney shrugged: People make mistakes, Bill.

Yeah, said Bill Betz, counting down the names on THE CRIME SCENE board. Five, six, seven, eight of them? To date, so far. That's how many folk are claiming to have seen Shimoyama hanging round the tracks that night. So far.

Harry Sweeney shrugged again: It's early days, Bill.

Yeah, said Bill Betz again. That's my point, Harry. This is only going to get more screwed up. The more people come forward, the more newspaper reports, the more witness statements. You know that, Harry. You know how it goes.

Harry Sweeney nodded, looking from board to board, from column to column: Yeah? So what you saying, Bill?

I'm saying we should just let them get on with it, said Bill Betz. Not try and do their jobs for them.

Harry Sweeney turned to Bill Betz, laughed, and said, Yeah? You going to go tell Sir Charles that, are you, Bill?

Bill Betz shook his head, smiled at Harry Sweeney, and said, Look, Harry. I'm not trying to pick no fight here. I'm just saying this already looks screwed up. An' I reckon it's only going to get more screwed up. I just don't see why we should be the ones busting our balls trying to unscrew it.

Harry Sweeney turned back to the boards, back to the columns, nodded, and said, I know, Bill, I know.

But hey, Bill, said Susumu Toda, pointing from THE MITSUKOSHI STORE to THE CRIME SCENE board. Maybe it's not that screwed up? This car reported stolen from outside Mitsukoshi on the morning of the fifth, it's the same color and size as the one Satō's secretary saw and then the one seen around Ayase later that night, right?

You mean they're all big and black, laughed Bill Betz.

You never know, said Susumu Toda. They find that stolen car, get some prints, case might solve itself?

Come on, laughed Bill Betz again. You're going to abduct the President of the goddamn railroads in broad daylight, then drive around town with him all day in a stolen car? You think that was their plan, do you, Sherlock? Jesus.

Maybe it was spur of the moment, said Susumu Toda. Maybe it wasn't that well planned?

Most things aren't, said Harry Sweeney, his head still moving back and forth from board to board, his eyes still going from left to right, column to column, up and down, then back and forth, over and over, each board and each column.

Sir, said one of the Nisei translators, the one who called himself George, coming back from downstairs, another pile of newspapers in his arms. The morning editions are in, sir.

Harry Sweeney looked down at the big pile of newspapers in the man's arms, looked up at the black rings round his red eyes, all the black rings round all their red eyes, then Harry Sweeney turned back to the boards and the columns, the three boards and twelve columns, with all of their numbers and all of their letters, in white on black –

Come on, Harry, said Bill Betz. You been up all night. You need a break, Harry, we all do.

Harry Sweeney nodded: I know, Bill, I know we do.

That's all I wanted to hear, Harry, laughed Bill Betz, grabbing his jacket and hat, heading for the door, an exit. Anyone needs me, I'll be hitting the canteen, then the hay . . .

Harry Sweeney called out, Hey, Bill –

Yeah, yeah, said Bill Betz, not stopping, not turning back. I know, and you're welcome, Harry. Don't mention it.

Harry Sweeney smiled, turned to Susumu Toda, George, Dan, and Sonoko, and said, Same goes for you guys. You should all take a break, too. And thank you.

What time you want us back here, sir, asked Dan, already putting on his jacket, picking up his hat.

Harry Sweeney glanced at his watch, the face still cracked, the hands still stopped, and shrugged: Susumu?

You guys both billeted here, asked Susumu Toda.

No, said George. Over at the Yashima Hotel.

Say one o'clock then, said Susumu Toda, looking at his watch, then back over at Harry Sweeney –

But Harry Sweeney had turned back to the boards and the columns, their numbers and their letters, not answering Susumu Toda, not watching the two Nisei leave.

Sir, excuse me, sir, said Sonoko, standing next to Harry Sweeney in front of the middle board, the MITSUKOSHI board, looking across the columns on the board, then back down at the piece of paper in her hand.

What is it, sweetheart, asked Harry Sweeney.

Well, sir, whispered Sonoko, I don't mean to get the other

man, Mister Bill, in trouble, sir, but I think he forgot this report, sir. Forgot to write it on the board, sir.

Don't worry, laughed Harry Sweeney. Wouldn't be the first time, won't be the last. Let me see –

And Harry Sweeney took the piece of paper from her outstretched hand, looked down at the piece of paper, read the words on the paper, read them twice over, then went over to his desk, through the papers on his desk, all the newspapers on his desk, all the reports on his desk, scattering them this way, scattering them that: Where the fuck is it . . .

Where the fuck is what, asked Susumu Toda. What you looking for, Harry? What you lost?

That yellow pad, the one I always keep on the desk.

Why, asked Susumu Toda, coming over to the desk, picking up the papers from the floor. What is it?

Harry Sweeney stared down at his desk, shook his head, then reached for his jacket: Screw it. Call the pool and get a car, will you, Susumu. We're going out . . .

Sir, excuse me, sir, said Sonoko, standing frozen in the middle of the office, her head bowed, her hands at her side in two tiny balls. Have I done something wrong, sir?

Harry Sweeney picked up his hat, walked over to the girl, gently raised her chin in his hand, looked down at her face, into her eyes, then smiled and said, No, sweetheart. You've done something right. Just don't tell anyone.

In the shade of the Mitsukoshi department store, alongside the doors to its south entrance, Ichirō pulled in and parked up.

Back again, said Toda, getting out of the car.

Harry Sweeney had his door half open, then stopped: Hey, Ichirō? If I told you I was going to be five minutes, but then didn't come back, how long would you wait?

What do you mean, sir, asked Ichirō, turning in the driver's seat to look at Harry Sweeney.

I mean, how long would you sit here and wait for me? Before you called someone?

Call who, sir, asked Ichirō.

My office? Or the motor pool?

But what would I say, sir?

So you'd just sit here all day, waiting, would you?

Sir, if I may say, said Ichirō, the driver was just doing his job. Just like we all would, sir.

Harry Sweeney nodded: I see. Thanks.

You're welcome, sir, said Ichirō, turning in his seat, back to the wheel, to the view through the windshield.

Harry Sweeney got out of the car, crossed the narrow side road, and caught up with Susumu Toda, already standing in front of the south entrance to the store –

What was that about, asked Toda.

Harry Sweeney shook his head: Ichirō would wait all day for us and then some, if we don't come back.

They all would, said Toda, pointing at the other cars and their drivers, all parked up in a line down the south side of the store. They're used to it. Used to waiting.

Harry Sweeney nodded, took out his notebook from his jacket pocket, flicked back a few pages, and said, They got a statement from a driver who was parked behind the Shimoyama car that day, right? You read that, yeah?

Yeah, said Toda, taking out a handkerchief, mopping his face, wiping his neck. The guy's a chauffeur for Nippon Seiyaku. They got an office inside, up on the fourth floor. So he's a regular here, parked up most days, I guess.

And he's corroborated what Ōnishi said, saying he saw Shimoyama getting out of his car, walking into the store.

Yeah, said Toda again. Give or take a couple of minutes, here and there. It all matches, yeah.

Harry Sweeney looked down at his notebook again: What about this other car he saw? This Prism 36 which pulled in behind, shortly after? Claims he saw four or five men getting out, following Shimoyama into the store.

It's only the Nippon Seiyaku chauffeur saw them. And twenty minutes later, he saw them come out again.

They traced the Prism yet?

Not that I've heard, said Toda. No.

Harry Sweeney nodded: Okay then, let's go –

And Harry Sweeney and Susumu Toda walked into the Mitsukoshi department store, through the doors, glass and gold, this time clear and open. Through the same doors Sadanori Shimoyama had walked through. They passed through the Cosmetics section. Through the same Cosmetics section where a nineteen-year-old shop assistant thought she had seen a man fitting the description of Sadanori Shimoyama walking back and forth for a while, before heading toward the north side of the store. They walked through the Miscellaneous Goods section. Through the same Miscellaneous Goods section where a twenty-year-old shop assistant also thought he had seen a man fitting the description of Sadanori Shimoyama walking in the direction of the elevators on the north side of the store. They passed through the Shoe section. Through the same Shoe section where a twenty-one-year-old shop assistant thought she had seen a man fitting the description of Sadanori Shimoyama briefly stop to look at some traditional Japanese sandals in a display case. Then they took Staircase H on the north side of the store, down to the basement and the customer service desk by the doors to the underground passage and the subway. The same customer service desk where a thirty-five-year-old employee – whose job it was to count the number of customers who entered the store from the subway – thought she had seen a man fitting the description of Sadanori Shimoyama leaving the store sometime between ten and ten fifteen, followed out of the store by three other men. She could not be sure if these three men were with the man fitting the description of Sadanori Shimoyama, but she thought these three men were all in their late thirties, and one of them she remembered quite clearly, with his suntanned face, his old black suit and dirty felt hat. Harry Sweeney and Susumu Toda took the short flight of stairs down to the doors, came out of the store into the underground passage, and stopped, standing on an iron plate where the store met the passage. The same iron plate where a number of ladies of differing ages thought they had seen a man fitting the description of Sadanori Shimoyama talking with three other men in low voices at various, conflicting times. One of the ladies described one of these three other men as being around fifty years old and very short, at around four foot nine, with a swarthy, triangular face and gold-framed glasses, wearing a dark striped suit with a white shirt, open at the neck. His shoes were pointed at their tips, she said, and he carried a bag –

Thought the guy looked like a school principal, said Toda, mopping his face, wiping his neck again.

Harry Sweeney laughed: School for pimps maybe.

Like a goddamn sauna down here, said Toda, looking up and down the passageway, watching uniforms and detectives milling about among journalists and photographers, the customers for the store and the commuters for the subway, the busybodies and the rubberneckers.

Harry Sweeney was looking at Toda: You okay, Susumu? You don't look so good.

I feel like shit, said Toda, wiping his face again. Think I must have got the summer flu or something . . .

Harry Sweeney nodded: You been up too long, I'm sorry. Take the car back, go catch some zeds.

You sure, Harry?

Yeah, said Harry Sweeney. Go on –

And Harry Sweeney turned and walked off through the uniforms and the detectives, the journalists and the photographers, through the customers and the commuters, the busybodies and the rubberneckers, heading north down the passageway, past the ticket gates for the subway, until he saw the hair salon and the tea shop up ahead, saw the sign up ahead: COFFEE SHOP HONG KONG.

Harry Sweeney took out the piece of paper Sonoko had given him, glanced down, read it over once again, then took out his PSD badge and pushed through the crowds – two deep at the window, queuing up by the door – and into the coffee shop; every seat in the shop taken, the air thick with cigarette smoke, a waiter and waitress rushing back and forth with their trays from the kitchen to the tables –

Excuse me, said a man in his late fifties, standing behind the cash register by the door. But we're full.

Harry Sweeney held up his PSD badge: Good for you and good for business, yeah, the Shimoyama Case? You the manager?

Yes, said the man, shifting his weight from foot to foot behind the cash register. I'm the manager, Niide.

Harry Sweeney smiled: I can see you're busy, so I'll make this brief, but I need to speak with you and your staff.

I see, said the manager. Here?

Harry Sweeney looked around the low-ceilinged room, pointed to a door toward the back: That the kitchen?

Yes, said the manager. But it's very small.

Harry Sweeney nodded: One at a time, it'll be fine.

Who first, asked the manager.

Harry Sweeney smiled again: From the top, so you.

The manager nodded, called over the waiter, and told him to mind the cash register. Then he led Harry Sweeney down the aisle, between the tables, toward the back of the shop, the toilets to the right, the kitchen to the left, a telephone, a directory, and an ashtray on a stand between the two doors –

That the only phone in here, asked Harry Sweeney.

Yes, said the manager. You need to use it?

Harry Sweeney shook his head: No.

Okay then, said the manager, with a shrug. In here –

And Harry Sweeney followed the manager into a narrow, windowless, oil-stained strip of a kitchen, where a thin, middle-aged octopus of a man in a stained apron was busy frying onions and meat on a hot plate, stirring a pot of thick curry, while dishing out bowls of miso soup and rice.

This is Goto, the cook, said the manager, with a sigh. You want him to step outside while we talk?

Harry Sweeney shook his head, then asked the cook, You see President Shimoyama in here, did you? The morning of the fifth, when your colleagues say he was here?

No, sir, said the cook, shaking his head, not looking up from his pots and his pans. Don't see nothing from here, sir.

But you saw him, right, said Harry Sweeney, turning to the manager, asking, With four other men, yeah?

The manager nodded: Like I told the papers, then the police, I think I did, that's all, sir.

Go on then. Tell me what you told them.

The manager closed his eyes, stroked his cheek, then opened his eyes and said, It was about ten o'clock, I guess. We open at nine thirty, same as Mitsukoshi, but I didn't get in till then, till ten. When I came in, there were five of them, sitting there, well dressed, you know. In suits. Drinking Japanese tea, not coffee. Had some cakes, I think. Talking.

Describe them to me.

The manager blew out the air from his mouth and shook his head and said, I didn't really see so well, sir. Two of them were maybe late thirties, the other one older, the one that was maybe President Shimoyama. Other two, I couldn't say.

How long did they stay?

The manager shook his head again: Kazu-chan, the waitress, yeah? She served them, she'd know better than me.

But you remember them paying, yeah?

The manager shook his head: No, sir. See, they must have settled up at the table, sir. With Kazu-chan.

You still have their bill, right?

The manager shook his head again: No, sir. I had to give it to the police, sir, the Japanese police, sir.

Okay then, you remember anyone else, asked Harry Sweeney. Any of the other customers that morning?

No, sir. Not that day, sir, no.

What about regular customers? You must have some?

The manager nodded: Yeah, we do. But not at that time. Lunchtime is when we get the regulars in, sir.

I see, said Harry Sweeney. Okay.

The manager smiled: You want to speak to Kazu-chan?

Yes, said Harry Sweeney. But the waiter first.

The manager shrugged: I'll go get him then, if you're finished with me? I'll be out front, if that's okay, sir?

Harry Sweeney nodded, taking out his handkerchief, mopping his face, wiping his neck, watching the cook slicing and dicing, frying and boiling: Pretty hot in here, yeah?

Keeps me slim, laughed the cook.

How about your boss, asked Harry Sweeney. He keep you slim and all, does he? Or is he all right?

Long as we're busy, laughed the cook again.

Excuse me, said a tall, gaunt man in his mid- to late twenties, in a white shirt with a black bow tie. I'm Kojima, the waiter. You wanted to speak with me, sir?

Harry Sweeney nodded: Yes, and you know why?

About President Shimoyama, sir?

Harry Sweeney nodded again: Yeah. So you were working the morning of the fifth, is that right?

Yes, sir, said the waiter.

And you also saw a man fitting the description of President Shimoyama in here that morning?

No, sir, I didn't. Not personally.

You didn't? But you were working here, yeah?

Yes, sir, said the waiter. But at that time, I'm usually in here, in the kitchen. Mister Gotō here, he doesn't usually start until later, toward lunchtime. So I'm usually in here, sir.

Harry Sweeney nodded: You never come out?

Sometimes, sir, said the waiter. But not that morning, or not that I remember, sir. I was in here, sir.

Harry Sweeney stared at the man – this nervous man, gaunt and tall, touching his bow tie, his collar damp – and Harry Sweeney said, I want you to think very carefully, Mister Kojima. Has anyone – maybe a journalist, maybe a police officer, maybe even Mister Niide, your manager – anyone told you to say or not say anything about the morning of the fifth?

No, sir, said the waiter, shaking his head.

You're absolutely sure about that?

Yes, sir, said the waiter.

Harry Sweeney nodded, then pointed toward the doorway and said, Okay then, one last question. That telephone out there, did you see anyone using it that morning?

No, sir, said the waiter. Not that I remember, sir.

Harry Sweeney nodded again: Okay then, thank you. Would you ask the waitress to step in here, please?

The waiter nodded, turned to leave the kitchen, then stopped, turned back, and asked, Is Kawada-san in trouble, sir?

Harry Sweeney shook his head: Why would she be?

I don't know, sir, said the waiter. But she's a good girl and she works hard, I know that, sir.

Harry Sweeney smiled: You don't need to worry, son. Just ask her to step in here, please.

The waiter nodded, turned, and went out of the kitchen.

Kojima-kun, he's sweet on her, said the cook, dishing out another portion of rice and curry onto a plate.

Harry Sweeney mopped his face and wiped his neck again and said, How about the manager? He sweet on her, too?

I guess so, laughed the cook. Customers seem to like her, so she's good for business. Pretty face and –

Excuse me, sir, you wanted to see me?

Harry Sweeney turned to the doorway, to a twenty-year-old girl in a black dress and white apron, her hands clasped together in front of her apron. Harry Sweeney smiled, nodded, and said, Yes, thank you.

This is about President Shimoyama, I suppose?

Harry Sweeney, still smiling, still nodding, said, But there's nothing to be afraid of or nervous about. I just want you to tell me in your own words what you told the police, then maybe answer any questions I might have. Okay?

Okay, the waitress nodded. I see. Well then, it was quite soon after we opened, not long after half past nine, when the two gentlemen came in. The man who looked like President Shimoyama, he was wearing a mouse-colored suit with a white shirt. I remember he wasn't wearing a hat and he had on those glasses, those Harold Lloyd-style frames, they call them. I also remember he had quite distinctive eyebrows. They were thick and sloping downwards; that's why, when I saw his photograph in the paper, I thought it must've been him.

Harry Sweeney nodded: How about the other man?

I don't remember him so well, I'm sorry, said the waitress. You see, they were sitting at a table near the door, and the man who looked like President Shimoyama, he had his back to the door, so he was facing me as I was coming and going. But the other man, he was facing the door with his back to me, so I didn't really see him very clearly at all. But I had the impression he was a bit younger, maybe late forties?

But there were just the two of them?

Well, that's what I thought, she said. But Mister Niide, our manager, when he came in he thought there were more of them. Another three men, I think he said.

Harry Sweeney asked, But you don't think so?

I can't be sure, she said. I mean, there were three other men at the next table, just across the aisle. That's true.

But you're not sure they were together?

No, she said, shaking her head. I didn't think they were. I mean, I never saw them speak to each other or anything.

But this other party, these three other men, they came in and left separately then, did they?

I think so, yes, she said. I mean, I'm not sure, but I think they came in after the other two, then left after them, yes.

Harry Sweeney nodded again, smiled again, then asked, So the man you think might have been President Shimoyama and this other man, how did they seem? How were they speaking? Like they were maybe friends?

Not really, no, said the waitress. I mean, the man who looked like President Shimoyama, he hardly spoke at all. He was just sat there listening. Had his hands together, folded on the table. I remember that because when I brought their order over, he had to move his hands so I could put the drinks down. Sort of hunched over, you know? Looked dispirited, really.

"Dispirited" in what way?

You know, worried. Like he was getting bad news.

Harry Sweeney nodded: I see. Did you catch any bits of their conversation, any fragment at all?

Not really, no, said the waitress again. I mean, I couldn't hear at all what the other man was saying. It was like he was whispering, almost. But President Shimoyama – I mean, the man who looked like him – he was just sort of grunting.

"Grunting"? Like how?

You know, sort of um, um, like that. Um, um.

Harry Sweeney nodded again, said again, I see. And so how long did they stay, the two of them?

Not more than thirty minutes.

And they paid at the table, is that correct?

Yes, said the waitress.

And separately, then, from these other three men, the men on the next table, across the aisle?

Yes, said the waitress again, nodding. That's why I'm pretty sure they weren't together.

Harry Sweeney said, Sorry – what did they order?

The man who looked like President Shimoyama and the other man? Er, the other man had Japanese tea, and the man who looked like President Shimoyama, he had a soda.

Harry Sweeney nodded: Did they smoke?

No, sir, not as far as I remember.

And which of them paid?

I'm sorry, sir, she said. I don't know. See, when I came back, back from in here, the money was on the table and they'd already left. But it was the other man who'd asked for the bill, so I'm assuming it was him who had paid.

Harry Sweeney nodded again, smiled again, then said, You're probably right. Now I want you to think carefully, very carefully, and see if you can remember who else was in here that morning. Maybe a little bit before they arrived? Maybe they used the telephone, that one just out there?

Yes, said Kazuko Kawada, the twenty-year-old waitress of the Coffee Shop Hong Kong nodding as she looked Harry Sweeney in the eye, as she said, There was someone, yes. Using the telephone. How did you know?

Harry Sweeney took the stairs up to the street, two at a time. He headed south down Ginza Street, through the lunchtime crowds, over the Nihonbashi Bridge, until he came to the crossroads with Avenue W. He stopped on the corner opposite the Shirokiya department store and took off his jacket. He glanced over his shoulder, then turned to the right, walking west up Avenue W, past the Yashima Hotel, until he came to Gofukubashi. He glanced over his shoulder again, then crossed Avenue W and headed south along 5th Street, past the Yaesu entrance to Tokyo station, until he came to Kajibashi. He put his jacket back on as he waited to cross, took out a cigarette and lit it, then walked west up Avenue Y, under the tracks, until he came to 4th Street. He turned right, crossed the road, and walked along the street until he came to the extended canopy of the Yaesu Hotel. He dropped his cigarette butt into the ashtray by the door, then turned to look back down 4th Street. He saw a man standing on the corner, in the shade of the Chiyoda Bank. He stared down the street at the man. The man turned and disappeared around the corner, back onto Avenue Y. Harry Sweeney took out another cigarette and lit it. He stood under the canopy, smoking the cigarette, watching the corner by the Chiyoda Bank. Harry Sweeney finished his cigarette, dropped it into the ashtray, then went through the doors into the Yaesu Hotel. He crossed the lobby to the elevators, nodded at the boy stood inside number five, and said, Fourth floor, please.

Very good, said the elevator boy.

That's "very good, sir," said Harry Sweeney.

Very good, said the elevator boy, not turning around, closing the doors, waiting for a beat to say, sir.

You're new here, yeah, said Harry Sweeney to the back of the kid's head, the elevator going up.

Yes, said the elevator boy, with a nod and another beat before he said, sir.

Uniform or no uniform, said Harry Sweeney, you address every man as "sir" and every lady as "ma'am," okay?

Yes, sir, said the elevator boy, with another nod, as the elevator stopped, as he opened the doors. Fourth floor, sir.

Thank you, said Harry Sweeney, stepping out.

It's not lucky, you know, sir, said the boy.

Harry Sweeney turned around: What's not lucky?

The number four, smiled the boy. In Japan, sir.

Harry Sweeney reached up, held open the doors, and stared at the boy as he said, You speak good English, kid. Probably went to a good school. But you got a smart mouth and a bad attitude. Ain't my fault your country got its ass kicked, ain't my fault you're working this elevator here. Ain't my fault, and it ain't your fault either, I know that, kid. So let's lose the smart mouth and bad attitude and just get along. Okay?

Okay, said the elevator boy. Sir.

Harry Sweeney looked at the boy – the privileged face, the resentful eyes – then shook his head, turned, and walked away, down the corridor to the door of his room.

Harry Sweeney took out his key, put it in the lock, turned the key, and opened the door. He slammed the door shut behind him. He crossed the room, drew back the curtains, and sat down on the bed. He took off his shoes, then stood back up. He took off his jacket, his shirt, and his pants. He walked over to the washstand and turned on the faucets. He washed and he shaved. He changed the bandages around his wrists and then his underwear and socks. He found a clean shirt, a dark tie and put them on. He picked up his jacket and pants from the bed and put them back on. He walked back over to the washstand and picked up his watch. Its face cracked, its hands stopped. He put on his watch, over the bandages on his left wrist. He adjusted the cuffs of his shirt and jacket, then straightened his tie. He picked up his hat and his key, opened the door, and stepped out of his room. He closed the door, he locked the door, then walked back along the corridor toward the elevators. He walked past the elevators and took the stairs, the four flights down to the lobby. He walked through the lobby toward –

Mister Sweeney, sir, called out Satō-san from behind the front desk. Excuse me, but you've got some mail, sir.

Harry Sweeney turned, smiled, and said, Thanks, Satō-san, I'll pick it up later. I gotta dash now . . .

And Harry Sweeney walked out through the doors of the Yaesu Hotel, under the length of its canopy, to a cab sitting on the curb. He stopped to glance down the road, over at the corner of the Chiyoda Bank. He saw a man standing on the corner, in the shade of the bank. He stared down the street at the man, the man just standing there, not moving, looking back in the direction of Harry Sweeney. Harry Sweeney opened the door of the cab, got in the back, closed the door, and said, Seishōji temple, Shiba, please.

They had come in black and in white, in their hundreds and their thousands, to stand in lines and in queues, lines and queues which stretched all the way back to the trees of the park. In black and white, in hundreds and thousands, the lines and the queues, edging forward, slowly, slowly, step by step, hour by hour, under the sun, the afternoon sun, toward the gate, toward the temple. In black and white, in hundreds and thousands, in lines and queues, slowly, slowly, step by step, hour by hour, under the sun, the afternoon sun, to pay their respects and mourn the man, to mourn Sadanori Shimoyama; to mourn him as a public figure, a man they had not known, had only ever read about, maybe only even in his death; or to mourn the private man, their classmate or alumnus, their colleague or their boss, the engineer or bureaucrat, their friend or relative, their cousin or their uncle, their brother or their son, their husband or their father; the public figure or the private man, all had come to mourn Sadanori Shimoyama –

Through the black and white, through the hundreds and thousands, the lines and queues, edging forward, slowly, slowly, step by step, shuffling forward, trying not to push, not to shove, gently and quietly, Harry Sweeney weaved his way among the mourners, up the steps and under the first gate, made of stone and made of wood, slowly, slowly, gently and quietly, Harry Sweeney walked over the gravel and up more steps, then under a second gate, out into the main precinct of the temple, its central pathway lined with baskets of flowers and wreaths on stands, the smell of incense and the sound of sutras, on the air, in the air, the scents and the chants, across the precincts of the temple, over the thousands of mourners, from out of the main hall, the ceremonial hall –

Inside the large hall, in its long shadows, the air thick with clouds of incense, heavy with the drone of the sutras, Harry Sweeney stood at the back, staring over the rows of bowed heads, watching the chief mourners, the bereaved relatives, in their black suits and kimonos, their cleaned and pressed uniforms, all seated in rows to the left and the right of an altar draped in white and decked with flowers, giant wreaths towering on stilts over the altar, over the chief mourners, the bereaved relatives, Harry Sweeney counting the wreaths and the baskets of flowers – the one hundred and sixty-two wreaths and baskets of flowers, from the Emperor and the Prime Minister, from cabinet members and members of the Diet, from the Minister for Transport and from General Headquarters, from Railroad executives and Railroad employees, from the union and its members; but from the back of the hall, from among its long shadows, Harry Sweeney's eyes kept coming back to the chief mourners, the bereaved relatives and family, to Missus Shimoyama in her black kimono, to her four sons, three still in their school uniforms, pressed and clean; this family bereft and diminished, beneath the tall wreaths, lost among the flowers, the incense, and the chants, beside the altar, before the altar, draped in white cloth, decked with more flowers, with its candles and with its photograph; the single, solitary photograph, framed in black, bordered in black, the formal portrait of a man, a husband and a father, in his best suit and tie, a portrait of Sadanori Shimoyama, the eyes of Sadanori Shimoyama staring sadly, sadly back across the mourners, over their heads and into the shadows, back into the eyes of Harry Sweeney –

Harry Sweeney blinked, rubbed, and wiped his eyes, bowed his head toward the altar, toward the portrait of the man, then turned and gently, quietly edged his way out of the shadows and out of the hall, made his way across the precincts and down its paths, down its steps and under its gates, weaving his way through the hundreds and thousands, the lines and the queues, until he was standing on the street, taking out his pack of cigarettes and –

Well, that's just grand, said Lieutenant Colonel Donald E. Channon, coming up on the blind side of Harry Sweeney. Not only they got half the goddamn Jap police here on crowd control, we got our own police investigator here, too.

Harry Sweeney put away his pack of cigarettes, took a step back, and asked, Is something wrong, sir?

You goddamn bet your life there is, said Colonel Channon, red in the face, rye on his breath. You think you gonna catch his fucking killers at his funeral, do you, Sweeney?

Harry Sweeney smiled: I think maybe we should find your car, sir. Maybe get you home, sir . . .

You should find his goddamn fucking killers is what you should do, Sweeney, said Colonel Channon, two fingers prodding into the chest of Harry Sweeney, flicking up his tie. 'Stead of hanging round his funeral like a spare fucking prick.

Harry Sweeney took another step back, stared at Lieutenant Colonel Donald E. Channon, and said, Maybe I thought I'd come take a look for myself at that goddamn nest of vipers you were telling me about, sir.

Hey, hey, now hold on there, Sweeney, said Colonel Channon, shaking his head, wagging his finger. Few kickbacks, bit of pocket-lining is all I meant by that. Didn't say nothing about fucking murdering no one.

Honor among thieves, think that's what they call it. That what you mean, sir?

Lieutenant Colonel Donald E. Channon tried to stare at Harry Sweeney, tried to jab his finger at Harry Sweeney, saying, Harp to a harp, fuck you, Sweeney, is what I mean.

Harp to a harp, I think you should go home, sir, said Harry Sweeney, turning away, starting to walk away –

Don't you fucking turn your back on me, Sweeney, said Colonel Channon, grabbing Harry Sweeney by the arm of his jacket, turning Harry Sweeney back around into his face. Don't you fucking walk away from me when I'm speaking to you. Not when I ain't done speaking to you, mister.

Harry Sweeney put his hand on the hand of Colonel Channon, gently, firmly loosening the grip of Colonel Channon round his arm, firmly, slowly removing the fingers of Colonel Channon from the sleeve of his jacket, then slowly, slowly taking a step back as he said, Go on then, please, sir, by all means. If you've something more to say, sir?

You bet I've got something more to say, said Colonel Channon, nodding to himself, flapping an arm in the direction of the temple, its gate, and its funeral: I say you should go back in there, arrest that goddamn Red bastard, is what I say.

Which goddamn Red bastard is that, sir?

That fucking guy Honda is who.

Honda, sir? I'm sorry, I . . .

Jesus, Sweeney, laughed Colonel Channon. You at the back of the church, day they was handing out the smarts? Ichizō Honda, Vice Chairman of the fucking union, is who.

And you say he's here today, sir?

Fucking nerve of the guy, said Colonel Channon, shaking his head, swaying on his feet. You believe it? Like a goddamn skull on a stick, he is, with the greased-back fucking hair, wanting to give his condolences, saying how fucking sorry he is, how much he liked and respected old Shimoyama. Now the man's fucking dead, in pieces on the goddamn tracks, like he fucking don't know who did it, goddamn lying son of a bitch, making with the condolences, the blood still fucking wet on his hands, the goddamn murdering Commie son of a bitch. His skinny yellow ass you should be hauling in, Sweeney, that's what you should be fucking doing, making with the third degree. Give him the old fucking third degree, he'll soon tell you what you need to know, tell you who fucking did it, you goddamn bet he will, Sweeney.

Harry Sweeney had taken out his notebook, taken out his pencil, had written down the name Ichizō Honda. Harry Sweeney closed his notebook over his pencil, put them back inside his pocket. Then he patted the left side of his jacket and said, Thank you, sir. Sure that's very useful information, sir.

You bet your fucking life it is, Sweeney, said Colonel Channon. Solves your fucking case for you, is what it does.

Harry Sweeney nodded, then smiled at Lieutenant Colonel Donald E. Channon and said, Thank you, sir, I'm sure you're right, sir. I'll just go tie up the loose ends . . .

Because he had not slept, because he never could, they were stabbing at his skin, they were slicing off his ears, drilling down the holes, poking round with wires, scratching at his skull, scraping along its bone, the birds in the sky, the insects through the air, the kids on the corners, the people on the streets, the boots on the sidewalk, and the tires in the road, marching and turning, pounding and screeching, putting on the brakes, coming to a halt, the voice from a car, calling from its window, Hey, hey, hold up there, detective, will you!

Harry Sweeney stopped in the street, halted his long march back to the office, turned to the car parked up on the curb, turned to see Detective Hattori leaning out of the window on the passenger side, and Harry Sweeney said, What is it?

You're a hard man to find, detective, said Hattori.

Harry Sweeney looked at Detective Hattori, smiled, and said, Obviously not that hard, detective.

Obviously not that hard, repeated Hattori, laughing. I like that, that's very good, detective.

What is it, detective? What do you want?

We want to take you for a little ride, said Hattori. If that's okay with you, detective?

Where and why?

Not far, said Hattori. Just to Headquarters. We got a witness there Chief Inspector Kanehara thinks you should meet. That is, if you would like, detective? If you got the time?

Harry Sweeney nodded: Sure.

Hop in then, detective, said Hattori, smiling. Let's go.

Harry Sweeney opened the back door of the unmarked police car and climbed in the back. He closed the door and then the car set off, speeding along, silence inside, north up Mita Avenue, then west onto 10th Street, turning north again onto Avenue B, past the Education Ministry and the Finance building, past the Construction Ministry and the Justice Ministry, left again at Sakuradamon, pulling up in front of the Metropolitan Police Headquarters –

Follow me, detective, said Hattori, getting out of the car, lighting a cigarette, leading Harry Sweeney inside the building, through the reception area and up the stairs, down a long corridor of many doors, the doors all closed, down the corridor to the door at its end –

In here, detective, said Hattori, dropping his cigarette into an ashtray of sand, then tapping on the door, then opening the door, showing Harry Sweeney into the room: a small room, a spartan room, a narrow strip of glass along the top of one wall, four chairs, and one table; a thick file on top of the table between the two people sat across from each other – a man and a woman, the man in a uniform, the woman in *monpe* pantaloons, the man in the uniform getting up from his seat, the woman in the pantaloons looking up at Harry Sweeney and Detective Hattori.

This is Missus Take Yamazaki, said Hattori, pulling out one of the empty chairs from under the table. Have a seat, please, detective, listen to what she has to say.

Harry Sweeney sat down in the chair, nodding at the woman across the table, looking at the woman across the table, her worn-out clothes and her sun-dried skin.

Now there's nothing to worry about, Take-san, said Hattori, sitting down beside Harry Sweeney, smiling across the table at Take Yamazaki. This foreigner is a detective, he works for GHQ. He's just come to hear what you told us, that's all.

I see, said the woman, nodding. I understand.

That's good, said Hattori, leaning forward in his chair, resting his hands on the file on the table, still smiling at Take Yamazaki. So you just tell him exactly what you told us.

Well, I saw President Shimoyama, didn't I . . .

Sorry, said Hattori, stopping the woman, smiling at the woman. From the beginning, please, Take-san.

Okay then, began the woman again. That evening, the fifth, sometime after six o'clock it was, maybe even more like half six, I was coming along the Jōban line tracks. See, I'd been to visit my younger sister and her husband. She lives up Ayase way, and I'm in Gotanno Minami-chō, so quickest way home for me is along the railroad tracks. Bit dangerous, I know; I shouldn't, but it's a shortcut. Lot of us use it, see. So I was walking along the tracks, the eastbound tracks, the ones going to Ayase, that way, because that's a bit safer, see. On the other side, the westbound side, ones heading to Senju, they can come up behind you, can't they? So

I'm heading down the tracks, toward where there's a bridge, that way, looking up that way, yeah, because you still have to keep your eyes open, case a train come, yeah. So, anyway, I'm looking that way and I see this man, this gentleman, up toward the embankment of the Tōbu line, like around where the bridge is? And he's at the foot of the embankment, right by the tracks, near where there's that steel pillar. And I think that's dangerous, that is, strange and all. What the heck's he doing there? Bit late to be working in the fields, specially dressed like that. I mean, he's got on a gray suit, like a businessman wears. But I suppose I must've been staring, wondering what he's doing there, because then he sees me, doesn't he, sees me staring at him, watching him, and our eyes meet, don't they? Then quick as you like, he looks away and heads off down the banking, off the tracks and into the field there. Must've made him nervous, me staring at him, me watching him. But as I'm coming off the tracks myself, I see him again, don't I? Crouched down in the field, he was, pulling up weeds.

These weeds, said Detective Hattori, taking an envelope from inside his jacket, opening the envelope over the file on the table, gently shaking out its contents, slowly dropping the contents on top of the file, one by one: five hard, pale-green, oval-shaped seeds. We call them *juzudama*.

Harry Sweeney leaned forward in his seat, looked down at the top of the file, stared down at the five hard, pale-green, oval-shaped seeds, and said, Job's tears.

Evidence in any language, said Detective Hattori. That's what I call it, detective. Evidence . . .

Harry Sweeney looked up from the five hard, pale-green, oval-shaped seeds, Harry Sweeney turned to Hattori, and asked, Where did you find it, detective?

In the right-hand pocket of the pants of the suit which President Shimoyama was wearing on the night that train hit him, said Hattori. That's where we found it, detective.

There was a knock, the door opened, and Harry Sweeney glanced up over his shoulder to see Chief Inspector Kanehara standing in the doorway. Harry Sweeney started to get to his feet, but Chief Inspector Kanehara stopped him, saying, Please, Harry, don't get up.

Good timing, Chief, said Detective Hattori, gesturing at the five seeds. I was just showing Detective Sweeney here the evidence, sharing it with him, like you said, sir.

Chief Inspector Kanehara nodded, glanced at the seeds on the file, then looked at Harry Sweeney and said, So what do you think, Harry? Detective to detective?

Excuse me, Chief, said Hattori. But we hadn't quite finished. I haven't told him what me and Sudō-kun found.

Chief Inspector Kanehara nodded again: I see. Well, go on then, Detective Hattori. This is important, Harry.

Yes, said Hattori, scooping the five seeds back inside the envelope, putting the envelope back inside his jacket, then opening the file on the table and taking out a photograph, saying, See, when me and Detective Sudō re-interviewed Missus Yamazaki here – this is up at her house, right – we asked her to show us exactly the place, the exact spot where she saw President Shimoyama pulling the heads off the weeds. So she takes us to the place, shows us the exact spot, and this is what we found there, saw with our very own eyes –

Harry Sweeney leaned over the photograph, the photograph Detective Hattori was tapping with his finger, looked down at the photograph of a patch of wild barley, a clump of Job's tears, stared down at their stems, their decapitated stems, their heads all gone.

Evidence, said Detective Hattori again. As I'm sure you agree, detective. That's what's called evidence.

Harry Sweeney sat back in his chair, glanced across the table at the woman sitting with her head bowed, looking down at her hands, then Harry Sweeney turned to Chief Inspector Kanehara: May I ask this lady a couple of questions, sir?

Chief Inspector Kanehara nodded, smiled, and said, By all means, Harry, please do. That's why you're here.

Thank you, sir, said Harry Sweeney, taking out his notebook and pencil, turning back to the woman, and saying, Now, as Detective Hattori said, there's nothing to worry about, Missus Yamazaki. Just a couple of questions, okay?

Yes, said the woman, nodding. Please.

Harry Sweeney nodded, smiled, and said, Now this man you saw, you said he was wearing a suit?

Yes, said the woman again. It was a gray suit.

What about his hat? What color was that?

Erm, said the woman, looking up at Detective Hattori, then over at Chief Inspector Kanehara, and shaking her head. Erm, I didn't see no hat. I don't think he was wearing a hat.

Harry Sweeney nodded again, smiled again, and said, That's okay. Like I say, there's nothing to worry about.

I see, said the woman, nodding.

Okay, what about his shirt?

I don't remember, she said, shaking her head again.

Okay, that's fine. How about anything else? Do you remember anything else he was wearing?

Yes, said the woman, looking up again at Detective Hattori, over again at Chief Inspector Kanehara and nodding. His shoes. He was wearing these chocolate-colored shoes. Remember them because they looked expensive, they did; not like the sort of shoes you go wearing in the fields, you know?

Harry Sweeney smiled and said, What about his build, his age, his face? You got a good look at him, right?

Yes, said the woman again. I did.

Go on then, can you describe him for me, please?

Well, he looked older than me, about forty-six or forty-seven, I guess. And he was quite tall, taller than average, but I couldn't tell you how tall, I'm sorry.

That's fine. Go on . . .

He was pale, quite white, you know, the skin of his face. Not like he worked outdoors, you know. Kind of round, chubby face, but with a tall nose, you know, prominent.

You think he could have been foreign? Like me?

No, no, she laughed. I don't mean like that. He was Japanese, definitely Japanese, he was. I know that.

How about his eyes? You said your eyes met?

Black, obviously. Sort of sad.

Was he wearing glasses?

That's the only thing, she said, looking again at Hattori, over again at Kanehara. Reason I nearly never said nothing. Because I don't remember he was wearing glasses, and when I saw his picture in the paper like, in all the papers, he's always wearing glasses, isn't he? But my husband, he said I better say, go to the police box and say what I'd seen. So I went and I said.

And we're very glad you did, Take-san, said Hattori. Very glad indeed, aren't we, Detective Sweeney?

Harry Sweeney nodded, still looking at Missus Yamazaki, still smiling at Missus Yamazaki as he said, Indeed, we are, Missus Yamazaki. Just one last question?

Yes, asked the woman. Please?

After you saw him pulling up the weeds, after you passed him, did you turn around, see what he was doing?

Yes, said the woman. I had a glance, yeah.

And so what was he doing then?

Well, he was just walking off, wasn't he? Like to the east a bit, sort of absent-minded like, you know?

You didn't see where he went?

No, she said. I lost sight of him. Never saw him again. Not till I saw his face in the paper, that is. Fright of my life I got, I tell you, sir. Fright of my life.

Harry Sweeney felt a hand on his shoulder, heard Chief Inspector Kanehara whisper in his ear, Harry, I've got to go see

Chief Kita. But there's something else. Can we step outside?

Harry Sweeney nodded. He looked across the table, over the photograph on the top of the open file, and smiled and said, Thank you, Missus Yamazaki. You've been most helpful.

You're welcome, said the woman.

Harry Sweeney turned to Hattori, smiled again, and said again, Thank you, too, detective.

Don't mention it, said Detective Hattori. We're all just doing our jobs, detective.

I can see that, said Harry Sweeney, getting up from his chair, pushing it back under the table, then he turned and walked out of the room, closing the door behind him.

So what do you think, Harry, asked Chief Inspector Kanehara again. Detective to detective?

Harry Sweeney nodded and said, The evidence of the weeds would seem to corroborate the lady's statement, sir.

The timing also fits with the statements we've got from the Suehiro Ryokan, said Chief Inspector Kanehara. And all the other statements we've got from the vicinity, too, all the other sightings. They all seem to match, Harry. It all fits.

Just not with the autopsy, sir.

Harry, Harry, said Chief Inspector Kanehara. You know as well as I do, these scientists, they're not policemen, let alone detectives. They know their science, but never the scene, not how it is, not like we do, Harry. You know that, know how they are. Especially these Tōdai guys, all books and privilege.

Harry Sweeney nodded again: You might be right, sir. But what you going to do about the Public Prosecutor then? Last I heard, he was still agreeing with those Tōdai guys and their findings, agreeing it was murder, not suicide.

Leave that to me, Harry, said Chief Inspector Kanehara. I'm going to go see the Chief now, ask him to bring in Doctor Nakadate – you remember him, Harry?

Yeah, I remember him.

Good man, solid. He's worked many cases for us, and not just in the library or the laboratory, you know. In the field and at the scene, listening to us, working with us. He'll clear all this up for us, Harry, you'll see. He'll sort things out.

Harry Sweeney shook his head, sighed, and then said, You mean sort it out as a suicide, sir, yeah?

I'm sorry, Harry, said Chief Inspector Kanehara, nodding. It's not what you want to hear, I know that.

Harry Sweeney shook his head again: I just want to know what happened, sir. That's all, sir.

I know, Harry, I know. I meant to say, not what GHQ want to hear. They want to hear we're arresting members of the union, members of the Communist Party, I know that, Harry.

Harry Sweeney sighed again: I don't know about all of GHQ, sir. But General Willoughby in particular, yes, sir.

Look, Harry, said Chief Inspector Kanehara. You know me and you know the Japanese police. There's not a man among us has any love for the Reds, you know that, Harry.

Harry Sweeney nodded: I know that, sir.

But if the evidence ain't there, Harry, it ain't there. I wish it was, I really do. Believe me, Harry, believe me. Nothing I'd like more than to be hauling in a bunch of union hotheads, charging some Commie bastards for this . . .

Harry Sweeney nodded again: I know that, sir.

Particularly now, Harry . . .

Harry Sweeney looked at Chief Inspector Kanehara, saw him lean in closer, heard him lower his voice as he said, Like I said in there, Harry, there's something else, and not something you want to be talking about, specially not on the day of the man's funeral, Harry . . .

Harry Sweeney waited for Chief Inspector Kanehara to lean in closer still, waited for him to whisper in his ear, then Harry

Sweeney stepped back from Chief Inspector Kanehara, stared at Chief Inspector Kanehara, and then Harry Sweeney shook his head and said –

Fuck, said Chief Evans, looking out of the window of his office, staring up at the sky, black and thick, shaking his head again and again. Fuck, fuck, fuck, Harry. Jesus. Fuck, Harry. Fuck.

Yep, Chief, said Harry Sweeney, closing his notebook, putting it back inside his jacket. That's what I said, sir.

No way it's just some bullshit rumor then?

Least not the way Chief Inspector Kanehara laid it out, no, sir, said Harry Sweeney. Like I say, he laid it all out pretty good, Chief. The money problems, the sleeping pills, the pressures of the job, and then, if all that ain't enough . . .

A goddamn fucking woman, sighed Chief Evans.

*Cherchez la femme*, as the French say.

This fucking funny to you, is it, Harry, said Chief Evans, turning away from the window, walking over toward Harry Sweeney. You see some fucking cause for levity here, do you? Something I'm fucking missing here?

No, sir, not at all, sir, said Harry Sweeney, his hands up, his hands out. Just saying what the press will say, sir.

You don't need to be worrying what the fucking press will say, hissed Chief Evans, standing over Harry Sweeney, looking down at Harry Sweeney. You need to be worrying what the goddamn General will say. You're shitting strawberries and cream, you think he's gonna buy this crap.

Harry Sweeney shrugged, looked up at Chief Evans, and said, Be honest with you, Chief, all due respect, I could care less what the General says, sir.

That right, is it, said Chief Evans, shaking his head, staring back down at Harry Sweeney. Well, you should goddamn fucking care. You make an enemy of that man, you'll regret it the rest of your life, I swear. But you get him in your corner, keep him on side, then you're farting through silk.

Still stinks, sir. Silk or no silk.

Fuck is wrong with you, said the Chief, turning away, walking back to his desk. This ain't the time to be playing the wise guy, Harry. It ain't the smart play, not today.

I'm sorry, Chief, said Harry Sweeney, rubbing his eyes, rubbing his cheeks. I ain't trying to play the wise guy, not with you, sir. But what can I do, can we do? It is what it is, Chief, we can't change what it is.

I know, said Chief Evans, sitting back down at his desk, rubbing his own eyes, squeezing the bridge of his nose. I know. But you know how it is, too, Harry, this place – this country, this Occupation – it's snakes and ladders, is what it is, you know that, Harry. Goddamn snakes and fucking ladders.

Harry Sweeney nodded, smiled, and said, Been a while since I seen any ladders, Chief, I know that.

Exactly, said the Chief, looking across his desk at Harry Sweeney, staring across his desk at Harry Sweeney. That's my point: you play this smart, you play it right, Harry, you sort it out, you make it right – somehow, just any-fucking-how – be a big fucking ladder waiting for you, Harry, I know that. Biggest one you ever fucking saw.

But a ladder to where, sir?

Anywhere you want, Harry. Anywhere you want.

On the dark side of the street, in the shadows from the park, Harry Sweeney opened the car door and climbed in the back.

Sorry to have had to call you at your office like that, Harry-san, said Akira Senju as the car set off, set off fast.

Harry Sweeney shook his head: It was good timing.

That's what I thought, said Akira Senju, patting the top of Harry Sweeney's thigh, squeezing the top of Harry Sweeney's thigh. Thought to myself: This is something Harry should know, something Harry needs to know now.

Harry Sweeney nodded, looking out of the window as the car bore right onto Avenue W, heading east.

Could prove serendipitous, said Akira Senju, still squeezing the top of Harry Sweeney's thigh, squeezing it tighter. That's what I thought to myself, Harry, the way I hear the investigation is going. Or not going.

Harry Sweeney nodded again, watching the city fly past, the car speeding through the night, through the night and onto the bridge, the Eitai Bridge, over the bridge and across the river, the Sumida River, across the river, into the darkness.

Very serendipitous, said Akira Senju again, letting go of Harry Sweeney's thigh, patting the top of Harry Sweeney's thigh again. Minute I heard they'd found the car, heard where they'd found the car, I thought to myself: This is too good to be true, I must be dreaming, such a stroke of luck. I had to pinch myself, Harry, pinch myself and then call you.

Harry Sweeney gestured with his thumb over his shoulder at the back window of the car, the sound from the road behind them, the two heavy trucks behind them, and Harry Sweeney said, Made some other calls, too.

Precautions, Harry, that's all, said Akira Senju, still patting the top of Harry Sweeney's thigh, his eyes staring straight ahead, fixed on the back of his driver's head, the car slowing down, the convoy pulling up. Just ten minutes from the center of the city, Harry, but it's a different country.

Across the river, in the darkness, they had stopped and parked up. Akira Senju squeezed the top of Harry Sweeney's thigh, then opened his door, and Harry Sweeney followed him. Across the river, in the darkness, Harry Sweeney and Akira

Senju stood in the headlights of the car and the two trucks and looked across a bridge, over a ditch; the bridge the only bridge, the ditch a moat. They saw the signs on the bridge, they read the words on the signs: NO ENTRY, RESIDENTS ONLY, DEATH TO ALL SPIES. They looked beyond the warnings, they stared over the moat, and they saw an island; the island a fortress, the island fortress of a different country –

Little Pyongyang, Edagawa-chō, Fukagawa, Kōtō Ward: not in the city, not in the river; an island adrift, a world apart. Eight rows of weather-beaten, two-storied clapboard tenements. Their wooden backs hard against the water of the river, its filth and its stench, their shanty fronts closed to the rest of the city, its venom and its violence –

That first building on the corner, on the other side of the bridge, whispered Akira Senju, that's a tavern, that's their lookout. They've got bells, they've got gongs. They're watching us, Harry, waiting for us to make the first move.

And then in the headlights from the car and the trucks, Akira Senju raised his right hand high above his head, and Harry Sweeney heard men getting out of the trucks, jumping down from the backs of the trucks, and Harry Sweeney saw Akira Senju lower his hand, then step to one side, making a space between them, a space for two men and a youth –

In the headlights from the car and the trucks, Harry Sweeney turned to glance at the youth, and Harry Sweeney saw a Zainichi kid, a Japanese-born Korean youth, his young face bloody and swollen, his old clothes ripped and torn, a rope around his hands, a rope around his neck.

Take out your Public Safety badge, Harry, whispered Akira Senju. Hold it up and follow me . . .

And Harry Sweeney took out his Public Safety badge, held it up, and followed Akira Senju, past the signs and their warnings – NO ENTRY, RESIDENTS ONLY, DEATH TO ALL SPIES – and onto the bridge –

Before they came to the end of the bridge, before they put a foot on the island, Akira Senju stopped, and Harry Sweeney stopped. Akira Senju and Harry Sweeney looked up at the tavern on the corner, they stared up at this lookout with its bells and its gongs, dark and silent, watching and waiting, and Akira Senju shouted, You know me, you know who I am, and you can see him, that kid over there, you know who he is. You can have him back, back tonight, if you do what I ask, if you let us speak with his brother.

And then on the bridge, before the island, still looking up at the tavern, still staring up at the lookout, Akira Senju and Harry Sweeney waited, and waited, and waited . . .

Until a door at the side of the tavern opened and two men stepped out of their lookout, both men thickset and armed, one with a machete, the other with a pistol. The machete beckoned to Akira Senju and Harry Sweeney, and Akira Senju and Harry Sweeney stepped off the bridge, stepped onto the island, and approached the machete and pistol –

Bad news for you, said the pistol. He ain't here.

Akira Senju shrugged: Ain't bad news for us, but it ain't so good for his little brother.

That is a shame, yeah, said the pistol, as other men stepped out of the tavern, stepped out of the shadows, other men thickset and armed. But then, what's one more dead punk when we've killed you, the Emperor of Shimbashi?

Akira Senju looked the pistol and machete up and down, then nodded at Harry Sweeney and smiled: Yeah, but what you going to do about him, brave man? You going to kill an American police investigator, are you?

Don't care about him, said the pistol. He can go running back to GHQ. This is between us, Senju.

Harry Sweeney stepped forward, Harry Sweeney stared at the pistol, and said, Anything happens to him, anything happens to me, General Willoughby will come burn this fucking shithole to the ground with all of you in it. Men, women, and children. Willoughby won't care.

Akira Senju laughed: Turns out the rumors are true: I'm the man who would not die, the man you cannot kill.

Is that right, said the pistol, stepping toward Harry Sweeney, staring back at Harry Sweeney. I wonder?

Harry Sweeney did not step back, Harry Sweeney did not blink: Well, you can keep on wondering. Or you can find out. Or you can give us the brother. Your choice.

You deaf as well as dumb, Yankee, said the machete. We already told you, the brother ain't here.

Harry Sweeney did not turn to look at the machete, Harry Sweeney kept staring at the pistol as he said, So?

So what, said the machete.

So where is he then?

We don't know.

Harry Sweeney stepped back, looked from the pistol to the machete, from the machete to the other men, thickset and armed, and Harry Sweeney said, Someone does.

On this island, in this different country, where the night was still heavy, where the air was still wet, the pistol and the machete and the other men, thickset and armed, they stared at Harry Sweeney and Akira Senju, with hate in their eyes, with hate in their hearts, until the pistol shook his head, until the pistol said, The father's dead, there's only their mother.

She'll do, said Akira Senju.

She's a *mudang*, said the pistol. A shamaness.

I don't give a shit if she's the reincarnation of your Queen fucking Min, said Akira Senju. Let's see her!

The machete and the other men laughed as the pistol said, You will give a shit, you'll soon fucking see –

And the pistol turned and led Akira Senju and Harry Sweeney between the tenements, down the alleyways, the machete and the other men walking behind them, down the alleyways, between the tenements, the air fetid, the air laden – the sound of prayers from some of the houses, the sound of songs from some of the houses; Christian manifestos and Communist hymns, the Lord's Prayer and the Red Flag – down another alleyway to another tenement, where the pistol tapped on the door, then the pistol opened the door, showing Akira Senju and Harry Sweeney inside the tenement and into a room, saying, These men are here about your sons, Auntie . . .

In a headband of black, with her hair in a bun, an old woman was kneeling on a mat in the center of the small room, among statues and bowls, a lamp and a saucer, candles and oil, water and food, and a knife, an iron knife, with ribbons attached to its handle, ribbons of red and ribbons of white . . .

Where's your eldest son, Auntie, said Akira Senju. Where's Lee Jung-Hwan?

The woman did not look up at Akira Senju, did not answer Akira Senju. She leaned forward and poured water into one bowl, put *kimpche* into another, then dried fish and seaweed, then peppers, red peppers, mixing in ash, stirring in salt, pouring the oil and lighting the wicks, flames flickering and smoke rising . . .

A car was stolen from outside the Mitsukoshi department store on the morning of July fifth, said Harry Sweeney. The car was found earlier today, close to here.

The woman did not look up at Harry Sweeney, did not acknowledge Harry Sweeney. She was bowing and she was muttering . . .

Mister Senju here is a man of many friends, a man who hears many things, continued Harry Sweeney. He heard your youngest son stole this car from outside Mitsukoshi. He found your youngest son, spoke with your youngest son.

Still the woman did not look up at Harry Sweeney, still she did not acknowledge Harry Sweeney. Muttering, then chanting, she got to her feet and she began to sway, to sway and then dance, dancing and chanting, chanting –

*The twelve gates all locked –*
*Open up! Open up –*
*Twelve gates –*
*Open up!*

Your youngest son, said Harry Sweeney, he told Mister Senju that he stole the car at the request of his big brother, for Lee Jung-Hwan and his friends.

On this fortress island, in this different country, in the tenement, in her room, amid the flickering flames, among the rising smoke, the woman was still dancing, spinning weightless in her robes, dancing and still chanting –

*O great spirits, hear us now –*
*We who are but beasts –*
*Our tenuous lives –*
*Hanging by threads!*

We're not interested in your youngest son, continued Harry Sweeney. He can return to you tonight, come home to you tonight. But we need to speak with Jung-Hwan.

Amid the flickering flames, among the rising smoke, her body was trembling, her eyes were shining – her body and her eyes free from all flesh, free from all bone, from all ground and all ties, the room gone and the ceiling gone, the island and the land gone, gone, she was spinning and swirling, weightless and free, under moons and under suns, stars falling and clouds racing, moons waxing, moons waning, suns rising and suns setting, before the gods, before the spirits, their gates unlocked, their gates open – her eyes shining, her body trembling, she was moving in circles, she was rubbing her hands, together in communion, together in prayer –

*O protect us please –*
*From all demons –*
*Protect and help us –*
*Help and save us!*

Just tell us where Lee Jung-Hwan is, said Harry Sweeney. Tell us and save your youngest son.

In her circle of flames and smoke, in her circle of statues and bowls, the woman dropped to the floor, the woman picked up a bowl. She drank from the bowl, held the water in her mouth, looked up at Harry Sweeney, stared up at Harry Sweeney, then she spat at Harry Sweeney, she screamed at Harry Sweeney, shrieked:

*Shoo, demon –*
*Shoo!*

Just tell us where he is, shouted Harry Sweeney, wiping her spit from his shirt, bending down to look in her eyes, to stare into her eyes and shout again, Tell us where he is!

On the floor, in her circle, the woman reached for the iron knife with its ribbons of red and its ribbons of white, and she picked up the knife, and she held up the knife, and she pointed with the knife, pointed up at Harry Sweeney and hissed, He lives with you, he works for you . . .

Where, said Harry Sweeney, pushing the knife away from his face, grabbing the woman by her shoulders, her head lolling back, her eyes rolling back, shaking the woman, then gripping her face: Tell me fucking where! Where?

The woman was grinning, the woman was laughing, grinning at Harry Sweeney, laughing at Harry Sweeney, muttering and whispering, He lives with you, he works for you. In the big mansion, in its big grounds . . .

Fuck this, said Akira Senju, pulling Harry Sweeney off the woman, pushing Harry Sweeney toward the door, throwing him out of the room and into the alleyway. Fuck this!

Told you you'd give a shit, said the pistol, the machete and the other men laughing in the alleyway, between the tenements. You're not in Shimbashi now, Senju.

Yeah, said Akira Senju, looking at the pistol, staring at the pistol. Well, let's see if you're still laughing in twenty-four hours, *chonko*. That's how long you got.

For what, said the machete.

You bring me Lee Jung-Hwan, said Akira Senju, not looking at the machete, still staring at the pistol. Bring me big brother, the kid can still walk. But you don't find him, or we find him first, then the kid is dead. And so are you.

His clothes still stuck to his skin, his hands still shaking, Harry Sweeney drained his glass of Johnnie Walker, his third double Scotch, and Harry Sweeney looked down the bar of the Dai-ichi Hotel, waved the empty glass at Joe the barman, saying, Hurry it up, will you, Joe. Man can die of thirst, you know . . .

Come on, Harry, said Joe the barman. Whatever it is, whoever she is, this ain't gonna help, you know that, Harry.

Hey, what are you, Joe, a priest or a barman?

Maybe I'm just being a friend, Harry.

Is that right, Joe, said Harry Sweeney, slapping the top of the bar with one hand, pointing at the bottles behind the bar with the other. Well, maybe I don't need no more friends, Joe, maybe what I need is just one more drink, Joe, please, Joe . . .

It's okay, Joe, said Gloria Wilson, sitting down on the stool beside Harry Sweeney, patting Harry Sweeney on the arm, smiling at Joe the barman. I owe this man a drink, so let's make it his one for the road, then I'll see him home, Joe.

Is that right, said Harry Sweeney, turning to look at the young woman with the large eyes and the large nose, her hand on his arm. You gonna take me back to Montana . . .

Gloria Wilson smiled at Harry Sweeney and said, Sure, Mister Sweeney, if that's what you want . . .

How about Muncie, Indiana?

Gloria Wilson laughed: I don't think you'd care for Muncie, Indiana, Mister Sweeney . . .

How'd you know what I'd care for, said Harry Sweeney, leaning into Gloria Wilson and her big eyes, as Joe the barman placed their drinks down on the bar.

Gloria Wilson gently turned Harry Sweeney toward the bar and the drinks: You're right, Mister Sweeney, I don't. But how about we drink these, then go back to the hotel?

You wanna go back to my hotel with me, said Harry Sweeney, picking up his drink from the bar. You really aren't like any librarian I ever met, Miss Wilson. You sure . . .

Mister Sweeney, please, laughed Gloria Wilson. What are you thinking? Your hotel is my hotel, the Yaesu Hotel.

They got out of the cab, they walked under the canopy and through the doors into the lobby of the Yaesu Hotel, Harry Sweeney leaning on Gloria Wilson, Gloria Wilson holding up Harry Sweeney. They crossed the lobby to the elevators, and Gloria Wilson smiled at the boy stood in number five –

Fourth floor, is it, asked the boy. Sir?

And the sixth, please, said Gloria Wilson.

Oh, really, said the elevator boy, not turning around, closing the doors. If you say so, ma'am.

What the hell you mean by that, said Harry Sweeney, trying to free his arm from Gloria Wilson, trying to step toward the boy. Apologize right now, you insolent piece of shit!

I'm sorry, sir, said the boy, still not turning around, the elevator going up. Thought you were both going to the same floor, sir. My mistake, sir.

You apologize to this lady right now, goddamn you, said Harry Sweeney, still trying to free his arm from Gloria Wilson, still trying to step toward the boy –

Gloria Wilson holding back Harry Sweeney, saying, Leave it, Harry, please, Harry . . .

Very sorry, ma'am, said the boy as the elevator stopped, as he opened the doors. Fourth floor, sir.

Gloria Wilson gently pushed Harry Sweeney out of the doors into the corridor, then she stepped back into the elevator, smiled at Harry Sweeney, and said, Goodnight, Harry.

In the corridor, before the elevator, Harry Sweeney looked at Gloria Wilson and smiled: Goodnight . . .

Told you it wasn't a lucky floor, whispered the boy as the elevator doors closed. Bad luck, sir.

Harry Sweeney reached up to try to hold open the doors, but the doors had already shut, the elevator already going up, heading to the sixth floor. Harry Sweeney cursed and shook his head, then turned and walked away from the elevators, down the corridor, his right shoulder banging into the wall on the right, his left shoulder then banging into the wall on the left, until he came to the door of his room. Harry Sweeney found his key, took out his key, dropped his key, picked up his key, stabbed his key at the door, then at the lock, but missed the lock, then found the lock, put the key in the lock, then turned the key and opened the door. He staggered through the door, over two envelopes on the floor in the doorway. He felt the envelopes under his feet, picked up the envelopes from the floor. He stared down at the two envelopes, one posted from America, with his name and the address of the hotel, the other hand-delivered, with just his name and his room number. Harry Sweeney cursed again and tossed the two envelopes back down on the floor in the doorway. He stepped back into the corridor and slammed the door shut. He walked back along the corridor, right shoulder into the right wall, left shoulder into the left wall. He came to the elevators and he pressed the call button. He waited until elevator number five arrived, waited until the doors of elevator number five opened, until the elevator boy smiled and said, Sixth floor, is it, sir?

And then Harry Sweeney reached inside the elevator, grabbed the boy, pulled him out into the corridor, threw him up against the wall of the corridor, and then Harry Sweeney raised his fists and –

# 4

## Until the Last Day

*July 11–July 15, 1949*

The fuck you do it for, Harry?

Harry Sweeney did not open his eyes, Harry Sweeney did not turn away from the wall. He lay on the cot in the cell and he waited for the voices to stop. For the cell door to close again, for the key to turn in the lock again. For the boots to march away again, away back down the corridor again, until the next time. Until the next time he heard the boots down the corridor, heard the key turn in the lock, the cell door open, and the voices start up again –

Come on, Harry, talk to us, tell us what happened.

Maybe the dumb fuck likes it in here.

The next time, the third time, with his eyes closed, his face to the wall, until the next time, the fourth time, he heard the boots, he heard the key, he heard the door, he heard the voices, the same fucking voices, the same fucking questions, over and over, and he opened his eyes, he turned his face from the wall, and he saw the two of them, standing over him, looking down on him. The Military Police. The one with the smile and the one with the scowl, always the same, the same fucking way, and Harry Sweeney said, Fuck you twice.

Hey, hey, don't make it worse than it need be, Harry, said the one with the smile. Delinquency Report is all it is.

Harry Sweeney shook his head: A Delinquency Report, yeah? For not taking any crap from an insolent little Jap?

Hell, you're just a regular patriot, is what you are, Sweeney, said the one with the scowl. Drink all day and fight all night, yeah? Fuck, way you beat that Jap kid up, they should be giving you a medal, that what you think?

I barely fucking touched the kid.

You even remember, Harry?

It was a slap on the cheek. It was nothing.

Not the goddamn way he looks, Sweeney, not the fucking way he tells it either. What's left of his mouth.

Harry Sweeney shook his head again: That's bullshit.

Look, Harry, said the one with the smile. Just give us your statement, you're out of here. We file the report, it goes up the chain. Be a rap on the knuckles is all.

Yeah, just better pray your knuckles have healed by then, champ, said the one with the scowl.

Harry Sweeney looked down at his hands, looked down at his knuckles, black and purple, scabbed and swollen.

Yeah, said the scowl again. You take a good look at them knuckles of yours, Sweeney. Might want to think again about that slap on the cheek you was telling us about.

Harry Sweeney stared down at his knuckles and Harry Sweeney shook his head: I didn't mean to . . .

We know, said the smile, crouching down beside Harry Sweeney. We know you didn't, Harry.

In the cell, on the cot, Harry Sweeney raised his hands, he raised his knuckles, black and purple, bloody and swollen. He held them up to his face, held them up to his eyes, looking at them, staring at them, black and purple, bloody and swollen, turning them over, turning them back, then he buried his face in his hands, buried his eyes in his hands, rocking back and forward, on the cot, in the cell, the tears from his eyes falling into his hands, his tears falling through his knuckles, black and purple, bloody and swollen, rocking back and forward, saying, I'm sorry, I'm sorry, I'm sorry . . .

*

Night turned to day, turned to night, turned to day, how many nights, how many days, he did not know, he could not tell. But with a copy of his statement and with the bandages around his knuckles, under the canopy, then through the doors, Harry Sweeney walked into the Yaesu Hotel and across the lobby. He saw Satō-san behind the front desk, saw him look away, and he saw all the other hotel staff, saw them all look away. Harry Sweeney almost stopped, he almost spoke. But Harry Sweeney did not stop, he did not speak. Harry Sweeney kept on walking through the lobby, toward the elevators. But Harry Sweeney did not take an elevator, he took the stairs instead. Four flights up to his floor, the fourth floor, then down the corridor, toward the elevators. Before the elevators on the fourth floor, Harry Sweeney stopped, and before the wall opposite the elevators, Harry Sweeney swallowed, then blinked. He saw the holes in the wall, he saw the stains down the wall, and swallowing again and blinking again, he reached out to the holes and the stains, and he touched the holes and the stains. His fingers in the holes, his fingers down the stains, the bandages around his knuckles, the bandages around his wrists, Harry Sweeney struggled to breathe, to hold back his tears, to turn away from the holes, away from the stains, and to walk down the corridor, down to his room. Before his room, before its door, Harry Sweeney took out his key, put the key in the lock, turned the key in the lock, and opened the door to his room. He stepped inside his room, picked up two letters from the floor. He closed the door, put the letters on the desk. He crossed the room and sat down on the bed. He took off his shoes, then stood back up. He took off his jacket, his shirt, and his pants. He walked over to the washstand and turned on the faucets. He took off his watch, with its cracked face, with its stopped hands, and placed it between the faucets. He unwound the bandage around his left knuckles, he unwound the bandage around his right knuckles. He dropped them on the floor. He unhooked the safety pin that secured the bandage on his left wrist, he unhooked the safety pin that secured the bandage on his right wrist. He dropped them on the floor. He unwound the bandage on his left wrist, he unwound the bandage from his right wrist. He dropped them on the floor and he turned off the faucets. He put his knuckles and his wrists into the basin and the water, he soaked his knuckles and his wrists in the water in the basin. He watched the water wash away the blood, he felt the water cleanse his wounds. He nudged out the stopper, he watched the water drain from the basin, from around his wrists, from between his knuckles. He lifted his hands from the basin, he picked up a towel from the floor. He dried his knuckles on the towel, he dried his wrists on the towel. He folded the towel, he hung it on the rail. He walked over to the desk, he sat down at the desk. He stared down at the two envelopes on the top of the desk: the one posted from America, with his name and the address of the hotel, the other hand-delivered, with just his name and his room number. He picked up the second envelope and he opened the second envelope. He took out a single folded piece of paper, he unfolded the single piece of paper. He read the single sentence on the single piece of paper: It's closing time, but Zed Unit are not to be blamed for nothing. He screwed up the piece of paper, screwed up the single sentence. He threw it on the floor, he picked up the first envelope. He opened the envelope, he took out the many folded pieces of paper. He unfolded the many pieces of paper, he scanned the many pieces of paper. Their many sentences, their many words: Betrayal. Deceit. Judas. Lust. Marriage. My religion. You traitor. Will never give up. Give you a divorce. I know what you are like, I know who you are. I forgive you, Harry. Come home, Harry. Please just come home. He put down the many pages, with their many sentences, their many words, put them on the desk before him. Then Harry Sweeney sat forward with his elbows and his arms on the desk, and Harry Sweeney looked down at his wrists and his knuckles. The scars on his wrists, the scabs on his knuckles. Then Harry Sweeney raised his hands toward his face, and Harry Sweeney brought his palms together. And he bowed his head, and he closed his eyes, and he said, Lord Jesus Christ, Son of God, have mercy on me, a sinner . . .

Breaks my heart, Harry, said Colonel Pullman. I can't tell you how much it hurts me, son, to see you like this, in this kind of mess. Hell, you're one of the best damned officers I've got.

Back on the fourth floor of the NYK building, back in the office of Colonel Pullman, stood before his desk, with his head bowed again, Harry Sweeney said, I'm sorry, sir.

You and me both, son, sighed Colonel Pullman. He put down the Letter of Resignation, then he picked up the Delinquency Report again. He sighed again, looked across his desk again, and said, It's not just this then, Harry?

Harry Sweeney looked up at Colonel Pullman, at the Delinquency Report in his hands, and shook his head and said, Just think that's a sign, sir, a sign it's time.

Sign you been working too hard, son, is all I think it is, said Colonel Pullman, waving the Delinquency Report across his desk at Harry Sweeney. Hell, I've had Chief Evans, Bill Betz, even goddamn Toda in here, all telling me how you've not been sleeping, been pulling twenty-four-hour shifts . . .

Harry Sweeney looked down at his hands, at the scabs on his knuckles, and he shook his head again: Sir . . .

Now I know everybody's got themselves all twisted up over this whole damned Shimoyama business, and I was there, don't forget, I was in the room, son, when old General Willoughby tore you a new one. And I felt for you, Harry, I really did, son. Because I know you're a conscientious officer, a diligent detective,

Harry, and so I know you're upset, you're frustrated, you have a few too many drinks and . . .

Harry Sweeney shook his head: Sir . . .

Hold on there, son, said Colonel Pullman. Now I'm not saying it's nothing. It's not. And I know you know it's not nothing, Harry, I can see that. But it's a severe reprimand, is what it is, not a goddamn resignation, son.

Sir, please, I've thought . . .

Hear me out, Harry, said Colonel Pullman, putting down the Delinquency Report again. Because you leave now, leave like this, with this on your file, this on your record, then what you going to do, son, where you going to go? What police force back home is going to take you, Harry? Not a goddamn one is who, son, not with this on your record, you know that, Harry. But see, this Occupation's already winding down. Two, three years tops, we'll all be gone. And thank God, son. Leave them to get the hell on with it with themselves, is what I say, Harry, it's their goddamn country. So all you need to do is sit tight, see out your time, son, stay out of trouble, away from the drink, Harry, then you're leaving with a clean record of service and a glowing letter of commendation from me, that's what I'll be giving you, son, that's what you'll be leaving with, Harry. Then you're walking into any goddamn force in the land, any goddamn force you choose, son. Maybe even being some sweet little sheriff in some sweet little town, Harry. Imagine that, son, how sweet would that be, right, Harry?

Harry Sweeney looked up from the scabs on his knuckles, and he stared across the desk at Colonel Pullman, and he shook his head again and said, I'm sorry, sir.

Look, son, said Colonel Pullman, picking up the Letter of Resignation again, holding it out across the desk toward Harry Sweeney. You're upset, Harry, I know that, I can see that, son. But maybe you're not thinking straight, or maybe you are. Either way, son, I can't let you just walk out of here, resign with immediate effect. Don't work like that, Harry, you know that. You got to give me notice so I can get you replaced, son. But here's what I'll do, Harry: I'll note down what you said, and the date that you said it, then you take back this letter and you put it in your pocket. Then come the end of the month, you come back in here, you come back to me, then you tell me what you're thinking, and if your thinking's still the same, same as in that letter, son. You got that, got that straight, Harry?

And Harry Sweeney looked at Colonel Pullman, at the letter in his hands, and Harry Sweeney nodded.

Very good then. Dismissed.

Harry Sweeney closed the door behind him and started to walk away, down the corridor. He stopped, turned, and walked back toward the door. He stopped before the door to Colonel Pullman's office, his right hand in a fist, his knuckles aching. He raised his fist, his knuckles to knock on the door again, but stopped again, lowered his knuckles, his fist, and his hand again, swallowed and turned away again, away from the door again, and he walked back down the corridor, back to Room 432 of the Public Safety Division. The office was quiet, the blackboards were gone, Betz and Toda, too; no sign of George or Dan; only Sonoko, at a desk, with her eyes down, her fingers moving, reading through reports, typing out translations. Harry Sweeney walked across the office, between the furniture, up to her desk, and said, Hey, where is everyone, Sonoko?

Oh, cried Sonoko, jumping back from the keys of her typewriter, her hand to her heart. I'm sorry, sir –

No, I'm sorry. I gave you a fright.

Excuse me, said Sonoko, flapping her hands, catching her breath. I wasn't expecting you, sir. How are you, sir? I hope you are feeling better now, sir?

Harry Sweeney smiled: I hope so, too. Thank you.

I think there's something going around, sir, said Sonoko. Mister Toda's been ill, too, you know, sir.

Harry Sweeney nodded: He still ill?

No, no, sir. He should be back quite soon. I think he just went down to the canteen, sir.

And Chief Evans and Mister Betz?

Well, I believe Chief Evans is in a meeting with the Public Prosecutor, sir, said Sonoko. But I'm afraid I'm not sure where Mister Betz is, sir. I'm sorry, sir. Would you like me to try and find out, sir?

Harry Sweeney smiled again: No, don't worry, sweetheart. I'm sure he'll turn up.

Sonoko looked at Harry Sweeney and smiled and said, Is there anything I can do for you, sir? Can I get you something to drink, sir? Some water, sir, some coffee, sir?

That's very kind of you, said Harry Sweeney. Some coffee would be good, thank you.

Very good, sir, said Sonoko, smiling broadly, springing up from her chair. Coffee coming right up, sir!

Thank you, sweetheart, said Harry Sweeney again, smiling back, then turning away, still smiling as he walked over to his own desk, still smiling as he sat down in his chair, smiling until he saw the police reports and the daily newspapers all piled up on his desk, until he saw the list of names and numbers, the telephone calls to be returned, if he returned, returned to his desk. Harry Sweeney put the list of names and numbers to one side. He stood back up, walked over to open the window, then back to his desk. He took off his jacket, hung it on the back of his chair, then sat back down at his desk. He picked up the pile of newspapers, turned them over to start from the bottom of the pile, then he began to flick through them, one by one, one after another, scanning the headlines: POLICE CONTINUE TO PROBE

DEATH OF SHIMOYAMA / NO DIRECT CLUE FOUND BY POLICE / POLICE CHECKING MYSTERIOUS CALL RECEIVED BY NRWU / STOLEN CAR RECOVERED / SHIMOYAMA DEATH REMAINS A MYSTERY / WAS RAILWAYS GOVERNOR MURDERED OR DID HE DIE BY HIS OWN HANDS? – NO SUFFICIENT PROOF TO DECIDE EITHER WAY, SAYS CHIEF PROSECUTOR / SHIMOYAMA DEATH STILL A MYSTERY / MYSTERY WRITERS OF JAPAN MEET: ROMAN KURODA VOWS TO CRACK "JAPANESE LINDBERGH CASE" / NO DIRECT CLUE FOUND BY POLICE YET / TOOK OUT IMPORTANT PAPERS FROM CHIYODA BANK SAFE / EYEGLASSES, NECKTIE, CIGARETTE CASE STILL MISSING / AUTOPSY FINDINGS CALLED INTO QUESTION – TIME OF DEATH UNCERTAIN / PROBE INTO SHIMOYAMA CASE EXTENDED GEOGRAPHICALLY / MANY FACTORS TENDING TO SUPPORT SHIMOYAMA SUICIDE THEORY UNEARTHED / GOV'T MAY OFFER ONE MILLION YEN FOR SHIMOYAMA CASE CLUE / CHIEF KITA DECLARES MUD FOUND ON SHOES IMPORTANT CLUE: IDENTICAL TO SAMPLES FROM THE VICINITY / CHIEF CABINET SECRETARY REBUKES KITA: NO DEFINITE PROOF EARTH ON SHOES IDENTICAL TO PLACE OF TRAGEDY / CHIEF PROSECUTOR ASKS POLICE TO INVESTIGATE SHIMOYAMA CASE ON ASSUMPTION OF HOMICIDE / TEAHOUSE PROPRIETRESS COMES INTO LIMELIGHT . . .

Harry Sweeney leaned back in his chair, loosened his tie, undid his collar button, then sat forward at his desk again. He put the pile of newspapers to one side, picked up the pile of police reports, turned them over to start from the bottom, then began to flick through them, one by one, one after another, scanning the sentences: There have been no firm developments in the case / Investigations continue into clues reported earlier / Press reports of "Mysterious telephone calls" are to be regarded as journalistic license / Shimoyama was in the habit of smoking "Chikari" cigarettes and, on occasion, a briar pipe; none of these objects or his lighter were found at the scene / He did speak of needing to purchase a wedding present with an employee of the RR prior to his disappearance / Checks are ongoing as to whether Shimoyama had any insurance policy, amount involved, beneficiaries, and whether recently acquired / There have been no definite developments in the case at this time / Checks are being made on trains which passed over Shimoyama's body in search for missing personal items such as cigarette lighter, Eversharp pen, necktie clip, and spectacles / Translation of letter received by Chief Inspector Kanehara of the MPD on 10 July 1949, mailed in plain envelope at the Tokyo Central Post Office, Marunouchi, on 7 July 1949, written on obsolete report form used by former Imperial Government offices: Mr. Shimoyama met Heaven's Justice. Though he dismissed 150,000 employees, it appeared he had no pity for them. It was a brutal act conducted for the reconstruction of Japan. It is said that those who lost their jobs will be hired by civilian companies, but this is lies and propaganda. More than half of the employees of the Toshiba Company were already dismissed into poverty and starvation. Of course, this brutal act was not done by Mr. Shimoyama alone. There will be another Shimoyama, there will be more victims. But remember: Heaven sympathizes with the Poor. Accordingly, even MacArthur will be killed by those he abandoned to poverty and starvation. You may be one of the victims, too. So stop your investigation work. No, do your investigation work as it is your duty. But remember: the efforts of Mr. Kanehara will be for naught / Hairs found on pillow at Suehiro inn used by guest suspected to be Shimoyama are being checked / 11.30 pm, July 5th, a man was observed leaning against a telephone pole in front of Suehiro inn / In response to

PSD query, a check showed that both the top two buttons on Shimoyama's shirt and undershirt were still attached to the cloth, while the remaining buttons had been torn off. This indicates quite conclusively to MPD that Shimoyama was not wearing a necktie at the time of the train incident and that the two top buttons were open / Correction: Shimoyama had been in possession of a cigarette holder, not a pipe as previously reported; this holder is of wood, brown, with a black stem. This item has not been found to date / The stolen car, recovered in the vicinity of Fukagawa, has been checked for prints. One found on rear-vision mirror. This has not been checked with Shimoyama print or any suspect as yet / The search at the scene of the disaster has now been extended to nearby drains and fields / Checks continue on the railway stations at Ueno, Asakusa and Kita-Senju for trace of Shimoyama / Report on identification of handwriting on anonymous letter received by MPD: expert TAHARA believes handwriting is that of young man with average schooling and education. Attempt was made on first page to disguise handwriting but was discarded in latter parts. Ordinary writing ink was used with brush. Writing on envelope same as letter / In response to GHQ suggestion on investigation procedure, preliminary check made with all police boxes in the immediate vicinity as to union members residing in area revealed: 17 current members of the RR union, 2 formerly employed by RR, and 5 suspected Communists, 1 definitely. Area to be checked will be expanded as investigation continues / No new facts which would confirm murder theory have been uncovered / Reinvestigation of alibi of Mrs. Nobu MORISHITA in progress . . .

One by one, Harry Sweeney went through the reports, not noticing Sonoko put down the cup of coffee on his desk, one after another, not noticing the cup of coffee go cold, one by one, Harry Sweeney not noticing Susumu Toda come back into the office, one after another, not hearing Susumu Toda speak, one by one, one after another, not noticing anything, not hearing anything, until Harry Sweeney had finished going through the reports, until Harry Sweeney heard Susumu Toda click his fingers and say again, Hey! Harry –

Hey, said Harry Sweeney, looking up from the reports, leaning back in his chair again, stretching and yawning. Then he turned to look up at Susumu Toda and said, How you doing, Susumu? You feeling better?

I'm okay, said Susumu Toda. But how *you* doing?

Not bad. Better, thanks.

You seen the Chief yet?

No, not yet. Just Colonel Pullman.

How'd that go, asked Susumu Toda. Okay?

Harry Sweeney smiled: Here I am.

Right, said Susumu Toda, glancing at Harry Sweeney's hands, looking away from Harry Sweeney's knuckles. Right.

Harry Sweeney sat forward in his chair again, his hands in his lap, under his desk, and said, Where's Bill?

Think he's with the Second Investigative Division, said Susumu Toda. The Chief's got him liaising with them.

Thought they were off the case?

For a day, laughed Toda. But I guess the General put some pressure on Chief Kita, so Kita sent them back up there, looking for union members and Reds in the area.

Harry Sweeney nodded: Yeah, I saw that in the reports. They found anything then, anything concrete?

Well, surprise, surprise, they've turned up some Railroad employees, all union members, couple of them possibly Commies, like you saw. But nothing to connect them to Shimoyama, not so far, last I heard.

But Bill's up there now?

I guess so, nodded Toda. Least that's where he told the Chief he was going. See, there's these Koreans as well.

Harry Sweeney turned in his chair, turned to look up at Susumu Toda, to look up and ask, What Koreans?

Hang on, said Susumu Toda. He walked over to Sonoko's desk, spoke with Sonoko, took a piece of paper from the top of the pile of papers on her desk, then he walked back over to Harry Sweeney and said, Here –

Harry Sweeney took the piece of paper from Susumu Toda. He looked down at the translation of the most recent police report and read: At approximately 2200 hours, 5 July 1949, five Koreans stopped at a Japanese barbecue stand at Ayase station on the Jōban train line (lower track, approximately 10 minutes' walk to the scene where Shimoyama's body was found), where they drank 15 glasses of Japanese liquor (similar to gin). According to information received, the Koreans remained there until 2345 hours, when they were observed taking the last train from the station at 2350 hours. Prior to the Koreans leaving, two of the Koreans had gone outside at approximately 2330 hours and were gone for what seemed to be a short while and then returned. This matter needs to be checked into more carefully as there may well be a discrepancy in the time when the two Koreans left the barbecue stand and when they returned.

It only came in last night, said Susumu Toda. But Bill seemed pretty keen to chase it up. The Chief, too.

Harry Sweeney nodded: I bet.

What do you think, said Susumu Toda, looking down at Harry Sweeney, at the piles of newspaper reports and police reports stacked up on his desk.

Harry Sweeney put the report on the five Koreans on top of the other police reports, looked down at all the reports, the piles of reports, police reports and newspaper reports, and shook his head, then sighed and said, Figures of eight . . .

Figures of eight, said Toda. What do –

Harry Sweeney waved his hand across his desk, across the reports: We're all going round in figures of eight, Susumu. Chief Kita and the First Investigative Division pushing the suicide angle, the Public Prosecutor and the Second Investigative

Division pushing for homicide, the doctors at Tōdai saying murder, Nakadate at Keiō saying suicide, the *Mainichi* backing the suicide theory, the *Asahi* going for murder, back and forth, murder then suicide, round and round, suicide then murder, in figures of fucking eight . . .

General Willoughby sure doesn't see it that way. Chief Evans neither. They're adamant it was murder.

Harry Sweeney looked down at his hands, looked down at his knuckles, at the scabs on his knuckles, and Harry Sweeney nodded, sighed, and said, I know.

I know you know, said Susumu Toda, his eyes on Harry Sweeney's knuckles, on the scabs on his knuckles. But what are you going to do then?

Me?

Yeah, said Susumu Toda. You.

Harry Sweeney looked up from his knuckles, from the scabs on his knuckles, looked up at Susumu Toda, looked up into his eyes and said, So it's "me" now, not "we," yeah?

Look, I'm sorry, I don't . . .

Harry Sweeney shook his head: No, don't say sorry, Susumu. I'm the one who's sorry, and I mean it, I am sorry, Susumu. I fucked up. End of the month, I'm gone –

Harry, don't say that . . .

What else is there to say?

We all make mistakes, said Susumu Toda, shaking his head, smiling at Harry Sweeney. You said so yourself.

Harry Sweeney shook his head again, held up his knuckles, and said, Not mistakes like this.

I'm sorry, said Susumu Toda. I've just made you feel worse, was maybe trying to make you feel worse . . .

You've every right, Susumu –

No, no, said Susumu Toda. That don't help me, that don't help you – don't help *us*. So come on then, Harry, come on, what *we* going to do?

*

They drove east up Avenue Y, through Kajibashi and Kyōbashi, through Sakurabashi and Hatchōbori. The young guy Shin at the wheel again, Harry Sweeney sat in the back with Susumu Toda. They crossed Takahashi Bridge, then turned left off Avenue Y and headed north along a straight narrow road, alleyways and houses off to the left and off to the right –

Shinkawa, sir, said Shin, slowing down.

Little further on, said Susumu Toda. The block at the end, where this road meets Eitai-dori, Avenue W.

Very good, sir, said Shin, going a little further on, then pulling in behind another large black car –

Shit, said Susumu Toda, looking at the car parked in front of them. You know whose car that is, Harry?

Harry Sweeney nodded: Yep.

You sure this is a good idea, said Susumu Toda. I mean, the Chief's not going to like this . . .

Harry Sweeney shrugged: Someone has to check it out. Doesn't mean we have to believe what we hear.

Just don't like the guy, said Toda.

Harry Sweeney laughed: Doubt his own mother likes him. Let's just get it done –

And Harry Sweeney and Susumu Toda got out of the car, closing the doors behind them, standing on the street, looking up and down the street, the alleyways and houses off to the left and off to the right, a thick, damp blanket of clouds overhead, the thick, rich stench of the river, the Sumida River in the air, part salt and part shit –

Jeez, said Susumu Toda. Not the place I'd come to forget my troubles, to get away from the world.

Depends on your troubles, depends on your world, I guess, said Harry Sweeney before the tiny, single-story wooden *machiai* with its shutters and its door, before another place of shabby, gloomy trysts and assignations, another place of secret rendezvous, this *machiai* known as the Narita-ya.

After you then, said Susumu Toda, gesturing toward the solid, wooden sliding door –

But the solid, wooden door was already sliding open, Detective Hattori stepping out of this *machiai* known as the Narita-ya, followed by a younger man, Detective Hattori jumping theatrically back, clutching his heart, blinking his eyes, and saying, What a fright!

And a very good afternoon to you, too, detective, said Harry Sweeney, with a short bow and thin smile.

Thought I'd seen a ghost, smiled Hattori. Heard you were no longer with us, detective.

Harry Sweeney smiled again: Shouldn't believe all you hear, detective. Don't need to tell you that.

Very true, said Detective Hattori. But how's your hand, detective? Heard you hurt it, hurt them both, in fact.

Harry Sweeney held up his hands in front of Detective Hattori, turned them over, turned them back again, and made them into fists, then held up the fists and said, As you can see, they're getting better, detective, thank you.

That's good to hear, said Detective Hattori, looking from the knuckles, from the fists into the eyes of Harry Sweeney. But you just be careful where you stick them, yeah? Never know, next time that somewhere might hit back.

Harry Sweeney smiled at Detective Hattori and nodded: You're right – you never know, detective.

Ah, excuse me for interrupting your conversation, said Susumu Toda. But we need to get back, so . . .

Of course, of course, said Detective Hattori, turning to Susumu Toda and smiling. I'm sorry, *Mister* Toda-san. Don't want to keep the General waiting now, do we? But before you go in, in with *your* questions, can you spare me a few minutes more of your very precious time . . . ?

In the street outside the Narita-ya, under the thick, damp blanket of clouds, amid the thick, rich stench of the river, the Sumida River, Harry Sweeney nodded and said, Go on –

See, I'm very pleased you're here, detective, and Chief Inspector Kanehara will be, too, I know that. Pleased you're obviously taking this lead so seriously. But I also know you're going to be taking it even more seriously when I tell you what I've got to tell you, detective, I can tell you that . . .

Harry Sweeney glanced at his watch, its face cracked and its hands stopped, sighed, and said again, Go on –

Sorry, sorry, smiled Detective Hattori. I know you're busy, detective, need to get back to the General and all that. But listen to this: minute we hear about this Missus Mori and her friendship with President Shimoyama, we get a couple of men over here, asking around, you know . . .

Is this with the *Yomiuri* reporters, asked Susumu Toda. Or was it separately, detective?

*Mister* Toda, smiled Detective Hattori. As I'm sure *Detective* Sweeney will agree, journalists, they have their uses. That is, if you know how to use them. Am I right, detective?

Harry Sweeney sighed: Just go on, please –

Of course, said Hattori, of course. So then, to cut a long story short, three years ago, after the surrender, this woman, this Missus Mori, this friend of President Shimoyama, she's selling peanuts by the side of the road, that's how she's living. But look at her now, with her own place, and wait until you see inside. Don't look much, right? But there's a little detached back room, two separate telephone lines – I mean, how much does one telephone cost, right? So two? We're talking big bucks, yeah? Someone's paying for it, right? And it ain't her husband, that's for sure. So we start asking about, the *Yomiuri*, too, and we start to hear things, things like the minute President Shimoyama comes on the scene – and he's on the scene almost every day, is what we hear – that's exactly when her luck starts to change: this house gets built, the telephone lines . . .

Harry Sweeney shook his head: We have read the fucking papers, you know? That's why we're here.

Patience, detective, patience, said Hattori, smiling. Obviously, the question is: Who's paying for all this? Like, Shimoyama's got money – more money than me, that's for sure – but *that* much money? That's what I ask myself, right? So I start to sniff around his finances, that's what I've been doing. And I tell you this, detective: they don't smell too good –

Harry Sweeney took out his handkerchief, wiped his face, wiped his neck, and said, Bit like this place then.

Exactly, detective, said Hattori. Very much like this place, and because of this place, is what I reckon. See, we put the word out among the pawnbrokers and the like, to see if they had had any dealings with Shimoyama, and guess what? He's been in and out of a place near here, owned by a feller name of Shōji Shioda, like it was the Bank of Japan. Antique vases, his wife's kimonos, diamond rings, sapphire rings, you name it; he's been trying to hock the fucking lot.

In the street outside the Narita-ya, under the thick, falling blanket of clouds, amid the thick, clinging stench of the river, the Sumida River, Harry Sweeney looked at Detective Hattori and said, Is that right?

You bet it is, detective, said Hattori, smiling, still smiling. But here's the thing: stuff wasn't selling. See, not being Japanese you wouldn't know this, detective, but it's a buyer's market. You might want sixty, seventy thousand yen for your wife's diamond ring, but you ain't getting it, no, sir, no way. And so then you know what that means, detective? That means old President Shimoyama, he's in trouble, big trouble, that's what that means.

The wife, the mistress; two households, no money. Enough to make any man think of –

You got any evidence for any of this, *detective*, said Susumu Toda. Any actual proof?

Yes, *Mister* Toda, I have, said Detective Hattori, not looking at Toda, still looking at Harry Sweeney, still smiling, smiling and saying, Aside from the books and ledgers that Shōji Shioda's firm keeps, with the dates and the things that President Shimoyama brought in and tried and failed to sell, aside from that written *evidence*, the clerks also remember seeing President Shimoyama coming into the store, and remember him coming into the store with a woman – a very pale woman, a very thin woman, a woman with the very particular air of a geisha. Now you've met Missus Shimoyama, detective, and I've met Missus Shimoyama, and she is a *madam*, a lady of breeding and class, but I would not say, and with all due deference, that she is a very pale woman, or a very thin woman, and certainly not a woman with the very particular air of a geisha, would you, detective? What would you say?

In this street outside the Narita-ya, outside this place of secret rendezvous, Harry Sweeney stepped toward Detective Hattori, looked into the eyes of Detective Hattori, and Harry Sweeney said, I'd say you've spent a lot of man-hours, and used a lot of manpower, digging up dirt, digging up shit on a man who the respected doctors of forensic medicine at the University of Tokyo believe had been dead for three hours before that train ran over his body and severed his face from his skull, that's what I'd say, *detective*, that's what I'd say.

Well, the respected Doctor Nakadate of Keiō University begs to differ, as you know, said Detective Hattori, not smiling, just shrugging. But hey, look, I'm just telling you where the facts have led me, just telling you what I've found, that's all I'm doing, detective. Because I just do what I'm told to do, go where I'm told to go. That's me, detective.

Harry Sweeney looked Detective Hattori up and down, then Harry Sweeney nodded and said, Yep, that's you, detective, that's you. And in a nice new pair of shoes, too.

The fuck are you to speak to me like that, said Hattori, stepping up closer to Harry Sweeney, staring up at Harry Sweeney. Beating up elevator boys, sleeping in the drunk tank, then coming to me on the high horse, giving it to me with the high hat, the scabs still raw on your knuckles, the whisky still stale on your breath, while I been working the goddamn case, solving the fucking case. Fuck you and your fists –

Hey, hey, said Susumu Toda, the other, younger man, too, both stepping between Harry Sweeney and Detective Hattori, pushing apart Harry Sweeney and Detective Hattori. Come on, we're all on the same side here –

Fuck you and your same fucking side, Toda, said Hattori, stepping back, walking away. Go talk to her or go the fuck home, what do I care? Politics and bullshit, is all this is.

Leave it, Harry, said Susumu Toda, his hands on the chest of Harry Sweeney, on the arms of Harry Sweeney, the fists of Harry Sweeney. Let him go –

Harry Sweeney watching Detective Hattori walk away, back to his car, hearing –

Man fucking killed himself, said Detective Hattori, getting into his car. Wouldn't be the first, won't be the last – happens every day, *detective*, happens every day.

A streetcar stop, a sudden rainstorm, a gentle hand on a damp sleeve, a proffered umbrella, a shelter shared, with a kind word and a sad smile, said the pale, thin woman in the pale, thin *yukata*. That's how I remember we met, Mister Sweeney.

Not selling peanuts by the roadside then, said Susumu Toda. Peanuts or maybe some other charms, no?

The neighbors, they do like to gossip, said Missus Nobu Morishita, on her cushion, on the mats, among the insect coils and the tobacco smoke, not looking at Susumu Toda, still staring at Harry Sweeney. And then the newspapers, they will insist on printing such gossip and rumors, the lies people tell. It ought to be a crime, don't you think, Mister Sweeney?

Harry Sweeney smiled, then said, It is a crime, Missus Morishita, telling lies. In the papers or under oath.

You know, she said, when you smiled just then, just briefly then, you really looked like him.

Looked like who?

Well, like the President, of course, Mister Shimoyama, said Missus Nobu Morishita, lowering her eyes and her face, touching her hand to her cheek.

So it's all just bullshit then, said Susumu Toda. All these things the neighbors are saying, all these stories the papers are printing about you and President Shimoyama?

In her single-story *machiai*, in this place of secret rendezvous, with its little detached back room, its two separate telephone lines, Missus Nobu Morishita placed her hand to her heart and looked back up, not at Susumu Toda, but at Harry Sweeney, and said, I just feel so sorry for Missus Shimoyama, the things people are saying, the stories the papers are printing, so very sorry for Missus Shimoyama, if she hears the things people are saying, reads the stories the papers are printing, the insinuations and the innuendo; how awful it must be for her, don't you think, Mister Sweeney? I feel so sorry for her, Mister Sweeney.

Then you should speak out, said Harry Sweeney. Describe clearly the nature of your relationship?

The pale, thin woman clutched her pale, thin *yukata*, stared at Harry Sweeney, smiled at Harry Sweeney, and said, But how can I, Mister Sweeney? Could you, could anyone? Describe a relationship in words, use words to describe what was never said? What was never said, but only felt? Yes, I could say, "We were just friends, only friends," but what do those words mean, what does "friends" mean, Mister Sweeney?

Well, you could try using facts, sighed Susumu Toda. You could start by telling us dates and times, how often you and your "friend" the President saw each other?

Harry Sweeney nodded, smiled at Missus Nobu Morishita: My friend is right, it would help us . . .

Then of course, said the pale, thin woman, nodding at Harry Sweeney, smiling at Harry Sweeney. I do believe, have believed for a long time, that my purpose on earth, the only reason I'm here, is to help people, help men, Mister Sweeney.

Harry Sweeney nodded and smiled again: Then you could help us, help me, by telling us how often you saw President Shimoyama. Once a week, once a month?

Of course, said Missus Nobu Morishita, not smiling now, but sighing now. So, as I've already said, already told the police, when he was a minister, I would see Mister Shimoyama almost every day. He'd come by car, just after noon, then stay all afternoon, stay until six, but no later than six.

Always by car and always alone?

Yes, said the pale, thin woman. Always by car, the same car, the black Buick; I can still remember its number, 41173, and the face of his chauffeur, Mister Ōnishi.

So the driver Ōnishi, said Susumu Toda, he'd be waiting outside in the car then, all afternoon?

Except on Sundays, whispered Missus Nobu Morishita, looking at Harry Sweeney, blinking back tears. On Sundays, Mister Shimoyama would come on foot.

In the small room, on the square cushion, Harry Sweeney put his hand in his pocket, took out his handkerchief, and offered it to the pale, thin woman: And why was that?

Thank you, she said, taking the handkerchief, clutching the handkerchief. But I'm sorry, I can't tell you why.

Maybe he was worried the neighbors would start to talk, said Susumu Toda. Him coming every day . . .

This was when he's a minister, cut in Harry Sweeney. But when he was appointed president –

Things changed, yes, nodded Missus Nobu Morishita. Like they always do, don't you think, Mister Sweeney?

Harry Sweeney nodded and said, But how?

Well, he could not come so often, only once or twice a month, and he could not stay so long, only five or ten minutes, just a cup of tea, a sweet he often left, he did not touch.

Harry Sweeney nodded again: He'd changed, too?

Yes, nodded the pale, thin woman, staring at Harry Sweeney, blinking through her tears, clutching his handkerchief tighter, twisting it in her hands, and whispering, Like they always do, don't they, Mister Sweeney?

Harry Sweeney nodded, glanced away, looked away as he asked, How had he changed, ma'am?

The job had changed him, the work he knew he had to do, she said. It had made him afraid, frightened for his life.

He told you that, did he?

Yes, said Missus Nobu Morishita, staring at Harry Sweeney. The last time . . .

Harry Sweeney looked back at Missus Nobu Morishita and said, I'm sorry, but when was this, ma'am?

Just two weeks ago, she said. Twenty-eighth of June, though it feels like a lifetime ago. But you know, Mister Sweeney, I just knew, knew then it would be the last time.

Harry Sweeney nodded, and waited –

You see, Mister Sweeney, he took me for lunch, like he used to do, to the place we used to go, an eel restaurant in Shibamata, a place called Kawajin; it was "our place," as they say, the place we always used to go, used to go before, but had not been, we had not been for months, you see . . .

Harry Sweeney nodded again.

And that was when he said he feared for his life, when he told me he thought he'd be killed . . .

And what did you say?

I laughed, Mister Sweeney. I laughed and said, Such things don't happen anymore, not in the "New Japan," not like before the war, when there were assassinations, the murders of officials and ministers; I said that was in the "Old Japan," and I laughed, Not in the "New Japan," Mister Sweeney.

I'm sorry, whispered Harry Sweeney.

So you see, Mister Sweeney, I knew, knew it would be the last time, he told me so himself.

I'm sorry, said Harry Sweeney again.

Well, that's very kind of you to say, Mister Sweeney, said Missus Nobu Morishita. You're the only person to come into my house, and to sit upon my mats, and to tell me that you're sorry, only you have said you're sorry, Mister Sweeney. But you're not the one he told, you're not the one who knew. You're not the one who did not help your friend, you're not the one who did not save your friend; that's me, Mister Sweeney, me.

Please, said Harry Sweeney. You shouldn't . . .

Shouldn't what, Mister Sweeney? I am the one he told, I am the one who knew. I am the one who did not help my *friend*, the one who could not save my *friend* . . .

Please, said Harry Sweeney again, trying to smile, trying to say, I'm sure you helped him –

There, she said, the pale, thin woman in the pale, thin *yukata* said. You did it again, Mister Sweeney.

Did what again, ma'am?

You smiled again, the way he used to smile, so fleetingly, so briefly, as though you'd both forgotten.

Forgotten what?

Forgotten you were sad, Mister Sweeney, forgotten who you were, forgotten who you are.

They were riding the elevator back up to the fourth floor of the NYK building, Susumu Toda still going on about the lady at the Narita-ya, still saying, You believe a word of that shit? Old fucking geisha, giving us a performance, wringing her hands, dabbing her eyes, telling us how sorry she feels for Missus Shimoyama. Not sorry enough to stop her pawning the poor woman's kimonos and rings, yeah? You know who she reminded me of? That woman at the Suehiro Ryokan, that's who, like they were reading from a script, the pair of them. The same script.

Sorry, Susumu, said Harry Sweeney, stepping out of the elevator on the third floor. I'll catch you up –

And Harry Sweeney walked away from the closing doors of the elevator, the muffled protestations of Susumu Toda, and along the corridors of the third floor of the NYK building, the corridors of the Historical Branch, FEC, SCAP, the whole of the third floor given over to this section, reading the numbers and the names on the signs on the doors as he went – American names and Japanese names – the doors all closed, the rooms all silent behind them, until he came to the sign on the door he'd been looking for, the number and the name which read: Room 330, Library. Harry Sweeney tapped softly on the wood, opened the door, and stepped inside.

The library of the Historical Branch was a large high-ceilinged room of three walls and many rows of bookshelves. In its middle were three long, high desks arranged in a U-shape to form a counter, in the center of which sat a middle-aged, aristocratic-looking Japanese lady talking quietly into a telephone. The lady looked up, saw Harry Sweeney walking toward the counter, hung up the receiver, and stared at Harry Sweeney: This is the library of the Historical Branch.

I had a hunch, said Harry Sweeney, smiling.

The lady did not smile back: So . . . ?

So I was hoping to speak to Miss Wilson, said Harry Sweeney, still smiling. I believe she works here?

She did, but not anymore.

Oh, said Harry Sweeney. I see.

The lady gave a brief, closing bow: Good day.

Er, sorry, said Harry Sweeney. Do you know where Miss Wilson has gone? Where she's been transferred?

The lady nodded: She left, she went home.

Home, said Harry Sweeney. America?

The lady nodded again: I believe so.

That was mighty sudden, said Harry Sweeney. I only saw her a few days ago. She never said anything . . .

The lady sighed: Family trouble, I think. But I don't know anything more, so please don't ask me anything more.

Hey there, said a tall, thin man dressed in a dark, well-cut civilian suit, stepping out from one of the alcoves with a book in his hands. It's Sweeney, isn't it?

Yes, said Harry Sweeney.

Dick Gutterman, said the man, walking toward Harry Sweeney with his right hand outstretched. We met last week, General Willoughby's office?

I remember, said Harry Sweeney, shaking the man's hand. Didn't realize you were one of the History Boys?

Me, laughed the man. Hell, no. I just pop in every now and again, bother Miss Araki here, get her to lend me a book.

You planning on visiting Formosa, are you, said Harry Sweeney, nodding at the map book in the man's left hand.

The man glanced down at the book in his hand, then back up at Harry Sweeney, and smiled: I'm impressed. Didn't know you could read Japanese, Mister Sweeney.

Why would you, said Harry Sweeney.

You know what I mean . . .

Yeah, I know what you mean, said Harry Sweeney.

Sorry, said the man. Didn't mean to offend you.

Don't worry about it, said Harry Sweeney.

The man nodded, smiled again, and said, So how's it going then? The Shimoyama Case? Any progress?

Reckon I should be asking you, said Harry Sweeney. That information of a somewhat confidential nature you were mentioning to the General last week?

Hell, said the man, you should be thanking me for that. Got the General off your ass for you, didn't I?

Is that all that was about then, said Harry Sweeney, smiling. You trying to save my ass?

Hey, look, said the man. Hongō heard a whisper, I didn't reckon it was worth much – turns out I was right – but I don't like to sit there and watch the General dressing down a man like that, not unless it's another general. I'd pay good money to see that any day of the week. But not a regular Joe like you, a civilian. You ain't done nothing to deserve that, right? So I thought, Hell, I'll cut in here.

Thank you, then, said Harry Sweeney.

Forget it, said the man. You'd have done the same. I can see how you are.

Well, thanks anyway, said Harry Sweeney again. Better get back to it, but good to meet you properly.

Likewise, said the man. But hey, what brought you down here anyway? The Shimoyama Case?

No, laughed Harry Sweeney. I was just looking for someone, someone who used to work here.

A friend, was it?

Don't know, said Harry Sweeney, smiling at the man, then turning toward the door. Might have been, could have been. Not sure what "friend" means these days.

Well, hell, you gotta friend in me, said the man after him. Anything you need, Mister Sweeney, you just call Hongō House and ask for Dick Gutterman, yeah?

The call came, like he knew it would, like it always did, and so he went, like he knew he would, like he always did: in the big car, down the wide avenues, across the river, the Sumida River, to a warehouse he'd not seen before and would never see again, among low factories and barrack houses, in a place that could be here, there, or anywhere, a place that was nowhere today, today and evermore, forevermore this place was nowhere; and here in nowhere, before the warehouse, he got out of the back of the car, like he knew he would, like he always did, and he looked up at the warehouse, made of concrete, iron, and wood, grays and rusts and browns, stained black against the same grays and rusts and browns, and he breathed in the stench of the salt and the stench of the shit, and he breathed out the stench of cowardice, the stench of pride, then he walked toward the warehouse door, through the warehouse door, like he knew he would, like he always did, he walked between the metal drums, the iron pillars and the hanging chains, walked through the pools of oil, the discarded parts and broken glass, until he came to the back of the warehouse, until he came to the half-circle of men, in their shirtsleeves or their undershirts, with their tools or with their fists, until he came to the chair in their midst, until he saw the man on the chair, like he knew he would, like he knew he would, the man tied to the chair, stripped and naked, beaten and broken, like he knew they would, like they always did, like he knew Senju would, Senju always did, and Harry Sweeney stood there, in the back of the warehouse, in the middle of nowhere, among the men, before the man, and Harry Sweeney said nothing, like Harry Sweeney knew he would, Harry Sweeney always did, because Harry Sweeney always said nothing, Harry Sweeney always did nothing –

Took your time, said Akira Senju. But Akira Senju did not turn to look at Harry Sweeney, Akira Senju kept his eyes fixed on the man on the chair: Two, three more hours, not sure he would have been with us anymore. And that'd have been a shame, the things he's been telling us . . .

Harry Sweeney stared at the man on the chair, the man tied to the chair, the cable round his chest and his arms and the back of the chair, the cable tight into his chest and arms, his naked chest and arms, his stripped and naked body, painted in the colors of bruises and wounds, the strokes of beatings and tortures, his head bowed and his face hidden, blood dripping onto his chest, blood upon blood, and Harry Sweeney swallowed and whispered, He's no good to me dead.

That's what I thought, said Akira Senju. Thought to myself, then said to the boys, I said, He's no good to anyone dead, boys. Ease up, boys, ease up. But it's like the war never ended, like they never heard the news. They were not defeated, not this lot, my lot; you know what I mean, Harry?

Harry Sweeney stepped inside the half-circle of men, stepped toward the man tied to the chair. Harry Sweeney crouched down beside the man tied to the chair, raised his hands toward the man tied to the chair. Harry Sweeney lifted up the face of the man tied to the chair, the swollen face of the man, wet with blood, and wet with tears, and wet with sweat. Harry Sweeney looked into the face of the man tied to the chair, the broken nose and cheeks, the eyes swollen and shut, the ears twisted and torn, saw the mouth of pulped lips and broken teeth, and Harry Sweeney saw the mouth, open in bubbles of blood and bits of teeth, and heard it whisper –

Help me, please.

Harry Sweeney let go of the face of the man, watched it fall forward again, then Harry Sweeney stood back up, turned around, looked at Akira Senju, swallowed again, and then said, Clean him up, then bring him out to the car, *please*.

You heard the man, boys, said Akira Senju, as Harry Sweeney walked through the circle of men, past Akira Senju, through the pools of oil, the discarded parts and the broken glass, between the metal drums, the iron pillars, and the hanging chains, past the stacked-up packing cases of God-knows-what – guns and bombs for someone, drugs and alcohol for everyone – and through the warehouse door, back outside to the grays and rusts and browns, the stench of salt and the stench of shit, back to stand and wait beside the car, to smoke one cigarette and then another, and another, like he always did, like he always did, until he heard the boots, he heard the voice –

Here you go, said Akira Senju. Meet Lee Jung-Hwan. He's all yours, Harry-san, all yours . . .

No longer tied to a chair, no longer stripped and naked, Lee Jung-Hwan hung on the arms of two men, dressed in clothes torn and stained with blood and oil, his shoes barely on his feet, with his head still bowed and his face still hidden.

Harry Sweeney flicked his cigarette into the dirt, looked at Akira Senju, nodded, and said, Thank you.

My pleasure, Harry, said Akira Senju, smiling. Told you, I'm here to help. So what now, *boss* . . . ?

Harry Sweeney opened the back door of the car: Put him in here. I want to talk to him. Alone.

Sure thing, *boss*, said Akira Senju, clicking his fingers, gesturing to the two men carrying Lee Jung-Hwan. And the two men dragged him through the dirt, half lifting, half pushing him into the car, propping him up on the back seat of the car.

Harry Sweeney closed the door, went round the back of the car, opened the door on the other side, then got into the back seat next to Lee Jung-Hwan and closed the door.

In the middle of nowhere, on the back seat of the parked

car, Harry Sweeney stared out through the front windshield, out at the grays and the rusts and the browns, and waited.

Thank you, said Lee Jung-Hwan, not raising his head, not showing his face, his voice dry and cracking.

Harry Sweeney kept staring straight ahead, straight out and into the grays and the rusts and the browns, as he said, Save your thanks until we're out of here –

*Until we're out of here . . .*

The words hanging in the trapped, damp air of the car, hanging between them –

Where's my little brother, asked Lee Jung-Hwan, the question choking in his throat.

Harry Sweeney looked away from the windshield, away from the grays and the rusts and the browns, looked away to stare at the beaten and bloody, bowed and broken man beside him, to stare and say, I don't know.

Is he still alive?

As far as I know, but the only way to be sure, the only way to save him and to save yourself, is to tell me everything you know about the death of President Shimoyama.

It won't save me, said Lee Jung-Hwan, raising his head, then showing his face, the remains of his face, to look at Harry Sweeney and say, And it won't help you.

Might help your little brother.

*Might*, whispered Lee Jung-Hwan, turning his face away, lowering his head again.

Harry Sweeney turned, too, back to the windshield, back to the grays and the rusts and the browns, and waited.

Are you CIC, asked Lee Jung-Hwan, not raising his head again, not showing his face again.

Public Safety. Why?

CIC won't like what I say.

He was staring into the grays and the rusts and the browns, losing himself in the grays and the rusts and the browns, as

Harry Sweeney said, CIC don't like a lot of things people say. That's their job, not to like the things people say.

I know. But it's my job to say them.

You a Communist, is that it?

I'm a code clerk at the Soviet Mission, said Lee Jung-Hwan, raising his head again, showing his face again.

In the middle of nowhere, on the back seat of the parked car, Harry Sweeney looked away from the windshield again, away from the grays and the rusts and the browns again, looked away to stare at the remains of the face of this man again, the broken nose and cheeks, the eyes swollen and shut, the ears twisted and torn, the blacks and the purples and the reds of the remains of the face of this man, so many shades of black and purple and red, and Harry Sweeney said, Can you prove it?

Not now, not here, said Lee Jung-Hwan, pulling at his clothes, torn and stained with blood and oil, their pockets empty. But if you take me to your office, if you make some calls, if you check, then you'll have your proof.

First, tell me why I should, tell me what you know about the death of President Shimoyama.

Now, here?

Yes.

Okay then, sighed Lee Jung-Hwan. Okay. Well, as a code clerk I've seen the official communications between Moscow and Tokyo about Shimoyama . . .

Go on –

So in April, I think it was, when the retrenchment program was first announced, you know, the mass dismissals, that was when the order came from Moscow. It was sent to Lieutenant General Derevyanko himself, ordering the Mission to gain the confidence of Shimoyama, by any means possible. The suggestion from Moscow was that the best way to do this would be to supply Shimoyama with confidential information, thus gaining his trust . . .

On the back seat of the parked car, in the trapped, damp air of the car, Harry Sweeney reached inside his jacket, took out his notebook and pencil, opened his notebook, then, writing in his notebook, asked, You're saying Derevyanko was in charge of this operation, in *direct* charge, *personally*?

No, said Lee Jung-Hwan. Not personally, no. There's a man called Rosenoff, he's in charge of all covert operations at the Soviet Mission in Tokyo. But, of course, he reports to Lieutenant General Derevyanko, as well as to Moscow.

So this man Rosenoff ran the operation?

Yes, said Lee Jung-Hwan. But soon after, Moscow sent a man named Ariyoshi for the specific purpose of handling Mister Shimoyama. He was in day-to-day charge of the operation, reporting to Rosenoff and Moscow.

You ever see this man?

Yes, said Lee Jung-Hwan.

Describe him –

About the same age as me, I guess, early thirties. His features might be mistaken for Chinese, but I think he's Japanese. Long face, thick lips, fairly heavyset, about two hundred pounds, I suppose, about five and a half feet, maybe a bit taller.

Harry Sweeney turned the page of his notebook, still writing as he said, Go on –

So Ariyoshi had this guy inside the union, the National Railways Union. This guy is a Communist, but a secret one, and so Ariyoshi gets this guy to make contact with Shimoyama, to start feeding him confidential reports, some of them true but most of them not. Meanwhile – and this is the bit your CIC are not going to like . . .

Go on –

There's this member of the Kudan CIC, he's also a member of the Communist Party of America. Simultaneously, this guy also approaches Shimoyama, requests Shimoyama start supplying him with any confidential information he receives from inside the union – you get it?

Harry Sweeney stopped writing, looked up from the pages of his notebook, looked out through the windshield again, out into the grays and the rusts and the browns again, the grays and the rusts and the browns turning, turning and spinning, and Harry Sweeney nodded and said, Yep.

They got Shimoyama going in circles, said Lee Jung-Hwan. Thinking he's passing on union plans, Communist secrets, passing them on to CIC, on to your lot, CIC supposedly checking them, your lot supposedly thanking him. But all the time, day by day, they're setting him up.

In the trapped, damp air of the car, Harry Sweeney blinked and rubbed his eyes, squeezed the bridge of his nose, then looked back down at his notebook and began to write again, as he said, For the fifth of July –

Yes, said Lee Jung-Hwan, quietly, slowly. Late June, the order came from Moscow, the order to terminate Mister Shimoyama and, specifically, to terminate Mister Shimoyama in a manner that would cause the utmost confusion, creating huge problems for both the Japanese government and GHQ, anticipating an extreme reaction against the Japanese Communist Party and the trade union movement, which would, in turn, lead the Communists and the unions to finally embrace the necessity of violent struggle and revolution, fighting back as the vanguard of an uprising by the Japanese proletariat.

Harry Sweeney stopped writing, looked up from the pages of his notebook again, out into the grays and the rusts and the browns again, staring into the grays and the rusts and the browns again as he said, All beginning with the abduction and assassination of President Shimoyama.

Yep, said Lee Jung-Hwan.

In the middle of nowhere, on the back seat of the parked car, Harry Sweeney turned sharply, spun from the grays and the rusts and the browns to the blacks and the purples and the reds of the remains of the face of this man, turned to this beaten and bloody, bowed and broken man and said, An abduction and assassination you were a fucking part of –

No, said Lee Jung-Hwan. No, no! I just saw the communications, just encoding or decoding them.

Not what your brother says –

He's got nothing to do with this, said Lee Jung-Hwan. Nothing to do with any of this –

So why'd you bring him into it then? Why'd you get him to steal that car for you?

I didn't, he didn't, said Lee Jung-Hwan, looking at Harry Sweeney, pleading with Harry Sweeney, then turning to the window of the door, looking out at Akira Senju and his men. I don't know what car they're talking about, what car you're talking about, please –

Outside Mitsukoshi?

Please, said Lee Jung-Hwan, turning back to Harry Sweeney, shaking his head at Harry Sweeney, his beaten and bloody head. It's all a mistake, he's made a mistake. Please just let me see him, let me to talk to him . . .

Okay, calm down, said Harry Sweeney. You just calm down. I'll be back in a minute –

And Harry Sweeney got out of the back of the car, walked round the back of the car, back toward the warehouse, the shadows of the warehouse, the smile of Akira Senju –

Quite a story, eh, Harry, said Akira Senju. Quite a story he tells, yeah? I trust you're impressed, Harry-san?

Where you got his brother?

Impressed and grateful, I hope, Harry . . .

In the shadows of the warehouse, before its open doors, Harry Sweeney stared at Akira Senju and said, I asked you where the brother is? I need to talk to him.

Well now, Harry, that might be a little difficult.

You're fucking joking?

That's exactly what I said, Harry, said Akira Senju, when the boys told me what happened. I said, You're fucking joking, boys? What kind of fool throws himself from the back of a moving truck into the river, the Sumida River, when his hands are tied? What kind of fool does that? I mean, I know the kid was a *chonko*, but you're fucking joking, right?

In the shadows of the warehouse, before its open doors, among the grays and the rusts and the browns, all stained black against the same, Harry Sweeney turned to look back at the parked car, at the face at the side window of the parked car, the remains of a face staring up, out at Harry Sweeney –

You want to tell him, Harry, or shall I?

In this place that was nowhere, in the middle of this nowhere, with its stench of salt, with its stench of shit, Harry Sweeney turned back to Akira Senju, and Harry Sweeney looked at Akira Senju, and Harry Sweeney clenched his teeth, then said through his teeth, his clenched teeth, Harry Sweeney said, Nobody's going to tell him anything. I'm going to take him back to Public Safety, and you're going to drive us.

Sure thing, Harry. You're the *boss*.

In the NYK building, on the fourth floor, in Room 402, the office of Colonel Pullman, before the Colonel seated behind his desk, sat beside Chief Evans, Bill Betz, and Susumu Toda, Harry Sweeney nodded, looked back down at the statement, and began to read aloud: On the morning of the fifth, President Shimoyama arrived in his car at the south entrance of the Mitsukoshi department store and then proceeded on foot to the north entrance, where Ariyoshi, Oyama, Kinoshita, and Chin were waiting in two black sedans. I think they were cars Nine and Ten – a black Chevrolet and a black Buick – belonging to the Soviet Mission. The plates had been made specially for this purpose, and one was 1A2637, but I do not recall the other. Ariyoshi and Oyama guided President Shimoyama into the first car, seating him between them. The cars proceeded through Ginza and Shimbashi to a property in the Azabu area, close to the Soviet Embassy, occupied by Russian personnel. Before approaching the property, Oyama struck President Shimoyama in the vital organs, using a karate technique, knocking him unconscious. Once inside the property, President Shimoyama was murdered through an injection in his right arm. Immediately following confirmation of his death, his body was stripped and placed in the bathtub, and a blood vessel on his right arm was cut to drain the blood. His body was then put in a rubber bag and placed in the garage to the side of the property. In order to confuse the investigating authorities, an individual with similar features to President Shimoyama was employed as a decoy. The man's name is Nakamura, and he is approximately the same height as President Shimoyama. I do not know where this man lives, but I believe it is in the Kansai area. He comes to Tokyo at least once a week and meets with two men called Tokuda and Nosaka. At the property in Azabu, he was given the clothes which President Shimoyama had been wearing and was then sent to the area where the body was later found. About 9 p.m., the body of President Shimoyama was placed in the trunk of one of the original cars and then driven toward the scene of the incident, first stopping at an unknown location, but arriving at the scene of the incident at approximately 10:30 p.m. The car stopped under the railroad tracks of the Jōban line, near to Kosuge Prison. Here the man called Nakamura arrived in order to change clothes so that the body could be dressed. After this was done, Nakamura left the scene in the car. The body was then placed on a portable cart and taken to the place where it was to be found later. The body was positioned so that the arm which had had the injection was placed on the rail. As soon as this was done, three members left the scene with the cart. Three other members remained in the vicinity until they had seen the train run over President Shimoyama's body. Those that were at the scene were Ariyoshi, Oyama, Kinoshita, Chin, a Russian, and a Ukrainian. Those that remained at the scene were Ariyoshi, the Russian, and the Ukrainian. In order that the car would not be stopped in transit, all those other than the Russian wore American uniforms and carried falsified CIC credentials. A car returned to pick up the last three at an agreed time and place, but I do not know where and when that was. I have described the men I have named – ARIYOSHI, OYAMA, KINOSHITA, & CHIN – on the separate, attached page, and I have told you all I know. Signed, Andorushin, R.J.K.C. 125 (name and number used in Soviet Mission); real or birth name, Lee Jung-Hwan.

Harry Sweeney stopped reading, looked up from the statement, and waited, the sound of the clock ticking on the wall, and waited, the sound of minutes passing, until –

Well, that is some story, Harry, said Colonel Pullman. Quite the story. What d'you say, Chief?

I don't know, sir, said Chief Evans, shaking his head. So I say we pass this up the chain, sir, to the General, sir.

Really, said the Colonel. To General Willoughby?

If you're asking me, sir, yes, said the Chief. I mean, this isn't a Public Safety matter, sir, this is CIC.

Really, said Colonel Pullman again, sitting forward at his desk, looking across the desk, first at Bill Betz, then at Susumu Toda, then at Harry Sweeney, asking, How about the rest of you? Any of you believe it?

Bill Betz nodded: I know it all sounds kind of far-fetched, sir – draining the blood, using a decoy – like something from the movies, sir, but it also kind of fits.

You think so, laughed Susumu Toda, turning to look at Bill Betz. Fits with no evidence, is the only way it fits.

Hey, you were the one going on about the stolen car, about all them sightings of big, black cars . . .

On different roads, said Toda. At different times.

Bill Betz shook his head: So what if some of the details don't quite match up? Maybe a witness gets the wrong time, the wrong street – it happens, and you know it happens. Or maybe what these Commies wrote in their report to Moscow ain't quite how it was, or maybe Mister Code-Clerk ain't remembering it right? Got himself confused in the telling – so what?

So what, said Toda. He could be a compulsive liar, a complete fantasist, is what he could be.

Bill Betz shook his head: So like the Chief says, we let CIC work it out, what his story is. Not our problem.

Harry, said Colonel Pullman. He's your baby, son. You brought him into the world. What do you say?

Harry Sweeney shrugged: I'm sorry, sir, but I agree with everyone, everything they're saying. I mean, we got no real evidence, no proof, as Susumu says. But like Bill says, bits of it, they sound like they might make some sense. So I'm with the Chief, sir, I'd let the General and CIC sort it out, sir.

Really, said Colonel Pullman, getting up from his chair, coming round from behind his desk, taking the statement from Harry Sweeney, looking down at the statement by Lee Jung-Hwan, and shaking his head. Really . . .

Chief Evans, Bill Betz, Susumu Toda, and Harry Sweeney looking up at the Colonel, waiting, the sound of the clock ticking on the wall, waiting, the sound of minutes passing, more minutes passing, until –

See, the difference between you all and me, said the Colonel, is you all are civilians and I'm a soldier. An old soldier, but still a soldier. And see, I can't decide if this story here is horseshit or gospel. I just can't tell, I just don't know. But what I do know, what I can tell you, is that if I pass this on up the chain, like you all are so keen I do, if I give this to General Willoughby, then we'll be goddamned lucky if we all ain't fighting World War fucking III by sundown.

Chief Evans started to stand up, to say, I'm sorry, sir. We can just set it to one side, forget we . . .

Hold on there, Chief, said the Colonel. That's not what I'm saying, not saying that at all. I just want to be certain, when I do pass this on up the chain, when the General does start calling for Soviet heads, demanding Commie blood, I just want to be certain it ain't horseshit we're feeding him.

Chief Evans nodded: Of course, sir. Absolutely, sir. You want evidence, sir, of course, sir.

Evidence and discretion, said the Colonel. That's what I want, Chief. So I'm going to hang on to this here statement, and I'm going to make some calls, some discreet calls, see if I can find any record of any of these here names. Meanwhile, you men are going to go back through the police reports, the witness statements, and see if you can find any descriptions which might match either the men or the cars mentioned in this statement.

Chief Evans nodded again: And if we do, sir?

Hell, then you go goddamn interview them, is what you do, Chief. Is that understood? Are we all clear?

Yes, sir, barked Chief Evans, Bill Betz, Susumu Toda, and Harry Sweeney. Understood and clear, sir.

Very good then, said the Colonel –

Harry Sweeney said, Sir . . . ?

What is it, son, asked the Colonel.

Harry Sweeney asked, And if you don't, if we don't? Don't find any record, don't find any corroboration? Then what, sir? What we going to do with him?

Then he's not our problem, son, said the Colonel. Then we let him go, or we turn him over to the Japanese police, let him take his chances with them. Either way, he's not our problem. That clear, son? Understood?

Yes, sir, understood, sir.

Very good then, said the Colonel again. Dismissed!

*

I don't know, said Kazuko Kawada, sat at the table by the door, in the empty Coffee Shop Hong Kong, the customers gone, the shop closed, the manager and the waiter and the cook at the next table, waiting to be allowed home, wanting to go home, glancing at Harry Sweeney and Kazu-chan, listening to Kazu-chan say again, But I don't think so. I'm sorry.

Harry Sweeney looked down at the descriptions of the four men and the decoy which Lee Jung-Hwan had given in his statement, then Harry Sweeney looked back up at this pretty girl, still in her black dress and white apron, and Harry Sweeney said, But you still think the man you saw that morning, you still think that man could have been President Shimoyama?

I think so, yes, said Kazuko Kawada. Because of his Harold Lloyd-style glasses, because of the way his eyebrows sloped downwards. I think it might've been, yes.

Harry Sweeney nodded, tapped the paper on the table, the statement by Lee Jung-Hwan, and said again, But you really don't think these descriptions match either the man who was sitting with President Shimoyama or any of the men who were sat at the table across the aisle that morning?

I'm sorry, said Kazuko Kawada again. The men you've described, they're all much younger.

Harry Sweeney nodded again, then lowered his voice as he said, And the man who used the telephone that morning, you still can't remember what –

No, said Kazuko Kawada, her head shaking, her eyes blinking. No, I'm sorry, I'm sorry, I've tried, but I can't.

Harry Sweeney reached out across the table to touch her hand, to pat her hand: That's okay, that's okay.

I told you, said Kazuko Kawada, pulling her hand away, taking out a handkerchief from the pocket of her apron. He had his back to me, his face turned away . . .

Could he have been a foreigner?

A foreigner, like you . . . ?

Maybe a Korean?

We get enough of them in here, these days, said the manager, Mister Niide, from across the aisle. Throwing their weight around, acting like they own the place.

Harry Sweeney turned to look across the aisle at Mister Niide and said, But you still take their money, yeah? Let them use the phone, do you?

Hey, said Mister Niide. As long they've got some, I'm happy to take it. Money's money.

Harry Sweeney looked from the manager to the waiter to the cook, then back to the waitress, and said, So anyone wanting to use that phone, they have to ask one of you, yeah? And so that morning, the fifth of July, one of your customers, he asked to use the phone, he asked one of you.

Had to have done, said the manager, nodding, looking at the waiter and the cook. Must have done.

So which one of you was it, said Harry Sweeney, turning to look across the aisle again, to stare at the waiter –

The waiter – the nervous man, gaunt and tall – pulled at the collar of his shirt and said, Okay, okay, it was me.

You, said the manager. Why didn't you –

Because you pay them fucking peanuts, said Harry Sweeney. So he pocketed the man's change, that's why.

Mister Kojima, the waiter, tore off his bow tie, threw it down on the table, put his hand in his pocket, pulled out a fistful of coins, and slapped them down on top of the table: There you go. Keep it all, I don't care, he said, standing up –

Sit down, barked Harry Sweeney. Save your walk-out until after I'm gone, till after we're done.

The man slumped back down at the table, scowling across the aisle at Harry Sweeney, not speaking, just waiting.

What did he look like?

Who, said the man.

The goddamn Emperor of Japan, hissed Harry Sweeney. Who d'you fucking think I mean?

Don't know, said the man.

Harry Sweeney stared at the man as he said, That morning, the fifth of July, sometime after half past nine, but before ten o'clock, you were in the kitchen, and a man stuck his head inside, asked to use the telephone. I know he did, and how I know he did is because then that man called me, and so you're going to tell me what he fucking looked like –

But I don't know, said the man, glancing over at Kazuko Kawada, the waitress trying and failing not to cry. I'm sorry, but I really don't remember . . .

Young, old – you must remember something?

Look, I was busy preparing the orders, said the man. The food, the drinks. I glanced over my shoulder, took his change, and then he was gone . . .

But he spoke to you, and so his voice –

Just a couple of words. Softly spoken, polite, I think. But that's all I remember . . .

*Too late, whispered the voice of a Japanese man, then the voice was gone, the line dead, the connection lost.*

I'm sorry, said the man.

Me, too, said Harry Sweeney, looking across the table at Kazuko Kawada, the waitress with her head bowed, her shoulders trembling, tears falling onto her apron and her dress. Harry Sweeney closed his notebook, put the notebook and his pencil back inside his jacket pocket. He picked up the statement by Lee Jung-Hwan from the table, folded it back up, and put it in another pocket of his jacket. He picked up his hat from the chair beside him and stood up. He stared down at the staff of the Coffee Shop Hong Kong, shook his head, then turned and walked out through the door, the door banging, slamming shut behind him.

Harry Sweeney walked down the underground passage to the ticket gate to the station. He showed his pass, went through the gate and down the steps, onto the platform. The trains for Asakusa to the left, the trains for Shibuya to the right, a blast of wind rushing out of the tunnel and along the platform, picking up the scraps of paper and the ends of cigarettes. Harry Sweeney gripped his hat, held it tight as a train for Asakusa pulled into the station, the screams of its wheels and brakes piercing his ears again. Harry Sweeney waited for the doors to open, for the people to get off, the people to get on, then Harry Sweeney stepped into the brightly lit carriage, the doors closing behind him, the train pulling out as Harry Sweeney walked through the carriage, then the next carriage, and the next, and the next, until he came to the front of the train, found a seat in the carriage at the front of the train, sat down, and took off his hat. He reached for his handkerchief to wipe his face and then his neck, but his handkerchief was gone, and so he used the sleeve of his jacket to wipe his forehead, to wipe his mouth, then he put his hat back on and looked up and down the carriage, then across the aisle, at the passengers. Men here, men there, some wearing hats, some carrying fans, some in jackets and some in ties, sleeping or reading, their book or their paper. Back pages and front pages, in their hands or left on a seat, an empty seat. Harry Sweeney picked up the discarded newspaper and began to read the headlines and the articles beneath: POLICE MEASURES TAKEN TO CHECK LAWBREAKERS: Not Aimed at Trade Unions, Says Hepler, Refuting Russian Allegations / SOVIETS WORKING FOR JAPAN CHAOS, U.S. COUNTERBLAST TO ACCUSATIONS AGAINST OCCUPATION POLICIES: Local Reds Instructed to Create Fear, Unrest, Confusion, Says McCoy / JAPANESE DUTY TO RESIST SOVIET OCCUPATION MOVE SAYS P.M. YOSHIDA / SHIMOYAMA WAS KILLED, ATT'Y GEN. PRONOUNCES: Mystery Death Caused by Foul Play –

Harry Sweeney stopped reading, looked up from the paper, its headline and its articles. The train had stopped, the carriage was empty. They had reached the Asakusa terminal, the end of the line. Harry Sweeney put the paper back down on the seat beside him, stood up, and got off the train, onto the platform. He walked up the steps to the ticket gate, showed his pass, and went on through the gate. He walked up the sloping passageway, past the basement entrance to the Matsuya department store, and up the steps to the Asakusa Tōbu line station. He walked up the second flight of stairs to the platforms and the trains. He showed his pass at the ticket gate and walked onto the platform. He went briskly down the platform, got onto a train to his left, a local train about to leave, but he did not look for a seat. He stood by the doors and watched them close, watched the train pull out of the station, on its elevated tracks, he stared out through the windows of the doors as the train crossed the bridge, crossed the river, the Sumida River, staring out at the river, the Sumida River, on this yellow train across this iron bridge, the river, the Sumida River, there down below him, stretched out before him, so still and so black, so soft and so warm, inviting and welcoming, tempting, so tempting, always tempting, so tempting, the river, the Sumida River, a man disappearing, a man vanishing, so tempting, very tempting, to disappear and to vanish, into the air, into the night, but then the river was gone, the Sumida gone, temptation gone, gone for now. Harry Sweeney blinked, blinked and wiped his eyes, the train going down the line, stopping at the stations, Narihirabashi then Hikifune, closing his eyes, opening his eyes, down the line, over the crossings, station after station, Tamanoi and on to Kita-Senju, then across another bridge, another iron bridge, across another river, the Arakawa River, closing his eyes, opening his eyes, the prison looming, Kosuge Prison, from out of the shadows, in the night, black on black, the tracks raised again, elevated again, on embankments and over girders, Harry Sweeney staring out through the windows of the doors, staring down at the other tracks to his right, crossing the Jōban line, they were crossing the Jōban line, crossing close to the scene, they were close to the scene, the scene of the death, the death of Shimoyama, Sadanori Shimoyama, down there, there on the tracks, there down below, stretched out before him, below and before him, stretched out and taunting him, Harry Sweeney blinking again, taunting and taunting him, Harry Sweeney wiping his eyes, again and again, Sadanori Shimoyama taunting him –

*Too late, whispered the voice of a Japanese man, then the voice was gone, the line dead, the connection lost.*

Harry Sweeney got off the train at Gotanno station. He walked with the men and the women, with their briefcases and their handbags, down the platform to the ticket gate. He held up his pass and he passed through the gate. He turned left and walked south down the main street of Gotanno, passing wooden shacks offering cheap food and strong alcohol, their lanterns floating in the thick, black, insect air, then past a sweetshop and a hardware store, a tobacconist and a greengrocer, already closed for the night, closed to the world. He came to a crossroads, turned left to walk east, and found himself opposite the Suehiro Ryokan. He stood on the other side of the street, staring across the road at the tall wooden fence, the tops of the trees smudged gray in the dark, smudged and shielding the shabby, gloomy, two-storied inn, hiding and obscuring that place of shabby, gloomy trysts and assignations, this hidden and obscured place of deception and lies. Harry Sweeney coughed, banged his chest with his fist, cleared his throat, spat upon the ground, then walked on, down the road, under the metal girders of the bridge, under the tracks of the Tōbu line, until he came to the Gotanno Minami-machi police box.

The young uniformed police officer, sat alone behind the small counter in the police box, looked up from his hands, blinked nervously, and asked, Yes?

Public Safety, said Harry Sweeney, taking out his badge again, holding up his badge again.

Yes, yes, excuse me, said the young officer, standing up behind the counter, bowing, and nodding his head. I remember you, sir. What can I do for you, sir?

Harry Sweeney put away his badge, took out his notebook, flicked through the pages, then looked up and said, Missus Take Yamazaki? Can you give me directions, please?

Yes, yes, said the young officer, nodding. But it might be easier if I came with you, if I showed you, sir?

Harry Sweeney shook his head, smiled, and said, Thanks, but that won't be necessary. Just the directions, please.

I see, said the young officer, nodding again, gesturing with his right hand, pointing out of the door of the police box. Well then, you need to head back under the tracks, then cross the road and follow the embankment south. You'll see rows of houses beside the embankment. It's a bit of a rabbit warren, so you're probably best just to ask again when you get there.

Harry Sweeney nodded, thanked the young officer, and then stepped back out of the police box and back into the night, the black night and its thick, wet, insect air –

Hang on a moment, said the young officer, picking up a handheld paraffin police lamp, lighting the lamp, offering it to Harry Sweeney. Best to take this and all. You need to watch out for the ditches and the drains . . .

In the light from the police box and from the police lamp, in the thick, wet, insect air, Harry Sweeney looked at the young officer and he smiled and he said, Thank you.

You know, said the young officer, quietly, softly, handing the lamp to Harry Sweeney, then looking down at his empty hands, holding out his empty hands, rubbing the fingers and thumbs of his hands together. You know, I can still feel him on my hands. No matter how many times I wash them, I can still feel the pieces of him . . .

The pieces of him, asked Harry Sweeney.

The pieces of his skin, the pieces of his flesh, whispered the young officer, staring down at his hands, the ends of his fingers. In the rain, that morning, when they made me pick up his clothes, made me put them in that box, from along the tracks, all along the tracks, all covered in mud, all covered in blood, there were pieces of his skin, pieces of his flesh, still on his clothes, all over his clothes. I can still feel them, still feel them, on my hands, between my fingers, no matter how many times I wash my hands, I scrub my fingers, I can still feel him . . .

I'm sorry, said Harry Sweeney, reaching out to put a hand on the shoulder of the young officer, to pat the shoulder of the young man, gently, softly. I'm sorry.

Will it ever stop, asked the young officer, looking up from his hands and his fingers, staring up at Harry Sweeney. You think it will ever go away, sir?

I hope so, said Harry Sweeney, quietly and softly, and then Harry Sweeney turned away from the young officer, walked away from the police box, carrying the lamp, holding up the lamp, heading back under the bridge and under the tracks, crossing the road, and then going south, following the embankment, through the night – things moving in the night, things crawling in the shadows, insects biting and dogs barking – until he came to the houses, the rows of houses, some with their lights on, some in darkness, darkness and silence.

Harry Sweeney stopped before one of these weather-beaten, moss-stained, barely-still-standing tenement houses, one with a light and a radio on, a thin, sad melody leaking into the night, mixing in the air with the smell of sweet potatoes and human excrement, and Harry Sweeney tapped on its lattice door, then slid open its wooden door: Excuse me . . . ?

What a fright, cried an old skinny man, sprawled on the floor in his underwear, half under a battered, low table, half propped up on a stained, thin cushion. A foreigner!

I'm very sorry, said Harry Sweeney, glancing around the single room, seeing a woman rising from her bedding in the shadows, watching the man trying to get his feet out from under the table, knocking over the empty bottle and glass on the table. I'm looking for Missus Yamazaki's house . . . ?

Too late, said the old skinny man, coughing and wheezing. Too late then, aren't you.

What do you mean?

They've gone, haven't they, said the man, waving his right hand around. Her and her husband, they've flit.

Flit where?

Damned if I know, laughed the man. But bet it's someplace nice. They come into money, didn't they.

You shouldn't say that, whispered the woman from the shadows. You don't know that.

You can shut up, said the man, coughing again, wheezing again. Know more than you, is what I know. Know she was talking to all them newspapermen, all them interviews she was giving them, telling them anything they wanted her to tell them, long as they paid –

Stop it, said the woman. Shouldn't say things like that. She's never been well, has Take-chan, always had it hard.

And we fucking ain't, said the man. Everybody's had it hard, still got it hard. She ain't doing so bad now . . .

You don't know anything about her, said the woman. You never spoke to her. I did. She was afraid.

Afraid, asked Harry Sweeney.

From her bedding, from the shadows, the woman said, Yeah, afraid. Told me she wished she'd never opened her mouth, wished she'd never got involved. It was her husband who made her, made her say all that . . .

Good on him, laughed the old skinny man. Hasn't worked out too bad for them, has it? Got them out of here.

In the doorway, on the threshold, holding up the lamp, looking at the woman, on her bedding, in the shadows, Harry Sweeney asked, But what was she afraid of, who was –

I don't know, said the woman, lying back down on her bedding, turning her face back to the shadows.

Don't know, my ass, said the man. The fucking cops is who she was afraid of, everybody knows that, and everybody knows why. Selling rice, wasn't she –

Shut up, shouted the woman, turning back round, sitting back up. Shut up, you old git!

Why, laughed the old skinny man. Not a secret, is it? Everybody knows, the cops know. That's how they got her to say what they wanted, do whatever they wanted, isn't it? Because she was selling rice on the black market.

I can't believe you've just said that, whispered the woman, shaking her head, looking at Harry Sweeney, shaking her head again, pointing at Harry Sweeney. You don't know who he is, you've no idea who he is, you stupid old fool. You could have just signed her death warrant . . .

*Too late, whispered the voice of a Japanese man, then the voice was gone, the line dead, the connection lost.*

So what, laughed the man, then coughing again, wheezing again. We're all going to die, ain't we.

On the threshold, in the doorway, Harry Sweeney turned and stepped out of this weather-beaten, moss-stained, barely-still-standing house, and slid the door shut, the thin, sad melodies of the radio drowned by shouting and screaming, the smell of sweet potatoes now gone, the stench of human excrement still strong, stronger than ever, the insects biting deeper, the dogs barking louder as Harry Sweeney walked away down the alley, along and beside the embankment again, heading south again, Harry Sweeney going south again, until he came to the place where the embankment met another embankment, where the tracks of the Tōbu line crossed over the tracks of the Jōban line –

In the thick, wet, insect air, the police lamp in one hand, Harry Sweeney clawed one-handed up the embankment of the Jōban line, up and onto the tracks of the Jōban line. Dripping with sweat, wiping a hand on his jacket, Harry Sweeney turned to the west and saw the lights across the river, the Arakawa River, the lights of Kita-Senju. Then, turning to the east and holding up the lantern, Harry Sweeney saw the metal bridge of the Tōbu line tracks overhead, saw the ballast, the sleepers, and the rails of the Jōban line tracks at his feet, saw them disappearing around the bend, vanishing under the bridge. Between the rails, over the sleepers, and through the ballast, Harry Sweeney followed the tracks around the bend and under the bridge, under its girders, under the tracks, under the bridge and along the tracks, walking along the tracks, pacing out the distance: one yard, two yards, three yards, four, until he came to the place, he came to the spot –

In the night, the thick, wet, insect night, on the tracks, between the rails and on the ballast, the chipped and broken, stained pieces of stone, someone had rested a bouquet of flowers, white chrysanthemums tied with black ribbon, on the tracks, in the night, left in this place to mark the spot. And in this night and on these tracks, between the rails, on the ballast, Harry Sweeney crouched down and set the lamp down, in this night and on these tracks, Harry Sweeney reached out to touch the petals, to hold the petals, and Harry Sweeney touched the petals, Harry Sweeney held the petals, he touched the petals and he held the petals, the night beginning to tremble, the tracks beginning to tremble, the rails humming and the ballast jumping, faster and faster, a train coming down the line, its wheels turning on the tracks, around the bend and under the bridge, closer –

*Too late, whispered the voice of a Japanese man, then the voice was gone, the line dead, the connection lost.*

Harry, Harry! The fuck are you doing –

Holding the bouquet, picking up the lamp, Harry Sweeney stepped off the tracks, away from the tracks, stepped back from the train, out of its path, turning his face, turning his body away from the train and away from the tracks, Harry Sweeney seeing two lanterns, seeing two men clambering up the embankment, climbing up toward him, the young officer and Susumu Toda clambering and climbing, calling and shouting, through the noise of the train, the sound of its wheels, the young officer and Susumu Toda reaching the top of the embankment, running down the tracks, the train disappearing up the line, vanishing into the night, the young officer and Susumu Toda running toward Harry Sweeney, reaching Harry Sweeney, Susumu Toda grabbing Harry Sweeney, holding Harry Sweeney, whispering, Harry, the Colonel, the Chief . . .

They don't believe you, said Harry Sweeney. We can find no record of you – of who you say you are, of what you say you are – no record whatsoever, and, of course, the Soviet Mission are denying any and all knowledge of you.

In the cramped basement storeroom of the NYK building, in a borrowed chair at a borrowed table, his face broken and swollen still, but stitched and bandaged now, Lee Jung-Hwan smiled and said, What did you expect them to say? What else could they say?

But there's not a single shred of evidence, said Harry Sweeney, not one single scrap of proof to back up one single word you've said.

Lee Jung-Hwan smiled again and shook his head: Apart from the dead man on the railroad track.

The Metropolitan Police have been receiving confessions by the hour, said Harry Sweeney. They're flooding in, now the government has offered a reward. The police are inundated, fucking drowning in them.

Lee Jung-Hwan shook his head again and pointed to his face, to the bruises and the cuts, the bandages and the stitches: I didn't come to you, you came to me. Just look at me, look what they fucking did to me!

Tell the police, the Japanese police, said Harry Sweeney. You're to be handed over to them later on today.

Why? What for?

So you can make a formal statement.

But I already have – to you!

Public Safety are not investigating this case, said Harry Sweeney. The Tokyo Metropolitan Police Department and the Public Prosecutor's Office are in charge of the investigation. Tell them what you told us, told me; they may believe you.

Like fuck they will! You know they won't . . .

I don't know that, said Harry Sweeney.

Lee Jung-Hwan banged his hands down on the top of the table: Yes, you fucking do –

I don't, said Harry Sweeney again. Ask to speak to the Second Investigative Division or to the Public Prosecutor's Office. But when you do, make sure you have some fucking proof, yeah? Some evidence to back up your story.

Lee Jung-Hwan slumped forward in his chair, his arms on the table, and whispered, What's the point . . .

Well, the point is, if you don't, said Harry Sweeney, if you don't come up with any proof, if they don't believe your story, then my bet is you'll be sent straight to Kosuge.

Lee Jung-Hwan looked up: For what? For getting beaten to within an inch of my life by the biggest gangster in Tokyo? For that I'll be sent to fucking prison?

For being an undocumented and therefore illegal alien, said Harry Sweeney. And so then to await repatriation. That is, unless you come up with any proof.

This is all a mistake, said Lee Jung-Hwan, looking across the table at Harry Sweeney, shaking his head at Harry Sweeney. This isn't what was supposed to happen . . .

Never is, said Harry Sweeney, pushing back his chair, standing up. Nothing ever is.

Wait, said Lee Jung-Hwan. What about my brother? You said you'd talk to him, said you'd let me see him . . .

I'm sorry, said Harry Sweeney.

What? What do you mean, you're sorry?

I mean, he's dead. I'm sorry.

But how? When?

It appears he drowned, said Harry Sweeney, gripping the back of the chair, pain shooting through the knuckles of his hands. Probably trying to get away from . . .

Lee Jung-Hwan slumped forward again, his arms on the table, his face in his arms, his shoulders shaking, his body trembling, groaning and sobbing, then springing back, his body and his shoulders, his arms and his face to the ceiling, screaming, No, no, no . . .

I'm sorry, said Harry Sweeney again.

Fuck, fuck, fuck. They killed him, the bastards. The fucking bastards, they killed him and they set me up.

Harry Sweeney pushed the chair under the table, turning away, saying again, I'm sorry.

Wait, said Lee Jung-Hwan. Wait . . .

But Harry Sweeney did not wait, he did not turn back. He walked toward the door and he –

Please. You've got to help me . . .

Turned the handle and –

Listen to me, please . . .

Opened the door –

Please, whispered Lee Jung-Hwan. I work for you, for Hongō House. I'm with Zed Unit.

*

Thanks, kid, said Harry Sweeney as he wound down the window in the back of the car, then sat back and closed his eyes to the strains of a sonata he just couldn't place, the car driving through the morning, driving through the city, along Avenue A, then up Avenue W, under the railroad tracks, through the crossroads at Gofukubashi and on past the Yashima Hotel, turning left by the Shirokiya department store, then over the river at Nihonbashi, past the Mitsukoshi department store, its glass and gold doors just opening, its two bronze lions sat watching, their car going on along Ginza Street, heading on through Kanda, across Manseibashi, on through Suehirochō to the Matsuzakaya department store, turning left at Hirokōji, up Avenue N, then right down a side street, up a back road, a slight slope, the car slowing down, the car pulling up, Harry Sweeney suddenly opening his eyes, suddenly barking, Too late!

Excuse me, sir, said Shin. But we're here.

Harry Sweeney wiped his mouth and chin, unstuck his shirt from his skin, and looked out of the windows of the car, saw the high walls and the tall trees, the red, English-brick walls and the dark, timeless trees, saw the gates and the sign, the closed gates and the sign which read: OFF LIMITS: STRICTLY NO ADMITTANCE.

The second movement of the sonata ending, the third movement of the sonata beginning, from scherzo to lento, Harry Sweeney smiled, looked at his watch, its face still cracked, its hands still stopped, then blinked and smiled again, opened the passenger door, and said, I'll be back in five minutes.

# II

# THE BRIDGE OF TEARS

# 5

## Minus Fifteen to Minus Eleven

---

*June 20–June 24, 1964*

*Ton-ton. Ton-ton. Ton-ton. Ton-ton . . .*

Murota Hideki twitched, jumped, and opened his eyes. His heart pounding, his breath trapped, he swallowed, he choked, he spluttered and coughed. He wiped his mouth, he wiped his chin, he blinked and blinked again, looking down at the desk, the sticky desk and brown rings, the dirty glass and half-empty bottle, looking up and around the office, the tiny office and yellow walls, the dusty shelves and empty cabinet. His desk, his office, all dirt and all dust –

*Ton-ton. Ton-ton. Ton-ton . . .*

He put his hands on his desk, pushed himself up and the chair back. He got to his feet and walked over to the window. He closed the window, closed the city, the stench from the river and fumes, the noise of construction and trains, always that stench, that noise: the stench of the past, the noise of the future; Edo stench, Olympic noise –

*Ton-ton. Ton-ton . . .*

He sat back down in his chair at his desk, his collar wet, his shirt damp. He took out his handkerchief. He wiped his neck. He tried to unstick his shirt from his vest, then to straighten his thinning hair, the smell of his clothes and his hair fighting with the stink from the sink in the corner, the trash can by the door, the ashtrays on his desk, the alcohol on his breath. That taste, that taste, always that taste. He picked up a packet of cigarettes from the desk, took out a cigarette, and lit it. He squeezed the end of his nose and sniffed, massaged his right temple with cigarette fingers and closed his eyes, the dream hanging over him still, all dirt and dust, all stench and noise, with that taste, that taste –

*Ton-ton . . .*

Trapped, stale –

He opened his eyes, stubbed out the cigarette, and then called out, Yes?

The door opened and a thin young man in a tight, gray-shiny suit stepped into the office. He gave the mess of the room the quick once-over, spent a moment too long on the empty bottles of cheap Chinese wine, did the same to Murota Hideki, then smiled and asked him, Is this Kanda Investigations?

Like it says on the door, said Murota Hideki.

And so you're Murota-san, the owner?

And sole employee. Next question?

Excuse me, said the young man, putting down his new and expensive-looking attaché case. He reached inside his jacket. He took out a silver-plated name card holder. He took out a card from the holder. He put the holder back inside his jacket. He approached the desk. He held out the name card in both hands, bowed briefly, and said, I'm Hasegawa.

Murota Hideki pulled in his stomach and got to his feet. He reached across the desk to take the card from the man. He read the name on the card, the profession, position, and company beneath. He shook his head, tried to hand the card back to the man, saying, Not interested.

The young man frowned: But you don't –

Yeah, I do know, said Murota Hideki. You're an editor. You work for a publishing house with a famous weekly magazine. But I don't talk to the press. It's bad for business.

The man gave the office the quick once-over act again, this time with a sneer: Business good, is it?

Good, bad, or gone-to-the-fucking-dogs, it's my business, not yours, said Murota Hideki, flicking the card at the man, the card falling to the floor. See, about once or twice a year, some skinny young hotshot like you shows up here, in their tight suit with their smart mouth, asking for one of two things: if I got any dirt on anyone famous to sell, or if I'll spill some sexy private-eye bullshit for the feature they're writing. Either way, each time I tell them what I'm going to tell you: you got the wrong guy, now go get lost.

The young man bent down. He picked up the card from the floor. He held it out toward Murota Hideki again, in both hands again, but this time in a longer, deeper bow as he said, Excuse me. I apologize. But thank you. Now I know you're the right man. And so I'd be very grateful if you would please just listen, at least just listen to what I have to say. Please.

Murota Hideki looked at the man standing there, with his card out and his head bowed. He rolled his eyes and sighed, then sat back down and said, Go on then, sit down.

The man looked up. He thanked Murota Hideki. Then, with the card still in his hands, he sat down, smiled, and asked, Do you by any chance remember the name Kuroda Roman?

Murota Hideki nodded: A writer, yeah?

I'm impressed, said the young man. You read a lot?

Murota Hideki shook his head: Just the papers.

Then you must have a good memory.

Unfortunately, smiled Murota Hideki. But that was what they call a good guess, you being in publishing.

So you don't remember Kuroda Roman then? You've never read any of his books then?

Nope. Sorry.

Don't be, said the man. Few people have these days. He was briefly popular during Taishō, then there was a period of mental illness and silence. He published nothing more before or during the war; a couple of translations maybe, that was all. But then he did have a few books published *après-guerre*, as they used to say. Mysteries, true crime, that kind of thing. I thought, in your line of work, there was a chance you . . .

Be the last thing I'd read, said Murota Hideki.

Really, said the young man, staring at Murota Hideki, smiling at Murota Hideki. But you were a policeman, right? During the war, after the war? I'd heard cops liked reading true-crime books? Just thought you might've read –

Murota Hideki held the man's stare, ignored his smile, swallowed, and said, Who told you that?

Told me what?

That I was a policeman?

Well, he did.

Who?

Kuroda Roman, said the man, looking away now, but still smiling. Well, not in person, in one of his books. You're in one of his books, you see. *Tokyo Bluebeard: Lust of a Demon*. It's the one about –

I can imagine what it's about, said Murota Hideki.

But you've not read it, said the young man, nodding to himself. Well, you've not missed anything, it's not that good. And you're only mentioned very briefly. About how –

I was dismissed, said Murota Hideki.

For improper conduct, yeah.

For fucking a *pan-pan* gal on my beat, said Murota Hideki, still staring across his desk at this man, this thin young man, in his tight, gray-shiny suit.

Yes, said the man.

Murota Hideki picked up the packet of cigarettes from his desk again, took out a cigarette, and lit it. He inhaled, then exhaled, blowing the smoke across the desk at the man, saying, It's no secret. It was in some of the papers, or a version of it.

Nearly twenty years ago now. So that's my story. Now you going to tell me yours, Mister Editor, tell me why you're sitting here? Or you going to keep on sitting there, wasting my time?

Excuse me. I apologize, said the young man again. That came across very badly. I just wanted to say, I know you're an ex-policeman. And I know you lost your job, but that it was a long time ago now. But I also know that you know how to keep a confidence. You don't betray people.

Murota Hideki said nothing. He glanced at his watch, his watch running slow again, losing time again.

The man coughed, cleared his throat, then said, Sorry, I'll get to the point: Kuroda Roman has disappeared. He's gone missing. And we'd like you to find him.

"We" being who exactly?

Our publishing house.

Why, asked Murota Hideki. You said yourself, no one's heard of this guy or reads his books these days.

Unusually, said the young man, lowering his voice, and somewhat foolishly, one of my predecessors advanced a number of quite substantial payments to Kuroda. Understandably, the owners of our publishing house are very keen to recoup the money. Or the manuscript.

Murota Hideki stubbed out his cigarette, looked up at the man, shook his head, and said again, Not interested.

Why, asked the man, frowning again.

Pre-marital background checks, divorce cases, some insurance, that's what I do, said Murota Hideki. Nothing heavy, no debt-collecting, that's not what I do.

No, no, no, said the young man. That's not what we want you to do. We just want you to find him, that's all.

Murota Hideki shook his head again: But you're not bothered about him, not concerned for the man's welfare, right? You just want your money back, yeah?

Yes, said the man. But you don't have to do that part; our lawyers will handle all that.

If you can find him.

If *you* can find him, said the young man, smiling again. That's why I'm sitting here, wasting your time.

Murota Hideki stared at the man, not smiling, saying, Just because I'm mentioned in one of his fucking books? That's why you're sitting here asking me?

Not only that, said the man, still smiling. Actually, that was my idea, asking you. See, I thought you might've met the man, met Kuroda Roman, back then, before.

Still staring, not smiling, Murota Hideki shook his head, But I didn't. Never met the man, even heard of him.

Doesn't matter, said the young man, reaching down to pick up his attaché case. Might have been a bonus, might have helped, but it's not important. What *is* important is that I'm sure *you* are the right man to find him.

Murota Hideki reached for another cigarette from his packet and lit it: What about the police, they know he's missing? Any family, friends reported him missing?

No, said the man, opening his case.

Murota Hideki inhaled, exhaled, then smiled and said, Popular guy, this writer of yours, yeah?

Used to be. Briefly.

When did you last see him?

Me, said the man. I've never seen him, never met him.

Murota Hideki inhaled again, exhaled again, then sighed and said, Great. So how long's he been missing . . . ?

About six months, we think . . .

You *think*?

We're not sure, said the young man, taking out a large brown envelope from his attaché case.

Look, Mister, er, Hasegawa?

Yes, said the young man.

This isn't one of your mystery novels, this ain't the movies. It's a big city, getting bigger by the day, in a big, big country. Believe me, this is a big place to get lost in, and six months a long time to be lost for, 'specially if a man don't want to be found. See, my guess is your man isn't missing, your man isn't lost; he just don't want to be found.

Mister Murota, said the man, the case on his lap, the envelope in his hands, I know this isn't a novel, I know this *ain't* the movies. But we need to find this man, we want our money back, and we want both done quickly. Now if you don't want the job, we'll engage someone else.

Murota Hideki stubbed out his cigarette: I didn't say that. But it would be negligent of me if I didn't warn you of the difficulty in finding missing persons.

I appreciate your honesty, said the young man. But we're well aware of the difficulty involved in finding him.

Murota Hideki stared at the man again, smiling at the man now: You aware of the expense involved, too?

Yes, said the man, nodding. And we're prepared to pay whatever it takes, pay whatever you ask.

Still smiling, Murota Hideki said, Well, I take my pay in US dollars. Fifty of them a day, plus expenses.

Expenses in yen, asked the young man.

Murota Hideki nodded: All in cash.

Of course, said the man. But you should also be aware that there will be a substantial bonus if this matter can be resolved by midnight on the Fourth of July.

How substantial?

Five thousand US dollars, said the young man. Cash.

Murota Hideki stared across his desk at this man again, this young man, this man who said his name was Hasegawa, and he whistled, then said, You really want him found.

Our owners do, said the man. Yes.

Murota Hideki glanced at the calendar on his desk, then looked back up at the young man: Why the rush?

The contract for the manuscript, for which the advances were made, expires at midnight on the Fourth of July.

Murota Hideki glanced at the calendar again, then looked back up again: And if it's not *resolved* by then?

Then we'd no longer require your services.

Murota Hideki nodded, then nodded again, then said, Of course, there is one other possibility, one I'm sure your owners must have considered: he may be dead.

Of course, said the young man. But dead or alive, the monies still need to be repaid, either by the man himself or from his estate if, in fact, he is deceased. So if you do find proof he's dead, you'll still receive your bonus.

Before the Fourth of July?

Before midnight on the Fourth of July, yes.

Murota Hideki glanced at the calendar again, reached for his notebook and pen, opened his notebook, looked up at the young man, and said, Okay, first I'll need some basic –

I do apologize, said the man. But we've been dancing for rather longer than I imagined, and I have another –

It was you who asked me to dance . . .

And I do apologize, said the young man again, placing the large brown envelope down on the desk in front of Murota Hideki. Then, reaching back into his attaché case, he took out another envelope, opened up this envelope, and began to count out two hundred and fifty US dollars in various denominations. He placed the notes down in a pile on the desk next to the large brown envelope, then began to count out eighteen thousand yen, again in various denominations, again putting the notes down in a pile on the desk in front of Murota Hideki, as he said, In that envelope you will find all the pertinent information we have about Kuroda Roman. The money I am giving you is for five days' work, plus some yen on account for expenses.

Murota Hideki nodded and said, Thanks.

You're welcome, said the man. I'll call again in five days, at ten o'clock on Thursday, the twenty-fifth, to see how you're progressing and to give you more money.

Murota Hideki nodded again: Thanks.

The young man smiled, reached inside his attaché case again, and took out a typewritten document. He placed it on the desk, on top of the envelope and the money, in front of Murota Hideki and said, I'd be grateful if you'd just write your name and address in the space provided and then add your seal. Just to acknowledge receipt of the money. I'll bring a copy for you when I come again on Thursday.

Murota Hideki filled in the form with his name and address, then took out his *hanko* from the top drawer of the desk and did as he was told.

Thank you, said the man, taking the piece of paper from Murota Hideki. He put it inside his attaché case, then closed and locked the case, smiled, and said, Until Thursday.

Murota Hideki did not get up, he just smiled back and nodded, then watched the young man in his tight, gray-shiny suit walk toward the door, watched him open the door, then turn back in the doorway to bow and to thank him –

One last thing, said Murota Hideki.

Yes, said the man, glancing down at his left wrist, at the cuffs of his jacket and shirt, the face of his watch. Yes?

This manuscript? This manuscript you say one of your predecessors *foolishly* advanced so much money for . . .

Yes, said the young man again.

What's it about?

The Shimoyama Case, I think it was, said the man, sighing, then saying, I'm sure you must remember . . .

Yes, said Murota Hideki. I remember.

But to be honest with you, said the man, no one believes he's actually written it, least not finished it. And that suits us just fine. We'd rather have our money back.

I see, said Murota Hideki, nodding, watching the young man bow again, thank him again, then turn again and step out of the office, closing the door behind him –

And then the man was gone –

The man was gone, and Murota Hideki was on his feet, out from behind his desk and to the door, and by the door, his ear to the glass of the door, Murota Hideki was listening: the man walking away, down the corridor, down the stairs.

Murota Hideki opened the door. He went down the corridor, to the end of the corridor, the stairs to his left, the toilet to his right. He went into the toilet, past the basin, past the stall, past the urinal to the window. The window already open, always open, Murota Hideki opened it wider, peering out, staring down, down to the street –

Down at the guy –

The guy who called himself Hasegawa, the guy walking out of the building toward an old gray car parked out front, possibly a Toyopet Master, but definitely not a taxi. The guy opened the rear passenger door, but he didn't get in. He just leaned in, leaned in for a minute, two minutes. Then he closed the door and the car pulled away, past the shrine and under the tracks. The guy who called himself Hasegawa watched it go, taking out a packet of cigarettes, lighting a cigarette, then the guy crossed the road, toward the tracks, and headed south, toward the station, just the cigarette in his fingers, no attaché case in his hand, the guy disappearing, out of sight.

Liar, muttered Murota Hideki as he pulled his head in, turning to the urinal. He undid his flies and he took a piss. He did up his flies, then turned to the basin. He ran the faucet, he cupped the water. He washed his face, he washed his neck. He caught a glimpse of himself in the grime, in the grime of the mirror above the basin: fifty-two, balding, fat, and gone-to-shit. He smiled and said, Not gone-to-shit, always shit.

He turned off the faucet, dried his hands on his trousers, taking out his handkerchief, finding a crumpled pack of cigarettes. He wiped and dried his face, put his handkerchief back in his pocket, took out the crumpled pack of cigarettes, one last, bent cigarette. He put the cigarette between his lips, crushed the empty pack of cigarettes in his hand, tossed it in the wire basket underneath the basin, then patted himself down: front trouser pockets, back trouser pockets, shirt pocket – nothing. He glanced back up at himself in the grime, the bent, unlit cigarette between his lips. He smiled again, took the cigarette from his lips, and said, Fucking liar.

He said goodbye to the mirror, bye to the toilet, and he went back down the corridor, back into the office, back to his desk and his chair. He lifted up the money, he lifted up the envelope. He moved his notebook, he moved his pen. He looked under the calendar, looked under the ashtrays. He sifted through all the other pens and pencils, all the scraps of paper and other bits of shit on his desk. He opened the top drawer of his desk, rummaged through the drawer, picked up a bunch of name cards, flicked through the name cards one by one, shaking his head. He stuck the name cards back in the drawer and closed the drawer. He pushed back his chair, looked under his chair, looked under his desk. He stood up again, walked around his desk, and looked under the other chair, on the other side of the desk, looking on the floor, picking up magazines, picking up newspapers, putting them back down again, down on the floor again, over the dirt and over the stains, saying, Dumb, dumb, dumb.

He shook his head again, cursed himself again, then walked over to the shelves. He picked up the phone book. He carried it back to his desk. He sat down and opened the directory. He turned the pages, found the name of the publishing house, the number for the publishing house. He picked up the handset of the phone on his desk, stuck his finger in the first hole, and began to dial the number. He heard the ringing down the line, heard a girl on the switchboard give the name of the publishing house, then he said, Hasegawa-san, please. Not sure which section he's in these days, sorry.

And who shall I say is calling, asked the girl.

Murota Hideki said, It's Murota.

Thank you, said the girl. Please hold –

And Murota Hideki held, cradling the handset between his ear and his shoulder, putting the bent cigarette back between his lips, reaching for his lighter –

I'm sorry, said the girl, Hasegawa-kachō is not at his desk, maybe not in the office today. But if you'd like to leave your number, then I'll be sure to pass it on.

It's okay, thanks. I'll try again on Monday, said Murota Hideki, and he put down the handset. He lit the cigarette, inhaled, then exhaled, blowing the smoke across the desk, over the money. He stared down at the money, then picked up the dollars. He counted the notes once, then once again, one by one, holding the dollars up, up to the light, the light from the window, the light from the river. Then he put them back down on the desk, stubbed out the cigarette, then reached down and opened the bottom drawer of the desk. He took out an envelope and put the dollars inside the envelope. He sealed the envelope, dropped it in the bottom drawer, and closed the drawer. He picked up the yen from the top of his desk and counted out the notes. Then he reached behind himself, taking out his wallet from his jacket on the back of his chair, opened up his wallet, and put most of the yen inside. He put the wallet back in his jacket pocket, then folded the rest of the notes in half and stuck them in his trouser pocket. He took another cigarette from the packet on his desk, lit the cigarette, and stared down at the large brown envelope on top of his desk, a long morning shadow falling across the large brown envelope, the long morning shadow of a half-full bottle of cheap Chinese wine. He looked at the half-full bottle of cheap Chinese wine standing on his desk in the light from the window, the light from the river, and he smiled to himself, he nodded to himself, and then he said to himself, Well, why not?

Murota Hideki reached over to the bottle, picked it up, and unscrewed its top. He held it over the glass, the empty glass, then tilted the bottle and filled the glass. He put down the bottle and picked up the glass. He held the glass up to the light, the light from the window, the light from the river, and he looked at the wine, the golden-brown wine, smiled at the wine, the golden-brown wine, then he put the glass to his lips and put the wine to his lips, tilting the glass, sipping the wine, the wine on his lips, in his mouth, down his throat, golden brown and mellow, down it went, down it went, then filling the glass again and tilting the glass again, sipping the wine, drinking the wine, the golden-brown and mellow wine, the room, this office golden brown and mellow, the world, this life golden brown and mellow, drinking and smoking and saying to himself, saying to her, Well, he may or may not be who he says he is, be who he claims to be, but his money, his dollars are real enough, real enough for you and me, for me and you to celebrate, my Nori-chan, yeah, we'll celebrate tonight, my Nori-chan . . .

And then smiling to himself, laughing at himself, Murota Hideki put the empty glass down beside the empty bottle and picked up the large brown envelope from the top of his desk. He opened the envelope, stuck his hand inside, and pulled out the papers, a thick, fat sheaf of them. He shifted the papers from hand to hand, turning through the pages, the densely packed, typewritten pages, with all of their characters and numbers, all their dates and their names, histories, and biographies, lists of book titles and photostats of articles, shifting and turning them from hand to hand, back and forth, one by one, from hand to hand, all these papers, these pages, back and forth, all their characters, their numbers, one by one, the past of a man, the ghost of a man, from hand to hand, all the pasts and ghosts of this man, this man, Kuroda Roman –

Fuck, you must be in here somewhere, said Murota Hideki, throwing down the thick, fat sheaf of papers back onto the top of his desk, screwing up his eyes, massaging both temples, then opening his eyes, looking back down at the papers, shaking his head, saying, But where are you?

Murota Hideki twitched again, jumped again, and opened his eyes. His heart pounding again, his breath trapped again, he spluttered and coughed, then reached for the phone, picked up the handset, and said, Hello, hello . . . Noriko?

He heard a coin drop, the sound of a station, then a voice saying, Murota-san? It's Nemuro. I'm at Kanda station. If you've got any news for me, I can stop by your office.

Yeah, said Murota Hideki, wiping his mouth, wiping his chin. But let's meet at the shrine next door.

When, asked Nemuro. Now . . . ?

Ten minutes, said Murota Hideki, and he hung up. He rubbed his eyes, rubbed, then slapped his cheeks, and sighed. He leaned forward, looked down at his notebook lying open on his desk, scanned the brief notes he'd made on Kuroda Roman; he'd left all the literary bullshit for the critics, just tried to find the man, the facts of his life – dates and places, family and friends, places of interest, people of interest – some flesh for the facts, some skin for that flesh. He closed the notebook over the pen, then picked up the Kuroda Roman papers and stuffed them back inside their large brown envelope. He reached down and opened the bottom drawer of his desk, dropped the large brown envelope on top of the envelope of dollars, then closed the drawer. He stood up, took his jacket off the back of his chair, and put it on. He picked up the notebook and his cigarettes, put them into different pockets of his jacket, and walked over to the door. He opened the door, stepped into the corridor, turned back, took his keys from his trouser pocket, and locked the door. He went down the corridor and into the toilet. He undid his flies and took a piss in the urinal. He did up his flies as he walked over to the basin. He ran the faucet, he cupped the water. He washed his face, he washed his neck. He cupped more water, rinsed his mouth, and spat. He turned off the faucet, dried his hands on his jacket, took out his handkerchief, and wiped and dried his face. He looked at himself in the grime of the mirror, smoothing his hair with his hand, sighing to himself, *Shikata nai* . . . It's who you are . . . It's what you do . . .

He turned away from the mirror, went out of the toilet, down the stairs, out through the lobby and onto the street. In the sticky, gray Saturday afternoon – the sort of Saturday afternoon, he said to himself, that makes you wish you were dead, muttering, wonder if you aren't already – turning right he walked along the street, then right again, under the stone *torii* and down the steps he went, into the shrine, the Yanagimori shrine.

Nemuro Hiroshi was already there. Aged and thin with worry and fear, he was standing with his head bowed in front of one of the smaller shrines. He finished his prayer, bowed deeply, then turned and saw Murota Hideki.

Murota Hideki nodded, then walked toward the two stone benches beneath the wooden *kagura* stage. He sat down on the edge of one, and Nemuro Hiroshi sat down on the edge of the other, their backs to the tall wooden stage which towered behind them, over them. There was a space of less than a meter between them, between the edges of the two stone benches, between the two men; no one else in the grounds of the shrine, just the occasional sound of the passing traffic on Yanagihara-dōri, above them to their right, the more regular sound of the trains going over the bridge behind them, over them, the stage, and the shrine, white gulls falling from the somber sky into the Kanda River to their left, the cats of the shrine sleepwalking here and there, here and there through the sultry afternoon air.

So then, asked Nemuro Hiroshi.

I'm sorry, said Murota Hideki, leaning forward, bending down to stroke one of the cats, which was moving between his calves, rubbing itself against his trouser legs. Three, four times he ran his hand down the length of the back of the cat, the cat quivering, the cat purring, then he glanced up at Nemuro Hiroshi, the man chewing the insides of his mouth, his hands gripping his knees, rocking back and forward ever so slightly on the bench. Murota Hideki stopped stroking the cat, sat up straight again on the bench, listening to the trains passing over the bridge behind them, watching the gulls rising and falling over them, and he waited –

He waited for Nemuro Hiroshi to ask, to ask as they always did, ask for the details, details they never needed to know, that would do them no good, no good at all, but which they thought they needed to know, they always wanted to know, always insisting, Please. Tell me, I want to know . . .

And so, as he always did, Murota Hideki took out his notebook, turned back through the pages, then reading from his notes he told him the time she had left their apartment complex, the streetcar she had taken, the department store she had waited outside, the time the man had finally arrived –

She waited so long for him, said Nemuro Hiroshi.

And as he always did, Murota Hideki neither agreed nor disagreed, he just kept on reading from his notes: the name of the cinema, how long they had spent inside the theater –

What was the movie, asked Nemuro Hiroshi.

Murota Hideki said, *Hakujitsumu.*

Enjoy it, did you, snorted Nemuro Hiroshi.

Murota Hideki shook his head and said, Not really, I was in and out. I went for a coffee.

And so then, said Nemuro Hiroshi, after they'd spent the afternoon watching pornography, I suppose they . . .

Murota Hideki nodded and said, Yes.

Where, asked Nemuro Hiroshi.

An inn in the Yoyogi area.

For how long?

They said goodbye outside the inn at five o'clock, so they were there less than two hours.

Less than two hours, laughed Nemuro Hiroshi. So she could still be back home to prepare my dinner, to greet me in the *genkan*, telling me she had run me a bath, urging me to relax in that bath, then to pour me a beer and serve my meal, asking after my day, hoping it hadn't been too stressful, while lying about her own day, her uneventful day, yet stinking of him, dreaming of him, talking in her sleep, moaning in her sleep.

I'm sorry, said Murota Hideki again, as he always did, closing his notebook, as he always did, waiting for the next question, as he always did, the question they always asked, sometimes sooner, sometimes later, but which they always asked, sooner or later, they always ask –

Who is he?

I can't tell you that, said Murota Hideki, as he always did, as he always had, since that one time he did say, the one and only time he had said.

Nemuro Hiroshi turned to look at Murota Hideki, the worry and fear all bled from him, drained from him, replaced by that predictable, corrosive cocktail of humiliation and anger: Can't say or won't say?

Won't say.

So you do know?

Yes, said Murota Hideki. But you don't need to.

Why not?

Because it'll do you no good.

He half said, half shouted, That's for me to decide.

No, said Murota Hideki, as calmly and as gently as he possibly could. That's for me to decide, and I've decided you don't need to know. Please, trust me, you really don't.

He was almost out of his seat, almost off the bench, almost touching Murota Hideki: So it *is* someone I know.

No, said Murota Hideki again, as calmly and as gently as he possibly could again. It's no one you know.

So just tell me then, said Nemuro Hiroshi, reaching inside his jacket, taking out his wallet. I'll pay you more –

Murota Hideki slowly raised his hand, slowly moved the wallet out of his face, and said, It's not about money, it's about you, Mister Nemuro, about what you might go and do if I was dumb enough to tell you the name of this man.

What do you mean?

I mean, you might decide to go visit this man, might then do something which wouldn't help you and which wouldn't help me, me being the person who'd been dumb enough to tell you the name of this man. That's what I mean.

I see, said Nemuro Hiroshi. I see.

Murota Hideki nodded: Good.

Yes, I see, said Nemuro Hiroshi, turning to Murota Hideki again, looking up into his face, turning on Murota Hideki now, as they often did, so many did, looking into his eyes and spitting, See, it's not about me, is it? It's about you, Murota, about you protecting yourself, isn't it? Well, what about me? How do I protect myself, Murota-san, protect myself, my wife, and my marriage from this man? This man I don't know, but my wife knows, yes, she knows, and you know, yeah, you know. Yeah, you know, you know so much, so you tell me what I should do. Go on, go on, you tell this cuckold what the hell he should do then.

Murota Hideki rubbed his eyes, his cheeks, his face, then sighed: You finished?

Nemuro Hiroshi looked away, down at his shoes, down at the gravel, the cat looking up at him, watching him.

Murota Hideki leaned forward, put his hand as gently and as softly as he could on the leg of this angry, broken man beside him, and said, Look, like I told you the first time we spoke, when a man or a woman thinks their spouse is cheating on them, ninety-nine percent of the time they're usually right. But most of the time it's a short-term thing; five minutes of fireworks, then finished forever.

Most of the time, said Nemuro Hiroshi, squeezing his wallet in his fist, staring at the cat. But not all of the time.

Not all of the time, no. But this time, yes.

How can you know that, said Nemuro Hiroshi, turning to look at Murota Hideki again, to search his face, his eyes for deception, for a lie. How can you be certain?

Murota Hideki shrugged, then said, I'm never going to tell you his name, but I will tell you this: he has a good job, a nice place, just like you, but he has a pregnant wife and one young son. He ain't going to be giving up all that, not for your wife.

So I just sit it out, asked Nemuro Hiroshi. Wait for the fireworks to finish, that what you're saying?

Murota Hideki nodded again: If you're not going to divorce her, if you still love her, and you obviously do, then yeah. Makes you feel any better, maybe go even things out.

Even things out? What do you mean?

Murota Hideki glanced at his watch, his watch running slow. Maybe go get yourself a *turko*. But if you're going, you'd best go quick. They're clamping down, with the Olympics –

Hardly the same, is it, snorted Nemuro Hiroshi. Paying for it, paying some old fucking whore . . .

It was beginning to spit, to rain on Murota Hideki, his stomach starting to rumble, to growl. He stood up and said, Wise up, will you? He's paying for it, you're already paying for it. We're always paying for it.

Murota Hideki started to walk away, away up the steps and out of the shrine, away from this man, this pathetic, shameless little man, his big fucking voice –

That what you'd do, is it, Murota? Your wife was cheating on you, fucking another man? You'd go get a *turko*, that's what you'd do, is it? Is it . . . ?

Murota Hideki stopped, turned back, back down the steps, back into the shrine, back to the man, walked back to the man, and looked down at the man, this pathetic, shameless little man looking up at Murota Hideki, this pathetic, shameless little man with a smirk, a sneer on his pathetic, shameless little face, and Murota Hideki said, he said, My wife is dead.

Nemuro Hiroshi did not look away. He did not even blink. He just kept on looking up at Murota Hideki, looking up at him, staring up at him, tears welling in his eyes, blinking then, blinking now, tears rolling down his cheeks as he said, Please, I just don't want to lose her . . .

Murota Hideki did not tell him she was already lost, she was already gone, didn't tell him that he didn't blame her, didn't blame her one bit. Murota Hideki just stood there, looking down on him, stood there and lied to him: You won't.

But you can make sure, can't you, said the man, wiping his eyes, wiping his cheeks, opening up his wallet, taking out three ten-thousand-yen notes. He held the notes up to Murota Hideki, held the notes out to Murota Hideki, raindrops falling on the notes, falling on his hand, down on the man and down on Murota Hideki, on the shrine and on the city –

*Old city, new city, same city –*
I want you to make sure.

It was still raining and he was still hungry, so he walked quickly, following the tracks, sheltered by the tracks, down to Yasukuni-dōri, then under the tracks and along Yasukuni-dōri, over the crossroads and the streetcar tracks, through Kanda-Sudachō and Ogawamachi, along Yasukuni-dōri and into Jimbōchō. Still raining, still hungry, very wet and very hungry, he went from bookshop to bookshop, used-bookshop to used-bookshop, from stack to stack, from shelf to shelf, until off Yasukuni-dōri, down a side street, up an alley, in a bookshop called Gen'ei-dō, in a stack by the door, he found the book he was looking for. He took the book and two other books from the stack by the door, then walked to the back of the store, put the three books down on the counter, and said, How much?

The old man behind the counter looked up from the book he was reading, pushed his glasses back up his nose, then looked back down at the three pocket-sized paperbacks on the counter, picking up *Tokyo Bluebeard: Lust of a Demon*, then *Teigin Monogatari: Winter of the Demon*, then *Whereabouts Unknown*, opening up each book, turning to the back page of each book, reading the price on the back page of each book, the prices scribbled in pencil at the back of each book. The old man looked up from the books, pushed his glasses back up his nose again, then smiled and said, Ninety yen, please.

Here you go, said Murota Hideki, handing over the exact amount, smiling at the old man.

The old man reached down behind the counter, taking out a paper bag, putting the books inside the bag, and said, Is there some kind of Kuroda Roman revival going on?

What do you mean, asked Murota Hideki.

Well, you're the second person this month buying his books, said the old man, handing the bag to Murota Hideki.

Murota Hideki smiled again and said, Let me guess: it was a skinny young guy in a flashy new suit.

Hard luck, Holmes-san, laughed the old man, shaking his head. It was a foreigner.

You're joking?

Nope, said the old man, shaking his head again, pushing his glasses back up his nose again. I was surprised.

Murota Hideki glanced around the cramped and tiny store, lined and piled back to front, top to bottom with shelves and shelves, stacks and stacks of books and books, and asked, You get a lot of foreigners in here, do you?

We used to, said the old man. After the war, during the Occupation. But not these days, not yet.

Murota Hideki smiled again and asked, Not yet?

The Olympics, said the old man, nodding to himself. You never know . . .

You're right, said Murota Hideki, nodding himself, turning to go. You never know.

Just hope they're all wanting Kuroda Roman books, laughed the old man. We got a box of them upstairs.

The bag of books tucked under his left arm, Murota Hideki opened the door, saying, Popular guy.

Briefly, a long time ago now.

So they tell me, said Murota Hideki, stepping out of the shop, closing the door behind him, walking back down the alley, back through the rain.

He went down the side street, along and up another, then found himself on Suzuran-dōri. He crossed the road, went inside the Yangtze restaurant, picked up a newspaper from the rack by the door, then sat down at a table at the back. He ordered a bowl of cold Chinese noodles, a plate of fried rice, six gyōza dumplings, a glass of beer, and a half-bottle of Chinese wine. He ate the gyōza and drank the beer, reading the evening paper, reading about the capture of the Hokkaidō Cabbie Killer, of the *Zengakuren* and their demonstrations, of Sawako Ariyoshi and her divorce, skipping yet more Olympic crap about another new highway here, another new trainline there. Then, when he'd finished the gyōza and the beer, when he'd finished with the evening paper, he folded the paper back up, stood up, walked over to put it back in the rack, then returned to his table, and sat back down. He took out his packet of cigarettes and lit one, then he picked up the paper bag and took out one of the three pocket-sized books, the tatty, worn copy of *Tokyo Bluebeard: Lust of a Demon.* He ate the fried rice, drank the Chinese wine, smoking more cigarettes, ordering more wine, another half-bottle, as he flicked through the pages, scanned the paragraphs, searching for his name, until he found his name, and then he began to read the page, the paragraph beginning: *Murota Hideki is originally from Yamanashi Prefecture. But after he was fired from the police for his inappropriate behavior, after he was left without a job, Murota Hideki did not go back to his family's home in Yamanashi. Murota Hideki stayed on in Tokyo. And so Murota Hideki still lives in an old wooden row house in Kitazawa, not far from the Shimo-Kitazawa station, the same old wooden row house that Detective Nishi found listed as his address in his personal records, the same old wooden row house . . .*

Lighting another cigarette, drinking another glass, reading ahead now, scanning ahead now, through all of the names, all of these ghosts – *Detectives Nishi and Minami, Inspectors Mori and Adachi, the girls, the murdered girls, Abe Yoshiko and Midorikawa Ryuko, and the killer, their killer, Kodaira Yoshio* – through all of these names, all of these ghosts, searching for her, looking for her, until he found her, there on the page, until he saw her, in black and white, he saw her again *step out of the shadows and through the shabby curtain, dressed in a yellow and dark-blue striped pinafore dress*, he saw her again and he heard her, heard her again, saying again, *I won't pretend to be dead. I'm not a ghost.*

*But they'll come for you again . . .*

Murota Hideki twitched, he jerked, then peeled his cheek, his ear, and hair off the paper bag of paperbacks. He sat up in the chair, opened his eyes, and rubbed his cheek, his eyes, then both his cheeks, he rubbed them hard, then slapped them hard. He looked down at the desk, the bag of books on the desk, the handset lying next to the bag, droning on the desk, on the top of his desk. He picked up the handset, held it up to his ear and he heard the drone, the drone of the missing, the missing and the dead. He swallowed, he blinked, sniffed up, and said, Now, now, no, no. Don't be starting with them waterfalls again. He shook his head, he shook his head, blinked and swallowed and sniffed again, then placed the handset back down on the phone, down in its cradle, back in its bed. He pulled himself up out of the chair, and round the desk he went. He picked up his shirt and jacket from the floor, his creased shirt and damp jacket, and put them on. He checked the pockets of his jacket, patting his notebook then his wallet, and he smiled to himself and said to himself, Could be worse, things could always be worse. He walked over to the window, over to the light, pushed open the window just a bit, the morning just a crack –

*Ton-ton, ton-ton. Ka-chunk, ka-chunk . . .*

Even on a Sunday, he said to himself, walking to the door and out of the office. He closed and locked the door, then walked along the corridor and down the stairs, the four flights of stairs. In the narrow entrance, he checked his metal mailbox in the wall of metal mailboxes. He sifted through the advertising sheets and utility bills, stuffed them all back inside the mailbox, and slammed its metal shut again. Then he went out of the building, down the steps and onto the street, into the morning, the cast-over morning, noisy and dull –

*Ka-chunk, ka-chunk, don-don . . .*

But he did not go right, past the shrine and under the tracks. He did not go to Manseibashi to take a streetcar, did not go to Kanda to take a train. He went east to the corner and then turned north, over the Izumibashi Bridge, over the Kanda River, the river darker than ever, its Edo stench worse than ever. North through Akihabara he went, north into Okachimachi, through the crowds and through the noise, the pachinko crowds and the Olympic noise, even on a Sunday, a country mining for gold: pachinko gold vs. Olympic gold –

*Don-don, ka-chunk . . .*

He skirted Ueno, avoided Ueno – the movie and the zoo crowds, the park and exhibition crowds – down the side streets, the backstreets he went, through Shitaya and on through Inari-chō, but north, still north, crossing over Shōwa-dōri, passing through Sakamoto-chō, the city getting darker, wooden and more green, the city growing quieter, hushed and more muted, until he was walking under Uguisudani, coming to a place of shadows, he was coming to a place of silence, coming closer and closer, the shadows and the silence –

*They'll come for you again . . .*

Until he had come to the place of shadows, the place of silence, he was in the place of shadows, the place of silence; Murota Hideki was in Negishi.

He took out his handkerchief and wiped his neck, pulled his jacket from his shirt, his shirt from his vest, his vest from his skin, then wiped his neck again. He put away his handkerchief and took out his notebook. He opened the notebook and turned through the pages until he came to the address. He repeated it out loud twice to himself. He closed the notebook, put it back inside his jacket, and walked along the main road, Kototoi-dōri, looking for a map board, a guide to this quarter. In front of a temple, he found a map board, a faded, ink-drawn plan laid out on a battered old wooden board, the tiny handwritten numbers of the addresses etched inside little black squares in a labyrinth of hundreds of little black squares on the decrepit, rotting board. He found the address, the little black square he was looking for, and he took out his notebook again, and his pen this time, and he made a rough sketch of the area around the address, the little black square he was searching for. The notebook still open in his hand, he set off down the main road again, then turned right off Kototoi-dōri into a side road, more of a lane than a road. He went down the lane, dark and narrow, into a maze of lanes, the scent of incense in the shadows, a sense of mourning in the silence, somber and meandering, among temples of moldering tombstones, past houses with weed-grown gardens, isolated and secluded, deeper and deeper he went, into the maze, its labyrinth of lanes, sullen and winding, until he stopped, stopped before a house even more isolated than all of the others, and he stood, stood before this house more secluded than the rest, in the middle of the maze, at the heart of this labyrinth, for he had found, found the house of Kuroda Roman, hidden and hiding.

In this place protected by shadow, guarded in silence, this place of retreat, retreat and exile, he stared at a low wall, masked by shrubs, buried by weeds, at the bamboo fence which rose up, out from behind the wall, the shrubs and the weeds, the fence which screened the garden and house behind its bamboo, shielded whatever, whoever within from the lane and the world, the eyes of the world, the eyes of Murota Hideki. He put his notebook back inside his jacket, took out his handkerchief, and wiped his neck, then stepped closer to the fence, trying to look through the fence, to peek between bits of broken bamboo, splintered and fallen, through gourds and vines, between plants and trunks, thickets and copses of pomegranate and myrtle, plum and pine, gazing into this garden, through its tones and shades, trying to see where the house should be, to glimpse its silhouette in this garden of shadows, this garden of silence, peering, then squinting through its shifting tones, its shifting shades, pale then gray, dim then dark, where lizards darted and centipedes crawled, in the shadows, in the silence, the silence through which mosquitoes now rang, ringing in his ears, piercing his skin, finding the blood in his vessels, sucking the blood from his neck, his ear, his cheek, his –

Shit, he said, stepping back from the fence and the wall, out of the shrubs and the weeds, into the dirt of the lane, flapping his handkerchief around his face, rubbing the bites, checking for blood, and cursing again, Fucking mosquitoes.

He put away his handkerchief, took out his notebook and pen again, and began to walk the length of the fence to map the boundary of the place, taking five steps, six steps, seven, then turning a corner, still following the low wall and bamboo fence, sketching the border, tracing its outline, until he came to a gap in the wall, a space in the fence, the gap filled with taller shrubs, the space thick with giant weeds, the shrubs and the weeds hiding a gate, the gate to the house. He stepped into the shrubs and the weeds, waded through their stems and stalks, parting and pulling at the shrubs and the weeds, their stems and their stalks, two steps, three steps, four, until he reached the gate, could touch the gate. The gate was made of wood, of old, thick wood, higher than his head, taller than a man, covered with a roof, a roof of thatch and twigs. Under this roof, its sloping eaves, among the shrubs and the weeds, through their stems and their stalks, their flowers and their leaves, he fumbled blindly at the wood, the wood of the gate, groped for a handle, a handle to the gate. But there was no handle, no handle to the gate. He cursed and pushed at the wood of the gate, but there was no give, no give in the wood, no give in the gate. He cursed again and pushed again, then made a fist and knocked on the wood of the gate, then knocked again, he knocked and knocked again, and cursed and cursed again –

Fuck was the point of this, he said, stepping back through the shrubs and the weeds, back into the lane, its shadows and its silence. He put away his notebook and pen again, took out his handkerchief again, waving away the mosquitoes again, wiping the sweat from his neck again as he looked at the gate, shaking his head as he stared at the gate, cursing the gate and cursing himself, Dumb, dumb, dumb.

He coughed and spat in the dirt of the lane, then turned and walked back around the corner, back along the fence, turning at another corner, down another lane, walking past another low wall, another bamboo fence, both tended and weeded, the sound of birdsong from within, a whistle within, the whistle of a man whistling to the birds. Murota Hideki stopped, stopped before the gate to this house, this gate, this house not hidden, not hiding. He slid open the gate, stepped over its threshold, and said, I'm sorry, excuse me . . .

Yes, said an old, bald man, dressed in a summer kimono, standing on the veranda of his house, four or five birdcages hanging from its eaves.

Murota Hideki took two or three steps up the large stones of the garden path, saying again, Excuse me, I'm very sorry to disturb you, but I was hoping to speak with your neighbor, Horikawa-san, the writer Kuroda Roman?

Good luck with that, said the old, bald man, raising his eyebrows, smiling as he closed one of the cages.

He doesn't seem to be home, said Murota Hideki. Don't suppose you know where is . . . ?

I wish I did, said the old man, shaking his head. My son's been trying to speak to him for months.

Oh yeah? Why's that?

We got an offer on this land, said the man, gesturing at his house and his garden. Real-estate company wants to build some apartments and a car park. It's a good offer, but they want his land, too, Horikawa's land, or else they're not interested.

The company can't find him then?

No one can, said the old, bald man, shaking his head again. You must be the third or fourth person been round here in the last year, asking about him.

Popular guy.

Not him, laughed the old man. Just his land. He's mad. Last time I saw him, he was eating the flowers in his garden.

Really . . . ?

Yeah, said the man, nodding and turning, pointing over to the back of his garden. Used to be a hole in the fence back there, between the two gardens. The wife made me get it fixed up, she thinks there's foxes in his garden. I told her, the only fox in there is that crazy old fox Horikawa-san.

But you saw him then?

Oh yes, said the old, bald man. Saw him on his hands and knees, eating the petals off flowers, drinking the water from his pond, he was, talking to his teddy bear . . .

His teddy bear?

You know, said the old man, smiling at the birds in their cages, waving at the birds in their cages. One of them stuffed animals, stuffed toys kids have?

Murota Hideki nodded and said, Yeah, I know what you mean. But you say he was talking to this teddy bear?

Unbelievable, I know, said the man. But I'll never forget it, can still hear his voice now: Sada-chan, Sada-chan, he was saying. Must be thirsty, have some water, Sada-chan.

That was the name of the bear then, said Murota Hideki. No one else living there with him then?

Not these days, said the old, bald man. Least not as far as I know. He was married, though, long time ago now.

I heard that, said Murota Hideki, nodding. You know what happened to the wife, do you?

Killed herself, said the old man, lowering his voice, turning to the birds in their cages, nodding to himself.

In the shadows, in the silence, the shadows and the silence again, Murota Hideki swallowed and blinked, blinked and swallowed again, then said, Poor woman.

Yep, said the man.

Murota Hideki blinked again and asked, Did you ever see her, ever meet her?

Nope, said the old, bald man. Heard her, though, sometimes, practicing the samisen. She was a geisha, see, ex-geisha. His family disowned him when he married her, cut him off, never saw him again, that's what I heard.

I heard that, said Murota Hideki again, nodding again. So when was that, when you last saw him then?

In his garden, you mean?

Yeah, that time.

A year, maybe two years ago now.

You've not seen him since?

No, said the old, bald man, tapping on the bars of one of the cages. Thought they must have taken him away again. Been in and out of the asylum since as long as I can remember.

You know which one?

No, said the old man, shaking his head, smiling at the bird in the cage. If we did, my son would've been over there like a shot, getting him to sign and sell up.

He might not want to, said Murota Hideki, looking up at the house, looking round at the garden, this beautiful old house, this beautiful old garden.

Might not, said the man. But I reckon he would when he hears what they're offering, how much they're offering.

Must be a good offer, said Murota Hideki.

It is, said the old, bald man in his summer kimono on the veranda of his house, looking at Murota Hideki, asking Murota Hideki, So why you looking for him?

Murota Hideki reached inside his jacket, took out his wallet, took a name card from his wallet, and stepped toward the veranda, holding out his name card, saying, He owes his publisher some money, that's all.

I see, said the old man, taking the name card, reading the name on the card. That's interesting, very interesting.

Why do you say that?

Because it means he'll be even more likely to sell, said the man. If you find him . . .

Maybe, laughed Murota Hideki. If I find him.

Wait there, will you, said the old, bald man, disappearing into his house, his beautiful old house.

Murota Hideki nodded, then waited in the shadows, the silence, turning to look at the back of the garden, the fence at the back, the fence which separated this house from the garden and house next door, the house of Kuroda Roman.

Here's my son's name card, said the old man, coming back out onto the veranda, handing the card, together with a narrow, thin, weather-stained notebook, to Murota Hideki. You might as well take this as well . . .

Murota Hideki nodded, looking down at the book, then back up at the old, bald man. Thank you, but what is it?

His address book, said the man, smiling to himself, shaking his head. Least that's what we think it is.

Murota Hideki nodded again, opening the book, flicking through the pages, asking, How come . . . ?

He used to throw stuff over the fence sometimes, into our garden, laughed the old, bald man. Can you believe it? Course, we'd try and give the stuff back, but it was like raising the dead, trying to get him to open his gate.

I know what you mean, said Murota Hideki.

That's if he was even home, said the old man. But my son had a look through it, even tried a few of the numbers, seeing if he could track him down.

No luck, though?

First few numbers he tried, said the man. They'd never heard of him, so he gave up. Thought you might have better luck, you being a professional. You never know?

You're right, said Murota Hideki, nodding to himself. You never know. Thank you.

Just make sure you let us know, said the old, bald man. If you do find him.

Will do, said Murota Hideki, holding up the name card, then turning to go, saying again, Thank you.

From the veranda, among the birdcages, the old man called out, Where you heading now?

The asylum, said Murota Hideki, not turning back, not looking back, stepping through the gate, out into the lane.

He closed the gate behind him, put the name card inside his wallet, his wallet back inside his jacket, and then opened the notebook, this address book again, flicking through the pages, turning through the syllables – A, KA, SA, TA, NA, MA – stopping when he came to MA, reading down the list of names, the names beginning MA, MI, MU . . .

*Murota – 291-3131.*

In Negishi, in this lane, in the middle of the maze, at the heart of this labyrinth, in the address book of Kuroda Roman, on a narrow and weather-stained page of this book, he read his own name, he saw his own number, and then he turned the page back, and back again, back through NA to TA, and he looked down the page, read down through the list, the list of names beginning TA, TI, TU, TE, TO . . .

~~*Tominaga – 291-3131.*~~

And in the shadows, and in the silence, in this place of retreat, retreat and exile, he read her name, her name and his own number, a line through his number, a line through her name, in the silence, in the shadows . . .

*Come for you again.*

He got off the Keiō train at Hachimanyama station. He went into the toilet on the platform. He took a piss, then went over to the basin. He took out a necktie from the pocket of his jacket and put it on, took out his spectacles from another pocket, then put them on. He ran the faucet and rinsed his hands, then dried his hands on the front of his jacket and shirt. He left the toilet, he left the station. He found a cake shop and he bought the two cheapest, smallest cakes they had on display. He crossed over the tracks, went south down a quiet, narrow road, then turned left and passed through the West Gate of the Tokyo Metropolitan Matsuzawa Hospital, formerly known as the Matsuzawa Hospital for the Insane, with the box of cakes in his hand, smiling and nodding to the guard-man at his post, who nodded, smiled back, and said, Good afternoon. He walked along the driveway to the main entrance to the Main Clinical Building. He walked up the steps, went into the lobby, and made a big show of standing there, the box of cakes in one hand, scratching his head with the other, turning one way then the other, screwing up his eyes, squinting through his spectacles –

You looking for reception, asked a young nurse.

He nodded, he smiled: Yes, I am. Could you –

It's this way, she nodded, and she guided Murota Hideki down a corridor, up to a counter, and left him there, in front of a stern-faced, much older lady.

Good afternoon, said Murota Hideki, placing the box of cakes on the counter between them.

She gave the box of cakes an irritated glance, looked back up, and snapped, Yes?

Excuse me, said Murota Hideki. I'm not from Tokyo. I'm from Yamanashi. This is my first time. Not my first time in Tokyo, but my first time here, here at this hospital. You see, I'm here on business. Not at your hospital, I mean here in Tokyo. But because I'm here, here in Tokyo on business, my mother and my aunt, they asked me if I would try to come to visit my uncle. That is, if I had time, because I wasn't really sure I would have time, because I wasn't sure how the business would go. But as it turns out –

Name, she said, through gritted teeth, teeth flecked with specks of lipstick that had long since left her lips.

Murota Hideki, he said, bowing.

Not your name, she spat. The name of the patient, this uncle you are here to see?

Tamotsu, said Murota Hideki. Uncle Tamotsu.

Full name, she sighed. His family name?

Ah, so sorry, he said. Horikawa. Horikawa Tamotsu.

The stern-faced nurse looked at Murota Hideki, stared at Murota Hideki, his creased suit and shirt, his necktie and his spectacles, his puffy and unshaven face. He smiled at her, but she did not smile back. He touched the box of cakes on the counter, and she glanced at the box again, then back up at Murota Hideki again. He smiled at her again, again she did not smile back, but then she sighed again and said, Horikawa Tamotsu? Just a minute . . .

She got up from her chair behind the counter and went into an office set back from the counter, leaving him standing there, touching the box of cakes, tapping the box.

I thought so, she said, returning to her chair behind the counter, smiling now, gloating now, an open file in her hands. Your *Uncle* Tamotsu is not here.

Really, said Murota Hideki, scratching his head, pulling at the lobe of his ear.

Yes. *Really*.

Sorry, said Murota Hideki, but are you sure?

Yes, she said. I am *sure*, very *sure*.

Just a minute, said Murota Hideki, reaching into a pocket, then another pocket, then another, patting himself down. But my mother and my aunt, they told me this was the name of the hospital. I even wrote it down somewhere. I'm sure this is the right hospital, I'm sure this is the right place . . .

He *was* here, she said. But he's not here now. You have the right hospital; he's just not here, not anymore.

But they gave me the name of the doctor, the name of his doctor, said Murota Hideki, still going through his pockets. They wanted me to speak with his doctor . . . Doctor, Doctor . . . oh, what was his name? Where's the letter . . . ?

He is not here, she said again. You're too late.

But that can't be right, said Murota Hideki. We would have been told, someone would have said. Where would he go, what would he do? He's not a well man, he's a very sick man. Poor old Uncle Tamotsu . . .

There were people behind Murota Hideki now, queuing up behind Murota Hideki now, impatient and annoyed people, looking at the receptionist, the receptionist looking at them, gritting her teeth again, shaking her head.

. . . Are you really, really sure?

LOOK, she snapped and spat, slamming down the open file onto the top of the counter, next to the box of the cakes. Then she turned to the people stood behind Murota Hideki, smiling at the first people in the queue, asking them, Yes . . . ?

Murota Hideki blinked his eyes, scratched his head, and looked down at the file, turning it around, staring down at the page, reading the names and the dates, his lips moving as he blinked his eyes again, scratched his head again, then shook his head and shook his head again as he closed the file and turned it back around again, waiting for the receptionist to deal with the people in the queue, just standing there, waiting there, waiting for her to pick up the file and triumphantly say, See.

Yes, said Murota Hideki, quietly and sadly, reaching into his pockets again, searching through his pockets again. But I wonder if it would be possible just to speak with his doctor? Just to have a quick word with Doctor Nomura, please?

No, it would not be possible, said the receptionist, getting up from her chair again, taking the file away.

How about if I came back tomorrow?

She got to the door of the office set back behind the counter. She turned around, she looked at him and sighed, No. He retired in March. He's not here either.

Murota Hideki nodded, then nodded once again and turned and walked away from the counter –

Just a minute, she shouted.

Murota Hideki turned back, smiled, and said, Yes?

You forgot your cakes.

He smiled again, smiled at her and said, You keep them. They were for Uncle Tamotsu. Please, you have them.

She looked down at the box, then back up at Murota Hideki, shook her head, and said, No, thanks. You take them, take them back to Yamanashi, to your mother and your aunt.

Murota Hideki walked back over to the counter, picked up the box of cakes, nodded at the woman, bowed to the woman, and said, You've been very helpful. Thank you.

You're welcome, she said. Goodbye.

He bowed once more, then turned and walked away from the desk, back down the corridor, back through the lobby and back down the steps of the Main Clinical Building, then back down the long driveway and back through the gates, smiling and nodding again at the guard-man at his post, who nodded, smiled back again, and said, *Otsukaresama desu . . .*

Murota Hideki nodded again, then turned left and walked south down the narrow, quiet road, following the walls and the trees which hid the grounds of the Matsuzawa Hospital, those high walls and tall trees which screened the lawns and the ponds of the hospital, shrouded the patients, the inmates inside. He turned left again at the corner where the Hachimanyama police box stood and walked up a path of dirt and stones, following a high wire fence which marked the southern boundary of the Matsuzawa Hospital, looking through the links of the fence, staring across a baseball field at the tall trees, at more tall trees, at more screens and more shrouds. He turned left again at another corner and then came to a park, a very small park. He sat down on a bench in the park, this very small and empty park, and opened the box of cakes. He took out the first cake and stuffed it in his mouth, swallowed the cake and then ate the other, his first food of the day. He wiped the cream from his mouth and his lips, licked his fingers, and then took out his cigarettes. He lit a cigarette, his first of the day, and inhaled, then exhaled. He finished the cigarette, stubbed it out in the dirt at his feet, then took off his spectacles and necktie, put them back in the pockets of his jacket. He took out his notebook and pen from inside his jacket. He opened the notebook and began to write down names and dates, his lips moving as he wrote, whispering other names and other dates as he wrote: *Chief Inspector Mori, June 1946, purged and gone insane, committed to the Matsuzawa Hospital for the Insane . . .*

He stopped writing, closed his notebook over his pen, and put them back inside his jacket. He lit another cigarette, inhaled, then exhaled, blowing the smoke up into the sky, Murota Hideki looking up into the sky, the sky over to the east, cast-over and dull, over Kitazawa, the clouds over Kitazawa, its old wooden row houses cast-over and gone, long gone, long gone, they were all long gone, cast-over and gone. He dropped the cigarette into the dirt at his feet, stubbed it out under his shoe, then rubbed and wiped his eyes. He stood up, picked up the empty cake box from the bench, walked over to a concrete trash bin, and dropped the box inside. He walked out of the small park, turned left, and went north up another narrow, quiet road, following more walls and trees, the walls and trees on the eastern edge of the hospital grounds. He turned right when he reached another park, another small park, and followed the Keiō line tracks east to Kami-Kitazawa station. He bought a ticket and went onto the platform, waited for a train, then boarded the train when it came. He sat in the carriage and closed his eyes, not looking out of the windows, not watching the houses disappear, the apartments rise up, in towers, in blocks, as the train headed to Shinjuku –

*Furimukanaide onegai . . .*

He walked out of the station, walked through the crowds, the movie and pachinko crowds, the milk-hall and the jazz-club crowds. He climbed the stairs to a second-floor coffee shop. He drank a cup of coffee, ate a thick slice of buttered toast, then ordered a glass of beer and a plate of Napolitan. He ate the spaghetti, drank the beer, ordered another beer and then a highball, drinking and smoking, checking his watch, his watch running slow, time going slow, killing time until time was dead and he was standing in front of the mirror in the cramped, dank toilet of the coffee shop, looking at himself, telling himself, *Shikata nai . . .*

He got off another train at another station in another suburb west of Shinjuku. But he did not put on his necktie and spectacles, he did not buy any cakes. He took out his notebook to double-check the address, the address and the route. He put the notebook back inside his jacket and began to walk, to walk the way he had come last Friday night, last Friday night when he had followed the man, followed the man back to his home, his family home, his happy home. Maybe because it had been a little later then, a little darker then, or maybe because it had been a Friday and not a Sunday, but it had seemed a much nicer place then, a much better area then. Now it was just another ugly little concrete hutch in another ugly sprawling suburban development, with its silly little fence and its patch of yellow grass, so much better in the dark, so much nicer in the night.

Murota Hideki took out his sunglasses and put them on, took out a toothpick and stuck it in his mouth. Then he opened the stupid little gate and walked up the stupid little path. The lights were on in the living room, the television on, the baseball on, the faint smells of dinner, the soft sounds of voices, the smells of a family, the sounds of a family. He pressed the stupid doorbell of the stupid glass door, holding it down a little too long, just a little too long, listening to it ringing through their little family home, hearing little feet running to the door. Little hands opened the door and a little face looked up at Murota Hideki. He took his finger off the bell, the toothpick from his mouth, put a big hand on the little head of this little child, looked down through his sunglasses, and said, Is Papa home?

Of course Papa was home, he could see him now, see him coming down the little hallway, anxious and fearful. He could see Mama, too, see her standing in a doorframe down the hallway, anxious and fearful, too. Both anxious and fearful because they could see Murota Hideki, see him standing at the door to their house, on the threshold of their home, their little family home, their little happy house, with his sunglasses and his toothpick and a hand upon the head of their firstborn, their precious little boy, the boy turning his head, looking for his father, the father pulling him away from the man at their door, pushing his precious little boy back down the hall, back to his mother, into her arms, as his father turned to Murota Hideki, asking Murota Hideki, What do you want . . . ?

Murota Hideki stared past his face, over his shoulder into his house, down the corridor, straight at his wife as he told the man his own name and the name of his company. Then he smiled and said, That's you, isn't it?

Who are you, said the man. What do you want?

Looking through his sunglasses, still staring at the wife, Murota Hideki licked his lips, then smiled again and said, A little chat in your little garden.

The man glanced back at his wife, his anxious, fearful, pregnant wife, her arms around her firstborn, then the man turned back, stepped outside, closed the glass door behind him, and followed Murota Hideki down the little path to the little gate, where he stopped and said, A little chat about what?

A little chat about your little wife.

What about my wife?

Very pretty, your wife, said Murota Hideki, staring at the house, rubbing his crotch. A very beautiful woman.

The man was a little taller and quite a lot younger than Murota Hideki, but he was not a hard man, just a salaryman. But the man was already balling his fists, already adjusting his stance, already thinking thoughts it was best to stop –

More beautiful than Nemuro Kazuko, said Murota Hideki, turning from the house to stare at the man, to smile at the man. In my opinion, but, of course, you've seen more of them than I have. Much more of them both.

The man was not balling his fists, not adjusting his stance anymore. All his weight was in his feet now, his heart in his mouth now as he struggled for air, as he spluttered to say, to repeat again, What do you want?

Well now, said Murota Hideki, chewing on the toothpick. That's the question, isn't it? What do I want? See, I could want many things, couldn't I? Many things from you: information from you, information about your company, information that could be beneficial, beneficial to me and my friends, if we were interested in stocks and shares, if we were so inclined. Or I could just want money, couldn't I?

How much, sighed the man.

How much what?

Money.

Murota Hideki smiled, he laughed and put a hand on the shoulder of the man, squeezed the shoulder of this man, and said, I don't want your money.

His face full of fear, his eyes filled with dread, the man looked at Murota Hideki and said, Then what do you want?

Murota Hideki smiled again, squeezed the shoulder of the man again, leaned in close, and said, Your word.

My word to do what, asked the man.

Your word that you will go back into your house, your lovely little house, and tell your wife, your pretty pregnant wife, that everything's all right, everything is fine, that I was just some guy who had heard from a friend that you were looking to buy a car, a car on the cheap, some guy who was just passing by, just in the neighborhood. But you told me you weren't interested, told me not to call again. You think you can tell her that, you think you can remember that?

Yes, said the man. But –

But this is the important part, said Murota Hideki, gripping the shoulder of the man, holding it tight. The part you don't tell her, the part you never say, but the part you always remember, you never forget . . .

What, what . . . ?

You give me your word you will never see Nemuro Kazuko again, understood?

The man started to nod, to nod and to say, Yes, yes, of course, of course. But then he started to think, to think and to say, But she'll contact me, I know she will, she always does. It's her, not me, it's always her. Then what do I say?

Tell her what happened, the truth: tell her this ugly big guy in sunglasses showed up at your house, your family home, on Sunday night. Tell her this ugly big guy in sunglasses had seen you both going in and coming out of your favorite little love inn in Yoyogi last Friday. That this big ugly guy knows who you are, knows both of your names, that he followed you home, knows where both of you live. That he banged on your door and asked you for money, lots of money.

But what if she doesn't believe me, asked the man, shaking his head. What if she won't leave me alone?

Then I won't leave you alone and I won't leave her alone, said Murota Hideki. Your money and her pussy, because that's what I'll want, what I'll take. And if you won't give it, or she won't give it, then I'll tell your wife and tell her husband. Is that what you want, loverman?

No, no, said the man, wide-eyed and shaking.

Murota Hideki patted the shoulder of the man, smiled at the man, and said, But she'll believe you, because you'll make her believe you. And then she'll leave you alone, and then I'll leave you alone, you and your family. Okay?

Yes, said the man, nodding.

Good, said Murota Hideki. Now you take one last look at me, then you turn around, walk back up your little path, through your little door, into your little house, and you go back to your little wife, your little boy, and your happy little life.

By the time he got back to Kita-Senju, the time he got to his apartment building, time he ran up the rusted metal stairs stuck to the side of the old wooden building, went down the damp and humid corridor, unlocked and opened his door, tore off and slung his jacket into his room, picked up the plastic bowl, the flannel cloth, and ancient razor from the top of the shoebox in the thin strip of a *genkan*, closed and locked the door again, went back down the corridor and stairs again, ran around the corner, up the road and stuck his head through the curtains hanging in the doorway, it was almost closing time at the public bathhouse. But the old granny on the counter laughed and waved him in: Quickly, in with you then, you sweaty old git.

Murota Hideki laughed, thanked the old bag, and stepped out of his shoes, up into the bathhouse. He undressed, dropped his clothes in the basket, then took his bowl, cloth, and razor into the large communal bathroom. He walked through the steam to the side of the room, ran a faucet and rinsed a stool, crouched down on the stool and soaped his hands, then his face, and began to shave. He shaved his face, then rinsed his face. He soaped his hands again, then his body, and began to wash. He washed and washed his body, cleaned and cleaned his body. The sweat, the dirt, and the grime from his skin, the sweat, the dirt, and the grime of the city. Then he filled and refilled the bowl three or four times, rinsing his body clean of the soap and its suds, clean of the sweat, the dirt, and the grime. And then he wrung out the cloth, rinsed off the stool, and walked over to the big bath. He climbed into the bath, sat down in the bath, nodded to the last of the men still soaking in the bath, then he sank down deeper, deeper into the water, closing his eyes.

Come on, let's be having you, shouted the old granny from the door. I want to go home, even if you don't.

Yeah, yeah, laughed Murota Hideki, opening his eyes, the last man in the bath, pulling himself up, climbing out of the bath. He slopped back over to the stools and the faucets, ran a faucet and filled his bowl again, rinsed himself down again, then wiped himself down with his cloth. He rinsed and wrung out his cloth again, picked up his bowl and razor, then went out of the bathroom back into the changing room. He picked up a towel from the pile by the door. He dried himself, dressed, and then combed his hair. He picked up his bowl, his cloth, and his razor, and dropped the towel into the basket by the door. He stepped down, back into his shoes, said thanks and goodnight to the old granny closing up, then went back out through the curtains, out of the public bathhouse and onto the street.

He walked back down the road, bought a bottle of beer, three packs of cigarettes, and some dried squid from the store on the corner, then went back around the corner, back to his building. He climbed the rusted metal stairs again, went back down the damp, humid corridor again, the stench from the single, communal toilet on the ground floor tart and rank. He unlocked and opened his door, put down the bowl, the cloth, and the razor on top of the shoebox, closed the door, stepped out of his shoes into the room, and said, *Tadaima*.

He found and pulled the cord, switched on the bulb, put the beer, the cigarettes, and the squid down on the low table under the dim bulb in the middle of the tiny room. He turned back to the *genkan*, took the cloth from the bowl, and picked up his jacket from the floor. He walked over to the tattered, torn paper of the *shōji* screen which covered the single window on the opposite wall. He draped the damp cloth over a coat hanger, hung it from one of the lattices of the screen, then hung his jacket on a nail in the wall. He took off his shirt, his trousers, his socks, and his underwear again. He hung the trousers on another nail, then put on clean underwear. He screwed up his dirty underwear, his socks, and his shirt in a ball and stuffed them in a corner on a pile of old underwear, socks, and shirts. He walked back around the low table to the sink next to the *genkan*, picked up a glass from the rack, and slumped down on the floor at the low table. He opened the beer, poured and drank a glass, chewing on a piece of squid. He leaned over, across the dirty mats, and picked up a thin towel from the floor. He wiped his face and neck, then wrapped and tied the towel around his neck. He poured another glass, listening to the sound of radios and voices, radios and voices from the rooms next door, the rooms below. He took another gulp of beer, the beer already warm, and cursed himself. He got back to his feet, went back over to his jacket on its nail. He took his lighter, the address book of Kuroda Roman, and his own notebook and pen from the pockets of his jacket. He carried them back over to the low table and sat back down on the floor. He drank the beer, chewed squid, and smoked cigarettes as he went through the address book of Kuroda Roman, looking for the last names and numbers on each page of the book. He copied out these names and numbers into his own notebook, drinking the beer, chewing on squid, smoking his cigarettes, then finishing the beer and drinking a glass of *shōchū* from a bottle under the sink, mixed with pickled sour plums from a jar under the sink, stirring the drink with a pair of chopsticks from the sink, making a second list of names and numbers from the address book of Kuroda Roman, a list of older names and numbers, stirring then drinking more glasses of *shōchū* and pickled sour plums –

Darling, she whispered, what are you doing?

He said, I want to find this man.

Please don't, she said, please stop.

But he poured another glass of *shōchū*, mashed the pickled plum into even smaller bits with the chopsticks, then took a long drink and said, No, no. I want to find who blabbed, the bigmouth who talked about us, who gave us up.

Long ago, she said, it's so long ago now.

He poured again, he mashed again, he drank and drank again, then said, Maybe to you, but not to me.

In tears, she said, it'll end in tears.

So what, he said, reaching for the bottle again, pouring again. It began in tears, it's always tears –

My tears, she said, not yours.

He picked up the chopsticks, smashed them down into the remains of the plums in the glass, again and again as he said, I need to know, I need to know, I NEED TO KNOW.

Darling, please, it will do you no good.

He looked up from the broken plums, the snapped chopsticks, the cracked glass, from the pools of *shōchū*, the splinters of wood and the spots of blood, looked up at the filthy, stinking sink, the single grease-coated ring, at the piles of dirty old clothes on the dusty, frayed mats, his soiled jacket and grubby trousers hanging by their nails on the grimy yellow walls, the dim, naked bulb dangling from the stained, warped ceiling, in the thick and foul, dank and insect air, looking for things that were not there, searching for people who were not here, talking to their shadows, speaking to their silence, he said, he said again, So what, so what? Is this some kind of good?

The Shimoyama Case, said Yokogawa Jirō, in the Yama-no-Ue Hotel in Ochanomizu. He was sitting on one of the black-leather-and-cherrywood sofas in the lounge of the lobby, filling his seat like it was some kind of throne, the pair of thick, red velvet curtains behind him adding a further regal touch to the scene. But instead of a jeweled crown, he was wearing a black beret with his brow-line glasses and his stiff, dark-green kimono, the beret giving him the appearance of a successful manga artist rather than the founder and chairman of the Mystery Writers of Japan. His face was even rounder, his lips even thicker than in his photographs, and he looked every one of his sixty-three years. He took another pull on his fat cigar, another sip from his whisky, then Yokogawa Jirō swallowed and said, Yes, I'm afraid that's what did for poor old Kuroda-sensei.

In the court of the Emperor of Mysteries, Murota Hideki nodded, sipped his own whisky, and waited. It was a slow, hungover lunchtime on the second day of the Rainy Season, Monday, June 22, 1964.

Ages ago now, said Yokogawa Jirō, after another pull, another sip. But it still sometimes feels like yesterday.

Murota Hideki nodded again, sipped again, and waited.

I'll never forget this one time, it was that summer, the summer of Shimoyama, Mitaka, and Matsukawa, must have been the August, I think. We called a meeting of the Mystery Writers of Japan, at the Tōyōken, up on the seventh floor of the Daiichi Seimei Sōgo building in Kyōbashi, where we always held our meetings back then. But we called it specifically to debate the Shimoyama Case, invited the press, asked certain writers to give their opinions, their theories on the Shimoyama Case, and then, at the end, we were to hold a vote on whether it was suicide or murder, whether President Shimoyama had killed himself or been murdered. It was all people were talking about – suicide or murder – back then, if you remember . . . ?

Murota Hideki nodded and said, I remember.

I'll never forget, said Yokogawa Jirō again. Right at the end of the meeting, after we'd had the vote, the doors burst open and in flies Kuroda Roman. You should have seen the state of the man! His *yukata* hanging open, underwear on display, holding his *geta* in his hands, his bare feet all cut and bloody, his hair all messed up, eyes wide and wild, he was almost foaming at the mouth, babbling and raving about how he'd cracked the case, solved the mystery of Shimoyama.

Murota Hideki asked, What was he saying?

I was at the other end of the room, said Yokogawa Jirō, shaking his head. So I couldn't really hear what he was saying, but apparently, I heard later, he was just babbling and raving on about time, about how time was "the mystery to the solution."

Murota Hideki said, The solution to the mystery?

No, said Yokogawa Jirō, shaking his head again. The other way around, "the mystery to the solution." I remember that, people repeating that later. But then he just started haranguing everyone, the writers and the journalists, as they were leaving, saying it was all just a game to us, another puzzle, that no one really cared. And he had a point, you know, but pretty soon after that he was committed, I think. It wasn't the first time either, or the last, from what I've heard.

But you've seen him since then, Sensei . . . ?

Another one, said Yokogawa Jirō, gesturing with his empty glass at his personalized bottle of whisky, standing next to the ice bucket on the cherrywood table between them.

Thank you very much, said Murota Hideki, nodding. He leaned over the table, picked up the whisky bottle, unscrewed the top, and poured them both another drink, then used the tongs to drop two cubes of ice into each of their glasses.

Yokogawa Jirō took another long pull on his fat cigar, then picked up his fresh glass, took a big sip, swallowed, then nodded and said, Maybe two or three times, I think. But not for a long time now. That's why I was quite surprised when you called, surprised he had my number. Because we were never very close. Not sure he was close to anyone.

May I ask you when these two or three other occasions were, when and where you did see him?

Well now, let me think, said Yokogawa Jirō, looking up at one of the chandeliers, puckering his thick, wet lips, then looking back across the glass-topped cherrywood table at Murota Hideki, nodding to himself as he said, Yes, once was soon after he came out of hospital. I remember because I was so surprised to see him. I didn't realize he was out. So that must have been late 1955, I think.

Murota Hideki asked, And where was that then?

The Imperial Hotel, at the Shinpi Shōbō *bōnenkai*, said Yokogawa Jirō, laughing to himself. Only way they could get people to go was if they held the party there.

Did you speak with him?

Oh yes, said Yokogawa Jirō, still laughing to himself but shaking his head now. Well, I mean, I listened to him . . .

And what was he talking about, do you remember?

What do you think, said Yokogawa Jirō, not laughing now. What did he ever talk about? The Shimoyama Case.

And what was he saying about it, Sensei . . . ?

He was just going on about the oil, the oil that had been found on the clothing of President Shimoyama, about the tests on the oil, about different types of oil, about factories where it could have come from, possible locations for these factories, but speaking so quietly, so quickly, faster than you could follow. Even if you'd wanted to, you couldn't keep up with him.

In the lounge of the Yama-no-Ue Hotel, on this slow, hungover lunchtime on the second day of the Rainy Season, Murota Hideki said, But you didn't want to . . . ?

Look, I liked him, and not a lot of people did, said Yokogawa Jirō, looking down at the end of his fat cigar, then back up at Murota Hideki, nodding to himself again. That's why I agreed to meet you, why we're talking now.

And I'm grateful for your time, Sensei, said Murota Hideki. I didn't mean to accuse or insult you . . .

No, no, said Yokogawa Jirō, shaking his head, waving his cigar across his face. I didn't think you were. What I mean to say is, and to give him his due, Kuroda-sensei was the first person to start talking about the Americans, about GHQ, saying some unit within GHQ had had a hand in the death of President Shimoyama. Of course, a lot of people think that now, but Kuroda Roman was the first person to say so, and to say so publicly, and then to write about it.

Murota Hideki looked across the glass-topped cherrywood table and asked, Is that what you think, Sensei . . . ?

Me, said Yokogawa Jirō, shaking his head as he stubbed out his cigar in the heavy glass ashtray. I long since gave up thinking about the Shimoyama Case.

Murota Hideki nodded and said, I see. So when were the other times, or the last time you saw Kuroda-sensei?

Probably around the time I stopped thinking about the Shimoyama Case, said Yokogawa Jirō, nodding to himself, smiling to himself. Would have been the ten-year anniversary of the death of President Shimoyama, so July 5, 1959, six years ago now. There was a sort of memorial service up at Ayase, at the scene of the crime, as they say. And he was there.

Did you speak to him again that time?

Nope, not that time, said Yokogawa Jirō, then he picked up his whisky again and took another big sip.

Murota Hideki nodded, waiting.

He was there with this guy, Terauchi Kōji. I mean, that was bad enough. You heard of this guy . . . ?

Murota Hideki nodded again and said, Vaguely, I think. Read his name in some articles . . .

Yep, said Yokogawa Jirō. That's where you'll find him, if you're interested. But I'm not going to sit here talking about him now, wouldn't waste my breath, except to say I think he's a complete fraud, a fantasist and a charlatan. But Kuroda-sensei, he seemed to fall under his spell –

Excuse me, Sensei, whispered a young man in a gray suit, another skinny young man in another flashy gray suit, crouching down at the side of Yokogawa Jirō. Your room is ready for you now, Sensei.

Yes, yes, said Yokogawa Jirō, waving the young man away, picking up and then draining his glass of whisky.

You're staying here, asked Murota Hideki.

Yokogawa Jirō put down his glass, wiped his thick, wet lips, and shook his head and said, I'm just writing here. You heard of "canning," Murota-san?

Murota Hideki shook his head.

It's when publishers imprison their writers in hotel rooms, cutting them off from the outside world, all distractions and temptations, so they can deliver their latest work on time.

I can think of a lot worse prisons, said Murota Hideki, looking around at the plush lobby, the obsequious staff.

Yokogawa Jirō sighed, pushing himself up from the black leather sofa, then said, If you really want to find Kuroda Roman, then you'll find him in the Shimoyama Case.

I understand, said Murota Hideki, putting down his glass, getting to his feet, and bowing. Thank you, Sensei.

Yokogawa Jirō put a hand on the shoulder of Murota Hideki. Murota Hideki looked up at Yokogawa Jirō –

You told me you were a policeman, said Yokogawa Jirō, staring at Murota Hideki. And you say you're working as a private investigator now, and so I don't doubt you know how a case can sink its teeth into a man. But this case, this is different. Yes, it sinks its teeth into you, but then it sucks and drains the blood from you, takes away your perspective, your senses, and your reason. That's why they call it "the Shimoyama Disease," because it infects you, occupies and possesses you.

Murota Hideki swallowed, nodded, and then said, And so that's what you think happened to Kuroda-sensei . . .

I know it was, said Yokogawa Jirō, squeezing the shoulder of Murota Hideki. And he wasn't playing with a full deck to begin with, as they say, if you know what I mean?

Murota Hideki nodded again and said, Yes.

Well, I hope you do, said Yokogawa Jirō, releasing his shoulder, then turning away from Murota Hideki, walking away from Murota Hideki as he said, So you take care now, Murota-san, out there, and in there, in the Shimoyama Case, because he didn't. That was the tragedy of Kuroda Roman.

*

He went down the hill, down through the drizzle, back into Jimbōchō, back to its bookstores, their shelves and their stacks, from store to shop, the stores selling new books to the shops selling used books, through their shelves and their stacks he went, searching for all the books he could find on the Shimoyama Case, then buying all the books he found on the Shimoyama Case – *Black Tide* by Inoue Yasushi (1950); *To Solve the Mystery of the Shimoyama Case* by Dōba Hajime (1952); *Conspiracy: Postwar Inside Stories* by Ōno Tatsuzō and Okazaki Masuhide (1960); *Trap* by Natsubori Masamoto (1960); *The Black Mist Over Japan* by Matsumoto Seichō (1962); *The Case of the Mysterious Death of President Shimoyama* by Miyagi Otoya and Miyagi Fumiko (1963) – and then, with his bags of books, he went back out into the drizzle, back down the side streets, onto Hakusan-dōri, into Sankōen, and with the bags of books at his feet, he sat down at the counter and ordered a plate of gyōza, a plate of fried noodles, and a bottle of beer, eating and drinking and reading the paper; not the books in his bag, but the paper from the rack, reading about pickpockets and suicides, gang busts and baseball, the Giants beating the Swallows, the Kokutetsu Swallows, the team owned by the National Railways, no escape from the railways –

*Shu-shu pop-po, shu-shu pop-po . . .*

He finished the gyōza, the noodles, and the beer, picked up the bags of books, put the paper back in the rack, paid his bill, and left the restaurant. He walked through the drizzle and the showers, back along Yasukuni-dōri, through Ogawamachi and Kanda-Sudachō, over the roads and the streetcar tracks, then under the railroad tracks, the railroad and its tracks, along Yanagihara-dōri, past the Yanagimori shrine, along the street and back to his building, the Yanagi building –

*Ka-chunk, ka-chunk, ton-ton . . .*

He traipsed up the steps into his building, the bags of books in his hand. He checked his mailbox in the wall of metal mailboxes. He sifted through the advertising sheets and the utility bills, stuffed them back inside the mailbox, and slammed it shut again. Then he trudged up the one, two, three, four flights of stairs, the bags of books in his hand. He went into the toilet at the top of the stairs, dropped the bags of books down beside the basin. He plodded over to the urinal, undid his flies, and took a piss, a long piss. Then he did up his flies, picked up the bags of books, and left the toilet. He lumbered down the corridor to the end of the corridor, took out his key, unlocked and opened the door, then stepped inside his office –

*Don-don, ka-chunk . . .*

He closed the door, then the window on the noise and the stench, the noise of construction, the stench from the river. He dumped the bags of books on top of his desk, then slumped down in the chair at his desk and lit a cigarette. He finished the cigarette, sighed, and began to open the bags of books, taking out the books, one by one, flicking through the books, one by one, turning their pages, scanning their pages, these pages of suicide, these pages of murder, murder or suicide, suicide or murder, back and forth they went, back and forth he went, over these pages, through these pages, these pages of murder, these pages of suicide, with their descriptions of the scene, the scene of a crime or the scene of a suicide, their descriptions of the body, the body of a suicide or the victim of a murder, back and forth they went, back and forth he went, through police reports and autopsy reports, reports of a murder, reports of a suicide, back and forth, back and forth, they went and he went, over pages of statements, statements by witnesses, through the many statements by so many witnesses, witnesses to a suicide or witnesses to a murder, back and forth through the conspiracies and theories, the theories and conspiracies, through conspiracies of murder, the theories of suicide, suicide due to stress, stress or insanity, or murdered by Communists, Communists or Americans, murder or suicide, suicide or murder, back and forth, back and forth he went, until the light had gone and the room was dark, and all he could hear was the sound of a train, over and over, over the tracks and over the body, the sound of that train –

*Shu-shu pop-po . . .*

In the darkness of his office, he got up from his desk, up from these books, walked over to the wall, and switched on the light. In the electric light, in the middle of the room, he stared around the office, its yellow walls and dirty floor, its dusty shelves and empty cabinet. He sighed again and walked back over to his desk, slumped back down again into his chair, and lit another cigarette. He picked up the books again, one by one, flicked through the books again, one by one, turning their pages again, scanning their pages again, with all their names, their many names, but no mention of Kuroda Roman, no trace of Kuroda; yet some names he recognized, some names he knew, the names of policemen, the names of detectives, men he had known, once personally knew. He took another cigarette from the pack on the desk and glanced at the phone. He lit the cigarette, inhaled, and looked again at the phone, then exhaled as he stared at the phone. He finished the cigarette, stubbed it out, sighed, and took out his own address book. He turned the pages, found the name and the number. He stared down at the name and the number, then up at the telephone again. He swallowed, reached for the phone, picked up the handset, and began to dial the number, *Shikata nai . . .*

Never thought I'd ever fucking say it, slurred Hattori Kansuke, but thank fuck for the Olympics.

They'd been drinking for three, four damp and sticky hours at the damp and sticky counter of a damp and sticky bar, a hole-in-the-wall bar, under the tracks at Yūrakuchō. The first hour had been all beers and cheers, all slaps on the back and how long it had been, it had been too long, much too long, and you shouldn't be a stranger, never be a stranger, no matter what happened, it was all long ago, a long time ago now; and here, you remember thingy and what-was-his-name, from back when we were recruits, dick-swinging pair of recruits we were, eh? Hell, not like that now, I tell you, hell, not like that now, all fucking college boys, rich little mama's boys, heaviest thing they ever lifted were their own fucking chopsticks, yeah, all fucking textbooks and manuals and fucking exams, hell, that's what it is now, pair of country cunts like us, we'd have no fucking chance, pair of know-nothing bumpkins like us, hell, I mean, I could barely write my own fucking name when I joined, tell you, I tell you, you're well out of it, Hideki, well out of it, not the way you went out, nah, nah, that was wrong, fucking wrong, mean who ain't had a bit on the side, eh? Not like you was married or nothing, she was married or nothing, was it? Where was the harm, the fucking harm, that's what I said, said so at the time I did, no fucking harm done, but it was all that fucking Kodaira shit, wasn't it? Fucking psycho, he was, eh? That fucker couldn't keep it in his fucking pants for ten fucking seconds, could he? Sex fucking maniac, he was, eh? Always wanted to know, wanted to ask, ask him how many women he'd fucked, must have been fucking hundreds, eh? Fucking maniac, eh? Always wonder what happened to his missus, eh, you ever see her? She was fucking lovely, she was, very pretty, and she must've been used to it five, six, seven times a day from that fucker, I bet, bet she fucking missed it then, when he'd gone, fucking waste, fucking shame, a fine-looking woman like that, wanting it and not getting it. Fuck, it's good to see you, Hideki! Hell, so fucking good to see you, hell, I can't tell you . . .

Likewise, Murota Hideki had said, nodding and smiling along, pacing himself, pacing his drinks but keeping them coming, coming for Hattori Kansuke, smiling and nodding along, moving him on from the beer to the *shōchū*, keeping it flowing, flowing for Detective Hattori –

How much I need this, Hideki, night like this, with you, someone like you, from the old days, who knows what it's like, knows how it is, someone like you, because I tell you: this fucking case is driving me mad, it's sending me nuts, over fourteen fucking months of it now, fourteen fucking months of it, that's what I've had, and not a single fucking break, not a single fucking one. Poor little Yoshinobu-kun . . .

That poor little lad, Murota Hideki had said as he'd ordered them more *shōchū*, nodding and listening to Detective Hattori Kansuke go on and on, on and on about this case – the case of Murakoshi Yoshinobu, four-year-old Yoshinobu-kun, who'd been kidnapped from a park close to his home in Taitō Ward in the March of last year, this case that had transfixed the nation, this case that had stretched the police to breaking point – this case that was still going on and on, this case still unsolved, poor little Yoshinobu-kun still missing –

I dream about him, you know? Dream I can hear him, hear his voice, his little voice, calling to me, calling for me, but only his voice, just his voice, his little voice, never his face, never the place where he is, only his voice, just his voice, his little voice, calling out to me, that's all I can hear, just his voice, his little voice, calling out to me, you know? And sometimes, in my dreams, in these dreams, I'm getting closer, closer to his voice, his little voice, so close I can almost feel him, almost touch him, almost fucking save him, but then, just as I'm there, as I'm almost there, almost where his voice is, almost where he is, where he is, then I wake up, that's when I wake up, fucking wake up, sweating and panting like a fucking madman I am, wake up, yeah, wake up to then fucking read in the fucking papers, yeah, how fucking inept we all are, like we don't fucking know, already fucking know, know it in our hearts, feel it in our hearts, like we don't want to fucking find the poor little lad, like it ain't all we ever fucking think about, every fucking minute of every fucking day, every fucking day of our fucking lives, all we ever fucking think about, all we ever fucking talk about, ever fucking dream about, I mean, hell, never thought I'd ever fucking say it, but thank fuck for the Olympics! If it wasn't for the fucking Olympics, they'd never fucking leave us alone, them fucking bastards in the press, fucking . . .

Worse than Teigin or Shimoyama then, said Murota Hideki now, now it was time –

Seven months, laughed Hattori Kansuke. That's all Teigin was. From crime to confession, just seven fucking months. Nothing compared to this . . .

But Shimoyama?

Like I could give a fuck about Shimoyama, snorted Hattori Kansuke. Then or now. Politics and bullshit, that's all that was, then and still now, politics and bullshit. Man fucking killed himself, everyone knows, case fucking closed.

Must be annoying, people still going on about it, then, said Murota Hideki, nodding again as he poured a dash more *shōchū* into his own glass, then a big splash more into the glass of Hattori Kansuke. When you were so certain, yeah?

Certain, laughed Hattori Kansuke, picking up his glass. Certain? Fucking proved it was suicide, I did.

Oh yeah, asked Murota Hideki.

Hattori Kansuke turned on his stool at the counter, switching his glass from his right hand to his left. He held up the fingers and thumb of his right hand in the face of Murota Hideki, then began to fold them down, one by –

One: family knows best. I was up at the house, day he went missing. First thing wife says to me is, He might've killed himself. I just hope he hasn't killed himself, she said. I mean, I told her not to say such things, course I did. But that's my biggest regret, that whole fucking business, that we didn't listen to her, what she first said.

Two: he had a mistress, or an ex-mistress, whatever you like. But this woman, she was bleeding him dry, asking him for money, making him sell stuff, pawn stuff. Even selling and pawning his wife's rings and kimonos to keep this woman, this ex-geisha sweet, sweet and quiet, until he had nothing left.

Three: the wife, four sons, the mistress, and no fucking money, not to mention his job and all that bullshit, course the man's worried, he's stressed, not thinking right, not thinking straight. So I went up to the hospital, their own railroad hospital they have, spoke with his doctor, his own doctor, saw the man's records with my own fucking eyes, and there it was, in black and white: June 1, 1949, diagnosed with a nervous fucking breakdown he was. Doctor had prescribed him Brobalin, to help him sleep, to calm him down. But the guy got addicted to it, didn't he? Doctor told me so himself, the man was in and out every other fucking day, asking for more. Bags of it he was taking, that's why his wife is thinking he's killed himself, right? Said so herself, said to me she thought he might've taken an overdose. Suicidal, she knew.

Four: witnesses, twenty-fucking-three of them, I think it was, we had, all the way from Mitsukoshi up to Gotanno and Ayase. Two of them alone, though, they were good enough for me, and should've been enough for any-fucking-one. This old granny, she saw him standing by the tracks, then sitting by the tracks, pulling up the weeds he was. She took me to the place, showed me the spot, and there they were, these fucking weeds with their heads all pulled off, and guess what? The heads of them weeds, them very same weeds, we found them in his fucking pockets, didn't we? Pockets of his corpse. Hell, there and then that's case fucking closed for me. I mean, what more do you want, what more do you need? But if you wanted more, there was more, loads fucking more. This other guy, local guy, good job, respectable guy, he saw him, too, described his suit, described his shoes. See, the man was wearing these chocolate-colored shoes with expensive rubber soles. So we took this guy, this witness to headquarters and we showed him the shoes, showed him the suit, and of course he says, That there's the suit I saw, them there are the shoes I saw.

Five: the fucking forensics. All them fuckers who go on about the science, about how it all proves he was murdered, they don't know shit. Ain't going into all that now, can't be fucking bothered but the shorthand is this: Doctor Nakadate, up at Keiō, he knew and he proved it was just another suicide, and as for them blood tests, all them fucking luminol tests, traces of blood, tracks of blood, up and down the tracks, here, there, and every-fucking-where, all that fucking bullshit, know what that was? Menstrual fucking blood from the toilets of the trains, that's all that ever fucking was –

Detective Hattori Kansuke had folded up his fingers and thumb, made a fist of his hand. He held the fist up in the face of Murota Hideki, held it up for a moment, a long moment, a moment too long in the face of Murota Hideki, then Detective Hattori Kansuke slowly opened his fist into four fingers and a thumb again, held the four fingers and thumb up in the face of Murota Hideki, and slowly said, These five fucking fingers mean that man killed himself, mean case fucking closed.

Fuck, said Murota Hideki, raising his glass in a toast and nodding. You nailed it pretty fucking good, yeah?

Hattori Kansuke shook his head, turned back to his drink, and said, Fat lot of fucking good it did me. I was just a leg of the fucking horse, you know, no one listened . . .

They all thought it was the Reds, yeah?

Fucking wished it was, yeah. Especially the fucking Yanks, yeah, some of our own government, too. MacArthur and

Yoshida, suited them, didn't it, or would've done, if the Reds had fucking done it, and we could've proved it . . .

Pressure from above must've been . . .

Like you wouldn't fucking believe, said Detective Hattori Kansuke, shaking his head again. Hell, I tell you, almost ended up like you, I did, talking of booting me out, they were. Because you know me, I'm not going to just sit there, just suck it up. Kept telling them and telling them it was suicide, suicide, so they moved me, yeah, to silence me, shut me fucking up, moved a lot of us – you remember Chief Kanehara?

Murota Hideki shook his head: No . . . ?

Head of First Division he was, my boss he was, great boss, great detective. He knew what he saw, knew what it was, knew it was a suicide, just another fucking suicide. Well, they moved him out, didn't they, moved him out to fucking Sanya, some old fucking shabby station out there. No way to treat a man, a fine, loyal man like that, a great fucking detective.

Murota Hideki nodded: You're right . . .

Yeah, said Hattori Kansuke, nodding, patting the arm of Murota Hideki. Don't need to tell you . . .

Nope, said Murota Hideki, sighing then smiling, smiling then saying, It's funny really, isn't it . . . ?

What is, said Hattori Kansuke, reaching for the bottle, filling both their glasses, emptying the bottle.

Well, you know, like now, these days, everything you read about Shimoyama, read about the case, they're always blaming the Americans, all accusing GHQ, right . . . ?

Detective Hattori Kansuke turned in his stool at the counter, turned to look over his glass at Murota Hideki as he said, You read a lot about Shimoyama, do you?

Me, laughed Murota Hideki. Read a book? I'm from fucking Yamanashi, remember? I mean, everything you *hear*, *hear* all them fucking lefties blabbing on about . . .

Hattori Kansuke was nodding, laughing now, holding up the empty bottle, gesturing to the Mama-san for another, then lowering his voice, still laughing, he said, Actually, you know where all that bullshit started, all that American conspiracy shit? Comes from this Kuroda Roman guy, this fucking writer guy – you ever hear of him?

I'm from Yamanashi, said Murota Hideki again, shaking his head. What do you think . . . ?

Well, he's the one started it all, this Kuroda Roman guy, going on about GHQ, about Zed Unit, was it? But the guy was insane, stark-raving, completely fucking mad. Talk about loose screws, hell, his screws were long, long fucking gone!

Really, said Murota Hideki.

Yeah, laughed Hattori Kansuke. And I should fucking know, I fucking met him, didn't I? Few fucking times . . .

Murota Hideki turned in his stool at the counter to look at Hattori Kansuke, at his face, maroon and dark with drink, at his mouth, open and wet, his big fucking mouth, wide open and wet, and Murota Hideki said, said again, Really . . . ?

Yeah, said Hattori Kansuke again, pouring more drink down his throat, then wiping his lips, his lips and his mouth, his big fucking mouth. A few fucking times . . .

Never thought my old bumpkin buddy would be hanging around with writers, laughed Murota Hideki, shaking his head, picking up his cigarettes, then lighting a cigarette, then picking up his glass, then taking a sip as he waited, waited for that big mouth, that big fucking mouth to open again –

Nah, nah, *he* was the one who was hanging around with us, always hanging around headquarters, wasn't he, bugging the fuck out of us, you know? So one day, Chief Kanehara, he tells me to go fucking talk to him, set him fucking straight, shut him the fuck up, yeah? So me and him, me and Kuroda, we go have lunch one day, he's paying, right, so he takes me to one of them fancy restaurants they got in Hibiya Park, the Matsumotoro it was, you know the one I mean . . . ?

Hideki Murota shook his head again.

Curry rice, they got, but not like any curry rice your mama ever made you, I tell you. Anyway, I lay it all out for him, the Shimoyama Case, just like I did for you, right? Explaining all the evidence, proving it was suicide, and he's nodding along, fucking agreeing he is, saying, Yeah, yeah, yeah, it must've been suicide, has to have been suicide, so I thought that was it, right, job done, last I'd ever see of the fucker.

No such luck, eh, laughed Murota Hideki.

You're not fucking joking. See, now the old fool thinks we're best fucking friends, bosom fucking buddies, like we're fucking partners or something, me and him. Never fucking leaves me alone, does he? Calling headquarters, dropping in unannounced, telling me he's got this new evidence, that new evidence, never fucking shuts up, does he? Unbelievable . . .

So what the fuck did you do then . . . ?

Well, what the fuck could I do? See, we couldn't have him keep coming into headquarters, calling headquarters, could we? So I start to meet him every now and then, you know, agree to meet him every now and then, like to humor him, yeah? And, like, he might've been mad, right, but he had money, you know? So it was usually someplace nice, yeah? Good food, good drink, but I mean, don't get me wrong, it was still a pain in the fucking ass, you know, listening to him, all his fucking theories, all his bullshit fucking conspiracy theories . . .

Murota Hideki shook his head, lighting another cigarette, taking another sip of his drink, laughing as he said, So how long did this go on for then . . . ?

Until I went to his house, said Hattori Kansuke, shaking his head, sighing to himself.

You went to his house?

Yep, up past Ueno, Uguisudani way, said Hattori Kansuke, shaking his head again, sighing to himself again. Should see the place, creepy old fucking place it is, I tell you. And that's just the outside, the garden, right? Hell, I mean, I knew he was fucking mad, yeah, but when I got in there, inside his house, yeah, fuck –

What?

One of the rooms, yeah, it was just wall to wall Shimoyama, like a fucking cave to the case. Photographs, maps, diagrams – hell, I couldn't fucking believe it. I mean, I'd never seen anything like it, you had to see it to believe it. And hell, that's just the walls, right, the fucking decoration, see, then he starts . . . Ah, fuck it, and fuck him! The fuck we have to talk about him for, yeah? So long ago now, who fucking cares?

Yeah, right, said Murota Hideki, nodding, nodding but then asking, But what did you do, when you were . . .

In his mad house, snorted Hattori Kansuke. What the fuck you think I fucking did? Got the fuck out of there as quick as I fucking could, made sure I never saw the cunt again.

What happened to him?

Why the fuck you care what happened to him?

Murota Hideki laughed, patting the back of Hattori Kansuke, and said, Hey, come on! You're the one telling the story, painting the picture, like some fucking *rakugo* master, then you suddenly stop, clam the fuck up, leaving me hanging. Just wondered what happened to the man, is all . . .

Know what should've happened to him, I hope happened to him – the fucking grave.

Hey, come on, laughed Murota Hideki again, his arm round the shoulder of Hattori Kansuke, squeezing his shoulder. Can't be wishing a man dead . . .

You never met him, didn't know him, said Hattori Kansuke. If you had, if you did, and you had a heart, maybe you might say the same . . .

Oh yeah?

Yeah, sighed Hattori Kansuke, looking down at the drink in his hand, swirling the *shōchū* round in the glass. Last I heard, they were running five hundred volts through his skull every day, up at the Matsuzawa Hospital for the mad.

Fuck . . .

Yeah, fucking waste of electricity, is what that is. You know what they say, say's the only cure for the mad, yeah?

No, said Murota Hideki. What do they say . . . ?

Hattori Kansuke looked up from the drink in his glass, turned to look at Murota Hideki. His face still maroon and dark, but not with drink, no more drunk than the stool on which he was sat, he stared at Murota Hideki, reached up to the face of Murota Hideki, held the face of Murota Hideki in both his hands, and said, The only cure for madness is death.

He was drunk and the rain was drunk. He'd missed the last train, the last train of the night. He had enough money, money in his wallet, money for a taxi back to his office, even back to his room. But he didn't, he didn't. He was drunk and the rain was drunk. Falling along the sidewalks, wading through the puddles, the man and the rain dashed over crossroads, splashed across streetcar tracks, splattered under railroad bridges, sprayed alongside tracks. He was drunk and the rain was drunk. They hammered on through the city, on through the night, on and on, they poured north through the city, north through the night, on and on, the man and the rain, bucketing down side streets, tippling down backstreets, through the valleys of the city, the low parts of the night. He was drunk and the rain was drunk. The city becoming darker, the night becoming quieter, coming darker, coming quieter, the city and the night, sopping and slopping, the man and the rain, his head starting to clear, her clouds starting to drift, but still drunk, still drunk, the man and the rain, until they had come to the place, had come again to the place, the place of shadows, the place of silence, the place again, of shadows again, of silence again, sodden and soaked. He was drunk and the rain was drunk.

In the middle of the maze, drenched and wringing, at the heart of its labyrinth, he staggered and he stumbled, through the tall shrubs, through the giant weeds, stumbled back and staggered back, into the lane, into its mud, then staggered forward, stumbled forward, forward again, through the shrubs and through the weeds, into the wood, the wood of the gate, stumbling and staggering, back and then forward, forward again, into the wood, the wood of the gate, back again then forward, forward again, his weight in his shoulder, all his weight to his shoulder, his shoulder to the wood, all his weight in his shoulder, into the wood, the wood of the gate, his weight and his shoulder, into the wood and through the gate –

*Darling, darling, what are you doing . . . ?*

With a crack in the wood, with a crack from the sky, through splinters, in splinters, of wood and of rain, through gourds and through vines, through leaves of plants onto leaves from trees, falling and fallen, Murota Hideki fell through the gate, into the garden and the past of a man –

*Long ago, it's so long ago now . . .*

In the garden, the past of a man, in its shadows and its silence, its shifting tones, its shifting shades, pale then gray again, dim then dark again, he pushed himself up, he picked himself up, wiping the leaves and the dirt from his clothes and his hands, as he felt for the stones, overgrown with weeds, found the stones of the path, grown over with moss, the path to the house, the house of the man –

*My tears, not yours . . .*

Through the leaves, the leaves of the trees, onto more leaves, the leaves of the plants, the rain fell, through the shadows and through the silence, drip-drip-dropping, plip-plip-popping, onto the leaves, from the leaves, to his right in the shadows, into old stone basins, an ornamental pond, to his left in the silence, as he followed the path, overgrown with weeds, grown over with moss, step by unsteady step, by unsure step, under a trellis of woven twigs, the low branches of a pine, he weaved and he ducked until –

*It'll end in tears . . .*

In the shadows of the garden, the silence of the garden, from out of these shadows, out of this silence, the house, the house of the man loomed –

*In tears . . .*

Darker than shadow, deeper than silence, draped in vines, shrouded in weeds, the ancient wooden house, its rickety, rotten veranda, knelt, bowed before him, waiting for him, welcoming him –

*In tears . . .*

From the last stone of the path he stepped up, up onto the veranda, the warped planks of the veranda, and he trod, gently, softly, unsteady step by unsure step, along the veranda, across the veranda, the planks of the veranda, warped and loose, loose and moving under his tread, under his steps, gently and softly, he reached the shutters, the shutters of the house, reached out to the shutters, touched and tried each shutter, gripping one of the shutters, he prized, forced open one of the shutters, the shutters of the house, the house of the man –

*Darling, please don't, darling, please stop . . .*

Prizing back the shutter, forcing open the shutter, with a crack in its wood, another crack from the sky, he pulled open the shutter, then Murota Hideki stepped into the house –

*Darling, please, it will do you no good . . .*

In the house of the man, he stood and he listened, in its shadows, to its silence, the shadows of the man, the silence of the man, standing and listening, the rain falling on the roof, the roof of the house, rain dripping, dropping somewhere in the house, and then he groped, began to grope and to search, through the shadows, through the silence, along walls and over furniture, groping and searching until he found a candle, a candle in a stand. He put his hand in his pocket, took his lighter from his pocket, and he lit the candle, picked up and held up the candle, its flame flickering, wavering as he turned around the room, the candle in its stand in his hand, illuminating the room and its walls, its walls and furniture, a western table and two chairs, a dust-coated bottle of wine and a glass, an unfinished meal on the table, the food on the plate, too bone hard, rock dry even for the roaches now, the cockroaches which scuttled among the centipedes in the traffic of the matting, lizards twitching on the walls, fleeing from his own shadow, the monster of his own shadow, moving along the walls, moving toward the door, sliding open the door –

*Please, it will do you no good . . .*

Moving from one room to another, through one empty, musty room to the next, shielding the candle and its flame with the fingers of his other hand, looking into the farthest corners, all of the closets, he went from room to room, the rain falling on the roof, the roof of the house, rain dripping, dropping somewhere in the house, the house of the man, dripping, dropping behind a door, the wooden door –

*It will do you no good . . .*

The wooden door at the end of the corridor, the wooden door to a detached wing of the house, he slid open this last wooden door, the smell of camphor so strong it stung his nose, made his eyes smart as he held up the candle, the flame of the candle, his eyes blinking, blinking then wide as he looked into the room, stepped into the room, staring around the room, its walls of photographs, its walls of maps, its walls of diagrams, around and across the room he stared and he moved, this once spacious room made small by stacks and stacks of books, books and documents, piles and piles of documents, books and documents and a diorama, on a large piece of wood which lay on top of legs of books and documents, the diorama a scale model of a river and an embankment, a bridge and tunnel, a railroad bridge and tunnel, railroad tracks passing over and under each other, across the bridge and through the tunnel, a black, die-cast model of a D51 steam locomotive coming through the tunnel, pulling a train of freight cars, through the tunnel and down the tracks, down the tracks toward a man, a little model man lying on the tracks, dead on the tracks –

*Shu-shu pop-po, shu-shu pop-po, shu-shu . . .*

In the smoke from the candle, the smell of the camphor, Murota Hideki stepped back from the diorama, away from the model, the model of the crime scene, and turned to the desk, the desk of the man, a rosewood Chinese desk, spartan and bare but for a chipped and cracked celadon vase of dead, dry flowers and a bookstand of teak, a sheaf of manuscript paper open on the stand, open and waiting, waiting for him –

*Potsu-potsu, potsu-potsu . . .*

The rain coming in through the roof of this room, the rain dripping in a corner of this room, Murota Hideki held the candle over the bookstand, over the manuscript, a pair of horn-rimmed glasses lying on the papers, one thick brow of their frames pointing up, waiting for the man, the author to return, return to his desk, return to his work –

*Zā-zā, zā-zā, zā-zā . . .*

The rain pouring in through the roof of this room, the summer rain in the corner, falling in the corner, running down the walls, Murota Hideki put down the candle, down on the desk, he picked up the glasses, laid them down to one side, the candle flickering, its flame guttering, Murota Hideki picked up the sheaf of papers, up from the stand, in the guttering of the flame, the dying of its light, Murota Hideki held the pages in his hands, turned the pages one by one, one by one he turned them back, back, back to the title, and at the death of the light, at the edge of utter darkness, Murota Hideki read the title of the work, the title and its authors –

*Natsuame Monogatari*, or *Tales of the Summer Rains*, by Kuroda Roman, with Shimoyama Sadanori.

# 6

## Minus Ten to Minus Six

*June 25–June 29, 1964*

*Sima Qian [c.140–c.86* BC*], author of the* Shiji *[*Records of the Grand Historian*], was a man who remained to live on in shame. Whereas any man of high rank would not have cared to survive, this man did. Completely driven to bay, fully aware of the base and disgusting impression he gave others, even after his castration, he brazenly went about the task of living on in our world of red dust, feeding and sleeping on a grief that day and night penetrated his entire body, tenaciously persisting in writing the* Shiji*, writing it to erase his shame, but the more he wrote, the greater was the shame that he felt. Yet perhaps it is easier to go on living in shame than we might imagine, for I, too, am living on in shame . . .*

*After the defeat, the surrender, then occupation, as the days became weeks became months became years – already my heart in peaceful times had cracked / now I walked a road more desolate each day – the holes in my roof, nests of moonlight and rain, the clothes on my back, the skin on my bones, bed and breakfast for fleas and for lice. Still, as the ghostly genius counsels: stay drunken till the end of your days, for none pour wine on the earth over Liu Ling's grave. And so I would powder my face, paint a smile upon my lips, don my least-worst suit and, blowing on my imagined dragon flute, beating on my made-up drum of lizard skin, stride out into the city.*

*Though it is perhaps hard to believe or even imagine now, in those occupied days that occupied city was filled with a hunger for books, a thirst for words, and thus had the air of a boom town in a gold rush for writers and translators. But while my brothers of the brush, my pals of the pen seemed to discover nugget after nugget, strike vein after vein, as ever I dug up only gravel, washed only sand, my prose rejected, my poetry even mocked. Fortunately, GHQ had to approve every single word before it could be published, thus every single word had to be translated into English, and so though no publishers would commission me to write articles for their magazines, they would on occasion – no doubt having exhausted all other options – call upon me to translate the words of my contemporaries into English; such were the dry bones on which I was forced to suck, the stale crumbs on which I had to subsist. Still, suck and subsist I did, and those occupied days, that occupied city were debauched and decadent, if one knew which stone to look under, which hole to go down, particularly if one did not pay much heed to what or with whom one drank; beggars, as they say, cannot be choosers. And so, having panhandled some meager advance on a commission for a translation from some publisher or other, with my powdered face, my painted smile, I would immediately begin looking under the stones of the street, going down the holes of the city, seeking to turn bones and crumbs into tobacco and drink, drink, drink . . .*

*Yet those among us who follow the Way of the Cup know its currents and tides can carry us on streams and down rivers sometimes strange and often dark. So it was one night in the early summer of their year nineteen hundred and forty-nine, so it was my empty little cup and I washed up in a place much stranger and darker than I had ever been or seen before . . .*

*The day had started out blandly enough, even quite fortuitously. I had recently taken to dashing off "true-crime" books at the insistence of a certain Mr. Shiozawa, the owner of the publishing house Shinpi Shōbō. The first of the books had done reasonably well and, that afternoon, I had submitted the manuscript of a second such book. Mr. Shiozawa seemed in a celebratory mood, first proposing we toast delivery of the manuscript with a whisky or two from the bottle he kept in his office, then, encouraged by me, I admit, we adjourned to Bar Bordeaux in Ginza. From there, having become both drunk and hungry, he extended his largesse to dinner at Hachimaki Okada, and, of course, I was only too happy to partake of all that venerable old establishment had to offer, savoring as much of their fine sake as I could before it was time for them to close. Yet though the night, as they say, was still quite young, by now Mr. Shiozawa could barely stand and, had he not been in such a state, had he not been egged on by me, no doubt he would never have invited me to join him in one last drink . . .*

*So it was we staggered through the streets of Ginza, their traffic and their lights, toward Hibiya Park, then weaved our way along the paths of the park, among their trees and their shadows, through the park, then out onto the street, across the street to the government buildings, those ministries of finance, construction, and justice, where, somewhere among there, we came to a flight of stone steps at the side of one building, steps descending down to a door, a gray metal door with no handle or sign. Here at the foot of these steps, here before the door, Mr. Shiozawa fumbled through his pockets, found and opened his wallet, and took out what appeared to be a piece of metal, the size of a name card, yet blank and razor thin. First glancing back up the steps, then winking at me, he turned back to the door, bent down, and slid the piece of metal under the door. Moments later, the door opened inward and two smartly dressed, well-built men – Asian, but not Japanese, I thought – greeted us, handing back the metal card to Mr. Shiozawa, who then led the way down a bare, concrete corridor to another flight of steps descending down to another door, this one made of polished wood and which opened as we approached. Once again, two smartly dressed, well-built men – one man Japanese, the other Eurasian – greeted us, along with the sounds of music and conversation, the smells of tobacco and drink, and the sight of another room at the end of another, but much shorter, corridor. Again, Mr. Shiozawa led the way down this short corridor, this one softly carpeted and lit, toward the room of music and conversation, tobacco and drink. At its threshold, Mr. Shiozawa stopped, turned, put a hand over his mouth, and whispered, "Welcome, welcome to the Shikinjō, Sensei . . ."*

*The Shikinjō – the aptly named Forbidden City – was more than a club, more than one room, being many rooms of many things; an underground labyrinth of low-lit nooks and alcoves, all branching out, off from a large central cavern with a long, well-stocked bar running the length of one wall, its floor space filled with tables and chairs, a stage at the end, the far end, the style a curious collision of an English hotel bar and a Bavarian* bierkeller, *with the ambience of a Chicago speakeasy in old Shanghai, a mood accentuated by the Zhou Xuan lookalike up on the stage, backed by her Japanese band, singing "Crazy World" as waiters in stiff white jackets went from table to table, hostesses in kimonos or gowns fluttering from patron to patron –*

*Ah yes, the patrons! For, yes, it was the patrons – the mix of members and their guests – that were the sight which almost stopped one in one's tracks to the bar. For in those occupied days in that occupied city, East only ever met West on her knees or her back, but here . . . well, here they mingled toe to toe, sat cheek by jowl, whispering mouth to ear, slapping backs and shaking hands, with a nod and a wink, in a society of . . . well, yes, rogues: former Imperial Army officers, bureaucrats, politicians, businessmen, and yakuza – men I'd thought purged, imprisoned, some even dead – all rubbing shoulders with American officers and civilians, all swapping stories and name cards, sharing jokes and contacts, raising glasses, proposing toasts to the New Japan, same as the Old Japan, their underground lair, its smoke-filled air crackling and hissing with electricity, yes, black electricity . . .*

*"Do try not to stare, Sensei," whispered Mr. Shiozawa at the bar, handing me a glass of fine old American whisky. "This is, after all, a place not to think but to drink . . ."*

*"How right you are," said I. "How very right you are."*

*And so drink we did, we did, straight whiskies then Sazerac cocktails, we drank and we drank, first with rye whisky then mixed with cognac, mixed as they should be, drunk as they should be. And as we drank, we drank, the waves of whisky, the currents of cognac, carried our cups down different streams, on diverging tides, and so it was, it was, I found myself lost in a nook, an alcove, at a table of men, four serious men, men and their cards, their cards and their cash, their packs of cards, their stacks of cash, sipping my Sazerac, watching them play –*

*"Join us," said the man who was the bank, a respectable-looking Japanese man of about sixty, offering me a deck of cards. "We're playing Faro. Anyone can play . . ."*

*"Anyone but a writer such as I," said I. "For I am as poor as the proverbial church mouse . . ."*

*"Church mouse, my ass," laughed the only American at the table, dressed in his army uniform, his captain's hat pushed back on his head. Between the hands, while he waited, he'd take his pistol from its holster and twirl it around in his fingers. When he had his fresh deck, then he'd tilt his chair back on two legs, chewing on his cigar as he studied his cards. He appeared to have stepped straight from a Hollywood western, but for one detail: he did not drink. "Hell," he laughed. "I thought all you Japanese writers lived in big old fancy houses down Kamakura way."*

*"Regrettably, sadly, not I," regrettably, sadly said I.*

*"Hell, pal," laughed the American again. "Then you must be the last goddamn poor writer left in Tokyo, my friend."*

*"If only I were," said I. "Were the last writer . . ."*

*And it was then, yes, then, an evil, vicious plan began to congeal in the dregs of my intoxicated, poisoned brain. Perhaps it was his reference to Kamakura; yes, yes, it was the mere mention of Kamakura which conjured up a vision of my contemporaries, my rivals, in their Kamakura homes, their beautiful houses, swanning up to Tokyo to further feather their nests, their already soft and silky Kamakura nests, with yet another commission, another advance, then strutting around town, peacocks in a wasteland, preening and posturing, their pockets bulging, wallets too fat to close, eating and drinking, bellies ballooning, bladders bloated, then taking the last train, the last train of the night, the Yokosuka line, back to Kamakura, all sat together, in the last car, in their little social club, drinking and laughing, bitching and gossiping, counting their lolly, their loot, in their so-called little Last Club, in the last car of the last train of the night –*

*"If only that last train, its last car," slurred I with an evil, vicious burp, "if only it were derailed, overturned, they would all be annihilated, all be erased, then truly I would be the last writer, all my troubles, my sorrows at an end, an end . . ."*

*"Say no more," said the American with a nod, with a wink, gesturing with his thumb to the two Japanese men sat to his right. "These pals of mine, they're old hands at bombs on the tracks, the derailment of trains. There'd be no slip-ups with the cops."*

*"Really," whispered I, as wide-eyed I peered into the shadows to his right, at the two Japanese men – one with a patch for an eye, the other with a scar across his cheek – resurrected* rōnin, *spectral spies, puffing on their cigarettes, their cards to their chests. I coughed, cleared my throat, then said, "Forgive me, for I do not wish to appear ungrateful, but surely a bomb on the tracks would attract too much speculation, no?"*

*"But obviously," said the man who was the bank, "people would assume it to be the work of the Reds."*

*"Hell," laughed the American. "Bases loaded the way they are now, might be just the home run we been looking for, hit those goddamn Commie bastards right out of the park – BOOM!"*

*I coughed again, cleared my throat, and said again, "Forgive me, gentlemen, please, I fear my drunken, idle –"*

*"Or perhaps start with something more subtle," said the man with a scar from the shadows to our right. "One by one?"*

*"Can be done, yes," said his pal with the patch.*

*"Yeah," said the American, nodding and smiling. "Yeah, sow seeds of anxiety, reap fear and paranoia . . ."*

*"Tell us," said the man who was the bank, looking at me. "If you had to name just one of your contemporaries, your rivals, one writer you wished would cease to exist, then what name would you tell us, whose name would you give us?"*

*"What a question," exclaimed I, attempting to rise from my chair at this table in this nook, this alcove in hell, this ugly hell, that selfsame ugly hell which once gaped before Doctor Faustus himself. But as with the poor doctor, so with foul me, for it was too late, too late, much, much too late –*

*"Tough question, right," cackled the American devil, gripping my arm, pinning me back down to my seat in this hell. "But come on, man, spit it out – spill!"*

*"Yokogawa Jirō," whispered, whimpered I.*

*"An excellent choice," said the man who was the bank, nodding at the American. "The man is degenerate and perverse, Jack, and would serve as a lesson to all."*

*Captain Jack had his pistol in his hand again, tapping its barrel on the edge of the table, musing aloud, "But how?"*

*"Stage it as a suicide," said the man with the scar from the shadows to our right. "A very public suicide . . ."*

*"We lure him, we abduct him," said his pal with the patch. "Then inject him and sedate him . . ."*

*"We wait until it's night, for the last train of the night," said the scar in the shadows. "We lay his body across the tracks, then let the train do the rest . . ."*

*"Hell, yeah," said Captain Jack, his head nodding, his pistol nodding, gesturing to the other three men, the other three men and*

*I, foul and evil, vicious I, gesturing for us to raise our glasses, our glasses in a toast: "TO BLOOD ON THE TRACKS!"*

*Ton-ton. Ton-ton. Ton-ton. Ton-ton . . .*

His heart pounding, his breath trapped, Murota Hideki twitched, he jumped, he swallowed, he spluttered, and he coughed. He opened his eyes, raised his head from its manuscript pillow on the desk, he wiped his mouth, wiped his chin, then the manuscript, the dribbles and the drool, and he blinked and looked up and –

Quite some dream you were having there.

Murota Hideki blinked again and stared up at the two men standing in his office: one was a little younger and a little thinner than him, the other a lot younger and a lot thinner, both wearing similar raincoats, haircuts, and expressions. Murota Hideki shook his head, reached for his cigarettes, and smiled: Only cops don't knock . . .

Yeah, and only a jack-of-all-trades, *nandemo-ya* like you sleeps at their desk stinking of drink, said the younger of the two men.

Late night, said Murota Hideki, turning the manuscript face down on his desk. That a crime, is it?

The older man smiled and said, Maybe, depending on what you were doing so late, keeping you up all night.

I was drinking in a bar.

Which bar, where?

Place in Yūrakuchō, Rabbit-o Hole.

You drinking alone, were you?

Nope.

So who were you with?

Murota Hideki leaned forward, stubbed out his cigarette, looked up at these two cops, from the one to the other, then smiled again and said, My old friend Hattori Kansuke, Detective Hattori Kansuke of the First Investigative Division.

The younger man glanced at the older man, raising his eyebrows. The older man kept his stare fixed on Murota Hideki: And so what time did you two old friends say goodbye?

Well, you know, we'd drunk a lot, said Murota Hideki, still smiling at the two cops. So I couldn't tell you exactly, precisely, but maybe you can ask Detective Hattori . . .

Don't worry, said the older cop. I'll be asking him, but now I'm asking you what time – not exactly, not precisely; imprecisely will do – what time you said goodbye?

Murota Hideki blew out the air from his cheeks, shrugged, and said, After the last train, so maybe one-ish?

Then what did you do?

I walked back here, said Murota Hideki, gesturing to the office, to the desk. Did a bit of reading, fell asleep.

Alone, yeah?

Yeah, said Murota Hideki, smiling as he shrugged again. Unfortunately, my secretary, she don't exist.

Nor your cleaner, said the younger cop, laughing at his own joke, pointing around the office in case no one got it.

The older cop didn't smile, his stare on Murota Hideki: Raining pretty damn hard around one-ish last night.

Don't I know, said Murota Hideki, pulling at his damp shirt with his fingers. Soaked through to the skin . . .

So why'd you walk, not get a taxi?

You know how it is, said Murota Hideki. A walk, some air, clear the head, seemed like a good idea at the time.

And now, said the older cop, the crumb of a sneer in the corner of his mouth, you still think it was a good idea?

Murota Hideki sighed, held up his hands, and said, Look, you going to tell me why you're here? Or . . .

Or what, asked the older cop.

Murota Hideki shrugged again, laughed, and said, Or you just going to keep standing there while I keep sitting here, trying to imagine what it is you think I've done which I ain't? Or maybe to save us all some time, maybe I just call up my old friend Detective Hattori right now . . .

This your name card, said the older cop, taking a small evidence bag out of his pocket, handing the bagged name card across the desk to Murota Hideki. Your office?

Murota Hideki took the bag and the card, the card creased and rumpled, turned it over in his hand, then looked back up at the older cop and said, Well, seeing how you're standing in my office, talking to me, then I'm sure even you two wise guys have worked that out, no?

You're the only one playing the wise guy here, said the older cop. Just answer the question: Is it your name card?

Yes, said Murota Hideki, handing the bag and the card back to the older cop, nodding, and smiling. Obviously.

Obviously, yeah, said the older cop, looking down at the card in the bag in his fingers, tapping it against the palm of his other hand, nodding and smiling, too, as he looked back up from the bag and the card, then back over at Murota Hideki, saying, So maybe you'd like to explain how come this name card – this name card which is *obviously* yours, as you say – how come we found it crushed in the hand of a dead woman?

Murota Hideki swallowed, staring at the creased and rumpled card in the evidence bag, shaking his head.

Actually, to be *precise*, said the older cop, crushed in the hand of a dead and *naked* woman . . .

Murota Hideki swallowed again, still staring at the creased and rumpled card in the evidence bag in the hands of this cop, and he shook his head again.

In the hand of a dead and naked woman lying on the ground beneath the balcony of her fourth-floor apartment?

Murota Hideki looked up at the cop –

Yeah, said the older cop, staring at Murota Hideki, nodding. Lying on the ground beneath the balcony of her fourth-floor apartment in Higashi-Nakano . . .

Nemuro Kazuko, said Hideki Murota. She's dead?

Yeah, said the older cop again. Eventually.

What do you mean, "eventually"?

When she fell from her fourth-floor balcony, she landed on the top of a parked car, bounced off the roof of the car onto the ground, then died sometime later, never having regained consciousness, perhaps fortunately for you.

Murota Hideki swallowed again, shook his head again, then asked, Why "perhaps fortunately for me" . . . ?

Because *obviously* – among many other questions – she might've been able to answer why she either jumped or was pushed naked from her fourth-floor balcony clutching your fucking name card, Murota-san, right . . . ?

What does her husband say?

Hey, hey, hey, said the older cop. You ain't a policeman anymore, you're a suspect in a possible murder, is what you are, so you don't get to ask us a thing, okay?

Murota Hideki shook his head: I ain't a murder suspect, and you know it. Otherwise, you'd be talking to me on the judo mats in Nakano or whichever station you're from.

The younger cop stepped forward, closer to the desk, saying, Who the fuck you think you are –

Listen, wise guy, said the older cop, his hand on the arm of his partner but still looking down, staring at Murota Hideki. The only reason we're not hauling you in for questioning is your alibi, so you better hope your old buddy in First Division remembers last night the way you remember last night, or your feet won't touch the ground, we'll have you in so fast. But you still ain't told us how come your name card is in her dead fucking hand, so, alibi or no alibi, you better start telling us here and now – okay?

Murota Hideki had his hands up again, speaking as softly, as calmly and slowly as he could: Okay. Look, the only reason I mentioned her husband is I gave *him* my name card, not her. I never met, never spoke with her. Her husband is the person who had my name card, not her, that's all.

So go on, how come he had your card?

He called me up, couple of weeks ago, asked for an appointment, came here, I gave him a name card.

So he was your client then, yeah?

Murota Hideki sighed, smiled, and said, Come on, you know I can't say yes or no – right of privacy, you know that.

Fuck you and your right of privacy, Murota.

Not mine, his, said Murota Hideki. Up to me, I'd tell you everything I know, I got nothing to hide, but then he could sue my ass, and, as you can see, I can't be paying any legal fees, plus my reputation would be trashed, I'd never work again.

You work much, do you, laughed the younger cop.

Listen, said Murota Hideki, looking at the older cop. I'm not trying to tell you and your kid brother here how to do your jobs, but you speak to the husband, see if he'll tell you why he called on me, how come his wife has my card.

Gee, thanks for that, said the younger cop. Like we'd have never thought of doing that ourselves –

So what did he say?

The older of the two men sighed, shook his head, and said, You hard of hearing or just plain fucking dumb? I told you, you don't ask the fucking questions –

Hey, look, said Murota Hideki. I'm sorry. I just mean, if he's spoken to you, or speaks to you about me, and you tell me what he says, then I can tell you everything I know, that's all I'm trying to say because I want to help.

Don't worry, said the older cop, putting the evidence bag and the creased and rumpled name card back inside the pocket of his raincoat, taking out a name card of his own from inside his coat and jacket, flicking it down onto the top of the manuscript on the desk. You're going to get plenty of opportunity to help us

the light from the river, the gray, damp light from the window, from the river, gray, damp raindrop light on the window, down the window, and he looked at the wine, the wine in the glass, the muddy brown wine in the glass, and blinked and he blinked. He sniffed and he swallowed, then put the glass to his lips, the wine to his lips, tilting the glass, tasting the wine, on his lips and in his mouth, down his throat, muddy brown and thick, down it went, down it went, glass after glass, tilting and filling, gulping and gulping, down and down, glass after glass, the room, this office muddy brown and thick, the smell of the river, the drains and the toilets, the stench and the stink, the clothes on his back, his skin and his flesh, the man beneath, muddy brown and thick, the world, this life, the world and the life of this man, muddy brown and thick, inside and out, the blood cold in his veins, the blood fresh on his hands, muddy brown and thick, the blood on his hands, fresh on his hands, drinking and smoking, blinking and swallowing, drink after drink, swallowing and blinking, cigarette after cigarette, blinking and swallowing, the wine and the tears, in the gray, damp raindrop light, the tears down his face, the blood on his hands, fresh on his hands, his hands again, the blood on his hands, on his hands again, his hands again.

*I blamed myself, I blame myself, from then to now, that moment to this, from that moment, split moment, it came across the waves, over the waves, with a roll on the drums and the crash of a cymbal, over the waves, the radio waves, through the crackle and the hiss, the voice, that voice, it spoke, it said, in black electricity said,* The President Is Missing, *and I knew, just knew, and know, still know, I'd done, have done, a terrible, terrible, terrible thing, and I sprung up from my desk, grabbed my hat, found my wings, leaped from my house, out to the street, flew down the street, down street after street, through the twilight I flew, I flew, I flew to the store, but the store was closed, so I ran round the building, to the lions I ran, and I spoke to the lions, but the lions would not speak, I begged and I pleaded, but the lions would not speak, no matter how I begged, no matter how I pleaded, so I jumped from the lions, down from the lions, ran down the street, flew down the streets, my feet and my wings, down the streets, street after street to the park and its paths, through the trees and their shadows I ran and I flew, down the flight of stone steps to the gray metal door, and I banged on the door and I banged on the door, I bloodied that door with the fists of my hands, but the door would not open, the door would not open, so up the steps, back up the steps, I ran and I flew, my feet and my wings, round the corner, up the street, to tell the police, to beg the police to listen to me, please listen to me: They have lured him, they've abducted him, injected and sedated him, I know they have, just know they have, Japanese money and American guns, a man with a scar and his pal with a patch, they're waiting for night, the last train of the night, I know they are, just know they are, to lay his body across the tracks, then let the train, the last train do the rest, that's their plan, I know their plan, but there's time, there's time, still time, I know, so please stop the trains, the trains in their tracks, to stop the blood, his blood on the tracks, please, I beg you, beg you, please, to stop the trains and save the man, for there's time, there's time, I know there's time, but the police did not listen, they just would not listen, the police only laughed, they laughed and laughed, then threw me out, out onto the street, back into the night, with a punch to my ribs and a kick up my ass, onto the street, into the night, but I would not give up, I could not give up, so I picked myself up, back up on my feet, dusted myself down, the feathers of my wings, and off again I ran, I flew, for there was time, still time, I knew, as I ran down the street, flew past the palace, to the station, to Tokyo station, across the concourse, into the station, begging the staff, pleading with the staff, to stop, to stop, to please stop the trains, shouting and screaming, PLEASE STOP THE*

*TRAINS! But again they did not listen, again they would not listen, the staff they either turned away or threatened me – me, me, me – threatened to call the police on me, to have me arrested, for what, for what, said I, for causing a scene, for disturbing the peace, what peace, what peace, said I,* WHAT PEACE IS THIS, *asked I, the man has been lured and abducted, injected and sedated, the man who is your president, they are only waiting now, waiting for the train, the last train of the night, waiting to place his body on the tracks, then for the train, the last train of the night, then for the blood, his blood on the tracks, please, please,* PLEASE STOP THE TRAINS! *But still they did not listen, would not, could not listen, deaf or dumb, I knew, I know not which, for still they turned away, again they threatened me, so out onto the streets again, back into the night again I went, too tired to run, too tired to fly, through the city of the deaf, the city of the dumb, I wandered here, I wandered there, where somewhere, somewhere near, in this city of the deaf, this city of the dumb, they were carrying his body onto the tracks, they were laying his body down on the tracks, I knew, I knew, as I took out my watch, there was no time, as I looked at my watch, no time left now, as I heard the whistles, the whistles of the trains, the last trains of the night, north, south, east, and west they went, the last trains of the night, through the city, the city of the deaf, the city of the dumb, down the tracks, their tracks they went, toward the body, his body on the tracks, somewhere near, somewhere here in this city of the deaf, this city of the dumb, somewhere in this city, somewhere in this night, as I looked again at my watch, my watch now stopped, the time now gone, the time now lost,* TOO LATE, TOO LATE, *the rain, the rain, in drops, in drops, falling on the city, this city of the deaf, this city of the dumb, in drops, in drops, falling in the night, this night of tears, this night of blood, teardrops and blood-drops, falling on me, down my cheeks, the tears down my cheeks, falling on me, onto my hands, the blood on my hands, for I'd come to the bridge, the Bridge of Tears, of tears and farewell, forever farewell, and here, it was here, on the Bridge of Tears, with the tears down my cheeks, by the execution grounds, the old killing grounds, the blood on my hands, fresh on my hands, here, it was here I heard the sirens, the sirens in the night, across the city, through the night, they were coming toward me, then passing me by, over the bridge, the Bridge of Tears, across the grounds, the killing grounds, too late, too late, heading north and east, of course, of course, where the compass points, north and east, it points to demons, to demons and death, to death, to death, TO DEATH, with the tears down my cheeks and the blood on my hands, too late, too late, I know, I knew, I ran, I flew, through the night and through the rain, north and east, I ran, I flew, across the river, the Sumida River, following the sirens, the wailing of the sirens, north and east, to death, to death, I ran, I flew, across another river, the Arakawa River, night turning to dawn, with the light from the east, I came at last, too late, too late, at last I came, I saw, through the tears in my eyes, the fingers of my hand, the bloody fingers of my bloody hand, I saw, I saw, in pieces did I see, saw the pieces of the man, on the tracks, on the tracks, in pieces on the tracks, the pieces of the man, on the tracks, on the tracks, the pieces but no blood, no blood, no blood upon the tracks, the blood upon my hands, my hands, his blood upon my hands, then and now, I knew, I know: HIS BLOOD IS ON MY HANDS.*

*Darling, darling, what are you doing . . .*

He washed and washed and washed his hands, again and again and again, he washed and washed and washed his hands, shook his head, he shook his head, shook his head then squeezed his head, he squeezed and squeezed the temples of his head. He cupped the water in his hands again, drenched his face, his head and hair again, then turned off the faucet, ran his hands across his face, through his hair, wiped them down his shirt, and left the toilet once again. He went back down the corridor, into his office and back to his desk. He picked up the manuscript off the top of the desk, opened the bottom drawer of his desk, stuck the manuscript in the drawer under the envelope of dollars, then closed the drawer. He looked at his watch, his watch running slow, then picked up a pen from the desk, tore a piece of paper from his notebook. He scribbled a note to that guy Hasegawa, then picked up his still-damp jacket off the back of his chair, his keys and his cigarettes from the top of the desk. He put on his jacket as he walked to the door and out of the office. He closed and locked the door, folded and stuck the note to that guy Hasegawa in the frame of the door, then walked down the corridor, down the one, two, three, four flights of stairs and out of the building –

*It'll end in tears, in tears . . .*

Under a low and heavy morning sky of gray, through the damp and filthy city air, he crossed the river to the station, queued and bought a ticket, climbed the stairs to the platform, then queued again to board the train. Pressed and crushed among the bodies, the yellow metal carriage carried him west across the city, following the river he could not see, past buildings and palaces he could not see, pressed and crushed among the bodies, their limbs, their flesh, and their bones, all wrapped in clothes, in skins he could feel, he could smell, their secrets, their lies pressed and crushed and packed so tight, beneath their clothes, under their skins, these secrets and lies, all these secrets and lies, they stank, they stank, beneath his clothes, under his skin, he stank –

*Darling, please stop . . .*

Pressed and crushed, he fell from the train onto the platform, down the stairs, and through the ticket gates. He came out of the station, still carried with the crowds, these columns of workers, an army of ants, in their white shirts, their dark pants, all marching as one, marching to their companies, their offices, their chairs at their desks. He found the company he was looking for, walked through the door and up to reception. He gave the name of the man he was looking for to the girl on the desk, the pretty girl on the desk who was reluctant, suspicious. He told her it was an urgent matter, an urgent, personal matter, so she asked him his name, and he gave her a name that was not his name, a name that was a lie. The pretty, reluctant, and suspicious girl asked him to take a seat and to wait, to please have a seat and to wait. He thanked her and walked over to the seats, but he did not sit down. He took out a cigarette and lit it as he watched her pick up the phone and make the call, smoking the cigarette as he waited for the man to jump up from his chair at his desk, to leave his office as fast as he could, to take the elevator down to reception as quick as he could, to step out of the elevator into reception, as white as the shirt stuck to his skin, the man nodding nervously at the girl on reception, the man walking straight up to Murota Hideki, the man pleading, whispering, What the hell are you doing here?

What did you say to her, said Murota Hideki.

The man shook his head, struggling to breathe, to whisper: Nothing. I've not heard from her . . .

Murota Hideki stared at the man, this anxious, fearful man in his white shirt and dark pants in the reception area of his successful company, his precious little son at school, his pretty pregnant wife at home in their lovely little house, this man shaking, trembling before him, and Murota Hideki smiled and said, Well, I've got good news for you then, loverman: you're never going to hear from her again.

How do you know that, spluttered the man, shaking his head again. How can you be sure . . . ?

Murota Hideki smiled again, put a hand around the shoulders of the man, pulled him close toward him, and squeezed his shoulder as he said, Nemuro Kazuko is dead.

No, no, said the air in the man, said the soul of the man, exiting, fleeing the body, the shell of this man. No, no . . .

Yes, yes, yes, yes, said Murota Hideki, holding up the man, what was left of this man, telling the man, what was left of this man, Last night she fell from her balcony, landed on a car, bounced off its roof, onto the ground, and died.

Excuse me, said the pretty receptionist, no longer behind her desk, coming toward them, other people in the reception area stopping to stare at them. Is everything okay?

Murota Hideki let go of the man, let him fall to the chairs, fall in a heap, a broken, sorry heap in a chair, then Murota Hideki looked from the man to the girl, the pretty girl and to the people, the other people staring, and Murota Hideki shook his head and said, No, everything is not okay . . .

And Murota Hideki turned and walked away from the man, the broken, sorry man, all that was left of that man, away from the girl and the people, still pretty and still staring, walked away and out, out of reception, out through the doors of the company, this successful company, out and back onto the street, another prosperous street, out and into the city, this successful, prosperous, and resurrected city –

*In tears, in tears . . .*

He did not go back to the station, did not take another train, another metal fucking train, pressed and crushed among bodies of secrets, bodies of lies. He did not take a streetcar, a bus, or a taxi, just walked, he walked, away from the big companies, their offices, the shops and the stores, the department stores and the movie theaters, walking north, north and then west, through streets where there were little houses, little wooden houses in rows, still in rows with pots of flowers, flowers and wind chimes, though there was no sun today, no breeze today, walking under the still low and heavy sky of gray, walking through the still damp and filthy air, still the noise of construction, always construction, into the sky and on the air, walking, he walked until he came to the hill, the foot of the hill, and began to walk, walk up the hill. He did not look up, he looked down, down to the ground as he walked, up the hill, its rough-textured concrete, up this hill of narrow grooves. Halfway up he stopped to wipe his face, to wipe his neck, as a taxi and a mortuary ambulance slowly passed him going the other way, down the incline, down the hill –

*Darling, please . . .*

He put away his handkerchief, took out and lit a cigarette. He sat on the low guardrail and smoked the cigarette. He could hear the sound of children, the laughter, the shouts, the screams and cries of their play coming down the hill or maybe going up, he could not tell. He could hear the sound of crows, too, somewhere near, near here, but where, where, again he could not tell. He dropped the stub of the cigarette onto the ground, kicked it into one of the narrow grooves in the rough-textured concrete, then he started to walk again, walk up the hill again until he came to the top, the top of the hill, and then he looked up, up at the buildings –

*Please stop . . .*

The four-storied concrete buildings, the blocks and blocks of identical four-storied concrete buildings on the top of this concrete hill in the suburbs of this concrete city, each block the same height, the same color, the same two shades of gray and green, the same number of doors on each of the floors, four doors on each of the four floors. He took out his handkerchief, wiped his face and neck again, then walked toward the buildings, round the buildings to the back. He passed children on bicycles, children on roller skates, women with prams and women without. He came to the back of one of the buildings, walked along the back of this building, through a car park that was empty, empty of cars and empty of kids and their mums. He did not look up, did not look down, just walked along the back of this building until he came to the place, came to the spot, then he looked up, up to the fourth floor, up at the balcony, then he looked down, down at the ground, the stain on the ground, the concrete ground –

*Darling . . .*

He wiped his face again, then once again, then walked back around the building, back toward the entrance to the building, a concrete hole with no door, past the mailboxes to the stairs, the sixteen metal mailboxes in two rows of eight beside the stairs, then up the stairs, the concrete stairs he climbed, the one, two, three, four flights of stairs he climbed. At the top of the stairs he wiped his face again, then put away his handkerchief and walked along the passageway, the open, concrete passageway. At the end of the passageway he stopped before a white steel door framed in green. He swallowed, swallowed again, then pressed the white plastic buzzer and waited. Then he heard a lock turn, saw the door begin to open, open out toward him, smelt the incense from within, now saw the face of a man, and now heard the man ask, Yes . . . ?

Murota Hideki took a step back from the door and the man, this man in a black suit and black tie, his face unshaven, his eyes bloodshot. Murota Hideki bowed slightly, then said, Excuse me, may I speak to Nemuro Hiroshi please?

Yes, said the man in the black suit and black tie, with his unshaven face and bloodshot eyes, this man Murota Hideki had never met, never seen before. I am Nemuro.

On the fourth floor of this concrete block, on this open concrete passageway, before this open metal door, the smell of incense from within, before this man he'd never met or seen before, Murota Hideki blinked, blinked again, swallowed, and then stammered, Excuse me, I made a mistake . . .

What do you mean, said the man.

I'm sorry, said Murota Hideki with another bow, short and quick, then he turned to go, to walk away . . .

Wait, said the man, reaching out from the doorway to try to grab Murota Hideki, to stop –

Murota Hideki too quick for the man, not stopping for the man, walking away from the man . . .

But the man was in his shoes, coming after him, shouting, I know who you are! You're him, you're him! The man the police told me about, the name on the card –

Murota Hideki started to run, down the stairs, down the one, two, three, four flights of stairs . . .

Stop, stop, called the man after him, shouted after him. You're him, you're him. The man –

Down the stairs and out past the mailboxes, out of the building and back down the hill . . .

Who killed my wife –

As fast as he could, as quick as he could, his face as red as the blood on his hands . . .

Murderer!

*Darkness covered Tokyo, covered Tokyo again, an old and hidden darkness that had never gone away, that had stayed, silent, round corners, waiting in rooms, under floors and under stairs, silent and waiting, behind screens, behind doors, in the wood of a shrine, the pocket of a uniform, on the other side of sunshine, in the damp of a handshake, the space between words, the blank and empty spaces, of promises and toasts, behind the smile, behind the teeth, in the hollows of laughter, the cold black pupil of an eye, that in the blink of an eye was back again, all black again, that darkness back again, rolling over Tokyo, pouring over Tokyo, in clouds and in waves, so thick and so tall, with the clap of its thunder, the whistle of its train, which shook the night, which pierced the night, waking, it is said, MacArthur in his bed, in fright in the night, pale and deathly white, he screamed, Old soldiers never die, never die, Blackie and Uki, Brownie and Koko, howling with their master's voice, the terror in his voice, the Emperor, too, his other dog, the living dead, is said, is said, that night it's said he rose in dread, in robes of red, to light the lanterns for the dead, the* obon *lanterns for the spirits of the dead, the restless spirits of the dead, in whispered chants by lantern-light, the dead they said, In shades we fade, we fade away, but never, never go away, silent and waiting, we come again, we come again, so thick and tall, in cloud and waves, rolling over Tokyo, pouring over Tokyo, torrents of darkness, torrents of rain, over the tracks and over the cops, the darkness and the rain, so ferocious and strong it knocked the policemen from their feet, picking up the parts of his body from the tracks, the pieces of his flesh from the rails, they slipped and they fell, in the dirt and the mud, dropped the parts of his body, the pieces of his flesh, tumbling down the embankment, splattered here and there, the cops and the corpse, akimbo, akimbo, the cops and the corpse, dancing akimbo, divided and splayed, the cops and the corpse, forever akimbo, in their* ankoku *dance, dancing in the dark, the darkness over Tokyo, over Tokyo again, over Tokyo and me again, yes, me again, for there was I, yes, there was I, in the torrents of darkness, the torrents of rain, at the scene of the crime, the author of the crime, drenched and soaked, with his blood on my hands, dark to the bone, cowering in the shadows, weeping in the weeds, in blood drops and teardrops, cried I and said, Would I could raise the dead, resurrect the man from these tracks, the parts of his body, the pieces of his flesh, steal his body from this scene, save his flesh from this crime; yes, then and there, it was then and there, in the torrents of darkness, in the torrents of rain, yes, then and there, it was then and there, in the shadows and the weeds, vowed I and said, I will take the parts of his body, the pieces of his flesh, I will put them together again, stitch them back together again, word by word, sentence by sentence, put him together again, make this man whole again, line by line and page by page, I will raise the dead, resurrect the man, chapter by chapter, chapter and verse, I will write this crime –*

*I will right this wrong!*

Fuck, fuck, fuck, he shouted, slamming down the receiver on the dead tone and disconnected number written on the name card of the man he thought had been Nemuro Hiroshi. You dumb, dumb, dumb and stupid fuck, fuck, fuck –

*Darling, please don't, she said . . .*

Don't tell me don't, he said, picking up the bottle again, pouring another glass again. Please, not today –

*But it will do you no good . . .*

So what, he said again, waving the glass in his hand, spilling the drink across his desk. Nothing does me no good!

*Darling, just let it go . . .*

Let it go, he laughed. How can I let it fucking go, when it don't let me fucking go, they never let me go –

*He used you, like they always use you . . .*

I know he used me, he said, then he drained his glass, picked up the bottle, refilled the glass, shaking his head as he said, You don't have to fucking tell me, I know he fucking did, know they always fucking do, like it's the only fucking thing I'm good for, being fucking used, only fucking here to be used, people like me, to be fucking used, people like us –

*They see you coming, darling, they . . .*

See me coming, yeah, yeah, he said, nodding his head, sipping his drink, staring down at his desk, the manuscript there on his desk, looking back up at him, staring back at him as he whispered, You're right, they saw me coming –

*They set you up, she said . . .*

Putting down his glass, picking up the manuscript, and nodding again, Murota Hideki said, Just like they set him up.

*

*I banged and banged upon the door of his house in Den-en-chōfu, banged and banged until my knuckles were red and bloody raw, till at last, at last Mr. Shiozawa opened his door just a crack, a crack through which he said, "Why, Sensei – whatever is the matter? You'll wake the dead!"*

"Exactement," *said I, thrusting my papers and self through the crack in his door, stepping into his* genkan, *out of my* geta *and up into his house. "That's why I'm here!"*

*"By all means, please do come in, Sensei," said Mr. Shiozawa, following me down his wide hallway and into his large study. "Though you do know what time it is, Sensei?"*

*"I know what time they say it is," snorted I, plonking myself down on his beautiful velvet chaise longue. "But I say to them, 'You don't fool me! I know it's too late, too late!'"*

*"Or perhaps a little too early," said Mr. Shiozawa with a smile, as he wiped the sleep from his eyes, then adjusted his gown.*

*"Just you read this," exclaimed I, springing up from the chaise longue, throwing my papers in his direction, the sheets of paper falling over the low table between us. "Then you tell me if it's perhaps a little too early or, in fact, MUCH TOO LATE!"*

*"Of course," said Mr. Shiozawa, still smiling, gathering up my papers. "It's always a privilege and a delight to read your work, Sensei, even at an unexpected hour such as this, before the dawn. But please, dear Sensei, please do sit back down and please do calm down – you do seem to have a touch of the Russian."*

*"Russian! Ha," laughed I. "Why not, why ever not! And if not Russian, why not Chinese? Anyone red will surely do!"*

*"My dear, dear Sensei, please," said Mr. Shiozawa, in a soft and gentle, soothing voice, placing my papers in a pile on the table between us, then walking over to his well-stocked cabinet of drink. "Perhaps I might suggest, if I may, a little brandy for breakfast to steady your nerves, while I sit and read your words?"*

*"I never say no, as you know," said I.*

*"A quality we publishers admire in any writer," said Mr. Shiozawa, as he handed me a large glass of brandy, then sat down across from me, picking up the papers from the table between us.*

*"You'll be needing a large one of these yourself," said I, raising my glass of brandy in thanks, "after you've read –"*

"The Assassination Club," *read aloud Mr. Shiozawa from the title page in his hand, nodding. "A fine title, Sensei . . ."*

*"A fine title for a tale of foul deeds," declared I. "A tale that spits the truth in the faces of our gods old and new, our leaders and invaders, into all our faces, our guilty faces!"*

*"Then please, my dear Sensei," said Mr. Shiozawa, turning to the opening page. "Please relax with your brandy, and another, if you wish, and let me read of this truth in silence . . ."*

*"Say no more," said I, a finger to my lips, then the glass to those lips, reclining on the chaise longue, then rising from the chaise longue to freshen up my drink, then pacing around his large study as he read, admiring the books on his shelves, the scrolls on his walls, the quality of his brandy, the quantity of his brandy, idly wondering how on earth it could be that one such as he, a publisher who published such junk, including junk of my own, could afford all these books, all these scrolls, such a large study in such a beautiful home, testing again the consistency of the quality of his brandy, not finding it wanting, amazed our invaders, our occupiers had not requisitioned this house, his beautiful home, vainly pondering what on earth he must have said or done, what price he must have paid to keep our invaders, our occupiers, those foreign wolves from his door –*

*"Well, well, well," said Mr. Shiozawa, putting my papers down on the table, then looking up from his chair. "That's quite a tale indeed, Sensei, and my compliments to you indeed, Sensei."*

*"I come not for your compliments, just as I write not for compliments," slurred I, aware I was now a little light of head,*

*collapsing back down upon his chaise longue, aware, too, I was now a little unsteady on my pegs. "I come to challenge you to publish this, to print this, if you dare . . ."*

*"Of course, of course," said Mr. Shiozawa. "But forgive me, Sensei dear, forgive me, please, for as a publisher, your publisher, dear Sensei, I'm forced to ask you for proof – what proof do you have for that to which your fingers point?"*

*I inhaled, then exhaled and exclaimed, "Proof? You ask me for proof? It is in the very air we breathe – can you not taste it in the air, smell it and feel it? This is nineteen hundred and forty-nine, they say, and the gas, the sleeping gas is rising thick and rising fast – wake up, man, wake up!"*

*"Rest assured, dear Sensei, thanks to you I have awoken," said Mr. Shiozawa. "But as you are aware, only too aware, as a publisher I'm legally obliged to submit all materials I might wish to publish first to the censors at GHQ. However –"*

*"You dare not," snorted I. "I knew it, I knew it!"*

*"Sensei, please let me finish," said Mr. Shiozawa, leaning forward in his chair, picking up my papers once again. "For there is a way, if you'll please just hear me out . . ."*

*"All ears am I," said I, my fingers to my ears, pulling out my ears. "All ears . . ."*

*"Then perhaps you might consider changing the names, rewriting the piece as fiction, a work of fiction, perhaps?"*

*"Fiction," said I, letting go of my sore ears, sitting upright on the chaise longue, contemplating. "Fiction . . ."*

*"May still the censor's red pen," said Mr. Shiozawa, nodding. "And then we could publish . . ."*

*"Why not, why not," said I, declared I. "After all, as Cao Xueqin says, 'Truth becomes fiction when the fiction is true.'"*

*"'And the real becomes not-real when the unreal is real,'" said Mr. Shiozawa, nodding again, patting my papers.*

"Exactement," *laughed I.*

*"But," said Mr. Shiozawa, lowering his voice, "as in* The Story of the Stone, *be aware, dear Sensei, that less-than-gentle readers may still inquire after the origins of your tale . . ."*

*"Have no fear," laughed I again. "For I have no fear!"*

*"My only fear is fear for you, my dear Sensei dear," said Mr. Shiozawa. "Remember, please remember, not for nothing do they say he who speaks feels the cold on his lips . . ."*

*"Pah," laughed I again, and then exclaimed, "Rather the cold upon my lips than swallow the tooth with the blood!"*

*"Fine words, Sensei," said Mr. Shiozawa, tapping my papers. "As are the words in your story, fine and brave words, dear Sensei. But either way, the cold on your lips or the tooth in your belly, let us pray we won't need to call you a doctor . . ."*

He had found the house, to the north of the hospital, in a nice part of town, on the top of a hill, the hill he was climbing –

*Stop! Stop, she was whispering. Turn back . . .*

There's no turning back, he muttered, as he climbed the hill, another big hill, not a concrete hill, a pretty, wooded hill of big, monied houses. No turning back on a one-way ride.

*Please, she said. This is the Path of Error . . .*

But he had reached the top of the hill, the biggest house of biggest money. Before its tall wooden fence, its traditional gate, he took out his handkerchief. He wiped his face, he wiped his neck. He put away his handkerchief, took out his necktie from the pocket of his jacket and put it on –

*A noose around your neck . . .*

We'll see, we'll see, he laughed to himself, taking out his spectacles from another pocket, putting them on. He opened the gate, stepped under its eaves, into the garden and onto the stones of its path, another path of stones through another garden of trees, leading to another traditional, beautiful house.

He slid open the door of the house, stepped into the darkness of its *genkan*, and called out, I'm sorry, excuse me . . . ?

A middle-aged woman in an austere kimono shuffled toward him down the dim hallway: Yes?

Is Doctor Nomura home, asked Murota Hideki, adjusting his spectacles, smiling at the woman.

Her face pale and pinched, eyes black and cold, she stared at Murota Hideki: Who are you?

I'm Horikawa, said Murota Hideki.

There was a spark, the brief spark of flint on flint in the caves of her eyes: What do you want?

I'd like to speak with Doctor Nomura, said Murota Hideki, smiling again. About my uncle, Horikawa Tamotsu.

The woman lowered her dark eyes, her pale face in the slightest of bows: I'm sorry. My father is retired now.

I know, said Murota Hideki. And I'm very sorry to call unannounced, very sorry to trouble him in his retirement. But you see, I'm afraid my uncle has gone missing.

The woman looked up, a terrible contempt in the corners of her mouth: Well, your uncle is not here.

I didn't think he would be, said Murota Hideki, smiling still, standing still, looking past the woman, looking down the hall, looking past a carved bird of prey on a table in the hall, glancing at a telephone on another table down the hall, still smiling, still saying, But I'd like to speak with your father.

The daughter lowered her eyes, her face again, and tried again: My father is retired now. He would have no idea where your uncle might be, and so good day to you.

Still standing but not smiling now, Murota Hideki took off his spectacles, put them back inside the pocket of his jacket, then stared at her and said, I'd like to ask him myself.

That won't be possible, said the woman, a slight, slight tremor in her voice. My father is not a well man.

Neither is my uncle, Uncle Tamotsu.

He does not receive visitors.

Then you should bar your gate and lock your door, said Murota Hideki, leaning forward toward her. Otherwise, a man like me, he might get the wrong impression.

In her dim hall of old wealth, with no rings on her fingers, no husband or son in this house or her life, this dutiful daughter took a slight, slight step back, thinking about turning, but turning to where, turning to whom, knowing there was nowhere, knowing there was no one, nowhere but here, no one but him, her mouth dry, her voice cracked: Who are you?

I told you, he told her again. I'm just a man who wants to speak with your father, Doctor Nomura.

And I told you, she told him again, but not a statement, now a plea. That's not possible.

We can do this all day, said Murota Hideki, taking a step toward her, toward the next step, the step up into her house. But I am going to speak with him.

She steeled herself, to slow her breathing, to steady her voice, one last try, one last time: If you don't leave now, I'm going to call the police . . .

No, you're not, said Murota Hideki, as he took the next step, up into her house, as she turned, but turned too late, slipping, falling onto her face and the wood of the floor with a dull slap that echoed –

*Stop! Stop . . .*

Echoed through the house, the silence of the house, as he reached down, grabbed the back of her kimono by its collar, turning her over, gripping the collar as he dragged her down the hallway, her hands to the collar and his fingers, struggling to free her throat from the grip of the cloth, the grip of his hand, her white socks, her white legs kicking up the skirts of her kimono as he pulled her along, down the hallway, toward the telephone, using his free hand to snatch at the phone, rip its cord from the wall –

Stop, please stop, the choking woman tried to scream, but Murota Hideki would not stop, he did not stop, pulling her, dragging her from one room to the next, sliding open one door then the next, until he slid open the last door and found the room, he'd found the room he was looking for, found the doctor he was looking for, lying on a futon on the mats of this room, his face on a pillow, his eyes turned to the door, the sight in the doorway, Murota Hideki standing in the doorway, throwing the woman, spinning the daughter across the room, over the mats, toward the doctor, toward her father, the woman sprawling over the mats, across the mats, scrambling toward the futon, toward her father, spluttering then coughing, shouting and screaming, Leave us alone, please leave us alone.

Murota Hideki took out his handkerchief, wiped his face and wiped his neck. He put away his handkerchief, took out his cigarettes. He lit a cigarette, put the packet back inside his pocket. He smoked the cigarette, looking around the room, the large room with the large windows which looked out upon the large garden of large trees. He came to the end of his cigarette, walked over to a vase of flowers in an alcove. He bent down, took the flowers from the vase, lay them on the wood of the alcove, then dropped the end of his cigarette into the vase. He stood up, turned back to the man on the futon, the daughter holding the man, both looking up at him, staring up at him as he said, I'll leave when you tell me what I need to know. But if you don't, or you won't, then I'll start to do things to you, to both of you, to make you tell me what I need to know.

But I told you, he's ill, he's retired, pleaded the woman, holding her father tighter. He doesn't know anything.

Murota Hideki walked across the mats, squatted down beside the futon, beside the man and his daughter, and he looked down into the eyes of the old man and said, That's not true, is it, Doctor Nomura? You know many things.

His eyes blinking, watering, his voice parched with age, with cancer, the old man looked up at Murota Hideki and whispered, What do you want to know?

I want to know the truth about Kuroda Roman, said Murota Hideki, calmly and softly. I want to know what happened to him and where he is.

If he's not back in the hospital, if he's not at his house, said the doctor, coughing, then I don't know where he is.

Murota Hideki reached for a jug and a glass. He poured water into the glass. He handed the glass to the daughter, then raised the head of the man from the pillow so he could drink from the water in the glass in the hand of his daughter.

Thank you, said the old man, as Murota Hideki lowered his head back down to the pillow.

Murota Hideki took the glass out of the hand of the daughter, then turned back to her father and said, calmly and softly again, he said, The last time Horikawa was discharged, it was you who discharged him. Just like the last time he was admitted, it was you who admitted him. Just like each time he was admitted, each time he was discharged, it was you, always you, Doctor Nomura, signing him in and signing him out.

So many times, whispered the old man, his eyes closing, tears in their corners. I don't remember.

Please, said the woman, touching the arm of Murota Hideki. He really doesn't remember . . .

Murota Hideki patted the woman's hand on his arm, then wiped the tears from the corners of her father's eyes and said, It doesn't matter if he remembers or not, it's all in the file, in his own hand, isn't it, doctor?

But I don't know where he is now, said the old man again, opening his eyes again, staring up at the ceiling.

But you do know who brought him to the hospital, said Murota Hideki. And who picked him up, don't you?

The old man turned his head on the pillow, his dying eyes looking up at Murota Hideki, shaking his head and blinking his eyes, whispering, It's not what you think . . .

Then tell me, what should I think?

Papa, Papa, said the daughter, reaching out toward her father again, trying to stop him –

Murota Hideki grabbing her again, hauling her back and away again.

What does it matter now, said the old man, closing his eyes again. I'm dying, I know . . .

Papa, Papa, no . . .

Tell me.

I wasn't his doctor, I was never his doctor.

Papa, please don't, please . . .

Who was his doctor?

An American . . .

Don't, Papa . . .

Who?

His name was Morgan, said the old man, opening his eyes, staring up at Murota Hideki. Doctor Morgan.

You won't get away with this, screamed the daughter, the woman with the glass in her hand –

I know, said Murota Hideki, waiting for the glass in her hand, the glass to smash into his head. I know I won't.

*Telephones ring in rented rooms, the rented rooms of rented men, the rented men with rented hands and eyes and tongues; yes, my plan to beat the ground, to startle the snakes, had worked, and worked rather well, even if I say so, do say so myself; I had stated in the press that this was a crime, a murder most foul; I had boasted to the press that I had knowledge, knowledge of the crime; I had sworn in public that I would solve this crime, the Crime of the Century; I had published* The Assassination Club *as fiction, a fiction that was true; and then I had waited, waited for the snakes to come out of the grass, and come they had come, out of the grass, on their bellies, from the long grass they'd come –*

*"Just a moment . . . yes, you, sir."*

*Late and dark it was, still hot and damp, one summer night it was, less than a month after the crime, when this cold voice ran down the length of my spine, freezing my feet, stopping me dead. From the foot of the hill I had seen them creeping down the hill from Yanaka toward me, disappearing then appearing again, through the huddles of humid mist, floating up then sinking down again, but I had not heard the sound of their feet, only then, as they passed, that voice, that command –*

*"Just a moment . . ."*

*Like the cry of a crow in the dark, like the scream of a heron in the night; the stranger on the train who stares at you with contempt and hate, raw yet crisp –*

*"Yes, you, sir . . ."*

*That voice spoke to me, that command was for me, freezing my feet and stopping me dead. From out of the black summer mist, from the cemetery on the hill, one, two, three, four of them, four grave markers, in single file they passed me by: the first was a man tall and gaunt, dressed in a coat the color of this night, spun and woven from the shades of its mists; the second was short with a paunch, giggling and whispering into his hands, talking to himself; the third was a proud man in his middle years, his hair already white, his limbs lost in the long sleeves and skirts of an old kimono which brushed the ground as he passed, his face turned from mine; the fourth and last man, muscular and of military bearing, gripped the tails of the third man, hidden in his shadow, the most obscure of the four, yet I knew it was his voice which had frozen my feet, whose command stopped me dead, and I turned as they passed to look back and ask –*

*"Are you speaking to me?"*

*The one, two, three, four of them, in their single file, they stopped, two, three, four paces down the slope from me, but they did not turn to look at me, to look back up at me, yet the man at the rear, the fourth and last man, he let go of the tails of the third man and straightened to attention –*

*"I am speaking to you."*

*A curse flung at a barking dog, his answer both scolded and threatened me, the breath of hell itself, it mocked and frightened me, stopped the night and chilled the air, yet captured and tempted me to ask –*

*"What do you want?"*

*Still he did not turn, turn to look back up at me, but stared straight ahead, down the hill, as he said –*

*"I wish to speak with you."*

*"About what?"*

*Down the slope, on the tracks, a train was coming from Ueno, the last train of the night, heading toward Nippori, its wheels all fire and steam, on through the night, it whistles and screams, blind and into the night –*

*"It's closing time," he said, through the steam, through the screams, the ringing of a telephone, the whisper down the line. "But Zed Unit are not to be blamed for nothing."*

Were you followed?

No.

Under a twilit sky, on a bench, hidden by trees, in Hibiya Park, two men were sat together. One man was dressed in the white robes of a war veteran, a cane in his hand, a cap on his head, dark amber spectacles hiding his eyes; the other man had a dirty bandage wrapped around his head, specks of dried blood on his jacket and shirt. Terauchi Kōji glanced at Murota Hideki, then away again, and said, What happened to your head?

People don't like the questions I ask.

But still you keep asking them.

Yes, said Murota Hideki.

That's why you tracked me down, you called me up; to ask me questions I won't like.

Your name and number were in the address book of Kuroda Roman, said Murota Hideki. You've been in the papers, in magazines. You seem to like to talk.

Terauchi Kōji turned the top of his cane in the fingers of his hand, laughed, and then said, I choose to hide in plain sight, Murota-san. Makes it harder for them, that little bit harder. But for fifteen years now I've been looking over my shoulder, waiting for the push in the back on the crowded station platform, at the top of a steep flight of stairs, or off the curb of a busy street. For fifteen years, Murota-san, fifteen years I've been living in this nightmare, hiding in plain sight, seeming "to like to talk." But if that's what you think?

I try not to think, said Murota Hideki. I just want to find Kuroda Roman, ask him a question, listen to his answer, then get the fuck out of this city, away from all this.

The air thick and still, darkening and more stifling by the minute, Terauchi Kōji laughed again, into the gloom again, then said, That's very candid of you, Murota-san. And so if I may be equally candid, I would suggest you forget about Kuroda-sensei, forget about your questions, and get the fuck out now, away now, while you still can.

Murota Hideki turned to look at the man beside him on the bench, this pale figure in the dark park, and said, That sounds like a threat – are you threatening me, Terauchi-san?

No, said Terauchi Kōji, his peaked cap and tinted spectacles turning to face Murota Hideki. Not at all.

Murota Hideki patted the top of the thigh of the pale figure on the bench beside him, smiled, then said, That's good. Because I'm not going anywhere until I've found Kuroda Roman, until I've asked him my question, and nor are you, Terauchi-san, until you've answered my questions.

That's why I'm here, why I came, said Terauchi Kōji. But I don't hear any questions, just a lot of –

Where is he – where's Kuroda?

Terauchi Kōji turned his peaked cap, his tinted spectacles back to the dark of the park, the shadows of its trees, smiled again, then said, I don't know, and I'm glad I don't.

Is that right? And why's that then?

Because maybe he's someplace you, me, we – all of us – someplace we cannot reach, someplace, then, they cannot reach, someplace far from them, out of their reach, that's why.

They, them, their reach, said Murota Hideki, gripping the thigh of the man, gripping it tight. You're them.

The pale man did not flinch, he just laughed again, into the dark, and said again, Is that what you think?

I told you, Murota Hideki told him again. I don't think. But I see and I see you, and you're either one of them, working for them, or a fraud, a fantasist, and a charlatan.

The air thicker still and still more still, pitch black and suffocating, Terauchi Kōji said, I am not one of them, have never worked for them, nor am I a fraud, a fantasist, or a charlatan. But I had the misfortune to know some of them and for one of them to tell me what they had done that night, that terrible night in July 1949, that night that changed the course of history. I am not a Communist, nor even slightly sympathetic, Murota-san, but they had disobeyed orders and murdered an innocent man, a good and decent Japanese man. And so I made a choice, for it was my choice and mine alone, to share what I'd been told, the truth that I'd been told.

But why choose Kuroda Roman, hissed Murota Hideki. Why drag him into all this, him of all people?

I gave him a choice, I warned him. And he made his choice. But he was already fucked, already rotting – just like you're already fucked, already rotting, Murota-san, just like I'm already fucked and rotting, too – but fifteen years ago, almost fifteen years ago to the day, to the night, we sat on this bench, this very bench in this park, and I warned him –

*"Too late, it's too late . . ."*

*"No, no," shouted I, springing up from the bench, running as quick as I could through the shadows of the trees, to the gates of the park, muttering and vowing, "It's never too late, too late . . ."*

*But I was going to be late, was going to be late, I knew, stuffing my pocket watch back up inside the sleeve of my* yukata, *up there along with the rolled-up papers, my notes on the crime, the things he had said, the truth he had told, as I ran through the gates to the curb and looked left then right, but there were no buses, were no taxis, only cars and only trucks. "Just my luck!"*

*The lights at the crossing about to change, I started to run across the road, but halfway across, with the lights now green and the traffic advancing, the thong of my left* geta *tore –*

*I stepped out of both* geta, *bent down, picked them up, then sprinted barefoot for dear life, dear life, toward the other side, where, narrowly, and ironically, just missed by a taxi, I collapsed on the curb to a chorus of motor horns and whistles, police whistles and yells –*

*"You there – yes, you there, there on the curb: STOP!"*

*Heavens, no, not now, thought I, and I jumped up, bowed deeply in the direction of the police box on the other side, then turned and set off, with my* geta *in one hand and the hem of my* yukata *hitched up in my other, sprinting barefoot again, down side roads and up back alleys, first to Ginza, past department stores and street stalls, then to Kyōbashi, all the while humming the finale to the* William Tell *Overture, just to keep up my spirits and chin, to stop me from thinking, "Too late, it's too late . . ."*

*Until at last, at last, devoid of breath and hum, I hobbled on my bruised and bloody feet up the steps and through the revolving doors, into the foyer of the Daiichi Seimei Sōgo building, where I fair flung myself onto the sign board, which announced that the monthly meeting of the Mystery Writers of Japan was taking place in the Tōyōken on the seventh floor, clinging thankfully to the board, relieved it had yet to be taken down, that the meeting was still in session. But there was no time, no time to rest, was no moment, not a moment to lose, so I peeled myself from the board and limped over to the wall of elevators, only to find they were all out of order: "Typical, bloody typical."*

*I stared up, up, up, up, up, up, up at the stained-glass ceiling in the roof of the building, sighed, then staggered over to the staircase, hitched up the skirts of my* yukata *once again, and began to whistle the "Flight of the Bumblebee" as I climbed up, up, up, up, up, up, up the one, two, three, four, five, six, seven flights of stairs to the imposing, grand, and closed double doors of the Tōyōken up, up, up, up, up, up, up on the seventh floor, where, heaving open the heavy doors with the very last ounce of my strength, I stumbled inside with a loud, "DA-DAA!"*

*But there at the back of the meeting room, through a thick fog of cigarette smoke, I was greeted by the words of the much-lauded and best-selling founder and chairman of the Mystery Writers of Japan, as he announced, "That concludes our special meeting to debate the death of the late Mr. Shimoyama Sadanori, President of the Japanese National Railways . . ."*

*"No," cried I from the back. "No!"*

*"Thank you all for your attendance and for your many contributions to our most lively debate . . ."*

*"Wait," exclaimed I. "Wait!"*

*"Until next month . . ."*

*"I know who did it!"*

"Otsukaresama."

*"Exactly who did it, who killed President Shimoyama," shouted I, banging together my* geta. *"You have to listen –"*

*But the members of the Mystery Writers of Japan would not listen to me, they were not listening to me –*

*"For they are planning to kill again, and kill again soon, but there's time, still time, it's not too late, too late, for there's time, still time, for I am the Mystery –"*

*But the members of the Mystery Writers of Japan were not interested, were not interested in –*

*"The Mystery to the Solution!"*

*The Mystery Writers of Japan were packing up their things, heading to the doors –*

*"Stop, stop," shrieked and cried I. "Don't any of you care? Is it all just a game –"*

*Looking forward to their dinner and drinks, lots of drinks, pushing straight past me –*

*"A puzzle for the train, a quiz before bed?"*

*Brushing me off, walking right through me, as if I didn't exist, wasn't even there –*

*"But I know you can see me, know you can hear me, and I know what you think –"*

*Laughing and joking, gossiping and bitching: Has-been, never-was, drunk again, drunk and mad again, not even a mystery writer, nor even a writer, can't call that writing, what we would deem writing, that's what they thought, what they said –*

*"I know, I know, don't think I don't know –"*

*Leaving me alone, alone in that room, my* yukata *shamefully gaping undone, my battered, broken* geta *in my bloody, ink-stained hands, alone, alone, alone again –*

*"Go on then, ignore me then," whispered I, struggling to hold back my tears, my tears of rage and sorrow, of guilt and grief. "But I'll show you all, all of you, you'll see –*

*"I'll publish and be damned. I'll be damned, but so will you, all of you – we'll all be damned –*

*"Damn . . . . . . . ."*

*Most unfortunately, by the time I had dried the tears from my eyes and my cheeks, pulled myself and my* yukata *together, and limped back down the seven, six, five, four, three, two, one flights of stairs to the foyer, the Daiichi Seimei Sōgo building was lit only by stained-glass moonlight, its revolving glass doors and two side doors all padlocked and chained for the night. "Just my luck . . ."*

*I tugged on the chains and rattled the doors to confirm my sentence, then leaned my forehead against one of the panels of the revolving doors and stared out at the deserted night streets of the now seemingly abandoned capital, waiting for a passer-by to pass by, but who never passed by. "Typical, bloody typical."*

*After who knows how long, and having decided the entire city must have gone to bed early, but still cursing my ill luck and its repetitions, I stopped staring out at the forsaken streets and decided to find another way out of the building.*

*Over on the front desk there was a telephone; a stroke of luck for a change, thought I, as I picked up the receiver –*

*"What number, please," asked a female operator.*

*"Excuse me," whispered I, "but I don't need a number. I've been locked inside the Daiichi Seimei Sōgo building in Kyōbashi, and so I would be extremely grateful if you could please inform the appropriate authorities of my situation, thank you."*

*"Hello? You'll have to speak up, please."*

*"I'm sorry," said I, in my most normal voice. "But I've been locked inside the Daiichi Seimei Sōgo building in Kyōbashi, and*

*so please, please could you let the appropriate people know of my predicament – this pretty pickle I find myself in."*

*"Hello? Hello? Is anybody there?"*

*"Yes, yes," shouted I, "I'm here!"*

*But the line went dead.*

*I placed the receiver back down in its cradle, then picked it up again –*

*"What number, please," asked the same female voice.*

*"My name is Kuroda Roman," shouted I down the line. "And I've been locked inside the Daiichi Seimei Sōgo building in Kyōbashi! Could you please, please, PLEASE inform the appropriate authorities, and do so immediately!"*

*"This isn't funny," said the operator.*

*"I know that," laughed I.*

*But the line went dead again.*

*And so off I set, down the corridors of the ground floor of the Daiichi Seimei Sōgo building, along all the corridors, trying all the doors, the handles of every door I came to, only to find them locked, all locked. "Just my luck, just my luck . . ."*

*Back at the front desk, I glanced at the telephone, but thought better of it. I picked up my* geta, *looked down at my feet, my bruised and bloody and very dirty feet, and I sighed and said, "I'm sorry, dear feet, so sorry . . ."*

*And then slowly this time, I hobbled back up the first flight of stairs, then along the corridors of the mezzanine, past the closed-up restaurants, trying all the doors, and some of them twice, just in case, until –*

*"Eureka!"*

*– the handle of the door to the ladies' bathroom moved and I could open the door. No lights were on and all was quiet inside, but, just to be on the safe side, always best to be on the safe side, I called out, "Excuse me . . . ? Emergency . . ."*

*There was no answer.*

*I found the switch on the wall, turned on the lights, stepped inside, and, straight ahead, saw an outside wall with a window, a big window, and a big window which opened. I leaned out of the window, looked down at an alleyway some twelve or so feet down below, and said, "Could be worse."*

*I looked left along the outside ledge of the window, and there, at its corner, spied a thick and most solid-looking drainpipe running down the length of the wall, right down to the ground. "Could be a lot, lot worse, in fact."*

*I turned back to the sink. I ran the faucets, washed my hands, washed my face, and smoothed down my hair. Then I unthreaded both the broken and unbroken thongs from my* geta *and used the material to secure the sleeves of my* yukata *and their contents. Then I pulled up both corners of my* yukata, *knotted them together, and stuck the knot inside the belt of my* obi. *Then I clambered up onto the sill, through the window, and out onto the narrow ledge, where, clinging to the painted metal frame of the window, I turned myself around so I faced back into the bathroom and began to edge along the ledge, inch by inch, toward its corner and the drainpipe. Then, with the fingers of my left hand still gripping the last of the frame of the window, I stretched out the fingers of my right hand toward the drainpipe. Then, as the fingers of my right hand clutched the drainpipe, I leaned slightly back, let go of the window frame, and in a missed beat of my heart had the pipe in both hands. "Praise be! Hallelujah!"*

*Just below the window ledge, running parallel, a horizontal pipe met the main drainpipe, and so, still clutching that main pipe in both hands, I crouched down, taking my right foot off the ledge, searching for the junction where the two pipes met. Mission accomplished, my left foot then joined my right foot, so I was now off the ledge, completely attached to the main drainpipe. Then I hooked my poor, sore right foot around the main pipe, then my equally poor and sore left one, and began to tentatively, inch by inch again, descend the drainpipe, thinking how most fortunate it was, indeed and in fact, that I had spent so many hours of my days clambering up and down the myrtle tree in my garden; far from being a waste of time, it turned out now to have been very good and valuable practice –*

*"Sensei . . ."*

*"What the –" said I, looking up for the source of the voice from above, to find a very round and most peculiar, brown and furry face looking down at me from the window of the bathroom, waving some pieces of paper in both of its paws –*

*"You've forgotten these," said the face at the window, "with your mystery to the solution."*

*"What the –" said I again, but, at that very moment, I felt the drainpipe begin to move, to detach itself from the wall, to come and then to fall away . . .*

Fuck, said Murota Hideki. He put down the phone, looked at his watch, his watch running slow. He picked up the glass from his desk, drained the last of the wine from the glass. He put down the glass, picked up the manuscript, stuck it back in the drawer. He closed the drawer with his foot and stood up –

*Ton-ton. Ton-ton. Ton-ton. Ton-ton . . .*

He looked at his watch again, his watch still running slow. He picked up his jacket from the back of his chair and put it on, then his keys and his cigarettes from the top of his desk. He walked over to the door of his office, then turned –

*Ka-chunk, ka-chunk, ton-ton . . .*

He stared round the room, the tiny office and its yellow walls, at the dusty shelves and empty cabinet, the sticky desk with its brown rings, the glass and the bottle both empty and finished. He blinked, blinked again, tried to smile, to laugh, but turned back to the door. He opened the door, stepped out into the corridor, closed but did not lock the door –

*Ton-ton, don-don, ton-ton . . .*

He walked down to the end of the corridor and into the toilet, past the basin, the stall and the urinal. He opened the window wider, peering out, staring down, down to the street. He pulled his head in, then looked at his watch, his watch running slow. He turned to the urinal, undid his flies, and took a piss, a long piss. He did up his flies as he walked to the basin. He ran the faucet, he cupped the water. He washed his hands, washed and washed his hands, then looked up into the grime, the grime of the mirror above the basin: fifty-two, balding and bandaged, fat and gone-to-shit, always, forever shit –

*Don-don, ka-chunk . . .*

He cupped the water once again, washed his face and washed his neck. He turned off the faucet, dried his hands on his trousers, down the front of his shirt. He put his hand in his pocket and took out his handkerchief, his handkerchief stained with dry blood, his own dry blood. He wiped and dried his face in the stains of his own dry blood, then put his handkerchief back in his pocket and took out his cigarettes. He put a cigarette to his lips, lit the cigarette and inhaled, then exhaled, blew the smoke at the mirror, the smoke over the mirror, the grime in the mirror, his face in the grime, hidden in the mirror, lost in the smoke. He tried to smile, to laugh again, but failed again and blinked, then blinked again and said, Fucking liars –

*But you knew that, darling, know they're . . .*

Cunts, he spat through the smoke, into the mirror, then turned from the mirror, away from the smoke, glanced at his watch, his watch running slow, then dropped the cigarette butt into the sink, down the plughole, and walked out of the toilet, into the corridor and down the stairs, the four flights of stairs, out of the building, onto the street, across the street, into the shadows, the shadows of the morning, in the shadows of the alleyway, across from his building, to watch –

*Don't, darling, please, please . . .*

From the shadows of the alleyway, in the shadows of the morning, under a damp and rodent sky, all fur and teeth, amid the stench from the river, the river and fumes, the noise of construction, construction and trains –

*Shu-shu, pop-po, shu-shu . . .*

He watched and he waited, watched for the car, waited for the car, an old gray car to come down the street, slowly, slowly down the street. He watched the car pull up outside his building, saw a passenger door open and a man get out, a thin young man in a tight, shiny suit. He watched the young man close the passenger door, saw the young man go up the steps, into his building, and then –

*Don't, darling . . .*

Murota Hideki stepped out of the shadows, ran across the street to the car and its door, its passenger door. He opened the door, climbed into the back, over the seat, toward a man, an old, old man in a white double-breasted suit, shouting, I know who you are –

This old, old man in his white double-breasted suit, in his round, tinted spectacles and Panama hat, nodding at Murota Hideki, smiling at Murota Hideki, as the driver reached into the back of the car, grabbing and pulling Murota Hideki –

You set me up, shouted Murota Hideki into the face of this old, old man. You set Kuroda up and –

That guy who called himself Hasegawa back out of the building and down the steps, joining the driver, grabbing and pulling Murota Hideki away from the man, out of the car, onto the street, hard into the ground, pinning him down, holding him down, ripping open the collar of his shirt as this old, old man stepped out of the car and onto the sidewalk, Murota Hideki pinned down, held down on the ground as the old, old man crouched down, down beside Murota Hideki, reached inside his white double-breasted suit, and took out a narrow velvet case, opened the case and took a syringe from the case –

I know, I know, screamed Murota Hideki, pinned to the ground, held down by their arms, their hands gripping his face, twisting his neck, the veins of his neck throbbing and bare, bare and exposed, exposed to the syringe, the needle of the syringe. You set up Shimoyama. You murdered Shimoyama.

# 7

## Minus Five to Minus One

---

*June 30–July 4, 1964*

*Yes, I was falling, yes, falling, toppling head first and long, long into darkness, falling down, slowly down, from the drainpipe, from the wall, past windows and their ledges, falling, still falling, down, slowly down, past walls, more walls, bookcases and cupboards, maps and pictures hung upon pegs, maps of the city, the Occupied City, pictures of the crime, the scene of the crime, falling down, slowly down, bottles and jars standing on shelves, a bottle marked "CLUES," a bottle marked "WITNESSES," a jar labeled "FICTION," a jar labeled "TRUTH," and as I fell, slowly fell, through the darkness, past the shelves, I reached for the jar, the jar labeled "TRUTH," and I took down this jar, this jar from the shelf, this jar labeled "TRUTH," the biggest, heaviest jar I ever had seen, seen or held, held in my hands, but as I fell, slowly fell, when I prized off the lid, when I opened the jar, to my great disappointment, my instant regret, all the truths blew away, flying up, up and away, back the way I'd come, up, up into the night, in a rainbow of butterflies, feathers, and petals, and as I tried to juggle the jar and its lid, tried to catch one truth, one butterfly, feather, or petal at least, one truth at least, this jar labeled "TRUTH," this jar now empty, it slipped through my fingers, it dropped from my hands, spinning off, spiraling down, slowly down, down and down, into the darkness, the darkness below –*

*"Look out," cried I. "Look out down below!"*

*No answer came up from the darkness below, just the echo of my voice, my voice in the dark: "Look out . . ."*

*But too late, too late came the echo of my voice, a warning in the dark, for thump! thump! thump! down I came upon a heap of broken jars, then bump! bump! bump! down something came upon my head, and I remembered –*

*Nothing more until I was not falling anymore, not in darkness anymore, not lying on a heap of broken jars anymore, nor in a pile of garbage in an alley anymore. I was being picked up, I was being carried along –*

*I opened my eyes: I was slumped on the back seat of a big car, with a sore head and aching bones, the car speeding through the night and the city –*

*"Thank heaven you've come round, Sensei," said the voice of the driver from the front, as I tried to sit up. "But I'd lie still, if I were you. Looks like you took an almighty tumble."*

*I nodded, but even that hurt. Still, I managed to blink a few times, to try to focus on the driver, the driver hunched in the front, a man too large even for a car of this size, dressed in a military coat unsuitable for late March, let alone for early July – assuming it was still early July – his hands on the steering wheel wrapped in winter gloves. But it wasn't winter, must be still summer, for I was sweating, soaked and dripping, my tattered* yukata *sopping wet through –*

*"So sorry about that, Sensei," said the driver. "But if I hadn't gone into the alley to answer nature's call, and if the stream of my call hadn't roused you, then I'd never have found you. Very lucky, all in all . . ."*

*"Thank you," said I, turning my face, and particularly my nose, away from the stench of my* yukata *toward the window, unfortunately closed.*

*"Think nothing of it, Sensei," said the driver. "I'd do the same for any man. But in your case, you being you, it's an honor. I am a great admirer."*

*"Really?"*

*"Oh yes," said the driver. "I grew up reading your books, Sensei. Your characters were like family to me, practically raised me, they did."*

*"Thank you," said I again. "Thank you."*

*"No, no," said the driver, "thank you, Sensei. In fact, it's funny me picking you up tonight because only the other day I was thinking to myself, I wonder whatever happened to Kuroda Roman? Because you've been a bit quiet of late, haven't you, Sensei? But it makes sense to me now. Because, and please don't be offended, Sensei, but I can see you've been having some problems. I just hope, and forgive me if I am being too blunt, but speaking as an admirer, I just hope you hadn't been trying to do anything stupid back in that alley, the open window and . . ."*

*"No, no," said I. "It wasn't like that. I fell."*

*"Right, right," said the driver. "It can happen."*

*"No, really," said I. "I got locked inside the building. I'd been at the Mystery Writers of Japan . . ."*

*"Had you now," said the driver. "Oh, I do envy you, Sensei. I'd have liked to have been a fly on them walls, I tell you. Bet you were all discussing the Shimoyama Case?"*

*"We were actually, yes."*

*"I knew it," said the driver. "I bet there were some theories flying around that room, weren't there?"*

*"A few, yes."*

*"But you know what annoys me?"*

*"No," said I. "What?"*

*"Headlines like THE CAR USED BY THE SUSPECT IS THE CLUE, and the way some of you writers blame the driver. I don't mean you, Sensei. At least, I don't think you suspect the driver, do you, Sensei . . . ?"*

*"I don't, no."*

*"Didn't think so," said the driver. "You're much too intelligent, I know. But one of your colleagues – forget his name, but a popular*

*writer – in one of the newspapers, he claimed the death of President Shimoyama is a case of murder and that the testimony of his driver, as reported in the newspapers, was highly questionable. He suspected that the driver had been blackmailed or threatened and that he should be considered the prime suspect. What an idiot, an absolute fool!"*

*"Quite," agreed I.*

*"And I'm not saying this just because I'm a driver. It's not as though all us drivers are part of some kind of secret brotherhood. It's just that I know the job. And so if he says he was asleep in his car outside the Mitsukoshi department store for five or six hours, I believe him. Because I know that's how the job is."*

*"Of course," said I.*

*"Actually, it's a shame you didn't come round a bit sooner, Sensei," said the driver, "because we passed Mitsukoshi, you know, 'one of the scenes of the crime,' just a bit back, back when you were still dead to the world."*

*"Is that right," replied I, looking hard out of the window, unable to tell where we were, the car traveling too fast, even accelerating, the inside of the car seemingly shrinking, the body of the driver ballooning.*

*"But if I may say so," said the driver, not waiting for I to say yes or say no, "I think novelists, even great ones such as yourself, Sensei, they should stick to their fictions, not get themselves mixed up in the facts. I mean, you of all people, Sensei, you know it's better not to go and get yourself mixed up in a real-life murder case –"*

*"Where are we going," asked I.*

*"Oh, I'm sorry, Sensei, you probably don't remember, what with you being in the state you were in, but I said I'd take you home . . ."*

*"Home," asked I. "You know where I live?"*

*"It's still Negishi, isn't it, Sensei," answered the driver, "that is, if my memory is correct?"*

*"Yes, thank you."*

*"Don't mention it, Sensei," said the driver. "It's my pleasure, Sensei. But hang on, what have we here . . . ?"*

*Suddenly, the driver braked hard and the car screeched to an abrupt stop, sending me forward, out of my seat, my head bouncing off the back of the driver's chair. "Owww!"*

*"Sorry about that, Sensei," said the driver. "I'm sure it's just routine, a formality, nothing to worry about."*

*I sat back upright, holding my neck, glimpsed the Matsuzakaya department store to my right, and realized we were in Ueno, not far from home, and I'd soon be home sweet –*

*"So sorry about this, Sensei . . ."*

*The back door on the left side of the car opened, and a rough-looking youth, dressed in military khaki and possibly Korean, climbed onto the back seat, the back seat next to me, then slammed the door shut –*

*"Excuse me," said I, politely, "but I'm afraid this car is taken, isn't it, driver?"*

*The youth turned to me, seized me by my throat with his left hand, punched me twice in my gut with his right, pushed my head hard against the side window, then said, "Step on it, driver!"*

*Crumpled on the back seat, clutching my stomach, my face pressed to the glass, I watched through the window, a window of tears, as the car began to move forward again, then to turn left, to pass the Shinobazu Pond, where the lotuses were closed and asleep for the night, then left and left and left again, up a hill, then down a slope, until all I could see were high walls and tall trees, their shadows and the night, and all I could hear was the youth whistling the Funeral March as the car slowed before a set of gates marked OFF LIMITS: STRICTLY NO ADMITTANCE, then passed through these gates, the gates closing behind the car, and up a long gravel drive, round to a large mansion, a mansion I recognized, the former residence of the Iwasaki family –*

*"I'm sorry, this is not where I live," whispered I.*

*"It is now," laughed the youth.*

*The driver turned off the engine, got out of the front, and opened the back door.*

*I looked up at him and said, "I'm afraid there has been a terrible mistake."*

*"Let's hope not," said the driver.*

*"Stop your blubbering and get out," said the youth, heaving me off the back seat, out of the car and down onto the gravel, the sharp, pointed gravel.*

*"Get up!"*

*"I'd rather not," said I, lying face down, trying to dig a hole in the ground, to tunnel my way out of here.*

*"Help me get him inside," the youth ordered the driver, and together they turned me over, picked up an arm and a leg each, then carried me squirming and writhing over the threshold, into the former Iwasaki Mansion, now known as Hongō House.*

*"I shall be missed," wailed I.*

*"In your dreams," laughed the youth again.*

*"Questions will be asked!"*

*"You're goddamn right they will be," boomed the familiar voice of an American, just a split second before –*

Knuckles and fists rained down on him, on the stones of the street, they punched and chopped him, in the broad light of day, packed and sent him, in the back of the car, their blows and the needle taking him down, knocking him out, down and out, out for the count –

*Don't fight them, darling, please don't fight . . .*

He drifted as they drove, just drifting, just drifting, in and out of the day and the city, the darkening day, the passing city, here and then gone again, gone again, gone –

*Just let them do, do what they want . . .*

Out of the car, the back of the car, they dragged and they hauled him, up stairs and down corridors, they kicked and they kneed him, into steps and into walls –

*For we could be happy, darling . . .*

They dropped and they threw him, again and again, across judo mats and polished floors, dropped and thrown, then rolled in a futon, wrapped tight in a futon, they smothered and they suffocated him, again and again –

*Darling, we could be happy . . .*

Smothered and suffocated –

*Happy and dead.*

*In a room underground, under the house, under Hongō House, in this tiny room, this cell of a room, under Hongō House, they tied me to a chair, tied me to a desk, bound my fingers to a pen –*

*And said, "I want you to write it all down."*

*"He wants you to write it all down."*

*Two figures in the room, this tiny room, under the house, under Hongō House, one in a black raincoat, one in a white raincoat, both masked, in masks: black-raincoat wears a smiling mask, white-raincoat wears an unsmiling mask –*

*"Who? What? When and where?"*

*"And the how? And the why?"*

*"The what and the where?"*

*"The who and the when?"*

*The light goes down, down and out, the light comes up, up and in; this is how time passes here, under the house, under Hongō House, where the weather is always the same, where the weather is always bad; this is how time passes here –*

*"Who? When? How and why?"*

*"Who–when–how–and–why?"*

*"WHO? WHEN? HOW? WHY?"*

*"WHOWHENHOWWHY?"*

*Light going down and out, light coming up and in, the weather always bad, bad and getting worse, the time passes here without seasons, only fall, my fall –*

*"Well?"*

*"Nothing."*

*"He didn't write anything?"*

*"No."*

*"He didn't write it then?"*

*"No."*

*"Not what we wanted to read?"*

*"Not what we wanted to read."*

*"He didn't say anything?"*

*"No."*

*"He didn't say it then?"*

*"No."*

*"Not what we wanted to hear?"*

*"Not what we wanted to hear."*

*"But did he weep?"*

*"Oh yes, he wept."*

*"And did he scream?"*

*"Yes, he screamed."*

*"Did he beg for mercy?"*

*"Yes, he begged for mercy."*

*"How did he beg? What did he say?"*

*"He said, and I quote, 'All that I give you is never enough.'"*

*"Are you sure that's what he said?"*

*"It's what's been written down."*

*"You weren't there?"*

*"I wasn't there."*

*"So you can't be sure?"*

*"I can't be sure."*

*"And so he might have said, for example, 'All that you give me is never enough.'"*

*"He might have said that."*
*"Might have said what?"*
*"'All that you give me is never enough.'"*
*"Really? The bastard said that?"*
*"The bastard said that."*
*"Right then. We'll have to give him the works."*

Yesterday, you attacked and assaulted President Shiozawa of the Shinpi Shōbō publishing house. Two days ago, a war veteran named Terauchi Kōji was found stabbed to death in Hibiya Park. The knife used to kill him was found in a drawer in your office in Kanda. On the previous day, you broke into the house of a Doctor Nomura, assaulted his daughter, and threatened the doctor. Meanwhile, Detective Hattori has told us he did not meet you, has not seen you for over fifteen years, and the proprietress of the Rabbit-o Hole bar in Yūrakuchō told us she was closed on the night in question, the night Nemuro Kazuko fell from her balcony, clutching your name card, the night you have no alibi for now. Furthermore, the whereabouts of your common-law wife, Tominaga Noriko, are unknown.

Murota Hideki looked up from the handcuffs around his wrists. He looked past the men sat opposite him, past the men stood behind them, over at the wall, then up the wall to the low ceiling, to the place where the wall met the ceiling, where a narrow, oblong-shaped air vent had been cut into the outside wall, the air vent covered in a black grid of metal bars.

Say something then, said one of the men.

But Murota Hideki said nothing, he just kept looking up at the air vent at the top of the wall, staring at the drops dripping down through its bars. Drop-drip, drip –

Talk, shouted another man.

Drop by drop, a dark liquid sweated out through the bars of the vent in black pearls, the color of ink or the color of oil, they trickled down the wall, caught the harsh light of the bare bulb, and turned red, a dark and ruby red, they dripped, they dropped, in a trickle, then a stream –

Confess, they screamed.

Crimson and scarlet, it was blood, it was blood, and in a river, now a torrent, Murota Hideki saw the blood run down the wall, watched the blood pool on the floor, falling faster down the wall, rising higher from the floor, Murota Hideki saw the blood lapping at his shoes, all their shoes, watched the blood covering his shoes, all their shoes –

Confess. Confess . . .

But Murota Hideki stamped his feet, his bloody feet, in the pools, the bloody pools, paddling and splashing in the tide, the bloody tide, up to his ankles now, all of their ankles, and Murota Hideki sprung up from his chair, jumped up and down in the blood of the tide, the tide of the blood now up to his shins, all of their shins, then his knees and their knees, then his thighs and their thighs, and Murota Hideki turned his face to the ceiling, the low ceiling of the room, raised his handcuffs to the light, the harsh light of the bulb, the blood of the tide, the tide of the blood now over his waist, all of their waists, then up to his chest, all of their chests –

Confess!

Up to his neck in the blood now, then over his chin onto his lips, Murota Hideki tasted the blood on his lips, the blood in his mouth, licked the blood, sipped the blood, the blood down his throat, the blood in his belly, drinking the blood, swallowing the blood, dark and ruby red, crimson and scarlet, the room, this station all dark and ruby red, the world, this life all crimson and scarlet, drowning and drowned, this life, his life in blood, in blood, Murota Hideki now drowned in blood.

*

*The works, the works, oh did they give me the works: injected and sedated, then doused and roused, slapped wide awake, punched in the ribs, kicked in the shins, throttled and choked, then injected again, sedated again, bound and then dragged, from pillar to post, from room to room, then car to car, and house to house: from Hongō House down to Yokohama, from Yokohama to a mansion in Kawasaki, from Kawasaki back to Tokyo, a big suburban villa in Den-en-chōfu, always tied to a chair or strapped to a bed, until I could stand it no more, no more, could take it no more, no more.*

*First, I tried to hang myself from a chandelier by my belt, but the lamp broke. Next, I tried to hang myself in the toilet, but my belt broke. Finally, having borrowed a pair of scissors from a sympathetic cook, I locked myself in the bathroom. I smashed the mirror on the wall, then with the scissors and the shards I set about my work. But we human beings are so frail and weak, so very frail and weak, and before my work was done I'd fainted and fallen to the floor, alas, not quite yet dead to the world.*

*Busybodies and do-gooders, or sadists and torturers, call them what you will, but there's always someone out there, out to save you from yourself, to break down the bathroom door, to wrap you up in bandages, to fill you full of pills, to strap you to a cot, to wire you to the mains and then to flick the switch.*

*On and then off, off and then on, again and again, day after day, over and over, night after night, they'd flick the switch and watch me twitch, twitch and writhe, writhe and thrash, with each of the shocks, their electric shocks, through the electrodes into my scalp, shock after shock, into my skull, into my brain, black electricity into my brain, into my mind, on and then off, off and then on, the black electricity into my mind, my mind.*

*"Release me," screamed I. "Release me!"*

*"If that's what you wish," they would sometimes say, and even sometimes do, driving me home, back to my house, my study and my desk, my pen and my papers. But no sooner had I picked up*

*my pen, put my pen to my papers, than I'd hear them knocking on my door, hear them whispering in my ear –*

*"Just checking how you are . . ."*

*And back they'd take me, kicking and screaming, back I'd go, bound and gagged, back to the Cuckoos' Wing of the Matsuzawa Hospital for the Insane, back –*

*"To save you from yourself . . ."*

*Dressed in soiled drawers and leather restraints, that's where I'd be, that would be me, lying in my own feces, choking on my own dribble, day after day, night after night, hearing only the sound of the rain and a clock – drip-tick, drop-tock – struggling to stay positive, to somehow have hope –*

*Drip-tick, drop-tock . . .*

*As the rain fell and the time passed – drip-tick, drop-tock – until late one cloudy afternoon, not unlike today, as I lay moored to my bed, bobbing up and down in my own private harbor of recollection and reverie, remembering lost times, dreaming old dreams, when in among the raindrops and the clock-tocks, stealing over the walls of the hospital and in through the bars of my window, I swear I heard –*

Shu-shu pop-po . . .

*Abandoning the sanctuary of my inner harbor, I dared to open my eyes and face again the stains on the ceiling, the cobs in the corner, and there I saw the colors begin to change, to shift, to smear, and then to run –*

*A moment later, even less, came a pale and sudden flash, then a clap of thunder so loud it shook my bed and bones, silencing the rain and stopping the clocks, the only sound now that sound of a train –*

Shu-shu pop-po, shu-shu pop-po, SHU-SHU POP-PO, SHU-SHU POP-PO . . .

*Louder and louder, faster and faster, nearer and nearer, shaking the walls, the ceiling, and floor, the noise of the train, the smell of the train, smoke through the window, steam through the bars, as I thrashed in my tethers and chomped on my gag, certain, so certain this was the end, the air grease and the air oil, the air coal and the air light, light flooding the room, the light from the train, coming down the line, coming down the tracks, through the tunnel of the window, round the bars of my window, the line and the tracks, up my bed, over my body, the tracks and the line, to the end, the end, where I was the end, the end of the line –*

SHU-SHU POP-PO, SHU-shu, shhh . . .

*But then and there, yes, then and there, at the end of the line, did the saintly moon of my salvation rise up before my face, take the sodden rag from out of my bloody mouth, put its cold finger to my chapped lips, its own sweet lips to my bandaged ears, then whisper, gently whisper, "Shhh now . . ."*

*But shhh now I could not – tears as big as pumpkins rolling down my cheeks, gasping for lost breath, struggling for forgotten words – finding his tongue and mine as I wept, as I begged, "Let me kiss you, my dear, dear Sadanori . . ."*

*For here at the end of the line, at the literal end of my tether, unfastening my restraints, massaging my ankles and wrists, here was Shimoyama Sadanori –*

*"Come back to set you free," he whispered. "But quick, there is no time for explanation, we must hurry."*

*And Sadanori helped me up from the bed, my feet to find the floor, to steady and then to guide me into clean drawers and next a white gown, then toward the door –*

*"Wait," said I. "My manuscript."*

*"Where is it," asked Sadanori, scanning my cell.*

*"Over there," pointed I. "Below the abandoned crucifix, under those vases of dead flowers."*

*"This," asked Sadanori, moving both vases to one side, then picking up my mighty tome.*

*"Indeed," said I, tapping the side of my head, giving him the knowing wink. "Cleverly disguised as a telephone directory."*

*"Say no more," said Sadanori, the book under his arm, now turning the lock, then opening the door, taking my hand, and leading me on. "Please follow me . . ."*

*And so down the corridor – that corridor of muffled cries and stifled screams, of thrashing beds and knotted sheets, to the applause of the thunder and the flashbulbs of the lightning; no nurse, no orderly, no soul in sight, all gone for the night – from room to room we went, stepping out of our paper world of words, out of the book, through its paper walls of pages, from all its fictions, knocking on doors –*

*Ton-ton. Ton-ton. Ton-ton. Ton-ton . . .*

Murota Hideki twitched, twitched again, his eyes open and his heart pounding. He swallowed and he choked, he spluttered and he coughed, swallowing and choking, spluttering and coughing, again and again, over and over, because he could not get up, he could not sit up. His body was strapped to the bed, his wrists and his ankles tied to the posts of the bed. He could only splutter, only cough, fight not to swallow his tongue, to choke on his own tongue, and wait for it to pass, then to close his eyes again, for all of this to pass again –

*Ton-ton. Ton-ton. Ton-ton . . .*

The muffled cries and stifled screams, of thrashing beds and knotted sheets, down the corridors, behind the doors, in this place of madness, time of madness –

*Ton-ton. Ton-ton . . .*

He did not hear the key turn in the lock, turn once and only once, if it did turn in the lock. He did not hear the door open, once and only once, if it did open. But he did feel the straps loosen on his chest, the ties fall from his ankles and his wrists as he opened his eyes, opened his eyes to see a figure in the moonlight –

*Ton-ton . . .*

In the moonlight of his cell, he raised himself up from the bed. He slowly swung his legs over the edge, slowly lowered his feet to the floor. Trembling and unsteady, Murota Hideki stood and stared as the silhouette stepped out of the shadows and came toward him, aged and skeletal, barefoot and dressed in a hospital gown, the specter had a thick book under his left arm, a teddy bear in his hands.

Kuroda-sensei, I presume, asked Murota Hideki.

Yes, yes, he replied with a sad smile. Unfortunately. But come, come, let us hurry, the rooms are about to be locked again, and we, we have an invitation to a séance . . .

Séance, asked Murota Hideki.

The book still wedged under his left arm, Kuroda Roman raised the teddy bear slightly in his hands. The teddy bear looked up at Murota Hideki, smiling sadly as he sadly said, Why, the séance in memory of my death, fifteen years ago tomorrow, and the mystery of its solution . . .

Out of the room, down the corridor they went, hand in hand, two barefoot men in their hospital gowns, led by a bear and a book, through flashes of lightning, amid crashes of thunder – 'Tis the storm of history, whispered Kuroda Roman with a gentle nudge and a sad wink – then down the stone stairs, flight after flight, then through the kitchens, down to the basement, then past the boilers, following the pipes, until they came to a door marked DEPARTMENT OF PSYCHIC SCIENCES –

After you, said Kuroda Roman, opening the door for Murota Hideki. But do mind your step . . .

Inside, the room was dim and stifling, but, guided by the hand of Kuroda Roman, Murota Hideki found a seat at a large round table, between one patient who-appeared-to-be a Westerner and one who-appeared-to-be Japanese, even vaguely familiar, but who did not look at Murota, acknowledge him, nor even his surroundings, but –

Ladies and gentlemen, interrupted another foreign man, lighting a candle in the center of the round table. I am Professor Peck of this department and I am very pleased to be able to introduce to you this evening Madame Hop . . .

Professor Peck, somewhat green around the gills, turned to nod and smile at a round-faced, red-haired lady seated beside him, then continued, As you may know, Madame Hop is one of the foremost mediums of our time . . .

They are Russian émigrés of the old school, whispered Kuroda Roman, leaning across the Westerner and the thick, black tablecloth to Murota Hideki. Berlin by way of Harbin, then back east again. Believers in the jinx and the hex, in numerology and demonology, black spots and evil eyes, the power of symbols and signs. Excellent –

Silence, please, exclaimed Professor Peck. Madame Hop needs to be able to discern a spiritual atmosphere before she can begin, so now let us all join hands, and give ourselves up completely, and concentrate . . .

In the faint, pale circle of the candle's light, Murota Hideki glanced around the table, watching the eight people – not counting the bear sat in the lap of Kuroda-sensei – all join hands, Murota, too, joining hands with the Caucasian on his right and the Asian to his left, their hands and his own, hot and clammy, the fingers and the palms. But hand in hand, in the dim, yellow circle, Murota Hideki found it hard to concentrate, to keep his eyes closed, peeking at the dark walls of velvet curtains, at the cards and pens and charts across the tabletop, the collection of megaphones and microphones dangling over the table, suspended from an unseen ceiling, but –

Concentrate on one thing, whispered Professor Peck, and one thing alone, emptying your mind of everything except the subject, and only the subject . . .

Still peering at the proceedings, Murota Hideki watched the Professor rise from the table, walk over to an ancient phonograph, turn its handle again and again, then return to his seat, as the strains of a somewhat scratched recording by Artur Rubinstein of Liszt's third "Liebestraum" tip-tip-tiptoed around the gloomy bunker –

We are calling you, said Madame Hop. Who is able and willing to talk to us . . . ?

The "Liebestraum" faded into silence, then into the silence, the waiting, then came a gentle, regular knocking, a tap-tap-tapping on the table –

*Ton-ton, ton-ton . . .*

They had gone from ward to ward, down corridor after corridor, from room to room, opening and closing doors, lifting sheets here, pillows there, turning faces to the light, their light, then moving on, slowly on, from floor to floor, down flights of stairs, through the kitchens, into the basement, past the boilers, the pipes until –

*Ton-ton . . .*

They are here, cried Madame Hop, as the table began to shudder, to shake, to tilt, and to rise. The Messengers are here.

The room was hot, then cold, now hot again, then cold again, in waves, on tides and on currents, of electricity, black electricity, hum, hum, black electricity humming, humming, louder, louder, something coming, coming, was coming –

*Is anybody there,* asked a voice, human-yet-not-human, from out of the biggest, blackest of the megaphones above the table and its sitters, then joined by other voices, also human-yet-not-human, from out of all the other megaphones, all speaking in chorus, *We said, IS ANYBODY THERE?*

Yes, stammered Madame Hop. We are here.

*Who are you,* they hissed, *this "we" . . . ?*

Madame Hop looked at Professor Peck, who looked to the foreign doctor on his left and asked, Doctor Morgan?

Doctor Morgan looked up from his pen and notepad, adjusted his glasses, touched his bow tie, coughed once, then said, Naturally. So then, anticlockwise, we have myself, Doctor Morgan, a visiting consultant here at Matsuzawa, specializing in the study and treatment of the long-term mentally ill. Then, to my right, Professor Peck and Madame Hop, former students of Gurdjieff and Ouspensky, well known in their field, and already to you, no doubt. Then, to their right, we have one of our longest-surviving patients, a former police inspector who went by the name of Minami, though he has not spoken a word since the day he was committed, back in 1946. Next to him, we have a recent arrival, Hideki Murota, charged with multiple murders, but whose mental competence to stand trial is currently under review. Beside Murota, we have a foreign national whose identity remains unconfirmed and who, again, has not spoken since being admitted to the hospital well over a decade ago now. Then we have Tamotsu Horikawa, better known as the writer Roman Kuroda, who has been in and out of here on a number of occasions. Finally, on my left, this is Sadamichi Hirasawa, the man convicted of the infamous Teigin mass poisonings in 1948. He is currently with us as part of an ongoing assessment of his mental competency, which, in turn, pertains to an appeal against his death sentence . . .

*Dark medicine*, whispered the voices.

Doctor Morgan touched his bow tie again, glanced up at the megaphones, cleared his throat, then said, So you now know who we are, but who, then, are you?

*We are legion*, giggled the voices in the megaphones, then laughing loudly, *For we are many.*

Very funny, said the doctor.

*Funny*, laughed the voices. *You think we are trying to be funny? We'll show you FUNNY –*

Instantly, the table rose up, then jerked in the direction of Madame Hop, Professor Peck, and Doctor Morgan, hitting all three in their chests, knocking them over, backwards in their chairs, sending all their cards and pens and charts falling from the tabletop, yet not the candle, which remained fixed to its spot in the center, though one moment lit, then not, then lit again, as the table came plunging back down to the ground.

Quietly, the doctor and the professor helped the medium back to her feet, then back into her chair, all three now seated back at the table as again the room turned hot, then cold, now hot again, then cold again, in waves, on tides and on currents, of electricity, black electricity, hum, humming again, louder, coming again –

*We are here because of you*, mumbled and muttered the voices, still from the megaphones, but different, quite different, sad, so sad, stifling, swallowing sobs. *Because of you . . .*

Thank you, said Doctor Morgan. We are –

*Shut up*, screamed the voice from the biggest, blackest megaphone. *One or more among you is an enemy . . .*

Somewhere near, or was it far, in another room, another world, where the year is zero, always, already zero, a gramophone began to play again, to sing –

*Oh so bravely, off to Victory . . .*

*Insofar as we have vowed and left our land behind*, boomed the gramophone. *Who can die without first having shown his true mettle? / Each time I hear the bugles of our advancing army / I close my eyes and see wave upon wave of flags marching into battle . . .*

*The earth and its flora burn in flames, as we endlessly part the plains / Helmets emblazoned with the Rising Sun, the Rising Sun, Sun, Sun . . .*

The needle stuck, the air became hotter again, much, much hotter than before, and filled with the strong scent of garlic, so strong it stung the eyes and tongues of the room, the hand of the man called Minami gripping, squeezing the hand of Murota

Hideki tighter, still tighter, crushing the fingers of his left hand, but then, just as suddenly, the noise of the needle stopped as the temperature fell, the stench and taste of garlic dissipated, the air colder, freezing, the sound of teeth chattering, of women wailing, weeping –

*Postwar,* après-guerre, *you say – he says, they say, all men say – but it's always been postwar, already* après-guerre.

*Conquered from birth, colonized for life, I have always, already been defeated. Always, already been occupied –*

*Occupied by you, by you, by you –*

*Born of me, the death of me. Blood of me, the death of me. Come in me, the death of me. Rob my name, the death of me. Born of you, the death of me –*

*In the snow. In the mud. Beneath the branches. Before the shrine. In the* genkan. *In the bank. On a street in China. In a wardrobe in Tokyo. With your poison. With your pen.*

In sorrow, whispered Kuroda Roman.

Nothing else remains, wept the man called Hirasawa. Only sorrow. Nothing else remains . . .

*It is you,* cried the voices of the women, still wailing, still weeping. *And only you . . .*

*Anata, darling . . .*

But now the temperature began to rise again as the voices of the women, their wailing, their weeping, began to fade and, in their place, the sound, the feel of hissing, then roaring – *sara-sara, sara-sara* – a shower of static, in the air, their blood – *sara-sara, sara-sara* – damp and clinging, holding the inside out –

*We are cold, we are wet,* the voices, the voices of children said, then asked, *Can't you see us? We are standing on the bridge, our little head between the narrow gaps in the metal railings, the marshaling yard of the station stretched out before us, we are spellbound by its sights and sounds, transfixed by its trains.* Shu-shu pop-po, *they go,* shu-shu pop-po. *We love to watch the shunting and the switching operations, the small trains pushing the goods wagons around the yard, connecting this wagon to that wagon, that wagon to this locomotive, marshaling the wagons, creating the train, the long, long trains, then waiting for the engines to be heated, for the coals to burn and the steam to rise, for the whistle to sound, and the wheels begin to move, to move and to turn, the train heading toward the bridge now, toward us now, passing under the bridge now, under us now, enveloping us in its thick black smoke as we turn to run to the other side of the bridge, through the clouds of smoke and steam, pressing our blackened face between the metal railings, watching the train steaming away, far, far away, on the tracks to some unknown place, so very, very far away.* Shu-shu pop-po, shu-shu pop-po. *We are three years old. We never tire of standing on this bridge, never tire of watching these scenes, of watching these trains.* Shu-shu pop-po, shu-shu pop-po. *We would stand here all day, every day, if they'd let us, just let us. But they won't let us* – shu-shu pop-po, shu-shu pop-po – *for they are murdering us . . .*

The sound, the scream of wheels and whistles, along with thick black clouds of smoke and steam enveloped the underground chamber, deafening the ears and blackening the faces of all who were sitting at the table, but then, just as suddenly again, the sound and the screams, the smoke and the steam retreated into the shadows, the corners, and now, in their place, the sound, the feel of rain, a summer rain, in the air, an insect air, and their blood, in their blood again, clinging, holding again, the inside out, turning the inside out –

*Behold, a summer landscape*, whispered a voice from a megaphone, softly-softly, rising gently-gently. *After the long border tunnel, again the defeated, occupied city appears, in the depths of the white night, again the landscape of a summer night, nineteen hundred and forty-nine. River. Embankment. Bridge. Crossing. Rails. Tracks. Road. Path. Fields and ponds. Prison walls and a rope hut. Here. They. Come. In the summer, in the night, beside the river, down the tracks, before the rain and before the train. Here they come: three, four men coming down the tracks, in blacks, in browns, in boots, in boots that once trampled Chinese dirt down, Manchurian earth, American dirt, and Indian earth, across the plains of history, from Wounded Knee to Nanking, all points before, between, and since, and yet to come, to come; here they come, beside the river, down the tracks, leading a child by its hand, they are leading him on, a Boy Who Loves Trains . . .*

*So easily led,* echoed voices from other megaphones, *first deceived, then tethered and led . . .*

*Down the line, along the tracks, looking for you, searching for you, calling for you . . .*

*But again the signals have changed, already the train has left the station,* announced a grating metallic voice from the biggest, blackest megaphone, repeating, *The signals have changed, the train has left . . .*

As the table began to shudder, to shake again, but then to rock, gradually increasing in speed as professionals and patients alike let go of each other's hands and tried to grip, to hold onto the tabletop –

*Again the coal has turned to fire, again the water turns to steam, again the wheels have begun to turn, again and again they turn and turn . . .*

And again the sound, the scream of wheels and whistles, again with thick black clouds of smoke and steam enveloping the underground chamber, again deafening the ears and blackening the faces of all who were trying to hold onto the table, the table violently rocking, faster and faster, rocking now racing, racing –

*The wheels of the locomotive, across the river, under the bridge, as the ground shakes, as the rails hum, hum . . .*

*Deceived, tethered, and led,* sobbed again a different voice, sad, so sad. *They have laid him down upon the tracks, across the rails, where he shivers, where he trembles but does not rise, he does not rise, for he is waiting, waiting . . .*

*WE ARE WAITING FOR YOU*, screamed a terrible, harrowing voice from the biggest, blackest megaphone above the rocking, racing table –

*For you, for you . . .*

*Who among you*, pleaded that different voice, so sad, so very sad, *who among you will take off your armor, your uniform, then climb aboard the locomotive of history – not to ride that train, but to halt that train – who among you will apply the brake, the emergency brake?*

*Too late, too late*, wailed the voices of the departed, as the table jumped up and out from the hands of the living, then came spinning straight back down, crashing round and into the circle of sitters, sending them flying into heaps of broken table and chair, piles of pulped skin and bone, all coated in ash and oil, rain and blood, wreathed in smoke and silence, apathy and stagnation, as somewhere near, yet far, a close but distant clock chimed midnight on the Fourth of July, Nineteen Hundred and Sixty-Four, and the fifteen-year statute of limitations expired, officially closing, sealing all investigations into the death of Shimoyama Sadanori, and from the wreck of the wood, the ruin of his flesh, Murota Hideki blinked and blinked again, choking, suffocating – struggling, now failing to breathe, he watched a tear fall from the button eye of a teddy bear, then heard a voice, a foreign voice to his right –

Too late, whispered Harry Sweeney.

# III

# THE GATE OF FLESH

# 8

## The Last Season of Shōwa

*Autumn und Verfall, 1988*

The Emperor was dying. Day by day, hour by hour, the hands of his Mickey Mouse watch were slowing to a stop. On the television and the radio, in the newspapers and the extras, the thrice-daily bulletins from the Court Physicians detailed his vital signs – temperature, pulse, blood pressure, and respiration – even his imperial stool, its temperament and consistency, all was revealed, shared, and retold. All told, all known, nothing private, nothing secret. Lying there, in the center of the city, the heart of Japan, behind his moats and his walls, his gates and courtyards, in his palace within a palace, in a second-floor bedroom, an eighty-seven-year-old man, frail yet stubborn still, reluctant to leave, fighting to stay, hour by hour, day by day, hanging on to dear life, the longest reign in history –

Frightened and scared of what is to come, came a voice in the dark, before the light, his voice in the night, before the dawn, woken by bells, fire-engine bells, kept awake by the rain, long, heavy rain, long before the light, before the dawn, already awake, still awake. He was always, already still awake, still awake. In these black hours, his eyes to the ceiling or the watch by his bed, its luminous hands, at first too slow and then too fast, the night-thieves and sleep-stealers, tripping alarms, then looting the golden kiss of slumber from his eyes. To the ceiling, to the watch, in these black, resentful hours, he tried to douse, to souse himself in half-remembered, almost-remembered quotes and lines: The loud notes swell and scatter abroad / *sā, sā*, like wind blowing the rain / the soft notes dying almost to nothing / *rei, rei*, like the voice of ghosts talking – *sā, sā, rei, rei*, the voices of ghosts in the rain –

See, they return, one, and by one, with fear, as half awakened; the curtain cracks, edges gray, whiten, then, at last, transparent light, scratched, stretched thin, then strained, he drifted then, now day, its light was here, dozed then, now dreamed, too late he dreamed: a shabby street, back street, half here, half there, a plaited fence, a shuttered house, the lady of this house, lost in exile and in thought, she writes a letter in the smoked, dimmed light, as the women weep around her, in the shadows weep around her, *Rei, rei* . . .

In fright, with a start, his body clawed and face wet, Donald Reichenbach woke, awoke, awake again. Grete had pushed open the door, jumped up on the bed, licking his face, asking to be fed. Yes, yes, I know, I'm sorry, he said. Your lazy Papa should be up and out of bed, I know, I know.

He gently turned to one side so the cat slipped from his chest onto the bed, one claw caught in his pajama top. He carefully unhooked her claw from the cloth. He reluctantly pulled back the covers from his legs and slowly got up and out of bed. He picked up his glasses from the table by his bed and put them on, then picked up his watch from the top of the book on the table, looked at its face and its hands, then fastened it to his wrist as he said again, Lazy Papa should be long out of bed, we know, hungry mouths waiting to be fed.

Grete danced and sang ahead of him as he padded in his slippers over the *tatami* mats of the bedroom onto the polished wood of the living-dining-kitchen room. He picked up her empty saucer and water bowl from the floor and walked over to the sink. He ran hot water over the saucer and bowl, then washed and dried them. He ran the water until it was cold, filled the bowl, then reached up to open the cupboard above the sink.

The tins of cat food were ordered and stacked so he could rotate them through the only three flavors deemed acceptable by Grete. This morning he took down, opened, and then served tuna as *la canette du jour*, placing the saucer and water back down on the floor to only the very briefest *meow-ci* from the lady of the house. You're angry, *ne,* he said, but lazy Papa said he's sorry. What more can he say?

He shrugged, walked back over to the sink, washed out the empty tin, then put it in the plastic bag beside the plastic trash box, the plastic bag he kept just for tins and cans, tins of cat food and cans of beer. It was a big bag, always full. He walked back over to the small square worktop between the sink and the stove, opened the jar of already-ground coffee beans, and began to prepare the morning coffee. The coffee on, he looked at his watch, went back into the bedroom, pulled back the curtains, and opened the balcony window slightly. It was a dull, gray day, a light drizzle falling on the trees across the road. He went from the bedroom into his study next door and opened the balcony window slightly here, too. He cast a brief-but-disappointed glance at the unfinished work on his desk, the unread books in their piles, then turned and went back into the living-dining-kitchen room, over to the silver radio-cassette player on the dining table, and switched on the radio. The Morning Music Promenade on NHK for today was Mozart's First String Quintet, and it had already reached the ending allegro. He looked at his watch again, then hurried to the refrigerator, took out a croissant, and placed it in the oven–toaster perched atop the refrigerator. He took out a plate from the cupboard under the worktop and a knife and spoon from the drawer. He turned back to the refrigerator, opened it again, and took out a jar of Staud's Viennese apricot jam, two of which he bought from Meidi-ya in Kyōbashi every month without fail: jam tomorrow, jam yesterday, *and* jam to-day, he liked to say, though not today. The oven–toaster pinged. He put the jar of jam down on the worktop, picked up the plate, opened the oven–toaster, and quickly dropped the piping-hot croissant onto the plate. He set down the plate again, opened the jar, and spooned out a generous helping of jam to keep the croissant company. He returned the jam to the refrigerator, lamenting momentarily, as he always did at this point, that butter had become a forbidden-though-never-forgotten pleasure. He carried the knife and the plate to the dining table and set them down, then walked back over to the kitchen to switch off and serve the coffee. He walked back to the dining table with the first-but-not-last mug of coffee and sat down just as the String Quintet ended, and smiled and said, Perfect timing, even if I do say so myself.

He glanced round to look for Grete, but, her own breakfast eaten, she had gone back to the bedroom and bed.

You always complain when I go out, sulk when I come back, he said as the seven o'clock news began and he started to break the croissant into three pieces. But you can't really blame me if I choose to eat out when you neglect me like this.

He took a tissue from the box beside the radio-cassette player and wiped his fingers. He picked up the knife and began to spread the jam on the pieces of croissant as he listened to the morning update from the Court Physicians: the Emperor had received a 200cc transfusion free of white cells, prompted by signs of further internal bleeding. However, the transfusion was carried out chiefly to treat the Emperor's anemia, said the Chief of the Imperial Household Agency's General Affairs Division, rather than to compensate for blood loss.

He swallowed the first piece of croissant and jam, took a first sip of coffee, then said, It'll be me next, you know, and then what will you do? They don't allow pets where Mister Kanehara lives, you know?

He picked up the second piece of croissant and jam, put it in his mouth, then reached for another tissue. The transfusion seemed to have been successful, as the Emperor's temperature had dipped below thirty-seven degrees for the first time since Tuesday. The Emperor had also been well enough to watch the last thirty minutes of the Olympic marathon race on television and then the closing ceremony. Lucky him, he said, somewhat bitterly; he had planned to watch the closing ceremony with Kanehara, but they had had a silly, drunken argument about the conduct of US athletes and news organizations at the Seoul Olympics and had parted on bad terms on Saturday night. He sighed, took another sip of coffee, then ate the last piece of croissant. He took a third tissue from the box and finished his coffee as the NHK announcer moved on to the news that talks between North and South Korea would resume on October 31, the hopes for improved relations despite the Olympic boycott by the North.

Not a cat in hell's chance, he said loudly, glancing at the bedroom door, then feeling his eyes begin to water. He took another tissue from the box, wiped his eyes, then put all the screwed-up pieces of tissue paper onto the plate, got up from the table, and carried the plate, the tissues, the knife, and the mug over to the sink. He tipped the tissues and flakes of croissant into the plastic trash box, then began to wash the plate, the knife, and mug, tears rolling down his cheeks. He wiped his wet cheeks with already-wet hands, then dried his hands, then the plate, the knife, and the mug. He sniffed, he sighed, then put the plate back under the sink, the knife back into the drawer, but left the mug on the worktop beside the coffee-maker.

I'm sorry, he said as he came into the bedroom, looking at Grete, oblivious, asleep on the unmade bed. Papa's in a very bad mood and he doesn't know why. He opened the closet, took a shirt and a pair of pants from their hangers, then underwear and socks from their drawers. Not that you seem to care, but I've a terrible feeling. I just wish I knew why.

Richard Strauss had replaced the news – thank God – as he carried his clothes through the living-dining-kitchen room into the bathroom, though it was his Cello Sonata Opus 6, of all things; nothing jolly, not these days. He took off his pajama top and began to wash, then put on his undershirt, took off his pajama bottoms, and put on his shorts, wishing that whenever he heard Richard Strauss, whose music he liked, and liked very much, he wasn't always reminded of that damn quote by Toscanini: *To Richard Strauss, the composer, I take off my hat; to Richard Strauss, the man, I put it on again . . .*

He felt suddenly breathless, his heart riven by palpitations, his eyes watering again. He gripped the edge of the basin, tried to catch his breath, to wait for the palpitations to pass. He blinked, wiped his eyes with his fingers, then blinked again and saw himself in the mirror above the basin. He stared at the reflection of the seventy-four-year-old American man, alone in the bathroom mirror of a fourth-floor apartment in Yushima, Tokyo, and he watched his eyes meet his own, saw his lips move, and heard him say, But you do know why, don't you, dear? You know damn well why –

*Rei, rei,* said the voices of ghosts, the ghosts talking again, the shadows around you again. *Rei, rei . . .*

Go away, he said and closed his eyes. Please.

But where would we go, what would we do? Wherever you have been, we have been; whatever you have done, we have done; wherever you will go, we will go . . .

Eyes closed, he said, Please, no.

Listen, they said, listen: the telephone is ringing.

You get the call, you heed the call: and you run, yes, you ran, to Frank in his palace, the Whiz in his Rat Palace, the black heart of our white sepulcher, in the middle of the American Century: between the Lincoln Memorial and the Washington Monument, by the waters of the Reflecting Pool, just a collapsing, crumbling, tin-roofed shanty, in a row of temporary War Department buildings, this is the Rat Palace, the set-up back then: they lead you down its dank corridors, drip-drop, pipes leaking, water falling, drip-drop, lights flickering, vermin scuttling: clickety-click, the rattles in the dark, the scratches from the shadows, clickety-click: they leave you in the Waiting Room, drip-drop, clickety-click, leave you waiting with the women: at two tables, in two chairs, the two women, one fat, one thin, dressed in black, under umbrellas black, one handle taped to a hatstand, one handle taped to a lampstand, drip-drop, clickety-click, they are knitting with black wool, their eyes downcast and never raised: they guard the approach, they keep the gate, the gate to the Director, the door to Frank.

Minutes click, they drip, pass into hours, then the thin one gets up from her chair, walks straight up to you, still with eyes downcast, still knitting with black wool, she whispers, You are expected. Knock once, then wait.

And you rise from your chair, and you walk to the door, and you knock once and you wait –

Come, shouts a voice, *his* voice, from behind the door, through the wood. Come, it said, and come you come.

Come in, Don, come in, says Frank, standing behind his desk, walking around his desk, shaking your hand and closing the door, gripping your elbow, sitting you down, in a single chair, before his desk: Frank back behind his desk, sat back on his throne, the piles of paper stacked up on his desk before him, a map of the world pinned up on the wall behind him: pinned and mounted, colored and defaced, mostly blue, partly red, with patches of black, a smudge of yellow.

Frank picks up a bottle of Johnnie Walker Red from his desk, unscrews the top, and says, Scotch, Don?

Thank you, you say. Thank you, sir.

Frank nods, Frank smiles as he pours out the Scotch, as he hands you your glass: Allen speaks very highly of you, Don. He says you're the man for me, just the man for the job.

Thank you, sir, you say again.

Frank offers you a cigarette, lights one for you and one for him, then says, Allen and Jim, they both agree. Tells me you speak the language, and Chinese, studied in Cambridge, England. They say you did a good job in Europe, too.

That's very kind of them, sir, you say.

Franks stubs out his cigarette, gets up from his chair, turns to the map, his palm over the East, the red and the yellow, and says, Kindness cost us half of Korea, going to lose us China. But I'll be damned if we gonna lose Japan, Don. The blood we spilled, the lives we lost. No goddamned fucking way we gonna lose Japan, Don. Time for goddamn kindness is over – you hear me, Don? You fucking hear me, Don?

Yes, sir, you say. I hear you, sir.

Frank stares at you, Frank nods at you. He downs his drink, you down your drink. He pours you another, then one for himself, shakes his head, and says, Country is a goddamn tinderbox, Don. One spark, Don, one fucking spark and the place is gone, Don, the place is fucking lost.

You drink, you nod, then say, What about SCAP, sir?

SCAP's the goddamn problem, Don, why I need you out there, Don. Mac's too busy playing God with the natives, while his High Priests fight their own little wars, feathering their nests and fucking the locals. Fine with me, Don, all fine with me, 'cept Mac won't let us anywhere near the goddamn place, hellbent on keeping us out, him and his little guard dog Willoughby. They've stood in our way since Day One, Don, slammed the door shut in our faces, Don, keeping us out and in the dark, sharing nothing, doing nothing, while the whole fucking place turns red under their goddamn noses, Don.

I see, sir, you say, then nod and drink again.

He fills your glass again, then his own again, stares at you again, and says, Do you, Don, do you really, Don? Because I see it, Don, I fucking see it, because I've seen it before, Don, I've fucking seen it all before – turning back to the map on the wall, slapping the map with his palm – France, Italy, and Greece, the whole of goddamn Eastern Europe, Don. I've had my hands full of this shit for the last three years, my hands full of shit and blood, Don. Argonauts betrayed, nightingales slaughtered –

From here to Shanghai and back again, we been robbed by gangsters, duped by Commies, but not anymore, Don, not in Japan, Don, not on my watch, Don, not in Japan.

Yes, sir, no, sir, you say. Of course, sir.

Frank sits down, downs his drink, then nods and says, We're deaf, dumb, and blind out there, Don. Deaf, dumb, and blind. You're going to be our eyes and ears, Don, the mouth that speaks the truth, Don, tells us what the fuck is going on.

Yes, sir, of course, sir, and so my cover, sir?

Frank moves the bottle, Frank opens a file, looks down, and reads, DipSec, a vacancy in the Economic Section.

I see, sir, you say, but then you say, But what about General Willoughby, sir? Won't he know, sir?

Frank closes the file, opens his mouth, and laughs, then says, Your grandfather was Bavarian, am I right, Don? You went to school in Cambridge, England, yeah? Baron von Willoughby, he'll be too busy trying to suck your damn cock, Don, to worry who the fuck sent you and why, right, Don?

Yes, sir, you say. I see, sir, thank you, sir.

Frank laughs again, Frank nods again, then Frank stands up again and says, Go down the corridor, go see the doc, then get yourself down to Arlington, on the first flight out to the coast, Don. Not a moment to lose, Don, yeah?

Yes, sir, you say again, standing up. Thank you, sir.

Good man, Don. Goodbye, Don.

You open the door, you close the door: clickety-click, back through the waiting room, down another dank corridor, drip-drop, to another door, to knock and to wait again for –

Come, sighs a voice, a tired voice, behind another door, through more wood. Come, and come again, you come.

Opened thirty-six new stations in the last six months, you know, says the old doctor, looking down at the forms on his desk. Anybody with warm blood and a pulse will do – so who are you and where we sending you, son?

Donald Reichenbach, doc, you say, to Tokyo, doc.

The doctor looks up from his forms, his face unshaven, sleeves stained with ink and with blood. He stares at you and says, Well, I hope you last longer than the last man we sent.

What happened to him, doc, you ask.

He smiles, he says, Hung himself, so I hear.

Oh, you say, and then, I see, doc.

He smiles again, stands up, and says, You've not been hearing voices, have you, seeing visions, I trust?

Not recently, doc, you laugh.

He does not laugh, does not even smile. He picks up a pair of calipers and a stethoscope, walks toward you in a pair of bedroom slippers, and nods, then says, Strip off down to your shorts and socks then, let me see and hear who you are then, see and hear what we're shipping out there this time.

Breathe in, said Doctor Morgan. And now hold it, please . . .

His socks not touching the floor, Donald Reichenbach sat in his shorts on a towel on the edge of the bed in the small examination room in the International Medical Clinic, breathing in, holding the breath, looking down at the paunch of his belly, the blemishes and the spots, the old scars.

And now out again, please.

He sat up straight, shoulders back, pulling in his stomach as he breathed out, his eyes watering again.

Doctor Morgan removed the ear-tips of the stethoscope. He sat back down in the swivel chair at the narrow desk and said, You're still not smoking, I hope?

For my sins, said Donald Reichenbach, sadly.

How much are you drinking?

Much less, said Donald Reichenbach.

Doctor Morgan shook his head, frowned, and said, And how much less is "much less" exactly . . . ?

No more whisky, just the odd glass of *shōchū* on a Friday, if that's still allowed, doc?

How about beer?

Don't mind if I do, said Donald Reichenbach, smiling at his own joke. Hardly counts as drinking now, does it?

Doctor Morgan sighed: You're putting on weight again and your blood pressure's up again. The weight is straining your heart and your lungs.

I grow old, I grow old, said Donald Reichenbach, smiling at Doctor Morgan. The bottoms of my trousers rolled.

Doctor Morgan smiled back at the old man in his shorts and socks perched on the edge of the bed and said, Quite, but we can still slow the speed of our exits, if we so choose.

Both men were around the same age; both had been here around the same length of time.

But one wouldn't want to outstay one's welcome, said Donald Reichenbach. That would be most impolite.

Doctor Morgan laughed: Don't be so dramatic, Donald. You're not yet seventy-five, man. Just look at the Emperor – he's got almost fifteen years on you. Why do you always have to be so goddamn dramatic about everything?

Whoever would have thought such a skinny little thing of a man would be such a stayer, said Donald Reichenbach, reaching for his clothes in the plastic basket beside the bed.

Doctor Morgan laughed again: Oh, come on. He didn't slit his belly back then, so he's hardly going to hurry off now, is he? Nothing if not a stayer, our *Tennō*.

Donald Reichenbach picked out his T-shirt from the basket and pulled it over his head as he said, How long has he got, do you think? In your expert, professional opinion?

As long as they need him, I suppose, to get things prepared, everything in order, in its proper place.

Donald Reichenbach stepped into, then pulled on his pants: They've had long enough.

Oh, come on, said Doctor Morgan again. They're completely useless at planning ahead, you know that. Always hoping the worst won't happen, and then, when it does, saying it can't be helped. Nothing to be done etcetera, etcetera.

Donald Reichenbach zipped up his flies, buttoned his pants, and fastened his belt: *Shikata ga nai*.

It's rather contagious, said Doctor Morgan, looking at Donald Reichenbach. Highly infectious.

Donald Reichenbach put on and then began to button up his shirt: You think he'll see in the new year?

He's a survivor, said Doctor Morgan. We all are, those of us who lived through all that. We had to be, didn't we?

Not all of us did, doc.

No, Donald, but *we* did, and we do.

Donald Reichenbach turned up his collar, put his tie around his neck, and began to fasten it: I often wonder how on earth we did survive, then why on earth we bothered.

Did you, said Doctor Morgan. Do you?

Donald Reichenbach picked up his watch from the bottom of the basket and put it on: Don't you?

Every day I sit in this surgery, Donald, I'm reminded of the greatest contradiction of our nature.

Which is . . . ?

We are self-destructive creatures, yet hellbent on self-preservation, laughed Doctor Morgan. Eternally so.

The internal telephone on the narrow desk buzzed once and flashed red, as it always seemed to do after fifteen minutes.

Donald Reichenbach glanced at his watch, then looked back up at Doctor Morgan and lowered his voice as he said, I've been having very bad dreams again.

The price of sleep, I'm afraid.

I received a letter from America, from a woman.

How very disappointing for you, said Doctor Morgan, his turn now to smile at his own joke.

Now she's here, she rang this morning, whispered Donald Reichenbach, his eyes watering again. She wants to meet, says she needs to talk.

About what?

But that's it, she didn't say.

Doctor Morgan stood up and said, Donald, dear, you're an institution, a Tokyo landmark, a sight to be seen and be met. Of course she wants to meet the Great Translator.

Other people's words, sniffed Donald Reichenbach. Ten, twenty years from now, it'll all be done by computers.

Doctor Morgan glanced at his watch and said, And so not worth reading, nor, then, worrying about.

Like my own poetry and prose, sighed Donald Reichenbach. Rejected, and not even politely.

Doctor Morgan had opened the door: Donald, dear, you're turning into your mother – didn't you say her heart had only enough room for her own miseries and sorrows?

You don't understand, said Donald Reichenbach, taking out his handkerchief, dabbing his eyes. I've got a very bad feeling, a terrible, terrible feeling . . .

Doctor Morgan patted Donald Reichenbach on his shoulder. He helped him to his feet, pushing him toward the doorway, the exit and out, laughing as he said again, Donald, dear, for as long as I've known you, since the day we first met, you've always had a very bad feeling, a terrible feeling.

Dread-filled and fearful, the flight makes you anxious, makes you nervous, and this is just the beginning: the beginning of the journey, the process: the flight from Washington to Los Angeles is routine, and scheduled; the flight from Los Angeles to Tokyo is not routine, not on any schedule. It leaves in the middle of the night, the American night, in the middle of the century, the American Century, from an airstrip on the edge of the airport: twenty-three passengers walk out to the airstrip with their luggage, report to a hut surrounded by barbed wire, guarded by a sentry: the hut dark, the gate locked, you set down your suitcase, your briefcase in the dirt and you look at the watch on your wrist, you bite at the nails of your fingers.

Don't worry, the sentry tells you. Them flying bastards only come along when they're good and ready. You best just sit yourself down on your bags and wait.

You take off your hat, toss it down on the suitcase, take out a pack of cigarettes from your raincoat, then a cigarette from the pack, search your coat, then your jacket for a light: you find the light, light the cigarette, then look up into the night sky, blow smoke up toward the stars, watch it drift across the moon, the summer moon, and wait.

Ten cigarettes, one hour later, the captain, the sergeant, and two other crew arrive at the gate to the hut: the captain, the sergeant, they crack jokes with the sentry, jokes about the passengers sat on their bags by the gate, then they go inside the hut, switch on the light, and then later, ten, twenty minutes later, they tell the sentry to let you bastards in now, all in now.

You stub out your cigarette in the dirt, pick up your hat, put it on, then pick up your suitcase, your briefcase and walk through the gate, into the hut: you sit down on a narrow bench, listen to the mandatory safety briefing from the captain:

Now see here, you bastards, the C-54 is a mighty good aircraft. But even the best aircraft in the world sometimes have to ditch, and the journey you're going on is mostly over water, over sea. Now I never heard of no C-54 ditching, but if she does go down, this is what you bastards do: you grab hold of anything yellow, because all of the life-saving gear is painted yellow, and everything yellow will float. That's all you bastards need to know, all you bastards need to remember –

Everything yellow will float.

You pick up your suitcase, your briefcase, follow the captain, the crew, your fellow travelers out of the hut, through the gate, along the perimeter of the airport to the airstrip, where the Douglas C-54 Skymaster is crouched, waiting.

You leave your suitcase with the other cases on the airstrip beneath the plane, then walk up the steps to the door: at the top of the steps you stop, put your hand on the brim of your hat, grip the brim of your hat tight, turn around, and look for the land, but the land is dark, dark and lost in the pitch of the night, you look up for the stars, but the stars are gone, gone and hidden away in the night: you turn back to the doors of the aircraft, take off your hat, step inside the plane: this C-54 is a troop carrier, with only benches, not seats: you sit down on one of the canvas benches along one of the sides of the plane, two straps hanging down behind you: you turn to your left, nod to the man on your left, you pull the strap down over your left shoulder and fasten it tight, then you turn to your right, nod to the man on your right, pull the other strap down over your right shoulder and fasten it tight: you put your hat on your briefcase, your briefcase on your knees, then pull the strap from the left and the strap from the right together and fasten them tight, then, your back against the metal hull of the plane, you wait.

The sergeant comes out of the cockpit, walks down the center of the aircraft: he shouts things to the passengers as he passes them, raises his thumb to them as he passes them, and they raise their thumbs back as he passes them: he shouts something to you as he passes you, something you cannot hear as he passes you, raises his thumb to you as he passes you, and you raise your thumb back as he passes you.

Now the frame of the Douglas C-54 Skymaster begins to shudder, harder, now the C-54 Skymaster begins to rattle, louder, now the Skymaster begins to move, faster, faster, down the runway, faster and faster, now the Douglas C-54 Skymaster begins to lift, higher, higher, into the night, higher and higher, into the sky, up, up, up and away, away from the land, away from America, the land below, behind you now, America below and behind you now, back down on the ground, prostrate in the dark, a hole in the ground, an open grave.

You loosen your grip on your briefcase and hat, lean back further into the hull, rest your head against the metal, feel the vibrations, the pulse of the plane, hear the hum, the drone of her engines: head back and eyes closed, you let yourself be carried now, carried by the hum and the drone, over the water, over the sea, from Los Angeles to Honolulu, the hum, the drone, over dark water and silent sea, the hum, the drone that rises and falls, with the currents, the tides, the hum and the drone, over the water, across the sea, from Honolulu to Midway, the hum, the drone, over bloated water and swollen sea, its currents, its tides, that hum, that drone, from Midway to Wake Island, over the dead, the sunken dead, that hum, that drone, that rise, that fall, in the deep, in its swell, ripped and torn, their bones picked clean, they hum, they drone, with the current, the tide, in their ships, their planes, from coast to coast, in the wrecks of their ships, the wrecks of their planes, the American dead, the Japanese dead, under the water, under the sea, they hum and they drone –

*Sā-sā, rei-rei . . .*

Eyes open, head forward: the plane jolts: the smell of grease, the smell of oil: the plane shudders: your palms damp with sweat, chin wet with spittle: the plane dips: the taste of leather on your lips, salt in your mouth: the plane drops: you wipe your chin, your palms.

The sergeant comes out of the cockpit again, tilts from left to right and back again as he walks down the center of the aircraft again, says things to the passengers again, thumb raised to the passengers again: he picks up your hat from the floor and shouts in your ear, You might want to hold on tight to that now, buddy. Captain's bringing us down into Guam.

You raise your thumb, he raises his: you tighten your grip on your case, your hat, sit up straight in your seat and close your eyes, keep them closed until you feel the wheels of the Douglas C-54 Skymaster hit the ground and bounce hard down the airstrip of the North Guam Air Force Base.

There's still the odd crazy gook out there don't know the war is over, don't know they lost, says the captain. So you bastards best stick to the base, your billet, and not be wandering off into the jungle. Because we ain't gonna come look for you, ain't gonna wait for you, either. This bird, she leaves at midnight, with or without you bastards . . .

You and your fellow travelers trudge along a muddy path in the sticky rain to your billet: the roof and walls of the building still pitted with bullet holes, large chunks missing from the stone steps that lead to your room on a second-floor corridor: a sentry in full battle costume, a carbine over his shoulder, paces slowly up and down the corridor: each time he comes to the end of the corridor, he takes a puff on a lighted cigar, then places it back on the window ledge: he tells you, You try sneak into them women's quarters, I'll shoot you dead, so help me God I will.

You close the door to your billet, set your briefcase down on the floor beside the low camp bed, take off your jacket, hang your jacket on the peg on the back of the door, hang your hat on top of your jacket, then sit down on the side of the low, hard camp bed and open your briefcase, take out two files, then the copy of Waley's *Genji* from the briefcase: you set the book to one side on the bed, then open the first file and you read: read through the file on the Hanged Man, his reports and his contacts, then you close the first file and open the second file: the file written in numbers, page numbers, line numbers, word numbers: you turn to the book on the bed, open the book on the bed, find the page, the lines, and the words, turning back to the file, then back to the book, from the file to *Genji*, then back to the file, decoding the file and translating the text until you've had enough, done enough for now, and you close the file, you close the book, put both files and the book back into your briefcase, close the case and lay it on the floor beside the camp bed: you take off your boots, stand them beside the briefcase and get up off the bed, unbutton your shirt and loosen your pants, then lie down on the low, hard camp bed and wait: you wait in the close, gray afternoon light, reciting your lines, rehearsing your part, learning your lines, learning those lies, your story, all lies: on the low, hard camp bed, not sleeping, just waiting, in the close, gray evening light, waiting for the flight to Tokyo, opening night and the show to begin –

The sentry knocks on all the doors of the second-floor corridor: Rise and shine, you lazy bastards . . .

You and your fellow travelers trudge back along the muddy path in the sticky night to a small and stuffy hut: you watch a short film of a Douglas C-54 Skymaster making a forced landing in the sea: the captain switches on the light, and says, Never gonna happen, but all you bastards need to know is everything yellow will float . . .

Strapped back inside the Skymaster, you stare at a spare yellow drum of aircraft motor oil strapped to the floor in front of the emergency exit: the sergeant taps you on your shoulder, shouts in your ear, You with us today, buddy?

You nod, thumb up, he nods, thumb up, in your face, then walks away: you tighten your hold on your briefcase, your hat, lean back in your seat on the bench and feel again the shudder, harder, hear again the rattle, louder, the vibrations and the pulse, faster and faster, the hum and the drone, higher and higher: you loosen your grip on your case, your hat, rest your head against the side of the small window to your left, and close your eyes, you close your eyes, the singing in your ears, hear them singing in your ears, they hum, they drone –

The dead, the dead –

*Sā-sā, rei-rei . . .*

Eyes open again: the inside of the aircraft is flooded bright with morning light: head forward again: the plane jolts: palms damp with sweat again, chin wet with spittle again: the plane shudders: you wipe your chin again, your palms again: the plane dips, the plane drops: you twist to look out of the small window by your left shoulder: the plane turns: you catch a glimpse of Mount Fuji: the plane circles: you lose sight of Mount Fuji: the sergeant taps you on your other shoulder, and you turn: the sergeant hands you your hat again and shouts, You want to get a leash for that, buddy!

You raise your thumb to him, he shakes his head at you, walks back down the plane to the cockpit again: the light inside the plane begins to dim: you tighten your grip on your case, your hat again, sit up straight in your seat again: the clouds outside begin to thicken, the plane begins to tremble, to shake, to shudder again: you close your eyes again, keep them closed again until you feel the wheels of the Douglas C-54 Skymaster hit the ground again, bounce hard down the airstrip of the Haneda Air Force Base, Tokyo –

Welcome to Japan, Mister Reichenbach, says the young American officer on the entry desk at Haneda Air Force Base as he hands you back your passport, your entry permit, inoculation records, and billeting slip.

Thank you, you say.

You're welcome, says the officer. Now you need to take the Northwest Airlines bus into the center of Tokyo. The bus is just to your left when you exit this building. The bus is direct, straight to the Ginza. So you get off the bus in the center at the

Ginza, then here's what you do: you go straight across the street from the stop to the Provost Marshal's Office. Because you need to report directly to the Provost Marshal's Office. That's the first thing you need to do. You're not legal here until you've done that. So make sure you do it now, straight away, before you do anything else here, Mister Reichenbach. Are we clear about that? You got that, sir?

Yes, you say. We're clear, thank you.

You're welcome, says the officer.

You put your passport, your entry permit, inoculation records, and billeting slip back into your briefcase, close the briefcase, put the briefcase under your arm, your raincoat over your arm, pick up your hat from the desk, put it on, then pick up your suitcase and walk out of the Haneda Air Force Base: you turn to your left, see the Northwest Airlines bus: you put down your suitcase, your briefcase again, take off your hat again and take out your handkerchief, wipe your face and then your neck, put away your handkerchief again, pick up your briefcase, your suitcase again and walk to the Northwest Airlines bus: you give the bus boy your suitcase, then take off your jacket, your hat and take out your handkerchief again: you climb on board the bus, walk down the aisle to the rear of the bus, put your briefcase on the rack above your head, fold and put the raincoat on top of the case, then sit down, lean your head against the window of the bus and close your eyes: you hear the engine of the bus start, feel the window of the bus quiver: you open your eyes again, stare out of the window, up at the nets of black cables overhead: you close your eyes, feel the bus go over a pothole: you open your eyes again, see a sea of rusted red roofs, and close your eyes again, then feel the bus swerve: you open your eyes again, out of the window again, see gangs of young boys on every corner, and close your eyes again: the bus stops, eyes open again: the bus boy shouts, Ginza!

You hand your passport, your entry permit, inoculation records, and billeting slip to the young American officer behind the main desk at the Provost Marshal's Office: he flicks through the papers, the pages of the documents, stamps the passport, entry permit, inoculation records, and billeting slip, then says, Now please go to the next desk, sir.

You walk over to the next desk and the next young American officer: he takes your fingerprints, left hand, right hand: you wipe your black fingers clean, walk over to another desk, another young American officer: he measures you, he weighs you, then hands you a board on which is chalked *Reichenbach, Donald / 276522*: he tells you to stand in front of a white wall, and you stand in front of the white wall, he tells you to hold up the board, and you hold up the board: he takes his photograph, your photograph, then tells you, You're done. Please report back to the first desk, sir.

You walk back over to the first desk: the young American officer hands you back your passport, entry permit, inoculation records, and billeting slip, then smiles and says, Welcome to Tokyo, Mister Reichenbach.

Thank you, you say.

You're welcome, says the officer. Now I need you to take your billeting slip round the corner to the Billeting Office for me. They'll confirm that this here address on this here slip is still the correct one. Most times it is, but sometimes it ain't. So if there's been a screw-up, then you're going to need to come straight back round here so we can amend your paperwork. But let's hope not. This place they've got you in, it's one of the best in town. You could do a lot worse, I can tell you, sir.

Thank you, you say again.

You're very welcome, sir, says the officer: now he watches you put your passport, your entry permit, inoculation records, and billeting slip back into your briefcase: watches you close your briefcase, put the case under your arm, your raincoat over your arm, then pick up your suitcase: he watches you walk out through the double doors of the Provost Marshal's Office, then looks away, turns back to his desk: doesn't see you turn, see you watch him pick up the telephone on his desk and dial four numbers, see you watch him wait, then see you hear him, hear him say, He's here, sir. Yes, sir, the Dai-ichi Hotel, sir . . .

Yes, I'm here, you whisper in the summer, *the summer of nineteen hundred and forty-eight*, and I'll still be here long after you're gone, all gone, I'll still be here.

At Kasumigaseki station, he got off the subway train and slowly climbed the steep stairs back into the drizzle of the day. He liked to walk through Hibiya Park, particularly when it was raining. But today he put up his umbrella, walked past the government buildings, the Tokyo high court, and police headquarters to Sakuradamon and joined the crowds as they crossed the moat, then passed through the gate into Kōkyo-gaien and the outer grounds of the Imperial Palace. Up ahead, he could see the long lines of people under their multicolored umbrellas, all queuing to enter the tent which had been erected beside the Sakashitamon Gate to house the books in which these well-wishers could register their well wishes for the recovery of the Emperor. But he did not join the queues; his black and foreign umbrella seemed somewhat in poor taste amid the sea of bright colors and local hopes. He turned and walked away, toward Nijūbashi, passing the kneeling and the standing, regardless of the puddles and the rain, their umbrellas down, unused and forgotten, their hands together and heads bowed, all faced toward the Imperial Palace, his dying majesty. He crossed back over the moat onto Hibiya-dōri, and then, for the first time since he could not remember when, he made a point – though what point, he was not sure –

of walking past the Dai-ichi Mutual Life Insurance building, the former palace of the blue-eyed *shōgun* himself, the General Headquarters of SCAP. But he did not stop, did not dillydally on Memory Lane, not today. No, he turned sharply left and up a side road to Yūrakuchō and then into the Denki building.

He took one of the north elevators up to the Foreign Correspondents Club on the twentieth floor, paid a quick visit to the bathroom, then walked down the short corridor to reception. He smiled as he handed his umbrella and raincoat to the new girl, whose name he could not remember, then went into the main bar. He was early, the lunchtime crowd not yet in, and had the pick of the tables, so he took one in the window at the far end of the bar and sat with his back to the room.

Twenty floors up, he looked out of the window into cloud and mist, the clouds so low and thick they smudged the skyscrapers, erased modernity, brought the city low again, smudged and erased again, just like when –

He stood up, turned almost straight into Hanif, almost knocked the glass of water and menu from out of his hands. He said, I'm sorry, Hanif, so sorry, but I'd forgotten something.

No problem, sir, smiled Hanif. No problem. You coming back later, want me to save you this table?

I'm sorry, he said again. But I don't think so, no, but thank you, Hanif, thank you.

No problem, sir, said Hanif again.

He walked quickly out of the bar, back over to the reception desk. He gave the plastic chit to the new girl. She brought him his raincoat and umbrella. Embarrassed, he mumbled apologies as he put on his raincoat and then said goodbye. He walked back down the short corridor to the elevators and pressed the button, then pressed it again –

Donald, old boy, boomed an all-too-familiar English public-school voice from over his shoulder. Where's the fire?

Jerry, how are you, he sighed as he turned with a reluctant hand out.

How are *you*, dear boy, is the question, grinned Jerry Haydon-Jones, not letting go of his hand. Thought you must be dead and buried, old boy. Food for the worms.

He freed his hand: Not quite, Jerry, not yet.

Just joshing with you, old boy, laughed Jerry, punching him in the top of his arm. Don't look so damn glum, man. Fact, only last week, when I dared to raise the mystery of your disappearance with the brothers at the bar, Bernie, I think it was, said, Don't you worry about old Donald, Jerry, he said, he'll be off somewhere lining his pockets with lovely lolly. Corporate jollies here, public speeches there, don't you worry, Jerry, Uncle Sam knows how to take care of his own, not like you beggars from Blighty, he said. Come on, confess to Father Jerry, where's it been: New York, Washington . . . Virginia?

The elevator had been and gone, mouth open then closed again, empty and hungry. He pressed the button again and said, Just here, Jerry, neither dead nor rich, sadly.

Now, now, no long faces, not on my watch, said Jerry Haydon-Jones, gripping his arm tightly, trying to turn and pull him away from the elevators. Come tell your Uncle Jerry all about it over a glass or three of firewater.

He freed his arm, his elbow knocking Jerry, and said, Nothing I'd like more, Jerry, but I really do have to go.

Like that, is it, said Jerry, feigning, perhaps, hurt and indignation, then gripping his arm again, pinching it tightly again. But only if you absolutely swear we will see you again, old boy, and see you very soon – you do promise?

Of course, Jerry.

You swear?

Believe me, Jerry, I will waste no time returning.

Then you are forgiven, said Jerry Haydon-Jones, letting go of his arm again. For now.

Thank you, he said, almost leaping into the mouth of the elevator, its doors closing –

But don't make me come dig you up again . . .

Rubbing his arm as the elevator bore him down to safety, he was breathless again, his heart racing. You old fool, damned fool. You don't like the place. Never have and never will. He stepped out of the elevator, turned right out of the building and back into the rain and Yūrakuchō. He put up his umbrella again, joined the hundreds of others, bustling and jostling their way, left and right, west and east along the sidewalk. So many umbrellas, so many people, almost banging into him, almost knocking him over, almost, but not quite. He made it to the curb, tried to catch his breath. A taxi splashed his trousers as he waited for the lights to change. A puddle filled his shoes as he stepped off the curb. A man almost walked straight into him as he crossed, an umbrella almost took his glasses from his nose, both cursed him as they passed. Don't these people know the Emperor is dying just up the road, an era coming to its end? He felt his eyes water again as he passed under the railroad tracks, walked up toward the Ginza, the sidewalk wider here, thank God. But he wanted to walk under the leaves and branches of trees, not under umbrellas and curses, see flowers, their petals bejeweled and wet, not these crowds and their faces, this apparition be gone, dear God, please, God, be gone. Increasingly wet with rain and sweat, he reached the Sukiyabashi crossing and the escape routes to the subway. He took down his umbrella, folded, rolled, and tied it up, then went down the stairs, almost slipping as he did, reaching and catching hold of the handrail just in time, the nick of time. He stopped, waited to catch his breath again, for his heart to slow again, then carefully, paying attention, he walked down the rest of the stairs, and still carefully, still paying attention, he made his way to the Hibiya line, bought a ticket, passed through the gates, and went down the escalator, then stood on the platform, waiting under the ground, thinking of all the things he had wanted to do on the

Ginza: browse the shelves in Kyōbunkwan and Jena Books; buy *sakadane sakura* and butter rolls at Kimuraya; treat himself to a bottle of French wine from Mitsukoshi or Matsuya; even lunch and a beer, *Bockwurst* and *Weissbier*, at the Lion Beer Hall. Oh well, he said out loud, as the train pulled in, trying not to ask, struggling not to plead. There'll be other times, another time?

These hours, first hours, in cellophane, they pass, pass into days, in cellophane, these days, first days into weeks, wrapped in cellophane, these weeks, first weeks, had you wrapped in cellophane: in Shimbashi, the Dai-ichi Hotel, in your tiny, cramped room; in Nihonbashi, the Mitsui building, in your cramped, tiny office, they had you wrapped in cellophane: part of the process, the cellophane, the waiting, all part of the process, the waiting in cellophane: the hotel bugged, the office bugged, you know, you know: just do your job, your day job: Diplomatic Section, Economic Liaison Section, where you compile and file reports, charts, and graphs, all then sent on to Washington and the State Department, but all first routed through Mac's military staff: Mac and his men, they are distrustful, disdainful of you soft-sell boys who spent your war in Foggy Bottom: but by the time you arrive, in the summer of nineteen hundred and forty-eight, DipSec is largely staffed by Foreign Service careerists, with even a sprinkling of rabid anti-Communists, and the hostility and suspicion, the violent prejudice of GHQ and SCAP is beginning to wane: everybody singing from the same hymn sheet, Red Purge and Reverse Course, at least in public, if you want to keep your job, your day job: so you read the newspapers, the financial pages, you study balance sheets, reams and reams of corporate balance sheets, and write reports on de-concentration, the dismantling of Japanese conglomerates and cartels: hour after hour, long day after long day, for damp week after damp week, hot month after hot month: in cellophane, that summer in cellophane, waiting and patient, all part of the process –

*Sā-sā, rei-rei . . .*

At twilight, most evenings, you go back to your tiny, cramped room at the Dai-ichi Hotel in Shimbashi: at first you take the bus, the bus provided for Occupation staff, but then, every now and again, you choose to walk: the city was still a battered city then, a city of black markets, prostitution, and poverty, and there are evenings, many evenings when you return to your room and you sit down on the edge of your bed and you weep: you weep for the men and boys who beg for cigarettes and chocolate outside the PX stores, for the women and girls who sell their bodies and their hearts beneath the railroad arches, in the shadows of the parks, weep for the destruction of this city, the ruin of its people: yes, you weep, but you study, too: in your room, which no longer seems so tiny and cramped, you study the language and the culture, the people and their history, in the secondhand books you find in Kanda and Jimbōchō, in the ventures you begin to make on your days off: to Tsukiji and Ikebukuro, but, more often than not, to Ueno and her park, the mortuary temples and graveyards close: all weeds and neglect, their fences broken down, you spend hours among the graves and their ghosts, their stones and their moss, gently trying to uncover their veiled engravings, to understand their melancholy testimonials, again in and through tears, your tears and theirs, their occupied tears –

*Sā-sā, rei-rei . . .*

They are weeping and you are weeping, weeping but waiting, waiting and watching, watching and testing: on these ventures you make, you are testing the waters, watching for watchers: in the stations, on the platforms, you often let the first train leave without boarding, bending down to tighten your shoelace, then you wait until every other passenger has boarded the next train, then slip on board just as the doors are closing: two stops later, you alight and catch a train in the opposite direction, the long way round the Yamanote line to Ueno, the advantage, the beauty of the circle that is the Yamanote line, round and round you go, getting on and getting off, testing these waters, watching for watchers –

*Sā-sā, rei-rei . . .*

Until you are sure, as sure as you can ever be, that you are not being watched, or watched no more if you ever were: and so as late summer passes into early fall, lying on your hotel bed, you decide you've waited long enough, been patient long enough, patient and cautious enough: you get up from your bed, take your briefcase from under the desk, open the case, carefully take out the two files from the case, then sit down at the desk: you switch on the lamp, light a cigarette, then warily open up the first file, vigilantly looking for the hair you had plucked from your head, had then placed in the file: the hair is there, still there, fair between the pages of the file: you stare down at the hair as you smoke, read again the words under the hair, then put out the cigarette, close the first file, and open the second file, find the second hair you plucked and placed there, still there, still there: you take Waley's *Genji* from the line of books propped up on your desk, open the book, turn to the chapter called *Yūgao*, find the page and the paragraph, its description of a shabby street, a secluded house, its lines and its words: you turn back to the file, then back to the book, from the file to *Genji*, then back to the file, decoding the file and translating the text until you're sure you've checked enough: you close the file, you close the book, put both files with their hairs back in the briefcase, the case back under the desk, then return Waley's *Genji* to its place in the line of books propped up on your desk: you get back up from the desk, go back over to the bed, then lie back down on the bed and wait: in the smoked, dimmed light, reciting your lines, rehearsing your part, learning your lines, learning those lies, your story, all lies: on the short, narrow hotel bed, not sleeping, just waiting, waiting for when the curtains will crack, their edges gray, then whiten, opening day, tomorrow: tomorrow the day the show will truly begin, the day you will visit the House of the Dead.

Yesterday, the Emperor's morning temperature had gone above thirty-eight degrees for the first time since September 19 and he had received another transfusion of 200cc of blood without white cells after further signs of internal bleeding had been noticed. By the time of the evening news conference, the Emperor's condition was stable and he seemed to have improved; his temperature had fallen to 37.4 degrees, pulse rate was eighty-four beats a minute, blood pressure was 134 over 56, and respiration rate eighteen breaths a minute. Kenji Maeda, head of the Imperial Household Agency's General Affairs Division, said the Emperor's high temperature could be attributed both to inflammation of the upper part of the digestive system and to the reaction of the Emperor's blood to donor blood. Since September 19, the total amount of blood given to the Emperor was 5,715cc.

You hear that, said Donald Reichenbach, glancing at the bedroom door as he wiped his fingers on a piece of tissue paper. 5,715cc of blood – that means they must have replaced every drop of his imperial blood!

An oxygen cylinder had also exploded outside the room where the Emperor lay gravely ill, but the eighty-seven-year-old monarch was undisturbed by the noise. Palace officials said a plumber working on renovations in the Imperial Palace Hospital was seriously injured when the cylinder exploded as he was inspecting the grounds. However, a palace official said, His Majesty apparently never even heard the explosion.

Oblivious to the end, said Donald Reichenbach as he carried the plate, the tissues, the knife, and the mug over to the sink. He washed and dried then put away the plate, the knife, and the mug as he listened to the rest of the morning news: news about the defeat of the Pinochet government, then the vice-presidential debate between Senators Bentsen and Quayle.

Defending his qualifications, Quayle had said he had as much experience as John F. Kennedy had when he sought the presidency. Bentsen had shot back, Senator, I served with Jack Kennedy. I knew Jack Kennedy. Jack Kennedy was a friend of mine. Senator, you're no Jack Kennedy –

He turned off the radio as he went into the bedroom, thinking of Stanford, a morning in Stanford, for it was morning on the Pacific Coast when Kennedy was assassinated. He had been invited over to give a series of lectures on classical Japanese prose, had gone ahead with the morning lecture as planned; it would have been impolite not to have done so, he had thought then, thought now. But the students hadn't agreed, all those healthy, good-looking sons and daughters of California, sullen in their blue-eyed grief, pouting at his poor taste. He smiled and took down a cardinal necktie from the rack in the closet, then giggled as he turned to Grete sleeping on the bed and said, Now, now, don't be jealous, Gre-chan dear, but Papa's got a luncheon date, must look his very luncheon best.

But he stopped smiling and giggling when he carried his clothes back into the living-dining-kitchen room, stopped before the radio-cassette player on the dining table. Richard Strauss had again replaced the morning news, but it was the *Vier letzte Lieder*, his *Four Last Songs*, of all things, *of all things*. Breathless again, heart riven again, in tears again, he sat down again, at the table again, clutching, cradling his clothes in his arms as Schwarzkopf, Szell, and the Berlin RSO carried him through "Spring," "September," "When Falling Asleep" to, finally, "At Sunset": Through sorrow and joy, we have gone hand in hand; we are both at rest from our wanderings now above the quiet land. / Around us, the valleys bow, the air already darkens. Only two larks soar musingly into the haze. / Come close, and let them flutter, soon it will be time to sleep – so that we don't get lost in this solitude. / O vast, tranquil peace, so deep in the afterglow! How weary we are of wandering –

He let go of the clothes in his arms, wiped his face, his cheeks and his eyes with the fingers of both hands, then reached to turn off the radio, but the radio was already off . . .

is this perhaps death?

In the small mirror above the small basin in the corner of the hotel room you shave, your eyes on the reflection of your neck, your cheeks, your chin, and top lip in the mirror: you wash your face, dry your face, then pick up your comb, straighten your hair, your eyes on the reflection of the teeth of the comb, the hairs on your head: you change your clothes, then straighten your necktie back in the mirror, your eyes on the reflection of the knot in the cloth, the tie around your neck: you know you are avoiding your own eyes, your own eyes in the mirror, not wanting to look into your own eyes, to see the anxiety in your own eyes, the fear in the mirror: you turn away from the mirror, pick up and put on your jacket, take your hat from the hook on the wall, the briefcase from under the desk, then you leave your hotel room, turning once to lock the door: you go down the corridor to the stairs at its end, take the stairs down to the lobby, then walk through the lobby, out of the Dai-ichi into Shimbashi: a late September morning, still sultry and warm: the light already different, the day already different, but the routine remains, must always remain, part of the process: the process is the routine, the routine is the process: you go into Shimbashi station, up to the

Yamanote platform, let the first train leave without boarding, bent down to tighten your shoelace, then wait until every other passenger has boarded the next train and slip on board just as the doors are closing: two stops later, at Tokyo station, you alight and catch a train in the opposite direction, back the way you came, back through Yūrakuchō to Shimbashi, on through Hamamatsuchō and Tamachi to Shinagawa: at Shinagawa, you get off again, cross to the other side of the platform, let the first train leave again without boarding, bent down again to tighten your shoelace, then wait until every other passenger has boarded the next train again and slip on board just as the doors are closing again: two stops later, at Hamamatsuchō, you get off again and leave the station, sure as can be you are not being watched, not being followed: you walk through Daimon to the grounds of Zōjō-ji temple and the Taitōku-in, another of the city's mausoleums for the Tokugawa *shōguns*, six buried here: but here, unlike in Ueno, the mausoleum and the temple were all burned, destroyed in the air raids of May, 1945: three years later, the grounds of Zōjō-ji, its National Treasures are still all ash and ruin, huge scorched trees lying still where they fell, their roots to the sky, branches charred, leaves lost: in the sullen, silent air, under the gray, overcast sky, you walk through this field of ash and ruin, round the remains of the temple and mausoleum, through other graves, overgrown with bamboo grass, weeds, and neglect: but you do not linger here today, not among these graves, not with their ghosts, their stones, and their moss, not today: today you must push on, through and in tears, your tears and theirs –

*Sā-sā, rei-rei . . .*

You emerge on the other side, the other side of these dead and their graves, out onto Avenue B: you stop by the side of the road, and you wipe your eyes, and you wait, and you watch, checking again you are not being watched, not being followed: an Occupation bus passes down the street, you turn away, then look back: bicycles and pedicabs pass in front of you, a cart filled with night-soil led by two oxen passes the other way, but no one emerges from the shadows behind you, the ground of the dead: you weave across the road, between the bicycles, the odd truck, then wait again, on the other side, you watch again: again no one emerges from the shadows across the road, the place of the dead: you turn away, turn off the main road, down a side road, into Morimoto-chō: a cluster of alleyways and houses, some large, some small, some burned, some not, some rebuilt and some not: a patch of waste ground here and there, where a house or a shop had once stood: through this patchwork of destruction and reconstruction you walk: the occasional smell of a household fire, a breakfast being cooked, the sudden sound of bedding being beaten and aired, *monpe*-clad ladies sweeping the mats of their houses, turning away when they see you coming, retreating back into their houses until you've passed: round the corners, at each corner, you stop, you turn and you wait, you watch: checking again and again you are not being watched, you are not being followed, until you come to the place, you come to the house: but you do not stop, you keep on walking: past the house, that secluded house, to the end of its street, its shabby street, round the corner you go: then you stop, and you wait, and you watch, then you walk on: back round the block, to double-check, then once again, to triple-check: no one is watching you, no one is following you: back down the shabby street, back to the secluded house, behind a stone wall, damp and tall, a wooden gate, plaited and warped: now you open the gate, and you step through the gate, into the garden, untended, unweeded, onto its path, half hidden, half lost, then you close the gate, turn back to the garden, and look up at the house: a two-story house, once painted yellow, now faded with weather and war, scorched black in part with soot from a fire, its shutters hanging broken and open, no glass in its second-floor windows, dark sockets in a pale skull: it is watching you, waiting for you: the yellow house, the House of the Dead –

*Sā-sā, rei-rei . . .*

You walk up the path, half hidden, half lost, approach the house, its front window, watching you, waiting for you: you shield your eyes, peer in through the glass, see a thick mattress on the floor, a table, three chairs, and a cabinet: you turn from the window, scan the garden, untended, unweeded: see the stacks of flowerpots, big ones and small ones, all chipped or broken: you walk over to the pots, bend down, and begin to search: under one stack of upturned, damaged pots you find a small mound of loose soil and ash: in this pile of dirt you find the key: you pick up the key, stand up, and walk to the door of the house: you put the key in the lock, turn the key in the lock, then the handle: you open the door and step inside, you step inside: inside the yellow house, the House of the Dead, you swallow but do not speak, do not call out: you stand in the doorway and listen: you hear the house breathing, hear the house murmuring, whispering –

*Sā-sā, rei-rei . . .*

You step into the hallway, close the door behind you: before you is a broken staircase and the hall: down the hall, to the right, a small, empty room, a kitchen and a toilet that both still function, still work: to the left, the large front room: you go into the front room, flick the light switch on and then off again, the electricity connected: you see the telephone, the radio on the wide table: you pick up the handset of the telephone, the telephone connected: you turn the radio on and then off again, the radio working: everything still working, everything still functioning, still connected –

*Sā-sā, rei-rei . . .*

You pull a chair from under the table, turn the chair to face the window, then sit down: in the yellow house, this House of the Dead, you sit and you wait, wait for them to come, come back again, return –

*Sā-sā, rei-rei . . .*

Return to you again: waiting in the chair, the chair at the table, watching the door, the door to the house, looking now and then, every now and every then at your watch, the hands of your watch, luminous in the shadows of the yellow house, this House of the Dead: waiting and watching, the door to the house, the hands of your watch: maybe you've got the wrong time: too early, too late, the wrong time again.

He was early, as was his wont, even when he didn't want. Early ripe, early rotten, that will be you, his mother had used to say. But she was early, too, this Julia Reeve he had never met before, sat at an angle to the window with its view of the pond, turned toward the entrance, shade across her face, a pale hand raised in a wave. You can never say no, that's your trouble, his mother and many others had also said, occasionally with kindness, more often with anger, frustrated by his moaning and regrets. But, then, when was he ever not filled with regret?

You're a friend of Anthony then, he said, after the handshake, the pleasantries, the easy bits had passed.

She smiled, she said, He suggested I should write when I told him I was coming. It was very kind of you to agree to meet, to spare the time. Thank you.

Spare the time, he repeated, then smiled. Well, one always tries to be welcoming.

She nodded, she said, You must have welcomed hundreds of people. After all these years.

And then waved them goodbye again, he said, then smiled again. Yes, I suppose I must have. After all these years.

She smiled, she said, Perhaps it suits you, saying hello, but then waving goodbye, always able to bid them *adieu*.

One just gets used to it, I suppose, he said, then smiled. But I don't know, you may be right. Perhaps I have acquired something of a sweet tooth after all these years.

She smiled again and said, I'm sorry, a sweet tooth?

Partings being such sweet sorrows, he said triumphantly, and then pointedly, Or so one always hopes.

She nodded, she said, You know, if I didn't know it, I'd never have guessed you were from Pennsylvania. You've not a trace of an accent; more English if anything.

More English than the English, he said, trying and failing not to smile, creases at the corners of his lips. That's what my friends, my chums at Cambridge used to say.

She smiled, she said, And Cambridge has stayed with you, then, even after all these years.

Just another of my many affectations, I fear. Born from – what's that word people use nowadays? – overcompensation, yes, that's it: overcompensation.

She nodded, she said, For what?

A Bavarian grandfather and a German name, he said. People were suspicious, you know, could be very unkind.

She smiled, she said, But you still kept your name, your family never changed it. Many families did.

I think my grandfather, and then my father, he said, I think they would have seen that as being rather dishonest.

She nodded, she said, A betrayal.

No, he said, rather too emphatically – for you doth protest too much – so he smiled and said, Much too dramatic.

She smiled, she said, You never felt the need?

My, my, you like to pry, he wanted to say, but smiled instead and said, The need to do what?

To change your name?

No, he said, then smiled again. Just to overcompensate, even "after all these years."

She smiled again and said, I'm sorry. I can tell I've offended you. But you look very well and, if you'll forgive me for saying so, much younger than your years.

Flattery is always forgiven, he laughed, giggled even. Though you wouldn't say that if you saw me plodding with my shopping up Muen-zaka – it means the Slope of the Dead, and I am sure I must look like one of them, one of the Dead.

She nodded, she said, The slope from *Wild Geese*? And you live at the top – how wonderful.

And how wonderful you know Ōgai, he said, smiling. I do often fear he's rather neglected, compared to others.

She smiled, she said, The Unremembered Dead.

Well, he said, if one wishes to be exact, to be precise, Muen-zaka most probably derives from Muen-ji, a temple which used to stand on the slope and which, it is said, was a repository for the souls of those travelers who had died anonymously in old Edo, unbeknownst to their relatives back home, thus unclaimed and unmourned.

She nodded, she said again, How wonderful.

Well, yes, he said, nodding. I suppose I am rather lucky, despite the climb. The Iwasaki Mansion is across the street, even visible from my windows, at least come wintertime, when the leaves don't interfere. Not many people can look from their windows at an Important Cultural Property.

She smiled, she said, Hongō House.

The devil are you, he wanted to ask as he looked at her, for the first time, properly looked, to see her, see who she was: her mouth and lips a little wide and full for her face, her nose and eyes, too, her eyes looking at him, watching him: the devil do you want with me, he didn't ask, but instead, just blushed, picked up the menu, and then said, Shall we order?

She smiled, she said, What's good?

What's good, what's good, he repeated, turning through the laminated pages of the Seiyōken menu as he had done so many times before, as he still did every single time he came, yet wondering if this would be the last time, why this felt like it would be the last time, blinking as he said, had said so many times before, The hashed beef rarely disappoints.

She nodded, she said, Sounds good.

The house specialty, he said, smiling as he closed the menu and then signaled to the waitress. And I usually have a beer. I shouldn't really, but I think will. And you?

She smiled, she said, Why not.

*Hayashi rice futatsu*, he told the waitress, smiling, *to biiru-o nihai, onegai shimasu.*

Julia Reeve turned to the waitress, smiled, and said, *Sumimasen, yaapari watashi-wa tai no wine mushi-o kudasai.*

*Nomimono wa*, asked the waitress.

She smiled again and said, *Daijōbu, arigatō.*

*Shōshō omachi kudasai*, said the waitress, collecting up their menus with a sympathetic smile at Donald Reichenbach.

Julia Reeve leaned forward, her hands on the table, then smiled and said, Don't look so hurt. It's Friday.

At least you're not a vegetarian, he said.

She nodded, she said, God, no. I used to live in Texas.

Did you now, he said. But you're not from Texas?

She nodded again and said, No.

And so where are you from, he said, his turn now.

She smiled, she said, Here and there.

And where might I find your here and there on a map, he said, smiling, with the bit between his teeth.

She nodded, she said, My father was in the military.

Was he now, he said. Ever in Japan?

She smiled, she said, Briefly, on R & R.

He served in Vietnam, he said.

She smiled again and said, MIA.

I'm sorry, he said, then again, I'm very sorry.

She nodded, she said, You served, of course.

Yes, he said. But in a very different war.

The waitress reappeared with their plates and two small bowls of salad, the glass of beer for him.

Julia Reeve picked up her knife and fork, then smiled at Donald Reichenbach and said, *Itadakimasu*.

Cheers, he said, holding up his glass of beer.

She put down her knife and fork, picked up her water, touched it to his glass, nodded, and said, Cheers.

That's bad luck, you know, he said.

She smiled, she said, I know.

You don't believe in luck then, he said.

She nodded, she said, No. Do you?

Not these days, no, he said, then took a sip of his beer, then put down the glass and picked up his spoon.

They ate in silence and occasional smiles, until she had almost finished, and he already had, so he could ask, before she could, And so what brings you to Japan?

She finished the last of her fish in its wine sauce, put down her knife and fork, then dabbed her lips with the napkin. She took a sip of water, then nodded, then said, My mother.

Oh, he said, and tried not to sigh in relief, even jump for joy. You should have said. She might have joined us?

She smiled, she said, I'm afraid she wouldn't be much company. She's got cancer, she's dying.

Oh, he said again, and then again, I'm sorry.

She nodded, she said, She hasn't long.

Here, he asked. But she's here?

She nodded again, then said, No. Indiana.

But you're here, he wanted to ask, as the waitress came to take away their plates, to ask if they'd like to order dessert, as he shook his head and said, I'd better not, no.

Julia Reeve nodded, then said, But you'll have another beer, won't you? Keep me and my coffee company?

Well, if you insist, he said, smiling.

She smiled back, then said, I do insist.

He ordered the beer and the coffee, this time without any contradiction, then turned back to Julia Reeve and smiled, then said again, I really am sorry about your mother.

She nodded, she said, She was here.

In Japan, he said pointlessly, his voice rising pointedly.

She smiled, she said, With the Occupation.

I see, he said – and you do, you do now – as the waitress brought over her coffee and his beer, as he almost took the glass from her hand, before it had hardly touched the table.

She nodded, she said, She knew you.

Your mother, he said, not putting down his beer.

She smiled, she said, Gloria Wilson.

I'm afraid, he said, bells tolling in his ears, in his heart, I'm afraid it's such a long time ago. I'm sorry.

She nodded, she said, She knew your wife, too.

My wife, he said, his voice rising again.

She smiled, she said, Yes.

Mary, he said.

She smiled again, then said, Yes, Mary.

My wife, he said again, then put the glass to his lips again, the beer already gone.

She nodded, she said, Would you like another?

Another what, he said, putting down the glass.

She smiled, she said, Another beer?

No, thank you, he said, glancing at his watch, his watch hidden up his sleeve. I shouldn't. Doctor's orders.

She nodded, she said, Go on, I insist, be a devil.

Well, then, if you insist, he whispered, blinking, then taking out his handkerchief, taking off his spectacles, dabbing his eyes as she ordered him another beer. Thank you.

She watched him put away his handkerchief, his glasses back upon his nose, waited for the beer to arrive, to let him take a sip, then she smiled and said, They kept in touch.

You know her then, he said. My wife?

She nodded, she said, No.

I see, he said again, and then again, I'm sorry. It's all so long ago. I'm old and I'm afraid I'm rather lost.

She smiled, she said, Don't be.

But I am, he whispered, holding his beer in both hands. I'm afraid I'm very lost. You'll have to help me.

She smiled again and said, That's why I'm here.

Then please do, he said. Please help me.

She nodded, she said, My mother said you'd know.

Know what, he said – but you know, you already know – as she reached across the table, took his hands from the glass, held his damp hands in her own, tight in her own.

She smiled, she said, What happened to Harry.

Harry who, he mumbled.

Don't be silly, dear. Harry Sweeney.

He pulled back his hands from hers, but she'd already let them go, and his hands, his arms flew back, knocking the beer from the table, the glass breaking on the floor.

She needs to know, I need to tell her.

Heads turned, people stared. The waitress came running over as he got to his feet, apologizing to the room and to the waitress, taking out and opening his wallet –

She knows you know . . .

Throwing a ten-thousand-yen note down onto the table, pushing back his chair, waving away the waitress as he stumbled toward the door, the exit, and out –

You were the goddamn Chief of Station.

We're all mad here, she says. I'm mad. You're mad.

In the yellow house, the House of the Dead, in the shadows of its front room, the chair at the table, you heard the gate to the garden open, the footsteps up the path, then the key turn in the door, the door open and then close again: you saw her step into the front room: tall, taller than you; fair, fairer than you: her left hand in the pocket of her coat, you watched her walk through the shadows, take her chair at the table, then you heard the words, those words pass from her lips: now you smile at her, you say to her, How do you know I'm mad?

You must be, or you wouldn't have come here.

And how do you know that you're mad?

Because I've been waiting for you to come, she says: her left hand under the table still in her pocket, she holds out her right hand across the table: her pale hand in the dark light, now she smiles at you, she says to you, Because I'm Mary.

In the shadows, across the table, you take, you hold, you shake her hand, and say, And I am Donald.

She does not let go of your hand, holds it tighter and says, Frank thinks we should get married.

But we've only just met, you say. We're such a long way from home. What will Mother say?

Tighter still, she holds, she grips your hand: her other hand, still under the table, still in her pocket: she looks into your eyes and says, I already asked her, Donald.

And what did she say, you whisper.

What do you hope she said?

In the yellow house, the House of the Dead, at your chair at the table, your own left hand on the table, flat on the table, you swallow, then say, I hope she agreed.

She did, Donald, she did, and so do I, she says, squeezes your hand once and lets it go, then takes her left hand, the pistol from the pocket of her coat, lays the pistol down upon the table and smiles again, and says, For the job, dear.

Yes, you say, your heart still pounding, the sweat running down your back, not looking at the gun, just smiling at your future wife, For the job, Mary.

She gets up from the table and the pistol, goes over to the cabinet, opens its doors, takes out a bottle and two glasses, walks back over to the table, puts down the bottle, the glasses beside the pistol: she uncorks the bottle, fills both glasses, then hands one to you and raises her own: To a happy marriage!

You stand up from the table and the gun, raise and touch your glass to hers, and say, To a happy marriage!

She puts the glass to her lips, you put the glass to yours, but you do not drink, she does not drink: you wait, you watch: she waits, she watches: now she smiles, a sad smile, then takes a sip, a big sip, then smiles again, a happy smile, and says, Happy marriages are built on trust, dear Donald.

So here's to trust then, my dear, you say, and down your drink in one, then watch her down her own in one: you reach for the bottle, she puts her hand on your arm –

We need to work, she says, her hand to your head, in your hair now: she pulls your face, your lips to her own: your mouths, your tongues entwined now: in the yellow house, the House of the Dead, now you go to work, you go to work.

*Im Abendrot, im Abendrot*, he was sat on a bench, *his* bench at the Shinobazu Pond, *meiner Heimat, meiner Heimat*, drinking cans of beer from a plastic bag: *wir trinken dich morgens und mittags, wir trinken dich abends*: hand back in the bag, can back to his lips, can after can: *wir trinken und trinken*: he sipped and he stared at the lotuses in their pond, shriveled and withered, dead where they stood, crumpled and brown and frail in their fall, he stared and he sipped: *wir trinken und trinken*: the last can drained, back in the bag, empty and crushed, he tied the handles of the bag, tied them in a plastic knot: *im Abendrot, im Abendrot*, he stood up from the bench, walked anticlockwise, back the way he'd come, back around the pond to the bins, dropped the bag in the trash, then left the pond and the park to stand at the crossing where Shinobazu-dōri meets Route 452, to wait for the lights to change, the light to change.

He crossed the road and turned left into concrete and neon, weaved down the backstreets of restaurants and bars, the smells of grilled meat and fried fish, through the maze of alleyways, the offers to press or suck flesh, then out onto Kasuga-dōri, across Kasuga-dōri and along another side street, into an *izakaya*, *his izakaya*, in hope, a last hope.

He greeted the Master, nodded to the regulars, then took a seat at the long L-shaped counter, not too close to the television, but close enough. He ordered the usual appetizers and a plate of deep-fried horse mackerel. The Master put his kept bottle of *shōchū* down in front of him, then a glass with two cubes of ice. He thanked the Master as he poured himself a measure, a generous measure, then he turned to sip the drink, to stare at the television: the Emperor's health was slipping, his blood pressure plunging. Because of the high number of transfusions the Emperor had received, his doctors were having difficulty finding suitable veins through which to administer transfusions. But despite the deterioration of his condition, the Emperor had not lost consciousness. Poor him, poor him, he thought but did not say, not here, of course, not here. But he did allow himself a slight smile as he picked at the dishes, as he sipped as he watched and he listened to the rest of the news, the other news: Bush had coasted to victory, and Takeshita had cabled the heartfelt congratulations of the Japanese people, who "felt extremely lucky and encouraged" by the election of the Vice President. And former director of the Central Intelligence Agency, he muttered to himself as he looked at his watch again, and wondered again if he would come, and then if he didn't, then what would he do, what on earth would he do?

You're smoking again, tutted Kanehara as he sat down in the empty seat at the counter next to Donald Reichenbach. You said you'd given up. You swore you had.

Donald Reichenbach sighed, stubbed out the cigarette, and said, I'm sorry. I'd forgotten I'd given up.

I don't care, said Kanehara. He ordered a beer, then lit a cigarette of his own, exhaled, and said, Do what you want.

Donald Reichenbach turned slightly to Kanehara, gently touched his arm, and said, Please don't be like this.

Like what, laughed Kanehara, leaning away.

You know what, said Donald Reichenbach, blinking, reaching into his pocket for his handkerchief. So cold.

Look, hissed Kanehara in a whisper, turning to Donald Reichenbach, his cigarette hand over his mouth. If you're going to make a scene again, then I'm going to get up and go.

Donald Reichenbach swallowed, took off his glasses, wiped his eyes, then his glasses, then put them back on. He looked up, down the counter, raised his empty glass of *shōchū* to the Master, and asked for a little more ice, please.

And if you're going to get blind drunk again, then I'm going, said Kanehara under his breath. I can't stand it.

I've no intention of getting drunk, blind or otherwise, said Donald Reichenbach, trying to smile, reaching for the bottle. I'm just very pleased, very grateful you're here. Honestly, I wasn't sure you'd come. Thank you.

You're already drunk, Donald, by the look and the smell of you, said Kanehara as he took the bottle of *shōchū* from Donald Reichenbach, poured just a splash over the glass of fresh ice, and then said, Honestly, after last time, I wasn't going to come. I really didn't want to, Donald, and I wouldn't have done – except you said it was urgent?

Yes, said Donald Reichenbach, holding the glass in both hands, but not raising it. And thank you, thank you again for coming, and I'm sorry, so sorry about last time, really.

Kanehara drained his draft beer, glanced at his watch, then ordered another beer and said, What's so urgent then?

It's about Grete, said Donald Reichenbach.

Kanehara lit another cigarette, blew its smoke up toward the ceiling, shook his head, and said, No.

No, what?

No, I'm not going to pick up your mail, water your plants, feed your fucking cat, and change her fucking tray again while you swan off to the sun again, Donald.

Donald Reichenbach blinked again, tried to hold his eyes open, the tears in their ducts, then swallowed again, tried to catch, to hold the sob in his throat, then said, tried to say, Please, it's just Gre-chan, just if something happened to me, I'm just worried what would happen to her –

If you're that fucking worried, said Kanehara, the hiss in his voice again, then stop fucking drinking and smoking so much. Because I'm not going to look after her. Or you.

Donald Reichenbach knew he was shivering, trembling. He gripped the edge of the counter, stared down at his hands, and whispered, Please, Yoshi, please.

No, said Kanehara, banging his beer down on the counter, standing up, then walking out –

Heads turned again, people stared again. The Master was shaking his head, telling Donald Reichenbach this was the last time, enough was enough, don't come again here, not with him again here, as Donald Reichenbach got to his feet, his face wet with tears, red with shame as he apologized again, again and again, paid the bill, then walked down the long counter, the long, silent counter, through the bead curtain, the sliding door, out of the *izakaya*, into the alley –

I won't let you blackmail me anymore, said Kanehara, waiting for him, turning on him. I've had enough, that's it.

It's not blackmail!

Then what the fuck is it, Donald?

I love you.

No, you don't. You never have, never will – never loved anyone, except for that fucking cat.

Please, don't say that . . .

What the fuck should I say, Donald –

I don't know, but . . .

Thank you? Is that what you want me to say?

No. Never. I just want, wanted . . .

What? What was this?

In the alleyway, off the main road, Donald Reichenbach reached out, held out his arms, his hands, and their palms toward Yoshitaka Kanehara, and said, I just wanted, want you to love me, like I love you.

Shut up, shouted Kanehara. Shut up! It's not love and it never was – he pointed down the alley, across the road – in that park, in the dark, you pulled me into the shadows, unzipped my flies, pulled down my pants, and sucked my cock, never looked at my face, just my cock – I could've been anyone. Anyone.

Is that how you remember it? Really . . .

How else should I remember it? That is how it was.

It wasn't like that . . .

Yes, it was. I was just another suck in the dark, a fuck in the park – I could've been anyone, Donald.

At the start, but . . .

But what? Then what? Your whore, then your nurse, your cook, your cleaner, your cat-fucking-sitter? Just because I was dumb enough, stupid enough to meet you again, then again, to fall for your tears, always with the tears –

No, whispered Donald Reichenbach, shivering, trembling as he pushed past Yoshitaka Kanehara, staggered past him down the alley to the road –

Yeah, go on, walk away, shouted Kanehara after him. Go on, like you always do, off to Zaza to drown your sorrows, dry your eyes in some young fucking crotch – don't think I don't know, Donald, just don't ever fucking call me again.

He waited at the crossing, not for the lights but for the hand, the hand on his arm, but the hand never came: the lights changed and he crossed, still shivering, still trembling; barely able to see, to think, he crossed the road: bustled and jostled, banged into and bumped, by the bubbles of the Bubble, the last of the bubbles, no respect for the dying, the nearly dead, the almost dead: he nearly fell, he almost fell, almost but not quite, he made it to the curb, steadied himself, then staggered on: off the main street, back along a side street, back through the puddles and the neon, the smoke and the lanterns, back out onto and then across Shinobazu-dōri, back to the pond –

The pond dark, the park dark, *his* pond, *his* park, dark and silent, silent, so silent, he took the long way, the long way around, walked anticlockwise, against the wisdom of clocks, against time, these times: the pond on his left, the city to his right, past the steps to the porno theaters, the backs of cheap hotels, under the trees, in their shadows, the swings, the slides, still in the shadows, still under the trees, the homeless in their boxes, on their plastic sheets, more and more, day by day, night after night, they return again, returned: before the zoo, the exit to the zoo, he turned, turned left again, crossed onto Benten Island, walked through the precincts of the Benten shrine, lit golden and red, warm in the night, still the scent of incense on the air, the rustle, the creak of stems, the dead lotus stems, on the air, in the night: *in der Nacht, der Nacht*, round the shrine, behind the shrine he turned, turned left again: *von Dunkel zu Dunkel*, round past the Boat Pond, back along the promenade, Hydrangea Promenade, back to the bench, *his* bench: again the rustles, the creaks of stems, the dead lotus stems, again their temptations, the temptations to drink: *wir trinken dich morgens und mittags, wir trinken dich abends*, to drink and not think, *in der Nacht, der Nacht*, but no, not tonight: tonight he walked on, pushed on, past the bench, its temptations: *von Dunkel zu Dunkel*, away from the pond, out of the park, *his* pond and *his* park, out onto the road, to wait and then cross, back across Shinobazu-dōri, back to the slope, *his* slope –

Up the Slope of the Dead he walked, unremembered, unmourned, and unclaimed, he walked, slowly, slowly, up through the shadows again, under the trees again, the trees of the Kyū-Iwasaki-tei Gardens, the wind through their branches, rising again, in the shadows again, up beside its walls again, walls of brick and stone, slowly, slowly, up he walked, through the shadows, past their walls, trying not to think, to listen to his thoughts, walls of brick and stone, to keep the darkness in: *von Dunkel zu Dunkel*, she smiled, she –

No, he spluttered aloud, at the top of the slope, and then again, No, as he stopped to find, to catch his breath again, slow and still his heart again: No, he said, No, then turned left, left again, then right and crossed the narrow street, right and straight to his apartment building, white in the night, the wind and now rain: through the doors, into the lobby, soft yellow and warm, warm and safe, past the mailboxes, his mailbox unchecked, he went, quickly, now quickly: to the elevator, up to his floor, along the corridor to his door: the key already in his hand, in the lock, he turned the key, the handle, the door open, he went inside, closed and locked the door: his back against the door, in the darkness of the hall, he caught his breath again, then switched on the light, blinked, and called out in tears again, *Tadaima*, Gre-chan. *Tadaima*, Papa's home, *tadaima* . . .

*Okaerinasai*, she purred, against his shins, his calves, between his legs, his trouser legs. He picked her up, up into his arms, stepped out of his shoes, up into the hall. He held her, stroked her as he carried her down the short hall, over the polished wood of the unlit living-dining-kitchen room, into the bedroom, onto the mats and the bed as he stroked her again and again, as he said, I know you're hungry, sweetheart, but we need to talk, to think, you and me, Gre-chan and Papa . . .

The wind, the rain against the window, its pane, the slight light of night, the night across the room, he slumped back on the bed, the cat in his arms, on his chest, still tight in his arms, she purred as he stroked her head, her back, felt her warmth through her fur, flesh and bones, quivering as he sighed and said, Don't worry, dear, don't worry. Papa will think of something, dear, some way out of all this . . .

Harder and stronger, the wind, the rain against the window pane, Grete had stopped purring, was staring into his eyes: her cat's eyes in the dark, looking into his eyes, into him, deep into him, they questioned him . . .

*Eine Gretchenfrage*, they asked of him in the dark, the night, the wind and the rain: a question by Gretchen, a difficult question, in the wind, the rain, in his heart, his soul: a question of belief, of belief in God, in his heart and his soul, the wind and the rain, now a storm: *wieder ein Sturm*, a storm again.

In a whirlwind, Don and Mary, a whirlwind romance, Mary and Don, married within a month. Mary wants you to leave the Dai-ichi Hotel, move into the house, the yellow house, the House of the Dead: Mary works for the Far East Network, and they agree, agree to the move to the house: the Diplomatic Section agree, too, agree to your move to the house: GHQ drag their feet, but then they agree, agree to and approve your move to the house: the yellow house with its fresh coat of paint, its stairs fixed, rooms cleaned and aired: not the House of the Dead now, now the House of the Newly Wed: Mary finds and hires a cook, hires a housekeeper, even a gardener: Mary has money, old or new, clean or dirty, she does not say, you do not ask: lots of money and connections, lots of connections: Mary knows everyone, everyone knows Mary: she throws open the doors of the house, the yellow house, an open house, most evenings and weekends: a whirlwind, a social whirlwind: All part of the job, dear, she says, all part of the job, Don: the drinks and the dinners, the receptions and the parties: Don and Mary, mainly Mary, first disarming the Occupation and the Occupied, then charming the Occupation and the Occupied: smiling and listening through the chitchat and the small talk, laughing and encouraging secrets to be slurred, let slip, and be shared: This is the job, dear, the job, Don: late nights, then long nights, remembering and recording, filing and reporting: this is the job, the routine and the process: the way of life, your life together, together with Mary, in a whirlwind together: by night and by day, day after day, night after night, blowing through the fall into winter, the winter into spring: the world turning, the wind blowing, the wind of change across a world of change: Whittaker Chambers appears before the House Un-American Activities Committee, accuses Harry Dexter White, Alger Hiss, and others of being Communists: the Republic of Korea is established, then the Democratic People's Republic of Korea is declared: the Foley Square trial of ten leaders of the Communist Party of the USA begins in New York: incumbent President Harry S. Truman defies all polls to defeat Thomas E. Dewey, Strom Thurmond, and Henry A. Wallace: the International Military Tribunal for the Far East sentences seven Japanese military and government officials to death: on December 23, 1948, all seven are hanged at Sugamo Prison in Tokyo: Give 'Em Hell Harry wanted photographs of the dead, hanging by their necks, published in the press: Dugout Doug, the American Caesar, defied Rome: Mac did not wish to further antagonize or embarrass the Japanese people, had never agreed with the trials, agreed instead with the last words of Hideki Tōjō: the leaders of the United States and Great Britain have made irreversible mistakes. Firstly, they destroyed a Japan that was the barrier against Communism; secondly, they turned Manchuria into a base for Communism; thirdly, they divided Korea into two and have created a dispute in East Asia. Therefore, the leaders of the United States and Great Britain have a responsibility to resolve these issues; thus, I am very pleased to hear President

Truman was re-elected since these mistakes need to be addressed and resolved. By order of the United States military, Japan has abandoned all her armed forces; this would be a wise decision, if the rest of the world will do the same. If not, it will create a paradise for criminals in which the police have quit their jobs and criminals can run amok. I believe it is necessary for humans to rid themselves of greed if we are to eliminate wars from the world. Unfortunately, in our present world, no other countries have abandoned greed or war; this might be the proof that it is impossible for humans and nations to abandon greed and war. In this sense then, World War III is inevitable and the main parties will be the United States and the Soviet Union. These two powers have completely different philosophies and values, so it will be impossible for them to avoid conflict. In World War III, the battlefields will be in the Far East, in China, Korea, and Japan. Taking this into consideration, I ask the United States to plan to protect an unarmed Japan; without doubt, this is the responsibility of the United States. Please create a path for the eighty million Japanese people to survive: the wind of change across a world of change, a cold wind, a cold world, white and red, a whirlwind of red and of white: by night and by day, day after day, night after night, until one night, one night she knocks on your door, comes into your room, sits down on your bed, hands you a file, an open file, a photograph, and says, Mary says, This is the man, Don, this is the man –

# 9

# The End of the Line

*Summer 1949, Winter 1988*

The Man Who Loves Trains leaves his British-style house in Kami-ikegami, Ōta Ward, between quarter past and half past eight every morning. Every morning, he gets into the black 1941 Buick Sedan, License Number 41173, provided for him by the National Railways, driven by his regular driver, Ōnishi. Most mornings, he will ask Ōnishi to take him directly to his office at the headquarters of Japan National Railways in Marunouchi, central Tokyo. He has recently been appointed the very first President of the newly created Japan National Railways; for the Man Who Loves Trains, who has always loved trains, you might think this job is the fulfillment of all his dreams, his childhood dreams as the Boy Who Loved Trains –

His nickname at school had been Tetsudō-sensei, "Professor Railroad," in recognition of his ability to recite – from memory, by heart – the name of every station in Japan, from Wakkanai in Hokkaidō to Kagoshima in Kyushu; not only the names of the stations, but huge chunks of the timetable, the individual names and numbers of each locomotive, and how many passenger cars formed each train. Later, after he had graduated from the Engineering Department of Tokyo Imperial University and started working in the Transportation Bureau of the Ministry of Railways, he became known as "the Owl," in part due to the Harold Lloyd spectacles he wore but also from his habit of slowly turning his face to look at someone when they addressed him. Throughout his career, he has always been popular among his colleagues; he refrains from alcohol due to a persistent stomach condition, but learned to compensate for this social handicap with a repertoire of magic tricks. He is also known as a devoted son to his mother; during his interview for the Ministry of Railways, when asked who he most respected in the world, he had replied, My mother, sir. He is an equally devoted father to his four sons and husband to his wife; when he had been sent abroad on a two-year tour of the railways of the world, from February 1936 to December 1937, he wrote almost six hundred and fifty letters and postcards to his wife and children back home in Japan. Back home in Japan, the National Service Draft Ordinance and the Mobilization Law had placed the nation in a state of Total War; in 1939, he was seconded to the Ministry of the Army, attached to the Third (Transportation and Communications) Bureau of the Imperial General Headquarters; he was sent on "missions" to Karafuto, Manshūkoku, China, Korea, and French Indochina, then later to Hong Kong, Thailand, Singapore, and twice to Malaysia and the East Indies. By July 1941, he was working as a technical officer for the Planning Board of the Prime Minister's Office; he was responsible for transportation and he had a vision: for war to become victory, transportation had to be efficient; to be efficient, transportation had to be modernized and standardized; modernization and standardization required rapid advances in science and technology; such rapid advances could only be achieved through the founding and funding of a separate new Agency of Technology. Following his successful lobbying of bureaucrats, politicians, and the military, the Agency of Technology was founded in January 1942, and he was appointed as head of the first department of its first section, in charge of General Affairs, with overall control of the Agency. His superiors, subordinates, and colleagues all noted that he had the rare ability to combine being both an engineer and a bureaucrat, of being able to explain complicated scientific and technological matters in a simple way to non-scientific and technological minds, particularly in the military. He was known to research thoroughly the backgrounds of every person he met – where they were born, which high schools and universities they had graduated from – and it was said he had inherited this political talent from his father, who had been a judge. But his family knew all the political and military machinations and maneuverings were taking their toll: he was hospitalized on a number of occasions for exhaustion and stomach ulcers. His family knew he just wanted the war to end and then to be able to return to the Ministry of Railways; he missed and pined for the railways and the trains, their absence only deepening, strengthening his enthusiasm and love. In late 1944, he got his wish, transferred back to the Ministry of Railways, promoted to Director of the Service Department, but it was only part of his wish: though defeat seemed inevitable, the war had yet to end; night after night, the destruction raining down from the skies grew only fiercer and fiercer, and, day by day, the difficulties in keeping the trains running only got harder and harder; the trains had to keep running, the railways being the lifeline of the country, but, he wrote, If I am to die, and I am certain I shall die, then I would rather die, and wish to die, in the service of that which I love most: the railways.

But he did not die and nor, in large part thanks to him, did his railways. After the defeat and the surrender, during the immediate Confusion and then Occupation, when repairing and maintaining the railways was a matter of life and death, this was perhaps his finest hour, the hour of his greatest achievement: the damage to the infrastructure of the railways, to both the railroads and the rolling stock, was tremendous, nigh on catastrophic, but he created and then implemented his "parallel diagram timetable," which allowed both passenger and freight trains to run on the same, single lines, at the same speeds, at alternating intervals. It was a simple idea, but only he had thought of it, and only he would have been able to persuade the Minister to accept and then implement it. His "parallel diagram timetable" proved the only way the country could maintain a reliable transportation system while repairing infrastructure and improving capacity. He had saved the railways, and thus allowed the people and the country to survive. In recognition, he became Director of the Tokyo Railway Bureau in March 1946, then Vice Minister at the Ministry of Transportation in April 1948, and, finally, the very first President of the new Japan National Railways in June 1949, with his own chauffeur-driven car.

But the Man Who Loves Trains does not particularly care for cars. So some mornings, between quarter past and half past eight, when he gets into the back of the black 1941 Buick Sedan, License Number 41173, he asks Ōnishi to drop him at Shinagawa station. He would like to take the train every day; he believes all employees of the National Railways, even executives, should always travel to work by train. But he worries if he always uses the train, then his driver will be laid off; a lot of people are being laid off, or are about to be laid off, by order of GHQ SCAP. As he walks into Shinagawa station, as he climbs the stairs, stands on the platform, and then, in the passenger car, on his way to work, he cannot miss the daily headlines on the front of every paper –

TIME HAS COME FOR JAPAN TO DECREASE DEPENDENCE ON U.S. AID, DODGE WARNS / DODGE SAYS JAPAN HAS BEEN LIVING BEYOND ITS MEANS FOR TOO LONG – Government Must Slash Expenditure at Any Cost, He Declares / LABOR UNIONS CONFIRM STRUGGLE POLICY – Stiff Fight Is Planned / GOV'T IS EXPECTED TO CUT PERSONNEL BY HALF A MILLION – Administrative Reform Bills Slated to Go Before Diet Next Week / OCCUPATION PERSONNEL WARNED TO STAY

INDOORS – Japan's Communists and Labor set to Celebrate Fourth Postwar May Day / PERSONNEL SLASH OF 267,000 IS SET – TPO Bill Puts Limit of Gov't Workers at 871,000 / MASS DISMISSALS SEEN AS BILL OK'D – 419,000 Gov't Workers Slated for Discharge / NEW RAILWAY BODY BEGINS WORK – the New Japan National Railway Corporation Began Functioning Yesterday with Former-Transportation Vice-Minister Sadanori "Lucky Boy" Shimoyama as First President . . .

He is no longer known as Tetsudō-sensei, no longer known as "the Owl"; now he is known as "Lucky Boy." But standing in the passenger car, on his way to work, reading the newspaper headlines, knowing what he has to do, knowing he has to dismiss one hundred thousand fellow employees, knowing the price the one hundred thousand fellow employees and their families will have to pay, he and his own family will have to pay, by order of the government, by order of GHQ SCAP, he does not feel a "lucky boy" at all; he feels cursed, he feels doomed, has done for months. I'm not sure, he told one friend in May, but maybe I'll be appointed President. And if I am, the dismissal job will be a tough one. I may even be killed. After he had been appointed President, when he was congratulated by the Chairman of the National Railway Workers Union, he said, It's embarrassing. I've been carrying around a letter of resignation in my pocket. Just waiting for the right timing. Large-scale dismissals are inevitable, he told his younger sister, in front of his wife, but it's not fair if the one who fires so many people then keeps his job, and so I will resign in June. I will leave the world of bureaucracy, he told another friend. Return to my hometown and rest for two years. But he could not resign, he could not rest, could not sleep: I'm unable to sleep, to eat, or even think straight, he told the doctor at Tokyo Tetsudō Byōin, the Railway's own hospital, due to the "strike issue." The doctor diagnosed a "mild nervous breakdown and gastritis," prescribed a course of vitamin injections, a glucose solution, and Brobalin to help him sleep. But still he could not sleep, could not rest or resign. They would not let him; they needed a scapegoat. I've been put on the chopping block, he told an old friend. Like a sacrifice . . .

Cursed and doomed, he feels marked and watched, and he's right; he has been marked, he is being watched: in his car to the office or on the train to his office, at his office and in his meetings, his meetings with his colleagues and with the unions, with politicians and with GHQ, whomever he meets and wherever he goes, he is always being watched; watched by people from the unions, watched by people against the unions, watched by people from GHQ, and watched by people who have been hired by Mary and you, and by other people, too, watched by people you didn't hire, people you don't know. In the summer of 1949, everybody is watching the Man Who Loves Trains, watching Sadanori "Lucky Boy" Shimoyama.

You're actually very lucky, Donald, said Doctor Morgan.

Well, I don't feel lucky, doc, not lucky at all.

Well, you should, said Doctor Morgan, what with all your smoking and drinking, the way you've carried on. Because there's really nothing wrong with you, Donald, least not physically, not seriously. It's all in your head, dear.

But you will give me more pills?

Yes, dear, sighed Doctor Morgan, turning back to his narrow desk and picking up his pen.

Donald Reichenbach swallowed, then said, Could you give me quite a lot, doc, save me keep coming back?

With pleasure, laughed Doctor Morgan. He stopped writing, tore off a sheet of paper, then turned back round from the desk and the prescription pad. As long as you do promise you're not going to do anything silly, anything dramatic, dear?

Donald Reichenbach took the prescription, shook his head, smiled, and said, Of course not, doc. Thank you.

Not planning to do a General Nogi on us, are you, dear, laughed Doctor Morgan again. Re-enact *Kokoro* in Yushima when old Hirohito finally shuffles off stage left?

Donald Reichenbach smiled again, then said, Only a matter of time now, I suppose, doc.

It's only ever a matter of time, said Doctor Morgan, standing up, walking over to open the door.

Donald Reichenbach swallowed again, then said, I saw her, you know? That woman I was telling you about.

That's nice, dear, said Doctor Morgan, the door open now. Good to get out, meet new people. Helps keep us young.

Donald Reichenbach said, Not in this case.

Oh, said Doctor Morgan, pointedly glancing at his watch, then the hallway. A disappointment, was she, dear?

She's the daughter of Gloria Wilson – you remember her, doc? She was asking about Harry Sweeney, wanting to know what happened to him. She knows what I used to do, doc, who I used to be. Even mentioned Mary . . .

Doctor Morgan closed the door again. He walked over to Donald Reichenbach still sat on the edge of the bed. He said, Donald, Gloria Wilson died childless of cancer fifteen, maybe twenty years ago now. What's her name, this woman?

Julia Reeve, she says, said Donald Reichenbach, taking out his handkerchief. How do you know she's dead?

Doctor Morgan shook his head, sighed, and said, Don't start blubbering, Donald, you hardly knew the woman.

Not crying for her, said Donald Reichenbach, taking off his glasses, dabbing his eyes. But how do you know?

If you must know, Mary told me.

You kept in touch?

Doctor Morgan laughed: Don't tell me you're jealous?

I'm not jealous, I just want to know . . .

Doctor Morgan shook his head again and said, Christmas cards, the odd letter, that kind of thing –

Dear Miles, Gloria Wilson's dead. Merry Christmas and a happy New Year, love Mary – that kind of thing?

Look, I don't remember, said Doctor Morgan. Mary just said she'd heard that Gloria had died, that's all. It must've been one of her last letters, if not her last, in fact.

Donald Reichenbach put on his glasses again, put his handkerchief away, and said, But you never said.

Really, Donald, sighed Doctor Morgan. Please do try and grow up, dear. There's still time, you know?

Donald Reichenbach stared at Doctor Morgan: Is there, doc? I hope you're right. But what about Harry?

Sweeney? What about him, Donald?

Did Mary mention him as well?

No, said Doctor Morgan. Why would she?

You know what happened to him, doc.

And so did she, and so do you.

Donald Reichenbach, still staring at Doctor Morgan, said, No, I know what *you* told me happened to him . . .

Donald, said Doctor Morgan, his voice low. What I told you happened to him *is* what happened to him: as soon as he was well enough, he was shipped back stateside.

And then, doc, then what?

I don't know, Donald.

Is he still alive?

I don't know, Donald, honestly, I don't.

And you don't care.

And nor should you, Donald, okay?

Donald Reichenbach nodded, then got up from the edge of the bed as he said, But she cares.

Who?

Donald Reichenbach looked up at Doctor Morgan, smiled, and said, This Julia Reeve woman. But don't worry, doc, that's what I'll tell her.

Tell her what, said Doctor Morgan, barring his way.

Just what you've told me, doc.

If I was you, Donald, said Doctor Morgan, his voice still low, I wouldn't tell her anything, or see her again.

She keeps calling. She knows where I live.

Then if I was you, Donald, said Doctor Morgan again, I'd tell her that if she calls or bothers you again, then you'll contact the embassy and the Japanese police.

Why would I tell her that?

Because this sounds to me like blackmail, Donald.

Donald Reichenbach stared up at Doctor Morgan again and said, How can it be blackmail, doc? If what you say happened *is* what happened, then I've got nothing to hide.

Oh, don't act so damn stupid, Donald, said Doctor Morgan. If it's not blackmail, then she's probably some kind of journalist or writer or something. Either way, you know as well as I do that the whole thing is still classified.

Donald Reichenbach smiled and said, In the interest of national security, right, doc?

The internal telephone on the narrow desk buzzed once and flashed red –

Exactly, said Doctor Morgan, glancing at the phone, then opening the door again. And so if you must see or speak to her again, Donald, then call her bluff. Tell her to save her damn questions for Washington and the State Department.

Donald Reichenbach looked down at the prescription in his hand, then back up at Doctor Morgan, and said, You know what Reeve means in Old English, Miles?

No, Donald, I don't.

Donald Reichenbach smiled again, then blinked, blinked again, and said, A steward or a bailiff.

This is the list of the men we want rid of, the names he's to make sure are included in the next round of dismissals, you say as you hand the envelope across the coffee-shop table, over the two cups and the ashtray to Kōji Terauchi –

Kōji Terauchi was employed on the railways prior to the draft and enlistment. He was captured in Manchuria and interned in a Soviet prisoner-of-war camp. Upon repatriation, like thousands of other former railway employees he was re-instated and re-employed on the railways. And like thousands of others, he joined the National Railway Workers Union, and he joined Nihon Kyōsan-tō, the Japanese Communist Party, or at least that's his story, so he says –

Kōji Terauchi is another of the men Mary found and hired, another of the eighteen native hires allowed under the finances provided by Frank, the ceiling dictated to the Rat Palace by Washington –

Kōji Terauchi takes the envelope, nods, then smiles and asks, Is it the same as the list I gave you?

With a few additions, you say.

Am I still on it?

Yes, you say. But don't worry, you've done a good job so far. And your work's not done yet. You'll be okay.

He nods: Thank you.

You light another cigarette, exhale, then lower your voice and ask, So when and where's the next meeting?

He's nervous, almost a wreck – I mean, you've seen all those KILL SHIMOYAMA posters all over town? He's had death threats, too, letters and calls – so he insists on somewhere public, a department store, either Shirokiya or Mitsukoshi.

You nod, you ask, When?

The morning after the first round of dismissals, says Kōji Terauchi. Early, before he starts work.

You nod, put out your cigarette, put the packet back in your pocket, pick up your hat, and stand up: Soon as you know the exact time and place, call the yellow house, okay?

Hey, he says. What about my money?

You lean down toward him, smile, and say, Mary's the one with the money, not me, you know that.

Please, he whispers. I'm broke, I got nothing.

You take some yen from the pocket of your pants, unfold a few notes, put them down on the table: That's all I got on me. Pick up the tab, then keep the change.

Gee, thanks, he says, looking down at the notes on the table, then laughs: You guys sure know how to beat the Reds.

You take your packet of cigarettes back out of your pocket, put it down on the notes, and say, Don't waste 'em, yeah? We're at war, and I got to get back to the front line –

You put on your hat, turn, and walk out of the Coffee Shop Hong Kong into the basement corridor. But you do not go up the stairs, back up and along the street, back to your cramped, tiny office in the Mitsui building. No, you check your watch, then the corridor, the faces, the eyes and the ears of the passers-by, the customers for the department store, and the passengers for the subway. You walk away from the coffee shop to the ticket gate, buy a ticket, then go through the gate, down the steps, down onto the platform –

You stand on the platform, watch the passengers getting off and on the trains heading east, the trains heading west. But you do not get on either train; you wait for the next trains, wait until every other passenger has boarded the next train heading west to Shibuya, then slip on board just as the doors are closing. You do not sit down; you stay stood up as the train passes through

Nihonbashi, Kyōbashi, and Ginza, then get off the train again at Shimbashi. You go up the steps but do not exit the station. You go into the toilets and you take a piss. You come out of the toilets, check the passengers again, their faces, their eyes and their ears, then walk down the other flight of steps, down to the platform, the platform for the trains heading east. You stand on the platform, bend down to tighten your shoelaces, and do not board the first train. You wait until every other passenger has boarded the next train, then slip on board just as the doors are closing. You sit down, take off your hat, take out your handkerchief, and wipe your face, then your neck. You put away your handkerchief, put your hat back on, looking up and down the car, then left and right across the aisle at the women with their empty shopping bags, the men with their newspapers, reading their headlines –

RED-LED RIOTERS STIR DISORDERS IN NORTH JAPAN – Agitators Seize Police Stations in Taira, Koriyama / RAILROAD WORKERS WARNED AGAINST USING FORCE – President Shimoyama Reminds Employees that Union Directive to "Resort to Force" is Illegal / RAILWAY SABOTAGE CASES ON INCREASE – Four Cases in Tokyo: Throwing of Stones Against Passenger Trains Reported on Jōban line / GOV'T HELD READY FOR EMERGENCIES – Situation After Personnel Cut Can Be Handled, Minister says / RED INDOCTRINATION – Repatriates Schooled in Ideas of Communism, Told Nothing About Truth Here / INQUIRY DEMANDED INTO RED ACTIVITIES – JCP Accused of Plotting Revolt in Japan: Revolution by Force Sometime in August or September –

– as the train carries you back through Ginza, Kyōbashi, and Nihonbashi, back to Mitsukoshi-mae and on to Kanda, where you stand up suddenly, get off the train quickly, just as the doors are closing, then stop on the platform again, bend down and tighten your shoelaces again. You stand up, walk down the platform, through the ticket gate, along the passageway, and climb the steps out of the subway to the street. You stop again, take out your handkerchief again, wipe your face, your neck again, then put away your handkerchief again. You check your watch again, then buy some cigarettes, two packs of cigarettes at a kiosk on the street. You light a cigarette, you start to walk, but feel spots of rain, the first spots of rain, then more spots of rain, now a shower of rain. You put out your cigarette, turn, and walk back to the station, buy another ticket, pass through another gate, and climb the steps up to the Chūō line platform. You stand on the platform, wipe your face, your neck again and watch the trains arrive and depart, the trains heading down to Tokyo station, the trains heading out to Tachikawa. Again you let the first trains leave, again you wait until every other passenger has boarded, then again you slip on board just as the doors are closing. You stand on the train for Tachikawa, but you do not sit down on this train, do not read the headlines on the papers of the passengers. You stare out of the window, watching the rain fall, the summer rain fall, waiting for your stop, the next stop, Ochanomizu.

He was already standing up as the train pulled into Shin-Ochanomizu station, the *Japan Times* already folded up, discarded on the rack above the seats, waiting for someone else to read in English, if they so wished, of the rally yesterday against the emperor system which had drawn a crowd of seven hundred and fifty to Yūrakuchō, so they said. But the Emperor, oblivious, is nothing if not resilient, he thought again, as he got off the train, walked along the platform, then stood on the steep escalator, gripped its red rubber handle, and tried not to look back down as up he went, up past the adverts for the Hilltop Hotel, its various restaurants. How long has it been now, he wondered, three months now? Hanging on for His Imperial dear life, the Court Physicians were amazed, were awed: just when they must have thought, but dared not say, of course, he'd breathed his last, then back he comes, back from the dead, thirsty for blood, more blood as on and on he hangs for dear life, clings to dear life, dear life. An inspiration to us all, he muttered again as he stepped off the escalator, passed through the ticket gate, then turned left and up the little steps, into the underground shopping center, along its short arcade, past the Cozy Corner café, the pharmacy and out through its automatic doors. Or maybe just afraid of what is to come, he thought now, standing at the foot of a flight of wide steps up to the city, the air and its light, and what he will face? He sighed, then slowly, slowly began to climb the steps to the street, stopping to catch his breath every now and then, every now and every then, slowly, slowly, until he'd made his way to the top of the twenty-two steps. Much more of this and he'll ruin Christmas and New Year, he thought as he stood again to catch his breath, pretending to look at the display of expensive, foreign-brand frames in the window of an optician, then said aloud, And we can't have that now, can we, Gre-chan?

He swallowed, he blinked, then swallowed and blinked again, but it was no good, no good. He reached into his coat pocket, yanked out his handkerchief, took off his glasses, then held the cloth to his eyes, to their tears, blubbering, yes, Morgan was right, blubbering, there was no other word for it, but one last Christmas together, is that really too much to ask?

He took a deep breath, then exhaled, wiped his eyes, his glasses, then put his glasses back on, handkerchief away, and said, aloud again, Of course not! Papa promised.

He looked up, faced the window, saw people – the customers and staff inside the store – now watching him, staring at him: Well, let them stare, enjoy the show. People always stare here, always have and always will; he'd a good mind to stick out his tongue, that would show them. But then, tongue poised and almost out, he caught sight of his reflection – in the glass of the store window, the spectacles on display – his own reflection, his reflections, all his reflections, now watching him, staring back and at and through him: You don't want to see us, see us, they whispered, but you do, yes, you do, they laughed, and we see you, see you, yes, we do, see you, too –

Quickly, he turned away from the window, the display and its spectacles, the eyes and the stares, these eyes and their stares which watched him, followed him, as he climbed the last five little steps up to street level and the road. He stopped to catch his breath again, watching the traffic – the trucks and the taxis, the cars and the buses, the bicycles and the people – flow over Hijiri-bashi, the Holy Bridge, then, breath caught, he went right, down the short, slight slope to the corner with Kōbai-zaka. Here again he stopped, not to catch his breath but to look up, up at the domes and the bells, the two pale-green domes, the dark, silent bells, their hours, their times, kept now, quiet now. He swallowed, blinked again, a deep breath again, then off he set again, round the corner, across and up Kōbai-zaka to the black gates of the Nikorai-dō, the Holy Resurrection Cathedral. Here again he stopped, paused to catch his breath again, to slow now, still his heart now as he swallowed, blinked again, then walked through the gates, the garden, the largely concrete garden, past its benches and the seminary to the steps of the cathedral, the five stone steps up to its doors, open to worshippers, the public, sightseers and tourists alike: So which are you, he sadly, sadly smiled, which today are you?

He looked up at the white walls of the cathedral, the arch above the doors, its metal Orthodox Cross, its painting of Christ and His Testament, then sighed as he slowly, slowly began to climb, climb the five large stone steps up, up to the doorway. How many steps have I climbed today, he thought, then wondered how many steps there were, how many rungs there were on the Ladder of Divine Ascent? Then remembered, yes, was sure, there were thirty, thirty steps, thirty rungs, as he paused again, at the top of the steps, to catch his breath again, to cross himself now, in the Orthodox way, in memory of the thirty years, the thirty years Christ lived in this world: renunciation of this world being the first, the very hardest step on the Ladder of Divine Ascent, he knew, as he crossed, crossed himself again, then the threshold into the cathedral.

An elderly Japanese lady in a rust-brown kimono was sitting at a long, narrow table where the narthex met the nave. There were books and calendars, postcards and candles on the table before her. She looked up at Donald Reichenbach and smiled, welcomed, then offered him a pamphlet about the cathedral, a candle to light, For one hundred yen, please.

He handed over his coin, but politely refused the pamphlet, the candle, and said, Actually, I was hoping to catch Father Ilya – is he about today, by any chance . . . ?

The lady smiled, nodded, asked him to wait, please, just a moment, please, as she got to her feet, left her post, and tottered off into the shadows of the cavernous nave.

Donald Reichenbach watched her go, get lost in the gloom, then let his eyes wander up, upward to the dome, head back and turning, then back down, down the walls, over the stained glass to the icons, the candle stands, their waxen prayers melted down to cold and varying lengths, their flames, their lights all out, already all out. Perhaps he should light, still light a candle, he thought, a candle for Gre-chan, dear Gre-chan, at least. He turned back to the table, his hand in his pocket, sifting its change, then noticed, beside the piles of books and candles, a small wooden box, read the sign on the box asking for donations for the victims and survivors of the recent earthquake in Armenia: How many dead, did they say? Thirty, forty, fifty thousand, is that what they said? But what did it matter when one old man was dying of natural causes in his gilded palace in the center of Tokyo, eh? He took his hand from the pocket of his pants, reached inside his coat for his wallet. He opened his wallet, took out a ten-thousand-yen note, then another, folded them once, then once again, and posted them through the narrow slot in the top of the box –

That's very kind of you, Donald, said Father Ilya, coming out of the shadows, his pale hands outstretched in the gloom. And very good to see you, too.

And you, too, Father, said Donald Reichenbach, smiling, then taking, kissing the hand of the priest. Thank you.

No, thank you, Sensei, laughed Father Ilya, holding Donald Reichenbach's hands in his own as he turned to the elderly lady sat back at her post: Satō-san, today we are honored. This is one of my oldest friends, the great Professor Reichenbach, the famous translator and scholar who has taught at Columbia, Stanford, and our very own Tōdai and Keiō.

The lady, on her feet again, bowed and gushed first with apologies, then wonder and compliments, now protestations as Donald Reichenbach bowed and blushed as he mumbled how his achievements were nothing special at all, his former positions of no importance, now he was retired . . .

How long has it been, said Father Ilya, leading Donald Reichenbach away from the lady, her table, back out through the doors of the cathedral. Five years? More . . .

I don't know, said Donald Reichenbach under the arch, its metal cross, shaking his head. I lose track . . .

Father Ilya smiled: Don't we all – but you've time for tea, or something stronger? I still keep a bottle in my room.

Thank you, Father, I'd like nothing more, said Donald Reichenbach. But first, would you mind if we sat outside? These days, I spend so much of my time indoors, inside.

Father Ilya nodded, smiled again, and said, Of course, Donald, whichever you prefer. Please, after you . . .

And the two men – these two old men, one Japanese, one American – began to slowly, slowly make their way down the stone steps and across the concrete garden, past the seminary building, to sit side by side, almost touching, knee to knee, arm by arm, on a cold concrete bench, under a sparse, crooked palm, close to the black iron gates.

Excuse me, Donald, said Father Ilya, looking at his watch, then standing straight back up again. If you don't mind, it's almost closing time. I'll just quickly shut the gates, save Satō-san the bother and us from unwanted interruptions.

In the fading, December-afternoon light, Donald Reichenbach shook his head, then watched his old friend – at least, the person he'd known longest in Japan – walk over to close the gates: his hair and beard were as long and full as ever, but now gray, almost white, snow white; he was stooping, too, his cassock trailing on the ground. Still, he moves well enough, much better than you, than me, he thought as he watched him close the gates, then come back toward the bench –

You know, Donald, if you'd called and let me know, said Father Ilya, smiling as he sat back down, we could've met at Rogovski, even the Kamiya, like the old days . . .

Donald Reichenbach nodded and said, I know, Father, I'm sorry. It's silly, I know, but I just don't really like to leave Grete too long, not these days, especially in the evenings.

Of course, said Father Ilya. Is she okay?

Donald Reichenbach nodded again, then laughed: Yes, she's fine, thank you. It's just me being a silly old fool.

Father Ilya turned to Donald Reichenbach, watched him reach into his coat pocket for his handkerchief, then take off his glasses, wipe and dry his eyes, then his glasses, then waited for him to fold up his handkerchief again, put it back inside his pocket again, so then he could ask, gently, softly ask, What is it, Donald? What's happened, what's wrong . . . ?

Donald Reichenbach shook his head: I don't know.

I think you do, said Father Ilya, nodding. And I think you want to tell me – that's why you came, isn't it?

Donald Reichenbach shook his head again, then said, I'm sorry, Father, I don't know why I came, I don't, I'm sorry.

I think you do, said Father Ilya again, reaching for the hand of Donald Reichenbach, then holding, squeezing his hand, gently, softly. You do know, Donald, you do. Just as you know why it's been so long, so long since you last came, Donald.

Donald Reichenbach sighed, nodded: Yes.

The past, said Father Ilya. Our past.

Donald Reichenbach swallowed, blinked, staring down at his hand, his hands in the hands, the hands of the priest, then swallowing again, blinking again, he nodded again, then said, It just keeps coming back, over and over, again and again.

I know, Donald, but it'll pass, it will pass . . .

I hope it's just the damn Emperor, all this time he lies there dying – why can't he just hurry up and die!

Quite, said Father Ilya. He should've gone years ago, the day he surrendered. But it'll soon be over, Donald.

Will it, though? Will it really?

Yes, Donald. Believe me.

But then what . . . ?

Then time can move on, said Father Ilya. And we can move on, Donald. Things will change, not only here . . .

What do you mean, Father? Where?

You know where, Donald: *there*.

Donald Reichenbach shook his head, turned to the priest, their hands still entwined, shook his head again, and said, No, don't say that. Please, don't say that.

They're already changing, you know that, Donald, but faster than they want, faster than you think, Donald.

But not all of it, surely not everything?

Yes, Donald, everything, whispered Father Ilya. Thaws become floods, floods wash things away . . .

In the concrete garden, the December twilight, Donald Reichenbach swallowed, freed his hands from the hands of the priest, closed his eyes, shook his head again, then sighed and said, What a waste, a pointless fucking waste . . .

We weren't to know, Donald.

Donald Reichenbach opened his eyes, turned to the man beside him, this man in his black dress, with his white hair and silver chain around his neck: Would it have made any damn difference to you if you had, if you had known?

I did what I thought was right at the time, said this Japanese man in his Russian clothes. We all did, Donald, did what we thought was right at the time.

But you were wrong, Kaz, we were all wrong.

We didn't know that, Don, not at the time.

But everything we did was wrong, everything that happened was wrong. We must have been mad . . .

What was the line from *Alice*, the line you used to like, Donald, said Father Ilya. "Like pilgrim's wither'd wreath of flowers / Pluck'd in a far-off land . . ."

Donald Reichenbach shook his head again, sighed again, then laughed and said, Is that what you tell yourself? How you live with yourself . . . ?

*My ne v izgnan'i*, said Father Ilya, clutching the cloth of his cassock, the cross on his chain. *My v poslan'i.*

Except the mission turned out to be a lie, said Donald Reichenbach, standing up. Only the exile was true, is real.

Father Ilya looked up at Donald Reichenbach, held out his hands, his palms toward Donald Reichenbach, and said, gently, softly said, It doesn't have to be exile, Donald. Please, stay here, with me, please, with Christ and with God . . .

Another mission, another lie? Fuck you, said Donald Reichenbach, turning away, walking away . . .

A flood is coming, Donald, said Father Ilya, watching Donald Reichenbach opening the gates. Please, Donald, I can help you hold on, hold on together . . .

Donald Reichenbach stepped through the black gates, turned to pull them closed again . . .

Please, Donald, you'll be swept away, washed away.

Donald Reichenbach glanced up through the iron bars, back at the man in his dress with his chain, on his concrete bench in his concrete garden, in the shadow of the cathedral, his ark and his cover, and smiled, then he turned and slowly, slowly walked away, down the slope, the hill, back into exile.

In the wet, black night, in the damp, yellow house, it is the Fourth of July, Independence Day, Nineteen Hundred and Forty-nine, and you are alone, yet not alone, here yet not here: tucked up in bed, in your single bed, with your books, all your books, your Japanese books: reading and studying, practicing translating, with *Genji*, always *Genji*: at night, by night, you love to take the retellings by Yosano and Tanizaki, love then to compare them – as best you can – with the original text, love then to return to the Waley translation, and then love, love to get lost, lost in these words, these characters and their world, at night, by night, in love, in love, with a different world, a different you, at night, by night: you look up from your books, your Japanese books, back from that world, back in this world: hear a car pull up outside in the street, then silence, in the silence, the long silence, you wait, you listen: hear a car door close, then the garden gate close, her heels up the path, then her key in the door: the door slammed shut, her heels kicked off, her stocking feet up the stairs now, you watch her fall through your door now, flop down upon your bed, your books, your legs, flat on her back, eyes open and wide, mouth open and wide, Mary giggles, then laughs: Happy Fourth of July, Donny – did you miss me, dear Ducky? Unbearably so?

You close your books, your Japanese books, prop yourself up, up on your pillow: you stroke her hair, her damp hair, and smile and say, *Inconsolablement, naturellement.*

*Merci*, she giggles again, *mon cher mari.*

Her lipstick smudged, dress ridden up, you play with a strand of her hair and ask, Did Mary-chan have a good time?

She sure did, she laughs. A swell time!

She sure smells sure swell . . .

Now, now, she says, turning onto her side to look up, smile up at you: to reach up to touch, to pinch, to pull your cheek. Don't be such a puritan Ducky, dear Donny.

You laugh: Go on then, dear, do tell . . .

Well, she says, rolling onto her stomach, still on your legs, still looking up, smiling up at you. There were parades and there were speeches, fireworks and songs, all the songs: "The Star-Spangled Banner," "God Bless America," "America the Beautiful," "My Country, 'Tis of Thee" – and she starts to hum, and then to sing – Sweet land of liberty, / of thee I sing; / Land where my fathers died, / Land of the pilgrims' pride, / From ev'ry –

Shh, you whisper, sat up straight now, your fingers to her lips, your head, your ear to the window, the street –

hear a car door close again, the garden gate close again, boots up the path, knuckles on the door: first tapping, then knocking, now banging on the door, your door –

Wait here, you say, pushing her off your legs, the books falling to the floor as you get out of bed, grab your robe, put it on, going out of the room, down the stairs –

at the foot of the stairs, you pause, you swallow, tighten the cord of your robe, then walk to the door, your ear, your lips to the wood of the door, you hiss, Who is it?

It's me, comes a voice. Terauchi.

You open the door, the door she left unlocked, see him

standing there, in the wet, black night, pale in the night: both pale with fear, with fright, you say, The hell you think –

I'm sorry, he says. But we need to speak –

Let him in, Don, says Mary behind you, coming down the stairs behind you, at the door now, beside you now, with her coat on now, her left hand in its pocket –

You open the door wider and let him in, show him through into the front room, sit him down, down at the table as Mary opens the cabinet, takes out a bottle and three glasses, puts them down on the table, uncorks the bottle, fills all three glasses, then smiles: Go on, Kōji . . .

He nods, takes a sip, a gulp from the drink in the glass, then begins to say, to babble, They're going to kill him, kill Shimoyama, that's what they say, tomorrow morning, that's what I heard. We need to warn –

Who, asks Mary.

He looks up, up at you both, from Mary to you, then back to Mary, and says, Shimoyama, President Shimoyama.

Yes, says Mary. But who's going to kill him?

He sips, gulps again, spills, dribbles his drink, then tries to say, to stammer, I don't really know who . . .

You take the glass, the drink from his hands, put it down, down on the table, then grab the tops of his arms, stare into his eyes, hold his arms, his eyes, and say, Slow down, Kōji, slow down, and go back to the start, the beginning, and then tell us everything, and I mean everything –

He nods again, looks again from you to Mary, then back to you; you smile, let his eyes, his arms go, and then you wait, you wait for him to start –

I was in the Tokyo Railway Club tonight, he says, in Yūrakuchō tonight, when I saw this man, this man who was one of my superiors in the Kwantung Army, in Manchuria, but I hadn't seen him since, though I knew he was back and was about, had heard he was doing well, well for himself, and . . .

What's his name, asks Mary.

Kōji Terauchi looks again from Mary to you, then back to Mary, then whispers, Shiozawa. He's a publisher now.

Go on, says Mary again, nodding, smiling.

Well, you know, so we start to talk, to drink, to swap and share stories, about the war, the people we knew, them who had died, those who'd survived, then about after, and now, who's doing this, who's doing that, and everything, what we're doing, we're thinking, about China, the Russians, America and Japan, you know, of course, all that's going on, with Yoshida, the government, the railways, the strikes, the Commies and the Reds, all the shit that's going on, what should be going on, how it should be done, what could be done, needs to be done, and we're quite drunk by now, yeah, him more than me, when he says, suddenly leans forward and whispers and says, We could use a man like you, Terauchi, we could, a man who served his Emperor, his country, who still loves his Emperor, his country, who wants to see the Emperor, the country restored . . .

And what did you say, asks Mary.

I said what you'd told me to say, he says, if anyone asks, drops any hints, invitations, just like you told me to say, I say, I said, Any way I can, I want to serve, still serve, and he nods, but then, very quiet, so I almost can't hear, he says, Remember back in China, how it was in Manchukuo, how sometimes we had to do bad things, things we didn't like, didn't want to do, but we had to do, still had to do, those bad things so good things, good things would come, would happen, good things for the Emperor, for Japan, you remember?

You look down at this man, this man who says his name is Kōji Terauchi, sat at your table, sat in your house, your yellow house, and say, you ask, And do you?

Shh, says Mary. Let him finish.

Kōji Terauchi, this man who says his name is Kōji Terauchi, he looks again from Mary to you, then back to Mary, then nods and says, Yeah, I remember, we all remember, and that's what I told him, Yes, I remember, and then he nodded, he nods and he says, Good, that's good, Terauchi, because it's the same, always the same, he says, Manchukuo then, Tokyo now, the battle's the same, the war is the same, and so we have to do bad things, things we don't like, if we want to win the battle, then win the war, for the Emperor and for Japan, you agree, Terauchi, do you agree?

And of course you agreed, you say, you said yes?

He looks at you, then at Mary, and he nods and says, Of course I agreed, I said yes, like you told me to say . . .

Just let him finish, Don, says Mary. Please –

Thank you, he says, thank you, because this is the part, the part you need to hear, because now he said, he says, The only way to beat the Reds, to crush the Commies, and to win that battle and then this war, is to turn the people of Japan, the people of the world, against the Reds and the Commies, and the way to do that is to shock the people, leave them appalled and horrified, and the only way, the only way to do that is to do a bad thing to a good man, to sacrifice a good man . . .

Sadanori Shimoyama, you whisper –

Yeah, he says. He said, I know President Shimoyama, met him in Manchukuo, a long time ago now, but he remembered me, took my call, listened to what I had to say, about information I had, about Commies and Reds in the union, the railway union, and so he wants to meet me, because he trusts me, asked me to meet him tomorrow, tomorrow morning at Mitsukoshi, the Nihonbashi Mitsukoshi . . .

You grab Kōji Terauchi, this man who says his name is Kōji Terauchi, and shout, This is a crock of shit. Either he's playing you or you're playing us –

Then why did I come here, he shouts back. Why'm I telling you all this, telling you to warn Shimoyama?

Let go of him, Don, says Mary, taking your arm, pulling your arm off this man –

Hell knows, you say, but this is bullshit, goddamn bullshit. He just happens to run into this guy he says he ain't seen since the end of the war, this guy who just happens to know Shimoyama and be –

Shut up, Don, shouts Mary, and then, softly now, she says, Please, Don, let him finish, let him tell us what the man wanted, why he's obviously sought him out . . .

Because he knows I'm back working for the railways, says Kōji Terauchi. Knows I'm in the union, so he wants me to go with him to the meeting, put Shimoyama at his ease, then help persuade Shimoyama to go with us –

Go where, you ask. Where?

He didn't say.

Kōji, says Mary, softly again, gently now. You think this man knows you're working for us?

No, says Kōji Terauchi.

Are you sure?

Yes, he says. He would have said, I know he would.

Mary nods, nods again, then asks, And tomorrow morning, what time is the meeting, and where?

Nine forty-five, he says. At the foot of the central staircase on the first floor of the store.

Mary looks at you, then back at Kōji Terauchi, and asks, What time and where had you arranged to meet Shimoyama?

He looks at you, then back at Mary, and says, Around half past nine, but at Shirokiya, not Mitsukoshi.

Good, says Mary. That's good; it means Shimoyama is still planning to keep his meeting with you, then to go on to Mitsukoshi to meet this guy Shiozawa.

Hold on, you say, turning again to this man, this man who calls himself Kōji Terauchi. What did you tell him? Did you agree, tell him you were in?

Yes, he said, then again, What else could I say?

Good, says Mary again. Very good, Kōji, you did the right thing, well done. So we stick to our plan –

What, you say, then, We have to –

We have to warn him, nods Kōji Terauchi.

Look, she says, says to you both. We need to give the list to Shimoyama, then Kōji can warn him.

But what about Shiozawa, you say, both say.

In the black, wet night, in the damp, yellow house, her coat still on, hand back in its pocket, Mary looks at you, looks at you both, then smiles at you, smiles at you both, and says, she says, I'll deal with Shiozawa, boys, trust me –

After all, she laughs now, turning to you, staring at you, we're all on the same side here – right, Don?

No, he said, shaking his head sadly, sadly smiling. No jam to-day, no jam to-morrow, as he put the jar back on the shelf and blinked, blinked again then turned away, wandering off down, down the aisle, then up, up another aisle. Even Meidi-ya, this store, his favorite store, seemed subdued, restrained, even in mourning, already in mourning. No Christmas decorations, piped carols this year, no, not this year. The same everywhere, all across town, the whole nation bowed, prostrate under this "Chrysanthemum Depression": sales of end-of-year gifts and New Year's cards were all down, people confused, uncertain whether it was appropriate or not to send cards which usually, traditionally carried celebratory messages, not when the Emperor was sick. Not sick, he's dying, he said, though no one else ever dared, ever did, then whispered, whispered again to himself, May already even be dead. No wonder a record number of people – mainly young people, according to the Japan Travel Bureau man in the paper – had booked flights out of here. Who could possibly blame them? And at least, he thought, looking down at the basket in his hand, Meidi-ya had not canceled their orders for *Stollen* bread: as his mother had often said, though rarely ever been, One must always be grateful for small mercies, dear Donald. And at the counter, the register, the two kindly staff who carefully wrapped, then packed his wine, his sausages, red cabbage, and *Stollen*, they seemed most relieved, even delighted to take his money, not appalled at his lack of self-restraint, not appalled in the least. They even smiled, kindly smiled as they thanked and handed him his bag, warning him it was heavy, asking him to take care, please take care. And he did, did take care as he walked, slowly walked out of the store, said goodbye to this store, his favorite store, and turned, slowly turned to the stairs down, down to the subway, stopping first to catch his breath at the top, the top of the stairs, then carefully, paying attention, holding onto the handrail, he made his way down, slowly down the stairs, then along the corridor, the underground corridor to the ticket machines. He bought a ticket, then walked slowly through the gate and down, carefully down the next flight of stairs, holding the handrail, down onto the platform of Kyōbashi station.

On the platform, under the ground, he put down the bag, the heavy bag, caught his breath as he waited for the train, the Ginza line train, back to Ueno, to Grete and home. He blinked, blinked again, then felt the wind come down the platform, out of the tunnel, blowing the skirts of his coat, his thin strands of hair. He turned, bending down, picked up the bag, the heavy bag, and watched the train pull in, the doors open, the people get off, quickly off, then he shuffled, slowly shuffled through the doors, onto the train, the busy train, looking right then left for a space, for somewhere to sit, to rest. A young woman rose, offered him her seat, and he blushed, bowed, and thanked her, but did not refuse her, just sat down with his face still red, he knew, bright red: *tomato-ojiisan*, no, always *gaijin-tomato-ojiisan*, he knew. No wonder people glanced, then stared his way, questioning, asking why he was here, this strange, old, foreign man with his bright, shiny, red face and strange, foreign food in his bag at his feet, why the fuck was he here, still here? All these eyes, their stares, all said, they said, Can't you see, don't you know, you've outstayed your welcome, it's time you went home, left and were gone? The doors were open again now, the train in Nihonbashi now, the kind young woman getting off now. He nodded, bowed his head, his thanks again, and though she didn't see, would never know, it made him feel better, a little better. But not for long, no, not for long, more people getting on, so many getting, pushing on, glancing again, staring again, he felt breathless again, chest tight again, struggling to breathe, the air in the carriage humid and sweet, so humid and sweet. He stood up to get off, had to get off, but the doors were closing, already closed now, the train moving, already leaving. He edged through the people, gently through the people, though some still scowled, he knew, they scowled, but did not care, he did not care, his head against the door now, the window of the door now, the darkness of the tunnel, the underground tunnel, waiting for the light, the air, he was waiting for the light, the air of the platform, the platform of the next station, praying for the next station and the doors, for the doors to open, open again –

Bumped, jostled as he stepped through the doors, people pushed and passed around him, he almost slipped, almost fell, but did not slip, did not fall, on the platform, stood on the platform, now he turned, suddenly he turned, back to the doors, the doors closing, already closed now, the train leaving, already leaving now, pulling away, carrying away his wine, his sausages, red cabbage, and *Stollen*, all carried, all taken away.

Damn you, damn you, damn you, he said, his hands, his fingers under his glasses, over his eyes, his tears, aloud he said, he cried, *Baka, baka, baka*, you stupid, stupid fool!

He wiped, he dried his eyes with his fingers, his hands, then swallowed, sighed, then turned away, away from the space where the train, his bag had been and walked, slowly walked down the platform to the stairs, then began to climb up, slowly up the stairs, one by one, one by one, stopping every now and then, every now and every then to catch his breath, his breath again and curse, curse himself again, until he came to the top, the top of the stairs and went through, slowly through the gates, looking for the office, the lost property office – Don't worry, Gre-chan, don't worry: silly old Papa will get them to call up the line, every station on the line; they'll find the bag, our bag, and keep it for us, dear Gre-chan, don't worry; this is Japan – but where *is* the damn office, the lost property office, he thought, still looking this way and that, that way and –

This is Mitsukoshimae, he realized now, suddenly now as he stared down the corridor, the low-ceilinged corridor that led to the store, the Mitsukoshi department store, with its marble columns, its tiled floor. In fright, shock, he turned, looked away, away from the corridor, into a corner, the shadows, he looked, saw and knew, knew where he was, this place was, in this corner, its shadows, this place that was not here, but still there, in the corner, the shadows, which whispered and said, You don't see us, they said, but we see you, see you, yes, we do, see you, in this place not here, not here but there, still there, see you, yes, we do, see you –

*Sā-sā, rei, rei . . .*

No, no, he said, but felt, now felt the ground tremble, then shake, beneath his feet, felt the plates move, then shift, under his feet, plates of time, plates of space, they trembled, then shook, they moved, then shifted, under his feet, from under his feet, knocking him back, pulling him down, but then, and now, back in the here, back in the now, he felt a hand, a hand on his back, his arm, holding him up, keeping him up, and he turned, slowly turned, saw her smile, heard her say, Is this a private apocalypse, or can anyone join?

You are following me –

She nodded, she said, Not me, no. I was just passing, saw you here, in this corner, smiling then sobbing, whispering to yourself, then shouting at yourself. I'm here to help.

I've lost something, left it behind, that's all.

She nodded again and said, Not something. Someone.

Hell is he, you hiss, walking out of the shade, the shadows of the Shirokiya department store, coming up to Terauchi.

He looks at his watch, shakes his head, and says, I don't know. It's not like him. He's never usually late.

Fuck, you say. Fuck. Come on –

And you start to walk, then run, the two of you run: through the morning, down Ginza Street, over the river, the Nihonbashi Bridge, then across the road, over to the store, the Mitsukoshi department store, the south entrance to the store: the cars down a side street, all parked up in a line: you walk down the line, pass a black Buick Sedan, Number 41173, its driver dozing, its back seat empty –

Fuck, you whisper.

In the shade, the shadows of this side street, this store, Terauchi wipes his face, his neck, looks again at his watch, shakes his head, and says, Hell we going to do now?

Come on, you say again, already crossing the road, walking toward the doors to the store –

He says, But Mary said –

Fuck Mary, you say, and walk through the doors, into the store, your hat pulled down low, but looking this way and that, that way and this, whispering, Where the hell is he?

At the foot of the central pillar on the first floor of the store, Terauchi wipes his face, his neck again, looks at his watch again, and says, Maybe he's stood us all up?

The fuck is his driver doing out there then, you say, looking at your own watch. We're too late . . .

Or maybe Mary warned him?

Then where the fuck are they, you say, and reach inside your jacket pocket, take out your notebook and pen, tear off a sheet of paper, scrawl a name, a number, then hand the sheet of paper, its scrawl to Terauchi: Go down to the basement, that Coffee Shop Hong Kong, the place we usually meet, there's a phone in there. Dial this number, then ask for this man –

Sweeney, asks Terauchi, reading your scrawl.

Yeah, you nod. A police investigator, Public Safety. Man's famous, broke up the markets and gangs.

But what the hell should I say?

Tell him President Shimoyama has been abducted, kidnapped at Nihonbashi Mitsukoshi.

We don't know that . . .

Yes, we do, you say. I fucking do, so just make the goddamn call, then wait for me there, you hiss, turning to start looking again, around the store, the first floor of the store, your hat still low, but still looking, looking this way and that, that way and this, walking through the Cosmetics section, Miscellaneous Goods, then the section selling shoes: past display cases, glass counters, the endless reflections, the tricks of the light: twice, twice you think you see him, spot him walking up ahead: sure, so sure it's him as you quicken your pace, pass and overtake, then turn to find, to see you're wrong, twice you're wrong: whispering over and over, It's gone wrong, gone wrong, then again and again, Where's he gone, he gone, as you check the toilets, the empty toilets, then take the stairs down, Staircase H down, down to the basement, still looking this way and that, then that way and this: past the customer service desk, then out through the doors, the underground doors, into the corridor, the underground passage, knowing he's here, somewhere he's here, still goddamn here –

I've found him, I've found him, says Terauchi, walking down the corridor, coming toward you –

You grab him, say, Where?

In the coffee shop . . .

Who's he with?

Shiozawa . . .

Fuck, you say, then, They see you?

He shakes his head, says, No, I don't think so. I was on the phone when they came in . . .

You spoke to Sweeney then?

He shakes his head again, says, No, I was waiting to, just about to, when in they come, Shimoyama and Shiozawa, so I hung up. Didn't know what else I should do, just didn't want them to see me, did I, so I just hung up . . .

But they're still in there?

He nods, says, I guess so – they've just ordered something to drink, look pretty deep in conversation, not like they're going anywhere . . .

You see anyone else, you say, looking around you, up and down the corridor, the passage. Recognize anyone else?

He shakes his head, says, No. Just them two.

Okay, you say, looking around you again, up and down the corridor, the passage again, thinking, wondering –

What we going to do, says Terauchi.

We wait and we watch.

What about Mary?

You see Mary?

He shakes his head again, says, No.

Right then, you say. Then you do what I say: you stand over there, by that column over there, and you watch the door of the Hong Kong and you wait, while I watch from here.

And when they come out, then what?

You do what I say, you tell him again. Okay?

Fuck, he mutters as he walks off, still shaking his head, off behind the column, to stand behind the column, to watch the door to the coffee shop and wait, and watch, and wait –

And watch, and wait, and watch: you keep checking your watch, watching the door, waiting and watching: thinking and wondering, The fuck you will do, do when –

The door to the coffee shop opens: Shimoyama and this man who must be Shiozawa step out, they shake hands, then part ways: Shimoyama heads for the gate to the subway, Shiozawa toward the stairs to the street –

Fuck, you say, running over to Terauchi, grabbing Terauchi, hissing, Quick, gimme the list!

He takes an envelope from inside his jacket, hands it to you, and says, What we going to do?

Just follow Shiozawa!

But what are –

You run toward the ticket gate, push through the gate, and fly down the stairs, almost tripping, almost falling, onto the platform: a train heading east to Asakusa and a train heading west to Shibuya, both pulling in, in at the same time, the platform already busy, already crowded: you push your way up the platform, through the crowd, bumping, jostling the people, the people getting off, the people getting on, scanning the crowd, searching their faces, their hair, and their clothes: you see a pale summer suit, a hatless head, the side of a face, the temple of a spectacle frame, a Harold Lloyd-style frame: you see the back of this man boarding the train, the train heading east, east to Asakusa: you jump on this train, this same train, two cars down, down from this man, the doors almost catching, trapping your arm: you pull your jacket loose from the door and walk down the car, your car, into the next car, to the end of that car: you stand by the door which connects the two cars, your car and his, and you watch the man: the Man Who Loves Trains, Sadanori

"Lucky Boy" Shimoyama, standing in the car, holding onto a handle, swaying, rocking, back and forward, with the motion of the train, his head down, face in shadow, lost in thought, in shadow: you put the envelope, the list inside your jacket pocket for now, then take out your handkerchief, wipe your face, then your neck: you put your handkerchief back in the pocket of your pants, then glance again through the door, into the next car, at the man in the next car, this Man Who Loves Trains, as the train goes on through Kanda, Suehirochō, Hirokōji, then Ueno, this train stopping at each station, but this man staying on: on through Inarichō, Tawaramachi to Asakusa and the end of the line: you wipe your face, your neck again, quickly, quickly, put away your handkerchief again, take out the envelope, the list and follow this man, this man Shimoyama as he gets off the train, onto the platform, along the platform and up the stairs: at the top of the stairs, as he passes through the gate, you give a coin, an apology to the staff on the gate, then follow this man, this man Shimoyama, up the sloping passageway: your eyes on his head, the back of his head, his suit, his pale suit, glancing behind you, back behind you, every now and then, every now and every then, to check and check again, no one is watching you, no eyes on the back of your head, the back of your suit as you follow this man, this man Shimoyama, past the basement entrance to Matsuya, another department store, with the envelope, the list in your hand: you are waiting for the moment, the right moment, to tap this man, this man Shimoyama on his shoulder, then to hand him the list: but he sticks to the crowds, the crowds of people, as he walks up the steps to the Tōbu line station, then buys a ticket, another ticket, then heads up more stairs, a second flight of stairs, up to the platforms, the Tōbu line platforms: Fuck, you think, fuck again, the fuck is he going, as you buy a ticket, then follow him up, quickly, quickly, up the stairs, two at time, then pass through the gates, onto the platform: see this man among the crowds, the crowds of people, see him waiting to board, then boarding a train: Fuck, you think, fuck again, as you glance behind you, behind you again, looking for eyes, eyes watching you as you board the train, another train again, two cars down again as the doors close again: again you walk down the car, your car, into the next car, to the end of that car: again you stand by the door which connects the two cars, your car and his, and again you watch the man on the train, this Man Who Loves Trains, Sadanori "Lucky Boy" Shimoyama, this time sitting down in the car, but again his head's turned away, staring out of the window, as the doors close, the train pulls away, out of the station, away from Asakusa, lost in thought, in shadow: again you put the envelope, the list back inside your jacket pocket, for now: But when, you think, then when, as again you take out your handkerchief, again wipe your face, then your neck: again you put your handkerchief back in the pocket of your pants, then glance again through the door, into the next car, the man in the next car, this Man Who Loves Trains, still turned to the window, staring out of the window as the train crosses the river, the Sumida River, and goes on, on and on, through Narihirabashi, Hikifune, Tamanoi, Kanegafuchi, Horikiri, Ushida, then Kita-Senju, again this train stops at each station, but again this man, this Man Who Loves Trains he stays on, on as the train, this train crosses another bridge, another river, the Arakawa River, on and on it goes as he stays, on through Kosuge, on past the prison, over the Jōban line, the Jōban line tracks, on to Gotanno: suddenly, quickly he gets up and off –

Fuck, you think, fuck, as you follow him off, off the train, onto the platform, down the platform: Fuck is he doing here, why here, you wonder as you watch him wander: with the people, through the gates, where he stops, briefly stops to say something to the staff on the gate: you hang back, glancing back, back behind you, to check, check again, no one is watching you:

watching you watching him as you follow him now, now through the gates, out of the station, Gotanno station: he turns left and begins to walk, walk south down a street, a wide, main street, past closed-up bars, closed-up restaurants, then a sweetshop, a hardware store, a tobacconist, and grocer's, until he comes to a crossroads, a crossroads and stops –

Fuck, you think, think again, as you stop, turn, and glance back: see the street almost empty, no one around, about, not a soul about: Now, you think, now is your chance, turning back round, taking out the envelope, the list: you quicken your pace, catch up with this man, this man Shimoyama as he starts to turn left, to walk east: you reach out, touch his sleeve, the sleeve of his suit, his pale summer suit, and you say, breathless you say, President Shimoyama . . . ?

What, he says, in Japanese, looking at you, staring at you through his Harold Lloyd frames, then again, What?

Excuse me, you say, in Japanese, too, looking at him, staring at him, this man in his Harold Lloyd frames, his pale summer suit, then say, I thought you were someone else.

He sneers, says, We all look the same, right?

If you want to, you say, if you try.

Still looking, staring at you through his Harold Lloyd frames, now he smiles, then he says, Of course, when we try. But remember: we're all on the same side now – right?

Who the hell are you, you say.

Just someone you thought you knew, he says, then turns, walks away, away to the east, crossing the road, then over a narrow ditch, and disappears through the wooden gate of a gloomy, shabby, two-storied inn –

Fuck, you say, aloud you say, Fuck, fuck, fuck, at this crossroads, in the middle of goddamn nowhere, under the sun, this burning afternoon sun: you put the envelope, the list back inside your jacket, then take off your jacket, take out your handkerchief, wipe your face, your neck, then look at your watch: Fuck, fuck, again you say as you turn back, to walk back, back from the crossroads, the middle of nowhere, under the sun, the burning sun, back toward the station, all the fucking stations, and the trains, the fucking trains, back down the line, both fucking lines: first to Asakusa, then on down the line, the Ginza line, back to Mitsukoshimae and where you came in: thinking, wondering, What the fuck's going on, hoping, praying something's being done, praying and pleading it's not gone wrong, not all gone wrong, as you go up the stairs and through the gates, walk past the coffee shop, the Coffee Shop Hong Kong, then along the corridor, the underground passage, back to the stairs, up to the street, onto the street, Ginza Street: again you look at your watch, again you think, Fuck, fuck, and turn left, along the street, Ginza Street: back toward the Mitsui building, your cramped, tiny office, thinking, wondering if you should've gone to Ochanomizu, should still go to see Kaz, glancing, looking again at your watch, thinking, knowing there might still be time, just enough time, deciding yes, yes, you should go, keep walking on, walking on: past your building, your office, you are walking away, when you feel a hand grab, grip your arm, and you turn, spin round: What –

You Don Reichenbach, says a hard, rough-looking young Korean man, in his gangster shirt and shades.

What you want?

Mary wants you to come with us, he says.

And what if I don't want to?

His grip still tight on your arm, he raises his shirt with his other hand, shows you the pistol tucked in his pants, his military pants, and says, That'd be dumb, Don, Mary says, even for you, Don, very dumb, Don.

You nod, you smile, then say, Please, after you . . .

No, he says. After you, Don, I insist, we insist –

And he turns you to the curb, the big, black car parked at the curb, its back door already open, open and waiting, and he moves, bundles you into the back, the back of the car, then climbs in after you, on the back seat beside you, closing, slamming the door behind him, and on you –

Step on it, he tells the big man up front, a big man in a big winter coat. We're already late . . .

May I ask where we're going, you say, turning to the window, watching the Mitsui building, your office, and Nihonbashi disappear as the car speeds down Ginza Street.

Not far enough, he says.

I see, you say, and blink, then blink again as you stare out of the window as the car speeds on: on through Kanda, on into Ueno, then left at Hirokōji, up Avenue N, then right down a side street, up a back road, a slight slope, the car slowing down now, before a set of gates, the gates opening now, the car passing through the gates, past a sign, the sign which reads: OFF LIMITS: STRICTLY NO ADMITTANCE.

They walked, side by side, in silence, through the gates of the Kyū-Iwasaki-tei Gardens, then up, slowly up the curving gravel slope, which led up, parallel to Muen-zaka, the Slope of the Dead, up and round to the old Iwasaki house, side by side, in silence still, they walked, slowly walked, until at the curve, the bend in the slope, he stopped, caught his breath, then said, At one time, you know, not so long ago, if one wished to visit these gardens, this house, then one had to apply to the Ministry of Justice for permission and an appointment, since it was their property, used to train Supreme Court judges, I believe.

She smiled, she said, Having first been confiscated by us, of course, these high walls and tall trees being perfect protection from prying eyes and awkward questions, hiding, keeping all the secrets, the black secrets of Hongō House.

I do wish you wouldn't keep using that name, he said with a sigh. No one calls it that now, if they ever did.

She smiled again, then said, But they did, you know they did, and so did you.

He sighed again, stared up the slope, through the gloom, the early-winter, late-afternoon gloom, up toward the weak yellow light of the ticket booth at its top, unfortunately still open, it appeared. He sighed yet again, then swallowed, then said, You asked me to show you the Iwasaki house, and, most reluctantly, I agreed. But if you do want to see it, and see inside it, then we should hurry – it'll be closing time soon.

She smiled, she said, That's why we're here.

Very well, he said as off he set, slowly set again. But we'll have no more talk of Hongō House then, please. This is now, and almost always was, the Iwasaki house, built for the founders of Mitsubishi, designed by Josiah Conder . . .

Who also designed your beloved Holy Resurrection Cathedral, the Nikorai-dō, did he not?

He stopped again, caught his breath again, then said, Not entirely, no, but in a manner of speaking, yes; the original plans were actually drawn up by a certain Mikhail Schurupov, a Russian architect and doctor of engineering. However, it is true to say Josiah Conder executed the original plans, yes.

And true to say, too, you do love the Holy Resurrection Cathedral, and spent many hours there, too, have you not?

In my younger days, perhaps, he said, setting off, off again, almost at the top now. But as you will see, if we're not too late, and there is still time, the Iwasaki house is essentially Jacobean but bears the trace and touch of many other Western, Eastern and Japanese styles, and thus serves as a monument to architectural syncretism, and all things Meiji . . .

But he was not looking, would not look at the house; no, he was looking, staring up, up through the trees, the bare winter branches of the trees, looking, staring at the white walls of his apartment building, beyond the trees, through their branches, the balcony, the windows of his home. He blinked, he swallowed, and said, It's getting late. Grete will be fretting, she'll be worried, she'll be hungry. I think I'd like to go home now, if you don't mind, I'd like to go home.

She smiled, she said, One of the mysteries to me, the mysteries of you, is why you chose to live where you do, so close to here, overlooking here, the scene of the crime . . .

What crime, he said, then shouted, There was no crime, no crime here, nothing happened here.

She nodded, she said, I mean, you could have lived anywhere, anywhere in Tokyo, in Japan, in the world. But no; no, you chose to live here, even waited until the right apartment became available, one with a balcony and a view, a view of these gardens, this house, and the scene of the crime . . .

What crime, he said again. There was no –

She smiled, she said, Yes, I see you, yes, I do, see you: on your little balcony, at your little windows, always looking out, already staring out, watching out, yes, yes: keeping watch, that was you, was it not? The Look-Out, the Watcher, making sure he didn't come back, they didn't come back, it all come back, yes, yes: that was you, your penance, your sentence.

No, he said, still not looking at the house, no.

She smiled, she said, But he has, they have, it's all come back, is back, returns, always, already returned . . .

Please, he pleaded. Please, not now, not yet.

She nodded, she said, It's too late, it's time. Look, listen, it's closing time –

The hell have you been, says Mary, running out from between the columns of the entrance of a big, old, British-style house as you climb out of the back of the big, black car –

Tailing his goddamn doppelgänger into the middle of fucking nowhere, you say, then, Is he here?

Is who here, Don?

Shimoyama!

Why would he be here, Don?

The hell is he then . . . ?

She walks toward you: takes your shoulders in her hands: leans toward you, kisses your cheek, then whispers, Please, Don, don't, Don, you're out of your depth here, Don.

And you're not, right, you say, pushing her off, back and away. You're just swimming along, everything swell.

Hey there, lovebirds, booms a voice, laughs the voice of a Texan. We're all on the same side here, yeah.

Don, says Mary, looking into your eyes, entreaties in her eyes, turning, twisting you round to face –

a tall, broad-shouldered man in uniform, an army uniform, his captain's hat pushed back on his head, a pistol in a holster slung low round his waist –

Don, she says again, this is Jack, Captain Jack Stetson.

Heard a lot about you, Don, says Stetson, grabbing your shoulder, your hand, kneading your shoulder, shaking your hand. From Mary here, and from Frank, Don.

You know Frank, you say, stepping back, pulling, breaking free from his grip and his shake.

Hey, Boss, interrupts the Korean, in his gangster shirt and shades. What you want us to do now, Boss?

Stetson turns away from you, from Mary, and grins, then says, Go get yourselves some chow, then some shut-eye. Gonna be another long goddamn night, kid.

Yessir, laughs the Korean, half saluting as he swaggers off with the big man in the big winter coat, brushing past, nudging into you as they head off, into the house.

Pair of mean sons-of-bitches, laughs Stetson, watching them go. Tell you, Don, glad they're on our side, but still gotta watch 'em, keep 'em on a tight leash, yeah?

You nod, then say again, So you know Frank?

Hell, everyone knows Frank, right, Don?

Mary touches, squeezes your arm and says, Jack's working with us now, Don.

Since when?

Since you guys lost Shanghai, Don, that's when, grins Stetson. When the goddamn roof fell in on y'all, Don.

Still touching, squeezing, holding your arm, holding you back, Mary says, Everything's changed now, Don.

In this summer, this twilight, you do not turn to look at her, turn to look at him: in this summer, this twilight, you look, you stare at this big, old, British-style house: hidden here, behind these walls, these trees, hidden and dark, you stare and then swallow, swallow then say, Shimoyama?

Don, she whispers, please, don't . . .

Hell, lovebirds, laughs Stetson, slapping his own face, splattering a mosquito. Let's get us indoors, do our yappin' in there, 'stead of gettin' eaten alive out here, yeah, kids?

Sure, Jack, nods Mary, turning away from you, turning toward the house, the columns and its entrance –

Hold up there, cowgirl, says Stetson, corraling you both, herding you off to the left of the house. You guys gotta see this old Billiard Room we got here . . .

And he guides, pushes you both through an open gate in a side wall, then down, round a short path, between more trees to a detached wooden cottage, a Swiss-style mountain lodge, here in this garden, in the middle of Tokyo: a log cabin, wooden shutters for its windows and doors, a long veranda, running its length, facing the garden, dark in the evening –

Wow, says Mary as she steps up onto the veranda, then in through the doors. Like a fairy tale, from *Snow White*!

Heigh-ho, heigh-ho, sings Stetson. Heigh-ho, heigh-ho, heigh-ho – come on, Don, sing along . . .

You do not sing along, but you smile, hum a different song

as you turn from the garden, the dark of the evening, into the light of the lodge: a bare electric bulb dangling, hanging down in the middle of a large wood-paneled room: there are shelves for books, but few books, but there are maps, many maps spread out over two large billiard tables –

Suddenly, a man rises from out of the floor, a hole in the ground, off to the left: a thin man in a dark, well-cut suit coming up steps from under the ground: he smiles at Mary, then sees you and stops, stops smiling, turning to Stetson, looking at Stetson, asking who –

Don Reichenbach, say "*guten Abend*," or whatever-the-hell-it-is-you-Krauts-say, to Dick Gutterman, says Stetson, then turns to Mary and laughs, I tell ya, Mary, we must be the only non-Krauts left in the whole of goddamn HQ!

I don't work for GHQ, you say, shaking the hand of Dick Gutterman. I'm DipSec, Economic Liaison.

Gutterman nods, smiles: I know.

Dick here knows everything 'bout everyone, don't you, Dick, laughs Stetson, then, Almost . . .

You got a call, Jack, says Gutterman.

One I need to take now?

Gutterman nods: Yes, Jack, now.

You two lovebirds make yourselves at home, yeah, says Stetson. I'll be back soon as I can, order up some chow, then we'll eat, talk some more, right?

Sure, Jack, says Mary.

You nod, watch Stetson follow Gutterman down the hole, disappear under the ground, then you turn, walk out of the room, out onto the veranda, to stare out at the garden, back into the evening, the dark, silent dark, almost, already silent –

*Sā-sā, rei-rei . . .*

Don, says Mary, softly, gently, with her hands on your back, touching your back. Frank wants us all to play nice.

You do not turn, turn to look at her: you look into the

evening, into the dark, and say, Yeah? Is that what Frank said, said to you? But who are they, who the hell are they?

Zed Unit, she whispers. Off the books, here and back home. Primary mission is China, counter-ops out of Taiwan, but they're putting together an army, ex-Jap military.

Mac, Willoughby, they know about this?

Sure Mac knows. He wants to retake China, roll the Reds right back to Moscow, then drop the goddamn bomb.

You shake your head, blink, then blink again, still looking, staring out, out into the evening, the dark, and you swallow, then say, The hell are we doing here then?

Her hands, her cheek now, on your back now, she whispers, she says, We're all on the same side now, Don.

You turn, raise your hands, grip her shoulders, grip them tight, stare at her, and say, And Shimoyama?

Bad news, kids, says Stetson, coming up the steps, from under the ground, out of the hole. That was the doc . . .

You let go of Mary, turn to Stetson: What doc?

The doc I sent to try help your pal Shimoyama . . .

The fuck are you talking about, Stetson?

Woah there, cowboy, says Stetson, walking toward you, his hand on his holster, the handle of his pistol: the pistol in his hand now, he smiles: I'm just the hired gun here, yeah.

You turn away from Stetson, look at Mary, but her eyes are on Stetson, staring at Stetson: she is shaking her head, shaking her head at Stetson, mouthing, No, no, no –

You turn back to Stetson, you stare at Stetson and say, you say, you shout, The fuck is going on?

He didn't make it, Don, says Stetson. Doc said he tried his best, but he's gone, Don. Your man never woke up.

The Emperor was dead. Day by day, hour by hour, he had received more blood, more and more blood, but his blood pressure had remained low, his breathing slow, until, on Thursday, he had slipped into a coma, become comatose, then at four this morning, Saturday, January 7, 1989, he had fallen into a critical condition, and at six thirty-three, in the sixty-fourth year of Shōwa, the Emperor had died, his time stopped.

Ah, was all Donald Reichenbach said, when the music stopped and the announcement was made. He blinked, blinked again, then looked at his watch, the luminous hands of his watch, but they had stopped, too, stopped at six thirty-three. He sighed, sighed again, then said, said again, Ah.

Oblivious, Grete danced and sang around him as he picked up her empty saucer and water bowl from the floor and walked, slowly walked over to the sink. He ran hot water over the saucer and bowl, then washed and dried them. He ran the water until it was cold, filled the bowl, then reached up to open the cupboard above the sink. He took down, opened, and served the tuna onto the saucer, then put his hand inside the pocket of his dressing gown. He took out the envelope and, crying softly, as softly, as quietly as he could, he mixed its ground contents into the tuna on the saucer. He placed the saucer and water back down on the floor but did not speak to her, could not speak or even look at her. He wiped, tried to dry his eyes but could not, could not stop his tears. He opened the refrigerator, took out the jar of apricot jam, the jar almost finished, almost done. He took a spoon from the drawer, then opened the jar, put the spoon in the jar, then in his mouth. He picked up the envelope, opened it and his mouth, tipped the rest of its ground contents into his mouth, swallowing the last of the powder with the jam. He screwed up the envelope, put it into the plastic trash box, then rinsed out the empty tin of tuna, the empty jar of jam, and put them in the plastic bag beside the trash box.

Meow, said Grete, against his shins, his calves, between his legs, pajama legs. He picked her up, into his arms, and held her, stroked her as he carried her toward the bedroom, stopping to turn off the radio, the announcement of the name of the new era: Heisei, the attainment of universal peace.

*Le roi est mort, vive le roi*, he whispered, holding Grete, stroking her as he carried her into the bedroom, onto the mats and the bed as he stroked her again and again, as he whispered and wept, I'm sorry, sweetheart, so sorry, sweet Gre-chan, I'm sorry, so sorry, *le mort saisit le vif* . . .

*Sā-sā, rei-rei, sā-sā, rei-rei* . . .

The rain, the wind against the window, its pane, behind the curtains, the curtains still closed, the curtain cracks, their edges gray, he slumped back on the bed, the cat in his arms, on his chest, still tight in his arms, as he stroked her head, her back, felt her warmth ebb away, away through her fur, from her flesh, from her bones, her breathing slow, slow as he waited, waited and wept, tried to hum, to sing, to sing as he wept, a lullaby, Dekker's lullaby: Care is heavy, therefore sleep you; you are care, and care must keep you . . .

No one cares, you say. They don't, we don't, the Japanese . . .

In his bed, his room, in the seminary, the shadow of the cathedral, its domes and its crosses, Kaz strokes your hair, wipes your cheek, and says, I care, Don, and you care, Don.

Not enough, you whisper. Not nearly enough.

Kaz wipes your cheek again, then kisses your cheek, then swallows, then says, We did what we could, Don.

Did we, you say, pushing him off and away, siting up in his bed, asking again, Did we? What did we do? Nothing! We just sat on our hands, let a man, an innocent man die.

Kaz sits up, shakes his head, then says, That's not true, Don, not true. Firstly, he wasn't innocent, not really innocent; he was dismissing, personally dismissing one hundred thousand workers, throwing them and their families into poverty. Don't tell me he was innocent –

But letting him die didn't save their jobs, their families from poverty, did it, you shout, getting up from the bed, reaching for your clothes. It didn't change a thing.

Kaz sits on the edge of his bed, looking up at you, nodding, Not yet, Don, not yet – but you know the plan, the strategy; this is what needs to be done, Don.

Yeah, you say, pulling on your pants, buttoning up your shirt. Well, I don't see any barricades, any revolution on the streets, do you? All I see is a man, an innocent man lying dead on a railroad track up in Ayase –

And one hundred thousand workers out of work, thanks to him, says Kaz, standing up. Him and his Yankee bosses. And *your* Yankee bosses, Don, don't forget, *yours*, not mine, Don.

You put on your jacket, stare at him, and say, Hey, I told you, I warned you; you said you'd let the Party know, make sure Moscow fucking knew – and you told me you did?

And I did, he says, I goddamn did, Don.

You pick up your hat, shake your head: So they knew, Kaz, they knew, but they just sat back and watched, waiting for someone else to do "what needs to be done."

We're at war, Don, at war –

Not anymore, you say, opening the door of his room. Not me – you tell them from me, it's over, I'm out.

It's not that simple, Don, says Kaz, standing there, staring at you. You can't just walk away –

Yeah? You just watch me, you say, walking out of his room, out down the corridor, the seminary corridor . . .

Not from them, or from me, Don.

But you're not listening anymore, not to him or to them, to anyone, not anymore: you just keep walking, out of the seminary, through the garden and the gates, not looking back, back at the cathedral, its domes and its crosses: down one slope, one hill, then up another, another slope, another hill, and into the station: you stand on the platform and wait for the train, the first train: but you do not bend down to tie your shoelace: no, you just board the first train to Tokyo station: you get off at the station, go down the stairs, through the gates, and walk as fast as you can to the Yaesu Hotel: you go under its canopy, into its lobby, up to the desk, the front desk: you ask the man on the desk for an envelope, and he hands one to you: you reach inside your jacket pocket, take out your notebook and pen, tear off a sheet of paper, and scrawl, *It's Closing Time, but Zed Unit are not to be blamed for nothing*: you fold up the single sheet of paper, put it in the envelope, seal the envelope: you turn back to the man on the desk, ask him for the room number of Mister Harold Sweeney of the Public Safety Division: he tells you the number, and you write it under Sweeney's name on the front of the envelope: you hand the envelope to the man on the desk and say, *Onegaishimasu*: the man on the desk nods, and you turn, walk away, out of the lobby and the Yaesu Hotel, and keep walking: through the morning, the afternoon, and the city, you keep walking, walking all the way back: back to the house, the yellow house, its gate, its garden and its path, its door and its lock: you take out your key, put your key in the lock –

You open the door, see her heels in the *genkan*, lying in the *genkan*: you step out of your own shoes, up into the house, and call out, I'm home, sweetheart, home –

She is sat at the table, a bottle, a glass, and her gun on the table: she looks up at you, smiles up at you, then says, she says, I know, Don, know what you've done, all you have done. But why, Don, why? Just please tell me why –

She smiled, she said, Do you despise, detest your own?

No, he said, and took another sip from the can, the last can of beer from the bag at his feet. I have no own.

She smiled again and said, Then why?

Indifference, he said. He took another sip from the can,

stared out across the pond of lotuses, shriveled and withered, still dead where they stood. I despise, detest indifference.

She nodded, she said, But not cowardice?

Perhaps before the war, he said. But since then, I would say, and still now, indifference is the greatest sin.

Not state-sanctioned murder . . . ?

Despite what you say, what you think, I was Chief of Station in name only.

She smiled, she said, So then what were you, Don – not in name, Don, but then really?

A false flag, he said, and a goddamn fool.

And a traitor.

I didn't know, not really know, he whispered. But then, when I did, as soon as I did, I quit. I quit and walked away.

She smiled, she said, And they let you just slink off and away – to teach, to translate, to do what you pleased . . .

Once I was out, I was of no use to them, neither Washington nor Moscow, as they say.

Footloose and fancy-free.

I wouldn't say that.

She nodded, she said, What would you say?

I have regrets, of course, bitter regrets. Everything I did wrong, I said wrong, gestured wrong. Every single day, everything wrong – a lifetime lived wrong.

She smiled, she said, There is a memorial to President Shimoyama, you know, close to the scene where he died.

I know, he said. I know.

She stood up, she said, Let's go.

Next time, he said.

She nodded, she said, It *is* next time, Donald.

He turned away from the dead lotuses, their stagnant pond, drained the last beer, his last can, put the can in the bag, empty and crushed, and said, said again, I know.

She smiled, she said, After you . . .

He tied the handles of the bag, tied them in a plastic knot, then stood up from the bench, no longer *his* bench, and walked away, quickly away from the bench, clockwise this time, away from the pond, away from the park, side by side, in silence now, clockwise they walked, away to the station, the platform, the train, then got on, stood on the train, side by side, in silence still, down the line, on down the line, over the crime, the scene of the crime, to the end, the end of the line.

The train pulled into Ayase station, terminated here, the doors opened, and he said, Please, after you.

She nodded, she said, No, after you.

He smiled, stepped off the train and onto the platform, the platform elevated, high above the shops and pachinko parlors. He looked down the platform to his right, the winter sun setting on the horizon, over the river, the city, then turned to her and said, It's that way. The West Gate exit . . .

She smiled, said again, After you.

He smiled again, sadly now, then started to walk, slowly, slowly down the platform, people stepping around him, passing and overtaking him, toward the top of the stairs, the stairs down to the ground, the exit and out –

At the top of the stairs, he stopped and looked down, down the steep, narrow flight of stairs. He blinked, smiled again, then reached for the handrail, felt a hand on his back, his body topple forward, his feet miss the step, the first step, leave the ground as forward, down he fell –

down the steps, down, down, down, down, down, down, down, down, down, down, down, down, down, down, down, down, down, down, down, down, down, down, down, down, down, down, down, down, down, down, down, down, down, down, down, down, down, down, down each one, each single one of the thirty-six steps to the ground,

the exit

and –

## It's Closing Time

In the twilight of the American Century, the American Season, they drove down Pennsylvania Avenue, traveled out through the slums, past the gas-storage depots, over a branch of the Potomac, into the wilderness of southeast Washington, the gray row houses and the empty lots, the dinosaur bones and the Indian graves, until they spied the elms above the walls, came to the red-brick gate, and said, This is the place.

They turned through the gate, headed up the long asphalt drive, the grounds sprawled out on either side in the haze of a gloom, and parked up outside the main buildings. They got out of the car, walked into the Center building, found the office of the Superintendent, gave their titles and names to the white-coated attendant at reception, stated their business, and made their request. The attendant consulted a card file, then gave them directions and pointed the way.

They walked back out of the Center building, across the asphalt and onto the lawn, the huge expanse of lawn, where men drifted about or sat upon benches, dumbly staring into space, among the tall clumps of boxwood, but where one man sits alone, dwarfed beneath the elms, reclining on a long camp chair, an empty chair to his right, another toppled on his left, this broad-shouldered man with a tangled gray beard and close-shaven head, his face seamed and yellow, cheeks high and hollow, with age and with weather, the ages of the world, the weather of the times, a figure exiled in a landscape the color of lead, the color of smoke, this old, dry man in dressing gown, striped pajamas, beneath his blanket, old army blanket he clutches, holds a teddy bear close, tight to his chest, aware of their advance, he senses their approach, turns his head, looks their way and waits, he waits.

At the declining of the day, in these final, violet hours, she smiled, she says, Police Investigator Sweeney?

Yes, speaking, he says, said again.

She nodded, she says, It is finished, it is done.

# END MATTERS

全 線
24.7.31
優待乗車證
24.6.30
特別觀覽券
電車優待乗車証
24.6.30
電車優待乗車證
24.7.31
東京都交通局
優待乗車證
24.9.30
24.9.30

## Author's Note

---

This novel draws on the lives, memories, and writings of many Japanese and Americans who lived through or participated in the US-led Occupation of Japan, particularly Kafū Nagai, Kōji Uno, and Ken'ichi Yoshida; Paul Blum, Donald Keene, Donald Richie, Edward Seidensticker, and Harry Shupak. However, and for the avoidance of any doubt, this novel is not meant to insinuate that any of these people had any part whatsoever in the death of Sadanori Shimoyama.

## Bibliography

Seventy years after the fact, the death of Sadanori Shimoyama on July 5, 1949, remains a mystery, officially unexplained. In Japan, hundreds of books and thousands of articles have attempted to solve the mystery. Novels, manga, documentaries, plays, and a film have also been based on the events of that night. At one time, it would have been no exaggeration to have compared the domestic political and cultural importance of the incident to the assassination of President John F. Kennedy, such was the level of public interest, the volume of publications, and proliferation of theories and conspiracies. However, as far as I am aware, the only substantial English-language accounts are to be found in *Conspiracy at Matsukawa* by Chalmers Johnson and *Shocking Crimes of Postwar Japan* by Mark Schreiber. The case also plays a fictionalized role in Osamu Tezuka's manga *Ayako*, which has been translated into English.

The case was widely reported in the English-language press of the day: the *Mainichi, Nippon Times*, and *Pacific Stars and Stripes*. These newspapers, along with the Japanese-language *Asahi*, *Mainichi*, *Yomiuri*, and *Tokyo Times*, have all been invaluable sources of information (and misinformation). The GHQ/SCAP record of the case—including crime scene photographs, hand-drawn maps, internal memorandums, and copies of the notebooks of the Public Safety Division—are available in the GHQ/SCAP Records (RG 331, National Archives and Records Service), Box 292, Shimoyama Case—Crime, July 1949–January 1950, and these files can be accessed digitally at the National Diet Library, Tokyo.

A lot of material pertaining to Japanese war criminals,

nationalist groups, and secret societies in postwar Japan has been declassified and can be accessed via the Library tab on the Central Intelligence Agency's own website. However, the sections for Japan in the weekly intelligence summaries provided by the Office of Reports and Estimates, CIA Far East/Pacific Branch remain redacted for the period around the death of Sadanori Shimoyama. And for only that period.

In the following bibliography, I have omitted texts already listed in *Tokyo Year Zero* and *Occupied City*.

*Ayako* by Osamu Tezuka, translated by Mari Morimoto (Vertical 2010, 2013)

*Black Blizzard* by Yoshihiro Tatsumi (Drawn and Quarterly, 2010)

*Blum-san!* by Robert S. Greene (Jupitor/RSG, 1998)

*Bōsatsu Shimoyama Jiken* by Yada Kimio (Kōdansha, 1963) and the film of the same name, directed by Kei Kumai (1981)

*Chronicles of My Life* by Donald Keene (Columbia, 2008)

*Conspiracy at Matsukawa* by Chalmers Johnson (University of California Press, 1972)

*Genji Days* by Edward G. Seidensticker (Kodansha International, 1977)

*Himitsu no Fairu: CIA no Tainichi Kōsaku* by Haruna Mikio (Kyōdō Tsūshinsha, 2000)

*Hōmurareta Natsu: Tsuiseki Shimoyama Jiken* by Moronaga Yūji (Asahi Shimbunsha, 2002)

*In the Realm of a Dying Emperor* by Norma Field (Vintage, 1993)

*Inside GHQ: The Allied Occupation of Japan* by Takemae Eiji, translated and adapted from the Japanese by Robert Rickerts and Sebastian Swann (Continuum, 2002)

*Japan Is a Circle* by Kenichi Yoshida (Paul Norbury, 1975)

*Japan Journals 1947–2004* by Donald Richie, ed. Leza Lowitz (Stone Bridge Press, 2005)
*Jungle and Other Tales: True Stories of Historic Counterintelligence Operations* by Duval A. Edwards (Wheatmark, 2008)
*Keiji Ichidai: Hiratsuka Hachibei Kikigaki* by Sasaki Yoshinobu (Nisshin Hōdō, 1975)
*Kuroi Shio* by Yasushi Inoue (Bungeishunjū Shinsha, 1950)
*Legacy of Ashes: The History of the CIA* by Tim Weiner (Penguin, 2008)
*MacArthur no Nihon* by Shūkan Shinchō Henshūbu (Shinchōsha, 1970)
*MacArthur no 2000-nichi* by Sodei Rinjirō (Chūō Kōronsha, 1974)
*Nisei Linguists: Japanese Americans in the Military Intelligence Service During World War II* by James C. McNaughton (Department of the Army, 2007)
*Remaking Japan: The American Occupation as New Deal* by Theodore Cohen, ed. Herbert Passim (The Free Press, 1987)
*Saishō Onzōshi Hinkyūsu* by Yoshida Kenichi (Bungeishunjū Shinsha, 1954)
*Sakuragichō Nikki: Kokutetsu o Meguru Senryō Hiwa* by Yamakawa Sanpei (Surugadai Shobō, 1952)
*Senryō-ka Nippon* by Handō Kazutoshi, Takeuchi Shūji, Hosaka Masayasu, and Matsumoto Ken'ichi (Chikuma Bunko, 2012)
*Senryō Sengoshi* by Takemae Eiji (Iwanami Shoten, 1992)
*Shima Hideo no Sekai Ryokō 1936–1937* by Shima Takashi and Takahashi Dankichi (Gijutsu Hyōronsha, 2009)
*Shimoyama Jiken* by Mori Tatsuya (Shinchōsha, 2004)
*Shimoyama Jiken: Saigo no Shōgen* by Shibata Tetsutaka (Shōdensha, 2005)
*Shimoyama Jiken Zengo* by Suzuki Ichizō (Aki Shobō, 1981)
"Shimoyama Sōsai Bōsatsuron" in *Nihon no Kuroi Kiri* by Matsumoto Seichō (Bungeishunjū Shinsha, 1960)

*Shimoyama Sōsai no Tsuioku* (Shimoyama Sadanori Shi Kinen Jigyōkai, 1951)

*Shinpan: Shimoyama Jiken Zenkenkyū* by Satō Hajime (Impact Shuppankai, 2009)

*Shiryō; Shimoyama Jiken*, ed. Shimoyama Jiken Kenkyūkai (Misuzu Shobō, 1969)

*Showa: A History of Japan* by Shigeru Mizuki, translated by Zack Davisson, four volumes (Drawn and Quarterly, 2013–15)

*Tales of the Spring Rain* by Ueda Akinari, translated by Barry Jackman (University of Tokyo Press, 1975)

*The American Occupation of Japan* by Michael Schaller (Oxford University Press, 1985)

*The Clandestine Cold War in Asia, 1945–65*, ed. Richard J. Aldrich, Gary D. Rawnsley, and Ming-Yeh T. Rawnsley (Frank Cass, 2000)

*The Human Face of Industrial Conflict in Post-War Japan*, ed. Hirosuke Kawanishi (Kegan Paul International, 1999)

*The Yoshida Memoirs* by Shigeru Yoshida, translated by Kenichi Yoshida (The Riverside Press, 1962)

*This Country, Japan* by Edward Seidensticker (Kodansha International, 1984)

*This Outcast Generation and Luminous Moss* by Taijun Takeda, translated by Yusaburo Shibuya and Sanford Goldstein (Charles E. Tuttle, 1967)

*Tokyo Central: A Memoir* by Edward Seidensticker (University of Washington Press, 2002)

*Wana* by Natsubori Masamoto (Kōbunsha, 1960)

*Yanaka, Hana to Bochi* by E. G. Seidensticker (Misuzu Shobō, 2008)

*Yonimo Fushigina Monogatari* by Uno Kōji (Kadokawa Shoten, 1955)

*Yumeoibitoyo: Saitō Shigeo Shuzai Nōto* by Saitō Shigeo (Tsukiji Shokan, 1989)

## Acknowledgments

The majority of the Japanese texts listed in the bibliography would have been beyond my ability to read in Japanese. I am therefore extremely grateful to Shunichiro Nagashima and especially to Junzo Sawa for the hundreds of pages of translations they provided me with, including from the Japanese press. They also discussed the case at length with me. However, this novel does not reflect their thoughts on the case, nor can it repay the debt I owe to them both, but thank you. Akiko Miyake also provided a lot of further information and translations, particularly in relation to Tokyo in the years 1964 and 1988. Akiko and Stephen Barber and I spent many hours walking the various sites in the novel, discussing the case, and the times, and the lives of expatriates and writers in Japan. I am very grateful to both Akiko and Stephen; thank you.

The sheer volume of material written about the case was, in part, responsible for the ten-year delay in completing the manuscript. I am very grateful for the patience and support of my publishers in the United Kingdom, the United States, Japan, France, Germany, Italy, Holland, and Spain, in particular. The joyless task of excusing and apologizing for the delay in delivery fell to my agent Hamish Macaskill of the English Agency Japan. I am very grateful to him for all his work on my behalf, and especially for his enthusiasm and belief in this book over such an extended period. Thank you, too, to Rob Kraitt at Casarotto Ramsay for his work. I would also like to thank the following people for their help during the writing of this book: Ian Bahrami, Matteo Battarra, Andrew Benbow, Phillip Breen,